ONE MAN'S EMPIRE

When John Butler's father leaves him nothing but a coffee plantation in Ceylon, he decides to sail there from Manchester in order to sign the deeds, sell the estate and pay off his gambling debts but, taunted by brutal plantation owner William Paget, John rashly decides to keep the estate and make a success of himself as a gentleman planter. Eventually his plantation begins to thrive and he falls in love with a local girl, but William Paget will stop at nothing to see him fail, and John is forced to risk everything he owns – and loves – on one last, epic gamble.

ONE MAN'S EMPIRE

ONE MAN'S EMPIRE

by

Geoffrey Bird

Magna Large Print Books
Long Preston, North Yorkshire,
BD23 4ND, England.

British Library Cataloguing in Publication Data.

Bird, Geoffrey
   One man's empire.

   A catalogue record of this book is
   available from the British Library

   ISBN   978-0-7505-3095-8

First published in Great Britain in 2008 by Macmillan New Writing
an imprint of Pan Macmillan Ltd

Copyright © Geoffrey Bird 2008

Cover illustration © Angelo Rinaldi

Magna Large Print is an imprint of Library Magna Books Ltd.

Printed and bound in Great Britain by
T.J. (International) Ltd., Cornwall, PL28 8RW

For Carmel

'The Bush produces the Leaf but it is the Processing that produces the Tea.'

Traditional tea industry saying

Contents

Part One

1874: THE BUD

'The first step is the plucking
of the fresh young shoot.'

One

Manchester

'You are a dissolute young man, John,' ran the letter, 'but perhaps there is still some vestige of hope for you. In recent years I have had the misfortune to see you cashiered from your Regiment, disbarred from the practice of Law and, by certain appalling conduct, demonstrate that you have no vocation whatsoever for the Church. I have frequently been obliged to make good on your various debts – including debts with tradesmen and those that you have incurred through your habitual gambling.

'Despite this dismal litany of failure, however, it was the earnest belief of your Mother, may God grant her peace, that you were not entirely beyond redemption, that it might yet be possible for you to make something worthwhile of your life. She clung to this belief despite whispered rumours that you have been involved in race-fixing, despite the curious circumstances surrounding your association with Mr Vincent Vincent and the horse known as 'The Rascal', and despite various other sorry tales of your self-indulgent, reckless and wholly irresponsible way of life.

'Were it not for her steadfast faith in you I would have no hesitation whatsoever in excluding

17

you as a beneficiary from my Will. However, out of respect for your late Mother's wishes I have decided to make the following bequest: I leave you my coffee plantation at Tondipgiri in Ceylon, in its entirety, including all assets and liabilities deriving therefrom. I make this bequest in the hope either that you will make something of it or that it will make something of you. I cannot pretend that I am hopeful in either regard.

'Your father,

'Edward Morrison Butler.'

'Is that all? No money?'

'The estate is the only item, Mr Butler.'

Butler grunted and tossed the letter on the desk. The chair creaked as he leaned back and stretched out his legs, one highly polished shoe crossing over the other.

'Bit of a disappointment, trolling up here just for that, but I suppose it's better than nothing.' He looked at the solicitor. 'Do me a favour would you, Mr Coutts, and sell the estate for me? You know the sort of thing, old fellow – interview all the prospective buyers then sell it to whoever offers the most.'

'I'm afraid it's not quite that simple,' said Coutts. 'You see, in order to sell the plantation you must first be in possession of the Title Deeds.'

'So throw them over, old fellow.'

'I don't have them, Mr Butler. Your father left the running of his Ceylon estate to a firm of trustees; it is they who hold the deeds. They will only release them to you on your signature.'

18

'You mean I've got to go and see them?'

'That is correct.'

Butler let out a bored sigh.

'All right, if I must. Who are these trustees?'

'It's a firm called–'

'Hold on, old fellow,' interrupted Butler. 'I don't suppose you've got a pen over there?'

Coutts breathed heavily. He didn't approve of young men who called him 'old fellow', even if, admittedly, there was now some grey in his impressive side whiskers; he didn't approve of young men who treated a bequest of property with a complete lack of the gravity the matter deserved, and he certainly didn't approve of young men with unruly hair and an easy manner about them. It particularly annoyed him when a visitor to his office didn't sit straight but sprawled in their chair, and in the case of this young man there was no excuse for it, no excuse at all. The young man wasn't exceptionally tall, the chair was a perfectly acceptable size, it was ridiculous that anyone should lounge in such a way. The intention, Coutts observed with a touch of peevishness, was doubtless to sport elegant tailoring designed to demonstrate that its owner carried no excess weight. Coutts sat a little straighter and pulled the lapels of his jacket together, conscious of his own developing paunch.

He passed Butler the requested pen.

'The firm is called–'

'Any paper, old fellow?'

Coutts controlled himself and passed Butler a sheet of paper.

'Right, carry on; what's their name?'

19

'It is the firm of Compton and Compton.'

'Address?'

'Chatham Street.'

Butler looked up.

'I don't know it. It's not in London, is it? Bit of a fag having to go all the way down there just to sign a piece of paper.'

'No, Mr Butler, Chatham Street is not in London. It's in Colombo.'

Butler looked blank.

'Where?'

'Colombo. That's in Ceylon,' and Coutts had the satisfaction of seeing total disbelief on Butler's face.

'Do you mean I'm supposed to go out to Ceylon? Just to sign for the deeds to this poxy little estate?'

'I don't think it's a *little* estate, Mr Butler–'

'Well, to hell with that.' Butler tossed the pen and paper on the desk. 'I've got better things to do with my time than swanning out to Ceylon.'

He stared at Coutts. 'Did you think this up? Was this bit of nonsense your idea?'

'Not at all, Mr Butler, your father arranged the whole thing himself – without any help from me, I assure you.'

'The silly old fool,' commented Butler.

The solicitor was silent and Butler stared at him.

'Well?' he said at last. 'Nothing to say, Mr Coutts?'

Coutts considered for a moment, then:

'What do you wish to do about the estate?'

'It's nothing to do with me,' said Butler,

standing up. 'Do what you like with it.' He went to the door.

'In that case I will instruct Compton and Compton to sell it.'

Butler turned back.

'That means I'll get the proceeds, won't I?' he asked eagerly.

Coutts shook his head.

'I'm afraid not, Mr Butler. In the event of you deciding against going to Ceylon your father's instructions were that the proceeds from the sale should be given to the workers on the estate.'

'Given to the natives?!'

'That is correct.'

'Rather than to me?'

'Again, correct. It was your father's wish that you receive no further funds with which to indulge your taste for gambling.'

Butler stared coldly at Coutts.

'The Old Man didn't have much of an opinion of me, did he?'

'I'm afraid that much is evident from his letter, Mr Butler. If you had established yourself in a career—'

'Let me ask you something, Mr Coutts,' interrupted Butler. 'Have you ever heard the word "scapegoat"?'

'Of course.'

'I can assure you that the chaps in the Army have heard of it too. They're quite capable of applying it to anyone who doesn't give unquestioning support to his fellow officers, no matter how dishonourable the things they get up to. You'd be surprised at what gets covered up in barracks, Mr Coutts, and when a chap says enough is enough it's very easy to make something up and pin it on him. That's the reason I was cashiered. It may interest you to know that they're not all "splendid fellows" in the Regiment.'

'Mr Butler, your father was disappointed in your abrupt withdrawal from what he hoped would be a promising career in the Law–'

'I've nothing to say on that matter, Mr Coutts. No doubt you and a lot of other lawyers who heard about the Rainford Lodge incident would like to know the name of the lady in question but I gave my word that I'd never reveal it. And, before you mention the Church, I chucked that because it simply didn't suit me; it's not my fault if I've no taste for making sermons,' and this time when Butler stepped to the door he didn't turn back. The door slammed behind him.

Two

A man at leisure in Manchester with a fancy for some illicit amusement after midnight could usually find it at the Boom Boom Club, an establishment catering for an assortment of tastes, lurking down an alley off a street near Deansgate.

Whichever end of the alley a man chose to enter, he would first be accosted by a pair of grubby street urchins squatting in the gutter. A

22

penny scrounged from the visitor would be considered a bonus to their wages, for they worked as crows – lookouts – for the club, employed to give advance warning of anyone who might be a plainclothes jack seeking to gain entry.

Butler tossed them a penny, which was caught expertly, and continued down the alley. Shadows shifted restlessly within the doorways, the figures of ex-boxers, thugs and bludgers, employed by the club to give a violent warning to anyone incautious enough to be venturing there, but Butler had no fear of them; he had been a customer of the Boom Boom Club long enough to have become a well-known face along the alley.

Standing in one of the doorways was a thickset man possessed of a nose that had been broken at least twice and never set correctly on either occasion. This was Maggs, and he was the Boom Boom Club's third barrier to unwanted callers. To get past Maggs the visitor had to pay half a crown; Maggs never asked for the half-crown, nor gave any sign that he had to be paid, but without it there would be no entry to the club. The regulars knew about the half-crown trick, but anyone who didn't and who tried to get in without offering it would find their entrance denied and then the bruisers in the doorways would emerge and escort the hapless unfortunate away.

And just in case someone not on the club's approved list, someone perhaps working on the sly for the police, knew about the half-crown trick and attempted to gain entrance, there was an additional element to the club's defences: upon every payment Maggs would grudgingly push open the door behind him and step back to allow the guest to enter the lighted hallway beyond. The false visitor would step into the lighted hallway, presuming he was entering the club, the door would close behind him and the next thing he would know would be waking up, severely beaten, in a lonely spot beside a canal, with a large sack and a lump of old iron lying nearby.

Only genuine members of the club knew that the opening of the door to the lighted hallway was a signal; as soon as the door was opened they would turn on their heels, cross the alley and open the rough and utterly anonymous door on the alley's opposite side that was the real entrance to the Boom Boom Club.

Butler paid his half-crown, waited for Maggs to open the hallway door, then turned to cross the alley, pushed the door open and entered.

The club was actually the insides of several adjoining buildings knocked into one. In the cellars were the 'pits', where dog-fights and ratting and badger-baiting could be had; the first and second floors hosted petty gambling on prizefighting, skittles, two-up, dice or billiards. The third floor was where the serious gambling took place and that was where Butler was going. No one knew what was on the fourth and fifth floors, but the few well-dressed visitors who had been seen going up there had been exceedingly careful to ensure that their faces were hidden by cloaks or by hats pulled well down. Whoever they were, they were most particular that their presence at the Boom Boom Club should not become public knowledge.

There was only one door on the third floor and Butler knocked on it and waited. A panel snapped back, suspicious eyes peered out, then the panel snapped shut and the door opened. Butler entered, nodded to the man who had let him in and went to the tables.

Mr Coutts, if he had seen Butler at that moment, would doubtless have disapproved of the location with its thick wreaths of cigar smoke, cards soft-slapping in the background against the murmurs of the players as they gambled. But he would have been compelled to revise his opinion of Butler as a lazy, idle fellow. At every table Butler exercised a shrewd intelligence as he studied the cards, carefully weighing up the style of the players, the size of the stakes, judging the pattern of play and, as always, calculating his prospects of winning.

He finally opted for a seat at a table where the game was Five Card Stud poker. Three of the four players were men he had seen before; he had studied their play and was confident that he knew when they were likely to take a risk and how they would play a bluff, but the fourth man was an unknown quantity. In view of the club's rules Butler judged it wise to exercise caution.

Five Card Stud at the Boom Boom Club was a risky business. The first of the club's rules was that instead of dealing a single hole, or hidden, card and then dealing the remaining four cards face-up, two hole cards would be dealt. Having only three cards visible and two hidden made it harder for players to calculate what their opponent might be holding. It therefore made the risks greater.

The second rule was that the cards should not be shuffled between games. This meant that by memorising the cards a good player – a *really* good player – could look at the face-up cards, recall what had come out with those cards earlier on and make an informed assessment of his opponent's hole cards. Such play required nerves of steel though, and a memory like a trap, and players who fancied themselves as having such were frequently – and expensively – proved wrong. Butler always took care to avoid players he knew to be memory experts and this new face at the table might be one such.

Butler played a subdued game, winning a few hands, losing a few, managing to gain a little more than he started with, but playing with no intention of raising his game until he had weighed up the stranger.

He studied the man's hands first. The fingers were short and stumpy, not the long, flexible fingers of a professional sharp. When he shuffled the cards it was with a beginner's shuffle; there was none of the dexterity and smoothness of one who spends a lot of time at the card table.

Butler soon christened him The Fidget.

To an untrained eye the man was calm and in control of himself, but by poker standards he was restless: occasionally scratching his chin or adjusting his collar, blinking slightly more rapidly

26

or breathing a little faster. The movements were small, barely noticeable, but Butler had been playing long enough to be on the lookout for giveaway signs from his opponents. Frequently The Fidget would lift his hole cards to check them, a sure sign of a beginner – an expert player would have weighed up his hole cards in one glance and have no need to look at them again. Sometimes The Fidget placed his bet a little quicker than usual and on those occasions Butler opted to play with restraint. His suspicions were borne out – on each of those hands The Fidget won.

The man made several high bets and twice he unconsciously patted his jacket. Underneath, Butler surmised, would be an inside pocket which, to judge by the bulge, held a fat wallet.

Butler summed him up: well off, able to play the game reasonably well but limited in experience and prone to letting his excitement or disappointment show. Against a more experienced opponent The Fidget would end up sadder, but wiser.

Butler decided to take him. All right, Mr Fidget, he thought, this is where you get a lesson in poker. It was Butler's turn to deal and he dealt for the first round.

The Management of the Boom Boom Club guarded the club's reputation jealously and took the non-payment of any debts incurred on its premises very seriously. Losers who either couldn't or wouldn't pay were assured of a visit from the club's 'punishers' – brutes who fancied themselves a cut above the common thug and who were employed for the sole purpose of delivering severe beatings. The Management were careful to ensure that all the club's patrons heard accounts of the 'punishings' that were handed out, and tales of broken or even severed limbs were usually enough to ensure that those incurring a debt did so only if they were supremely confident that they could honour it.

The man who had let Butler in at the door was the club's principal 'punisher' – a man called Jimmy Tupper. He looked strong and was; he looked pleasant and wasn't. He circled the card-room, watching the various games, and paused near one of the tables where a game of Five Card Stud was in progress. He wondered idly if his special talents would be called on tonight.

Butler dealt the players and himself two hole cards each and then dealt the first round of face-up cards. The opening bets were small, nobody wanting to announce themselves too early. On the deal of the second set of face-up cards one of the players shook his head, muttered 'Fold', and pushed away from the table. Now was the moment to put the pressure on and Butler put a hundred pounds in the pot.

'Too rich for me,' said one of the others and threw in his cards, leaving Butler, The Fidget and one other player at the table. The player looked wistfully at the sum in the pot, then he too shook his head and folded. Now it was just Butler and The Fidget.

The man stared at the pot, consulted his hole

cards, then looked at Butler and stared at the pot again. His hand went towards his inner pocket, then stopped and he put it back on the table. The fingers twitched. The Fidget looked at his cards again. He hesitated, then his hand went to the inner pocket again and this time it emerged with the wallet.

It was as fat as Butler had suspected.

The Fidget pushed his existing winnings into the pot and added enough from the wallet to match Butler's bet.

Now Butler dealt the third and final round of face-up cards. He had two Queens and a six face-up; his hole cards were another Queen and another six.

Three Queens and a pair of Sixes.

A Full House.

Only a Straight Flush – a run of five con-secutive cards in the same suit – or Four of a Kind were better hands.

The Fidget's face-up cards were a pair of fours and a three and Butler weighed his opponent's options.

The presence of the pair obviously ruled out any chance of a Straight Flush. The best he could possibly have would be Four of a Kind in fours, but Butler had been watching the cards carefully – the other fours had been played earlier, so that ruled out any likelihood of Four of a Kind. So that meant that the best hand the Fidget could possibly have was a Full House – probably three threes and a pair of fours – but Butler's three Queens and pair of sixes would easily beat that.

Butler put another hundred in the pot and, as

before, The Fidget reluctantly matched it. When he raised it was by only a small amount.

This was the pattern for several raises, and as his wallet emptied The Fidget became more agitated. He glanced nervously at Butler's impassive face and Butler detected the merest shake in the hand that lifted the hole cards to be examined yet again. There wasn't much left in the wallet now – perhaps two hundred, perhaps a little more – so Butler decided the time had come to take The Fidget to the limit. Which was just as well, because taking The Fidget this far had stretched Butler out.

Butler matched The Fidget's next small raise and raised by another two hundred and fifty. To match that amount would now clean The Fidget out – he would have nothing left and would be forced to take his chances and show his cards, hoping that Butler couldn't beat them. Or, if The Fidget couldn't match Butler's raise, he would have to throw his cards in. But, either way, Butler would take the pot – exactly one thousand, five hundred pounds.

The Fidget's hands were trembling. He stared at the pot and licked his lips nervously. His eyes kept flicking from the pot to Butler and back again. Butler stared back coolly.

Players from other tables had left their games and gathered to watch what was happening. The crush of onlookers pressing around the table was pushing the temperature up and the Fidget loosened his collar. He wiped his hands on his handkerchief, then picked up the nearly empty wallet. He pulled out the remaining notes – two hundred and fifty pounds – and his hands shook. He stared at Butler again, trying to read his face, searching for some clue as to what was driving his relentless betting.

He swallowed again then placed the notes on the pile.

Butler's hand automatically stretched out to his hole cards, the beginning of a triumphant move to turn them over and demonstrate to The Fidget the folly of betting against an expert like Butler, but his hand stopped.

The Fidget was reaching into his jacket, the other side this time. His hand came out with a thick bundle of notes, tightly rolled, which he opened and spread on the table. The onlookers murmured and sighed and shifted restlessly at the sight – a thousand-pound wad – and The Fidget put the lot on the pile.

'Raise,' said The Fidget, and his voice was cold and hard.

Butler was rigid.

Gone was The Fidget's restlessness, no more was he adjusting his collar, the previously trembling hands were completely still, motionless on the table top. The gaze was calm and steady and the nervous blinking had ceased. With sick certainty Butler realised he had been suckered in. The Fidget was no beginner after all.

Butler fought to maintain his composure, to force his mind to ignore the shock and concentrate on what was happening and what it meant. Now it was his turn to stare at the pile of notes in the centre of the scarred wooden table.

Two thousand, five hundred pounds.

Why was The Fidget suddenly so decisive? The only hand he could be holding that could justify betting like that was Four of a Kind. But the other fours had come out too recently to be figuring in this deal so it *must* be a bluff.

In which case The Fidget was a lunatic to be risking a thousand pounds. The man must be mad, concluded Butler, and looked up. The Fidget was staring right back at him and Butler began to feel doubt, a horrid core of cold somewhere inside him starting to expand.

It's a bluff, Butler told himself; the apparent composure must be a ploy that The Fidget relied on: an early show of nervousness then the appearance of supreme confidence later – an effective device which would rock many opponents and make them fold rather than call the bluff.

But ... what if it wasn't a ploy? What if this was the genuine thing?

The Fidget watched dispassionately and Butler mentally cursed him. That thousand-pound raise was demanding a response but Butler shied from the options.

He had nothing left with which to bet. The only way he could match The Fidget's raise was to put down a Note of Promise for a thousand pounds and then call. If The Fidget was bluffing then Butler was the one who would walk away laughing with two and a half thousand pounds in his pocket. But if it wasn't a bluff then Butler would be left owing a thousand pounds which he didn't have and Jimmy Tupper would come calling.

It was a bluff, Butler decided. He was certain that those fours couldn't possibly be coming out now.

Could they?

This must be another element of The Fidget's ploy: to shake his opponent so badly that cold, rational thought was an impossibility.

Think! Butler told himself and a bead of sweat trickled down the side of his forehead.

If he folded The Fidget would take the pot, would take everything Butler had put in, without even having to show his cards. The Fidget could win on the back of a massive bluff.

All right. Put a worthless Note of Promise in and call. Take the risk.

He looked up and stared at The Fidget. The man was staring back and now there was a mocking glimmer in his eyes. Butler almost called for pen and paper right then but he held himself in check. Standing right behind The Fidget was Jimmy Tupper and his expression wasn't encouraging.

Butler could have wept for being such a damned fool as to fall for The Fidget's deception, but he wasn't so foolish as to risk a visit from Jimmy Tupper. Butler was quite attached to his arms and legs and wanted to remain that way. No, the bitter fact was that he had been outsmarted by a better player. The only thing left to do was take the loss and walk away – with his limbs intact. He knew what he now had to say and for a moment the word stuck in his throat; he hated even the idea of having to say it.

'Fold,' he muttered, and there was another

collective gasp from the onlookers, followed by shouts and some cheers. Butler sat very still, wanting to be completely sure of his composure before he stood. He stared across the pile of money at The Fidget.

The Fidget was grinning as he raked in his winnings. The two hole cards still lay face-down and The Fidget noticed Butler looking at them. The Fidget picked them up and raised his eyebrows at Butler as if asking whether Butler wanted to see them. Butler gave a small nod and The Fidget grinned wider, then slowly and deliberately mixed them in at random with the other discarded cards.

Now Butler would never know if it had been a bluff.

The Fidget took his money and left. Butler stared rigidly at the deck of cards mocking him from the centre of the table, then a shadow fell across them and Butler looked up. It was Jimmy Tupper.

'I think it's time to go.' His tone was polite but his expression left no room for argument and Butler got to his feet. Feeling momentarily light-headed he held on to the table, then took a breath and walked out of the room, bitterly aware that the other card-players were watching him go. He gripped the rail tightly all the way down the stairs and left the club. Once outside he stood breathing deeply, ignoring the surly look he was getting from Maggs, then he turned and went up the alley.

He was flat broke but at least he had his limbs left, at least he could play another day.

But with what? He was cleaned out. Where was he going to get enough money to enable him to return?

There was no prospect of winning any because he had no stake with which to gamble. He couldn't think of anyone who might lend him some, nor anyone who had lent him money in the past who might be prevailed on to lend some more. The only thing left was to pawn or sell something. But what? He had nothing to sell.

Three

'Yes, Mr Butler, what can I do for you?'

'Good morning, Mr Coutts. Look, no beating about the bush, I'll come straight to the point – it's about that plantation. The fact is, I've been having a bit of a ponder and I think I might have been a bit hasty in saying I wasn't interested in it. On reflection I really think I should go out there and take possession of it. After all, the Old Man took the trouble to leave it to me, didn't he? Seems a bit ungrateful not to claim it.'

Coutts murmured something that might have been agreement.

'And would you give me that address again – the one for the firm of Trustees?'

Coutts wrote the address and Butler took it.

'By the way, old fellow, I've got a bit of a problem. I'm a bit short of the necessary for the boat fare. I don't suppose you could let me have a few pounds?'

'Your late father made provision for this eventuality, Mr Butler,' said Coutts. 'He expected that you wouldn't consider going to Ceylon unless you were completely devoid of funds so he put a sum aside for us to purchase a ticket on your behalf.'

'For *you* to purchase the ticket? You mean he didn't even trust me with enough for a boat fare?'

Coutts didn't answer that question.

'I'll arrange the ticket, Mr Butler,' was all he said.

Part Two

1875–1877: WITHERING

'During this stage the leaf is rendered pliable and made ready for the step that is to follow.'

One

Butler emerged on deck bleary-eyed, woken by the irritating clatter of the anchor chain. The Captain hailed him cheerily.

'There it is, Mr Butler, that's what you've been waiting for these past six weeks: Ceylon.'

Butler squinted in the sunshine and looked over the side. He wasn't impressed.

Ceylon seemed to consist of trees. Quite a lot of trees. Even the misty hills in the distance were covered with them. The tops of some buildings announced themselves beyond the waving palms but to Butler it all seemed uncomfortably primitive and he didn't look forward to going ashore. He fanned himself with his hat but a few moments of burning sun on his head were enough to make him put the hat back on. A blast on the steamer's whistle made him wait until he could make himself heard, then:

'When will you tie up to the quay?'

'This is as far in as we go, sir. Too many reefs and shallows to take her in any further.'

'So how do we get ashore if there's no gangway?'

'We'll lower a boat,' said the Captain. He sought to reassure Butler. 'It's quite safe, sir.'

Butler peered doubtfully over the rail at the clear water chopping around the boat and stared at the jetty. A crowd of people was gathering.

'I hear that the Grand Oriental Hotel's the best place to stay–' began the Captain, but Butler wasn't interested.

'Thank you, Captain, but I don't intend to be here that long. I have some business to transact and then I'm going back to England.' Butler pulled out a handkerchief and dabbed at the sweat trickling down his neck. 'Is it always so stinking hot?'

The Captain stared at him, surprised.

'This isn't hot, Mr Butler. Mind you, that blazer and flannels you're wearing aren't the best things for these parts. When you get inland, now that's where they say it's *really* hot. But I've heard it gets cooler when you get up in the hills.'

'I wish I was there now,' said Butler irritably. 'Dammit!' and he slapped at a fly on his cheek. 'When's that boat going ashore?'

'We're doing it now, sir,' said the Captain smoothly and turned away to direct the running out and lowering of the boat. Ten minutes later the boat swung at the bottom of the ladder and Butler regarded it sceptically. He descended slowly, hesitated, then ventured one foot on board. The boat rocked.

'Hold it steady, there,' called the Captain from above. Butler put his other foot in the bottom of the boat and sat down abruptly as the boat rocked again. There were laughs from above and two grinning seamen rowed the boat towards the jetty. Splashes from the oar-strokes sprinkled Butler and he scowled. The sooner he signed for the wretched deeds and got away from this God-forsaken place the better.

The little boat rolled and bumped as it came alongside the jetty and Butler clutched at the ladder.

'Thank God for that,' he muttered as he got to the top. He set foot on the jetty and a gaggle of grinning brown children immediately surrounded him, chattering rapidly and holding their hands out.

'Get off,' he ordered futilely as they pulled at his jacket. 'Enough of that. Clear off. Go on, get away.'

The children had no intention of abandoning their newfound friend and they accompanied him along the dock. Butler, however, had absolutely no intention of dragging round Colombo with an entourage of noisy kids getting in his way, so he fished a couple of pennies from his pocket and threw them on the ground. The children pounced on them and Butler hurried away through a gate in the wall.

Ten minutes of fruitless wandering made him acknowledge that there was more to Colombo than he had expected. All the streets looked the same with their long rows of two-storey buildings with arched verandahs and his eyes ached from the dazzling sunshine reflecting from the whitewashed walls. He pushed his way through the cram of people and rickshaws, got well and truly lost and found himself in the middle of a bustling vegetable and fruit market. Fending off insistent stall-holders he tripped up and sprawled headlong over pineapples, mangoes and avocado pears. He stumbled angrily out onto a street full of silk merchants and *saree* shops and after

41

another ten minutes of searching and cursing, his throat burning from the dust, he finally admitted defeat and asked for directions.

Chatham Street was lined with buildings on both sides and Butler breathed deeply. Coutts hadn't given him the exact address so Butler had to walk the entire length of one side and halfway back up the other, struggling through the pressing. crowd, before he spotted a brass plate by a door announcing the offices of Compton and Compton. Short-tempered and hot, he went in and up the stairs and opened the door.

The room was dim and cool and Butler sighed, glad to be out of the relentless sun. His eyes took a moment to adjust, then he saw that the room was divided by a wooden rail with a gate in the middle of it. Several well-worn desks stood on the other side. The only other person in the room, a rather elderly man, rose and came over.

'Good morning, sir,' he said. 'I'm Edwin Compton. Can I help you?'

Butler introduced himself. 'I believe you administered my father's coffee estate.'

'Mr Butler, this is indeed a pleasure,' and they shook hands. 'May I say what a fine man your father was. Please accept my deepest condolences.' Compton shook his head gravely.

'I'm here to sign for the deeds,' said Butler, impatient to conclude matters, and he slapped at a fly on his neck.

'Of course, sir,' said Compton smoothly. 'Won't you sit down?'

Butler sat, wiping his forehead as he watched

Compton search through a drawer. 'How do you cope with this heat?'

Compton paused.

'One doesn't cope with it, Mr Butler. One can only accept it as inevitable. I find it better to try to live with it,' and he returned to his search.

'Who told you my father had died?' asked Butler.

'We received a telegram from your father's solicitor.'

'Ah, yes, good old Coutts,' observed Butler sourly, and pulled his damp collar away from his neck.

'Here we are,' announced Compton. 'The Tondipgiri coffee plantation.' He brought a file over to the desk. 'There are various documents regarding the administration of the estate. If you would like to read them I think you'll find everything in order. I also have a set of accounts and—'

'Yes, yes,' said Butler. 'I'm sure everything's fine; I just want to sign whatever it is and get it over with. Then I can get out of this blasted country.'

Compton blinked, then inclined his head.

'As you wish, sir.' He withdrew a document from the file and laid it on the desk. 'Your signature is required here, and here,' and he watched as Butler used the scratchy pen to sign his name. 'I take it that it is your intention to sell the estate?'

'That's right,' said Butler. 'Once I've—' and he stopped. 'How did you know?'

'Your late father did advise us that you would

43

probably wish to sell,' said Compton as he signed the document and dated it. Butler leaned back.

'The Old Man seems to have shared his opinion of me with everyone; first old Coutts and now you. He really didn't have any confidence in me, did he?'

Compton paused and picked his words carefully.

'I believe he was of the view that your temperament was not that of one who builds for the future. I understand he felt your interest lay in exploring the more – er – immediate pleasures that life affords.'

'How very tactfully put,' commented Butler drily. He crossed to the slatted window and looked out.

'I presume you will be leaving Colombo as soon as you are able, sir?' asked Compton.

'That's right,' said Butler, looking down at people passing by in the glaring sun. 'I've got what I came for. No reason to stay,' and he turned. 'So I'll be off,' and he picked up the file.

'You're staying at the Oriental Hotel, I suppose?' asked Compton.

'No,' said Butler. 'I've had enough of this damned town – I'll sleep on board the ship. Then it's back to England.'

'That might prove difficult,' said Compton mildly.

'What do you mean?'

'The boat will have left by now, Mr Butler. It calls here to deliver mails, then departs for Australia.'

'They've left? But all my luggage was on

44

board!' and he departed Compton's office at a run.

He arrived at the jetty sweating and breathless. The ship was already a mile away and he bellowed after it but even as he did so he knew it was pointless. He stared at the departing stern, uncomfortably conscious of sweat running down his back, and he swore and kicked out viciously, sending a bucket splashing into the water. He scowled, breathing heavily, then noticed an old man sitting on a pile of luggage.

Butler's luggage.

'Here, get off that, you.'

'One shilling,' said the man, his brown face cracking into a wide smile showing yellowed teeth. 'One shilling for guarding bags. One shilling.'

Butler ignored him and pulled at his bags.

'One shilling,' repeated the man, agitated. 'One shilling for guarding bags.'

'Clear off,' said Butler shortly, and tugged at the bag the man was sitting on. The man wouldn't move and kept insisting on his shilling.

'No shilling,' said Butler. 'Move, damn you,' and he gripped the man by the shoulders, lifted him and set him aside.

The man sat on another of the bags.

'One shilling.'

'Get off that,' threatened Butler and the man ignored him. Butler threw him off that bag too but the man wasn't bothered; he merely went and sat on another of Butler's bags and repeated his demand.

Butler glared at him. This performance could go on all day.

'One shilling,' said the man again. 'One shilling for guarding bags,' and he grinned at Butler.

Cursing to himself Butler dug in his pocket for a shilling and threw it at the man. The man got up and Butler collected his luggage – two leather bags, a dressing case, a linen bag and a hat box – then he stared at the heavy and unwieldy trunk.

Carrying this lot by himself clearly wasn't on; besides, where could he carry it to? He wasn't registered at a hotel.

The thought brought him up short. If he was going to register he needed money and money was precisely what he lacked.

'Damn this filthy place,' he snarled, then remembered: Compton had said something about a set of accounts, hadn't he? So perhaps things weren't so bad after all – the contents of the plantation accounts should pay very nicely for a decent hotel room.

He fished out another shilling.

'Guard these bags,' he said to the old man and held up the shilling. 'Guard them and you'll get this.'

The man grinned widely and quickly sat on the trunk.

Butler put the bags round the man's feet and hoped the old fellow was trustworthy. At least he had looked after them well enough before. Butler gave him a doubtful look and left the dock.

Compton raised his eyebrows when Butler returned.

'Mr Butler. So soon. I presume the boat has departed?'

'Yes,' said Butler irritably, wiping his neck. 'It's gone,' and he changed the subject. 'You said something about accounts; how much money is there? How much cash?'

'It's detailed in the accounts,' said Compton, and held out his hand for the file. Butler passed it over and Compton consulted a paper within.

'Two hundred and three pounds and seventeen shillings on deposit at the Oriental Bank.'

Butler's face fell.

'Is that all?'

'Your late father made certain withdrawals some months ago; it's all detailed in the file. The cash should suffice to pay for hotel accommodation; I presume that's what you want it for.'

'Yes, it's for a hotel.'

Compton nodded as if in confirmation of some private thought and Butler stared at him. For some reason he couldn't fathom there was something about that nod and the comment about the hotel that bothered him. It was as if he had been insulted or denigrated in some way, yet there was nothing in the words, or the nod, that he could put his finger on. He felt uncomfortable and it bothered him. Then he understood and he frowned. He'd damn well had enough of this.

'You think I'm not going to visit the estate while I'm here, don't you?'

'You did say you intend to sell it, Mr Butler.'

Butler nodded. Being so predictable was starting to rankle.

'Well this may come as a surprise to you, Mr

Compton, and I know it will be a disappointment to Coutts and my Old Man – wherever he is now – but I've decided: I want to take a look at the place.'

Compton raised his eyebrows and Butler stared at him defiantly.

'You wish to see Tondipgiri, Mr Butler?' said Compton carefully.

'I just said so, didn't I?'

'It's a considerable journey.'

'So?'

There was a pause, then Compton made a small shrug as if coming to a decision.

'Very well, Mr Butler,' he said. 'If those are your wishes I will be pleased to take you there myself. But I suggest you go to the bank first and withdraw some money, then purchase tropical clothing. I think you'll find you need it.'

Two

Butler definitely didn't like Ceylon.

He had suspected he wouldn't and now his suspicions were confirmed.

It was about a hundred miles, Compton said, from Colombo to Tondipgiri, but only a few miles after they had struck away from the coast Butler began to regret his impulsive declaration that he wanted to see the estate.

Sweltering in the back of the ambling bullock-cart he sat on his luggage and cursed. The air weighed heavy and humid in the lowland country and the damp collar of his perspiration-soaked shirt chafed his neck and caused an angry rash. Occasionally the wheels of the cart would sink into a hole in the road, then jerk out again, and Butler would have to leave off mopping at sweat to simultaneously grab at the sides of the cart and clutch at his bags to prevent both himself and the bags from being tipped out and deposited in the road.

He scowled at everything and everyone. He was fed up with the blasted trees, fed up with the fields, fed up with the slow-moving rivers, fed up with the dust and the damned flies and, most of all, fed up with the vile heat.

Compton, sitting up front with the native driver, occasionally passed a comment or asked a question, but otherwise he said nothing and Butler groused to himself in the back, grumbling about the squeaking of the wheels, the rattling of the cart and the variety of noises issuing, with accompanying disgusting smells, from the bullock.

They made an overnight stop at a low-roofed building which Butler at first dismissed as a derelict shack but which Compton explained was a Rest House. To Butler the title seemed entirely inappropriate and he made a point of telling Compton so. He was still complaining at midnight, unable to sleep because of the heat and humidity, and he twisted on the rough wooden pallet, muttering and cursing.

He fell asleep just after one o'clock and ten minutes later the night was split by an agonised shriek, the hideous tortured cry of someone being sadistically disembowelled with a blunt hatchet. At least, that's how it seemed to Butler.

'My God, they're killing someone!'

'No, Mr Butler.' Compton's voice came from the corner of the Rest House, mild and unconcerned. 'It's merely the Devil bird.'

'The what?'

'That's what the natives call it.'

The scream broke and cracked and diminished into a bubbling sob and for a moment there was silence, then the night sounds of buzzing flies and vague shufflings from amongst the trees and bushes resumed.

Butler lay down and presently began to doze. The Devil bird started again.

'For God's *sake!*'

Butler went to the door and bawled at the bird to shut up. The bird ignored him.

'How long is it going to carry on like that?' he demanded of Compton.

'Who can say?' came the mild voice from the corner.

'Somebody should shoot the damn thing,' said Butler angrily and threw himself down on his pallet.

The Devil bird let out its night-shattering cry three times more then subsided.

After half an hour, senses screwed up, waiting for it to start again, Butler began to relax. He wriggled and twisted and finally found a position that was marginally less uncomfortable than any other he had tried and he began to drift off.

A deep throbbing booming began somewhere deep in the jungle and Butler thrashed about and got to his feet. He flung the door open.

'Shut up! Shut *up!*'

The booming continued from out in the darkness, a steady ceaseless threnody that seemed distant yet simultaneously all around.

'What's that?' he complained angrily. 'That's no damn bird.'

There was a sound that might have been a sigh from Compton's corner.

'Those are death drums, Mr Butler.'

'My God, you mean – you mean, they're about to kill someone?'

'No, I mean that someone is already dead. The drums are a lament.'

'This is ridiculous,' snapped Butler. 'How long do they go on for? I want to get some sleep.'

'They will probably cease at dawn,' said Compton.

'Dawn?!'

'I suggest you make the best of it, Mr Butler and try to sleep.'

'How do you expect a chap to sleep with that racket going on?' demanded Butler, but Compton made no further reply and Butler lay down again and buried his head in his blanket.

On the second day the cart burrowed through steaming rainforest, emerged to crawl up hills and descend into valleys, then plodded across dry scrubland and plunged into more dense undergrowth.

Butler had had more than enough, but the absence of complaints from Compton finally registered with him and he fell silent. The very evident low expectations which so many people had of him, the way in which everybody took it for granted that he would have no interest in the estate, still stung and he was determined that Compton, at least, should be proved wrong. He clung to the cart, the pristine tropical whites he had hurriedly purchased in Colombo grew rumpled and stained with the greenery of bushes, but he kept his mouth clamped shut, determined to bear it all from now on without voicing any further complaint.

The rough earth floor of another primitive Rest House was their bed for the second night, and Butler was stiff and sore and highly irritable when he climbed aboard the cart the following morning. He hadn't slept well, and although he tried to doze the endless swaying and jolting made him quickly abandon the attempt. He wedged himself in the back of the cart, his feelings deep, and spent his time fending away overhanging branches that seemed determined to swipe him in the face.

Lazily the road wound up into higher country and left the humid lowlands behind, but it didn't improve Butler's temper; the flies and dust were still with them and he sweated and slapped.

Compton seemed oblivious to the discomfort. It was as if the years of heat had baked all the moisture out of his skin, leaving it leathery and impervious to flies. The jolting and swaying didn't appear to bother him either.

As the wagon climbed up yet another interminable road, Butler, sprawling on his luggage, sullenly contemplated the fact that he was dirty, dishevelled, sweaty and smelly. He yearned for a bath and a shave and a comfortable bed with clean linen and he cursed the reckless gambling at the Boom Boom Club that had got him into this mess.

The cart suddenly halted.

'There it is, Mr Butler,' said Compton. 'Tondipgiri. That means "King Tondip's Hill" in the language, though how it got that name seems something of a mystery.'

Muttering to himself that the one thing he didn't need at that moment was a history lesson Butler got down from the wagon and walked forwards, avoiding the questing wet nose of the bullock. He stood in the middle of the dusty road, staring at what he had come halfway round the world for, and an eruption from the bullock's bowels seemed to sum it up for him.

The Tondipgiri estate straddled a long high ridge running directly away from them to the north. To their right, on the eastern flank, the hill dropped sharply to a wide river tumbling over rapids, bordered on the far side by dense untidy jungle. To their left lay the hill's western flank, covered thinly with trees and sloping gently to the road. Some buildings were down there, partially hidden by more trees.

So this was it.

When he had first heard that he had inherited an estate Butler had entertained a vision of the rolling expanses of choice land attached to the great houses of Cheshire and Derbyshire. Lush fields stretching away as far as the eye could see, broken only by thick stands of trees and dense woods teeming with wild game, perhaps with a rippling mere or two sparkling in the distance. It came as a jolt to find that his inheritance consisted of a single hill at the furthest end of the planting region, snugged up tight against steaming jungle.

He swatted at the flies buzzing around his head and turned back to the wagon. Compton was waiting patiently.

'All right, let's go and have a look at it,' said Butler sourly and he climbed aboard.

The road coiled down to the southern end of the hill, then went left along the bottom of the western slope, a stream bubbling beside them. Butler stared sulkily at the hill as they lurched along the road, then the cart turned off, crossed a stone bridge over the stream and went through a stand of trees. It came to a halt in front of a run-down single-storey building.

'This is the bungalow,' announced Compton, swinging down.

'Who lives here?' Butler asked, and Compton turned.

'You're the owner, Mr Butler – this is where *you* live.'

'Here?' said Butler incredulously. 'In this ruin?' and he stared at the bungalow in disbelief.

Holes gaped in the threadbare thatch of the roof and a shutter hung by one hinge, its partner missing. When Compton opened the door some small animal, startled by the sound of their arrival, darted out and scuttled into the undergrowth.

Butler's displeasure deepened when he went inside.

The furniture consisted of a dusty table and two simple chairs, and small piles of leaves occupied every corner. Butler sniffed in disgust and turned to Compton.

'Does this dump make much money?'

'Indeed,' said Compton, reassuringly. 'Tondip-giri was a profitable plantation in its day.'

'You mean it isn't profitable now?'

'We've managed the land in accordance with your late father's instructions but an estate needs someone on hand to supervise, to make decisions. Our instructions permitted us to maintain it as it was, but we had no discretion to make improvements or alterations. From time to time we would receive a letter from your father, but I fear it wasn't foremost amongst his business interests.'

Compton went outside and Butler followed.

'Like other plantations, the trees have been affected by the blight, with the inevitable consequence for the amount that can be cropped. The harvest has virtually dried up. There's barely enough income to sustain the workforce.'

'Blight? What blight?'

'It began several years ago,' explained Compton. 'Not far from here. It turns the leaves black, an orange powder appears, then the leaves fall off and the tree dies. Every estate is affected to some degree. Nobody's quite sure what to do about it.'

'Well that's just marvellous,' said Butler with heavy sarcasm. 'So I've got a diseased estate,' and he scowled and pulled again at his sweat-soaked collar.

He pointed at a square wooden building. 'What's that place?'

'The storehouse.'

'And what's that over there?'

'That's the coffee-house,' said Compton. 'That is where the coffee is processed and packed.'

Butler grunted.

'What about the workers?' he asked.

'They live over there,' and Compton pointed to low buildings visible through the trees.

Butler nodded and looked at the slopes.

'Is that a coffee tree?' he asked, pointing.

Compton nodded and followed Butler over to it.

'Where's the coffee?' asked Butler, and Compton shook his head.

'There are no beans, I'm afraid, the blight is quite severe.'

Butler pushed one of the lower branches aside and a yellow-orange powder detached itself from the underside of the leaves and shook itself over his sleeve. He brushed it off but a stain remained.

'Damn,' he muttered.

'That's the blight,' explained Compton helpfully, standing at his shoulder. Butler rubbed the mark harder but it smeared into the cloth.

'Dammit.'

He looked round.

'So this is it then – this mess is what I've inherited.'

'There is the far slope of course,' said Compton. 'You may wish to inspect it but the climb might be uncomfortable.'

Butler gave a short ironic laugh and spread his

arms wide.

'Well, why not? I'm filthy enough as it is. What difference will a bit more dirt make?' and he glared at Compton, then turned and started up the slope.

Various trees on the way to the top greeted their new owner with presents of the yellow-orange powder and Butler damned them all to hell. The slope pulled at his leg muscles, making him pant for air, and droplets of sweat beaded on his forehead and ran down his nose. He had to stop for breath halfway up and he stared at the estate on the opposite side of the road. Whoever ran things over there clearly had everything well under control: the trees ran in disciplined lines, unlike the untidy sprawl on this blasted hill.

He returned to his climb and found a breeze blowing near the top. He gasped, 'Thank God for that,' and stumbled onto the crest. He stood bent over, hands on knees, breathing in loud whoops and looked down at the steep eastern slope.

Not worth the climb, he concluded. More dejected coffee trees and squat bushes clung to the earth and the rumble of the rapids came up faintly from far below. The only other features were a rope bridge hanging precariously over the river and a path on the far side that vanished into the jungle. This was the extent of the estate of Tondipgiri.

Butler stared at the hills stretching away to the north and south and at the peaks that bordered the northern and southern flanks of the land to the west and gave a hollow laugh.

'Thanks for the inheritance, Father,' he said

aloud. 'Thank you very much,' and his voice was scornful. 'I hope you're finding all this amusing,' and he went back down the hill. He got to the bottom, went round the side of the bungalow to the cart and stopped.

'Hey, what are you doing?'

Compton turned from the cart and put the last of Butler's bags on the ground.

'Unloading your luggage, Mr Butler.'

'Put it back on; I'm not stopping here.'

'It's your plantation now; someone has to run it.'

'Yes and it's not going to be me. I'm going back to Colombo.'

'Not with me, you're not,' and Compton climbed back onto the cart. 'I have other business to take care of. I'm not going back to Colombo for a few days.' He looked past Butler. 'Besides, they're *your* responsibility now.'

Butler turned.

A score of dark-skinned men and women were staring at them from under the nearby trees.

'Who are they?' said Butler.

'Some of your plantation workers, Mr Butler,' and Compton called out, 'This man is *Durai*.'

'What?' said Butler. 'What was that? What did you say?'

'I told them that you are the *Durai* now, that means the man in charge.'

'They can look after themselves,' said Butler dismissively, turning back to Compton. 'I'm coming with you.'

'Out of the question,' and Compton nudged the driver. 'All right.'

'Hold on,' said Butler, and the cart stopped. 'Hold on. You can't leave me here.'

Compton stared down at him.

'Why not?'

'Why not?' echoed Butler. 'Why do you think, for God's sake? I don't know the language. I'm no planter; I don't know anything about all this,' and he gestured round with his arm.

'Then I suggest you learn,' said Compton coldly. 'And quickly. To be quite candid, Mr Butler, I don't much care for your attitude. I've lived in this country for many years and I've seen men of your stripe before. They came out here, young, arrogant, full of their own importance, contemptuous of the country and its ways, its people. Some of those men changed; they buckled down, they worked hard, they didn't whine – unlike you. They accepted the situation and they made something of themselves. They've become successful, respected. As for the ones who came here and scorned everything, the ones who came for an easy life or rich pickings, they didn't last long. When they found out this is a hard country which needs strong, determined *men* to work the land they scuttled back to England. And good riddance, I say.'

Butler started to speak but Compton bored on relentlessly.

'You've done nothing but complain since you got here. Your manner, your conduct, have been exactly that of those useless fops we're better off without. The sooner you leave, Mr Butler, the better, but I'll be damned if I'm going to nursemaid you around the country.' Compton nudged the driver again and this time the cart rattled away.

Butler stared, stunned.

'You can't leave me here,' he shouted. 'Come back. What am I going to do for food? I haven't even had any dinner, damn you!'

Compton didn't turn and the cart quickly vanished beyond the trees. Butler opened his mouth, about to shout something else, then gave up. He stared at the road, half-hoping the cart might reappear, but there was nothing. Movement away to his left caught his eye and the cart appeared beyond the trees, climbing to the top of the rise where Butler had got his first look at Tondipgiri. Then it was over the top and gone and Butler was on his own.

Except for the plantation workers – they were still watching him.

He looked at them, they looked at him, and Butler concluded that it was he who would have to make the first move. He walked over, stopped, and before he could say anything all the workers made small bows to him. He stood uncertainly, then made a short nod of his head in return.

'Does anyone speak English?' and he raised his eyebrows in question.

'Speak English?' he enquired again, louder this time, and the men and women stared at him without expression.

'I see,' muttered Butler to himself. 'So no one speaks English. This is going to make things interesting.' He mimed eating. 'Food? Do you have any food?'

60

The people stared at him, eyes wide, then a man whispered in the ear of one of the women and she hurried away. The others said nothing and kept staring with overt curiosity at the new owner.

Butler began to feel uncomfortable with the silence and felt he should do or say something. But what?

'Me – Butler,' he said at last, tapping his chest. No response.

'Butler,' he said again, repeating the gesture, then remembered the word used by Compton. 'Me – *Durai.*'

That produced a response. The people exclaimed and chattered to each other and Butler grinned and nodded, then the people fell silent again and looked at him expectantly.

Butler didn't know what else to say.

He put a serious expression on his face and nodded thoughtfully, hoping that he looked like a man in charge. The workers stared back.

Just when he had decided that to maintain that expression any longer would make him look stupid the woman came back through the trees with a bowl in her hand. She handed it to the man who had sent her for it, and then the man handed it to Butler, saying something in a language that Butler didn't understand.

The bowl was half full with rice and a pinkish-brown thing that looked like a potato. Butler stared at it for a long moment. Was this muck what people lived on out here? His feelings were deep and quite beyond polite expression, but at least, he finally consoled himself, it wasn't as bad as the weevil-ridden filth he had been expected to eat in the Army – that had been fit only for pigs, and what had passed for meat had been so tough it could have been used for repairing saddles. He looked up.

'Thank you,' he said to the man at last. 'Thank you,' he added, to the woman.

They made no response and didn't seem inclined to leave so he nodded again and turned back to the bungalow. When he reached the door he turned, expecting the people to have gone, but they were still standing there, in the shade of the trees, watching him. He nodded again and went inside the bungalow.

Once inside he realised he hadn't washed his hands and he went outside to go to the stream. Feeling as if he were a side-show laid on for the entertainment of the people standing under the trees he rinsed his hands, dried them on his handkerchief and went back to the bungalow. What he had thought was a potato turned out to be pleasantly sweet, but the rice was chewy and he grimaced. At least, thank God, it was edible.

The quality of the light inside the bungalow changed and he looked up. Wide brown eyes were peering through the slats at him and some of the bolder souls were openly staring through the shutterless window. He finished the meagre meal and went outside.

'Very nice,' he said, indicating the bowl and smiling. They said nothing, just stared, and Butler began to feel uncomfortable and annoyed to be so scrutinised.

Suddenly thirsty, he decided he needed a drink

of water and he went to the stream. He heard a shuffling behind and glanced over his shoulder. They were following him. He rinsed the bowl and sipped water from it, cold and sharp and fresh, then he gave the bowl back to the man.

'Thank you,' he said again and made a little bow.

The man smiled, showing discoloured teeth, and the people muttered excitedly amongst themselves. Butler decided he might as well make a closer inspection of the property he had come so far to claim and went towards the storehouse. His entourage followed.

They waited patiently outside whilst he examined the empty store and when he emerged they followed him along the foot of the hill to the northernmost point, where the plantation ended in rocky scree-covered slopes. They stepped aside respectfully as he walked back and stayed several yards behind him as he returned to the bungalow.

He bent to pick up his bags and looked across at the workers staring at him.

'Would you like to help? Carry bags?'

He sighed at the lack of response and took the bags into the bungalow then came back for the trunk. He lifted one end and dragged it through the dust and inside, then returned to the door. The plantation workers were still watching, seemingly finding him a source of unending fascination. He waved to them, then went inside and closed the door. After a moment he stepped slowly to the shutter and peered through the slats. He twisted his head to peer from side to side but the ground outside was deserted. He went to the door and looked out, then walked all around the bungalow.

They had gone.

There had been no sound, no sign of their passing, and feeling strangely bereft of their company he went back inside, noticing the sky turning orange in the west. Sooner than he expected the sun was down and he was left to the night.

He quickly found that he had exchanged one set of companions for another, this new collection much less respectful. The new visitors buzzed and fluttered and settled in his hair and on his skin, having no reservations at all about biting him, and Butler swatted and smacked.

The rough wooden affair which he supposed was meant to serve as a bed was as uncomfortable as it looked and he balled his jacket under his head as a pillow. He tossed and turned for a while, his attempts at slumber disturbed first by scufflings and movements outside, then he heard movement *inside*. He heard and felt something scratching underneath the bed and he got up. The scratching stopped, then started again when he lay down. He picked up a branch from the floor and poked and swiped under the bed and something dark and furry with a long tail squealed and scurried out.

He finally fell asleep just after midnight, only to be woken by the sound of something slithering across the floor. He stayed on the bed, cursing the lack of a light and swiped again with the branch. Something hissed and drew away with a

64

dry, leathery sound and Butler felt suddenly cold. He drew his legs up, not daring to attempt sleep again until it was light enough for him to see that he wasn't sharing the room with anything. Then, oblivious to the hard boards beneath, he fell asleep.

Three

Butler woke next morning, turned onto his side and groaned. He straightened and sat up, trying to bend his neck and work some of the soreness out of his shoulders, then he remembered the slithery visitor of the night and hurriedly drew his legs up. He checked underneath the bed but there was nothing there and he stood up and went through to the other room of the bungalow.

It felt hot and stuffy so he opened the door and nearly trod on a bowl covered with large leaves. On investigation he found it full of rice and something pale which he tentatively identified as some kind of fish. He looked to see if anyone was watching but saw no one. He took the bowl inside and sat down, then abruptly laughed out loud at the incongruity of it all. Two months ago he had been John Butler, frequent visitor to clubs, accustomed to fine dinners and crisp linen napkins and silver cutlery; now he was John Butler, the dirty, sweaty owner of a diseased coffee plantation, eating native food with his fingers.

Not any more, dammit, he decided viciously. I'm getting out of here and back to Colombo. *Today.* To do that I need transport and to get *that* I need to find someone who speaks English.

He finished the food, rehearsing angrily in his mind what he was going to say to Compton next time he saw him, then went outside to get some water and looked up at the Tondipgiri slopes. There were no workers up there and he presumed they were still in the buildings on the far side of the trees. But he didn't really care where they were – he wasn't going to be around much longer. He looked across at the neat and regimented lines of the plantation on the other side of the road, went back inside for his hat, then strode determinedly down to the road and along it to the turning to the plantation.

About a half-mile up the dusty track he rounded a stand of trees and saw a beefy man in whipcord riding breeches, a riding crop in his fist, striding across the yard in front of a well-kept bungalow. Butler hailed him.

'I say, can you help me?'

The man stopped.

'Who are you?' he demanded suspiciously, and as he frowned his heavy eyebrows met in the middle.

'The name's John Butler. I own the plantation over the road.'

The man grunted.

'Paget,' he said grudgingly, 'William Paget,' and his hand enveloped Butler's in a fleshy grip. 'For an owner you've not been out here much.'

'First time,' said Butler. 'My father owned the

66

place. He left it to me.'

'Thought you looked a bit new,' commented Paget. 'Those who've been out here a while look a lot browner.'

Butler grinned, acknowledging his pale skin. 'The fact is, old man, I'm stuck without any transport. Can you help?'

Paget shook his head. 'I've got nothing to lend you,' he said. 'But you might find something at the Planters' Club.'

'Where's that?'

'About twenty miles back down the road there's a turning. You must have seen it when you were coming up; there's a stone Buddha or some damn thing right next to it.'

'I didn't notice,' Butler confessed.

'Well, turn there and go up the road for a mile and you can't miss it.'

'Thanks.'

'Before you go, Butler, I'll give you some advice. You're the new boy here, you don't know the ropes, so just remember: don't take any nonsense from your coolies.'

'Coolies?'

'The natives who work your estate. Show them who's master right from the start. Keep them in line. And make sure they've always got something to do. See the shine on these?' and he indicated his glossy brown riding boots. 'I have these polished four times a day. If you let them think – for even one moment – that they can get away with slacking they'll do it. They're idle, lazy and dishonest – all of them. They steal from you the minute your back's turned,' and Paget lifted

67

the riding crop. 'Use this and use it often. And lay it on hard. "Spare the rod and spoil the coolie" is what I say. Thrash at least one every week and they'll respect you for it. If you don't,' and Paget shook his head, 'they'll rob you blind and sit around on their fat backsides all day.'

He turned and shouted towards the storehouse. 'Changarai! Get your lazy carcass out here!' He turned back to Butler. 'You have to watch them like a hawk. They do anything they can to avoid an honest day's work. Changarai!' he bawled again.

An old native in short baggy white trousers came trotting from the storehouse, a ledger in his hand. He was bald and his white beard and whiskers contrasted sharply with his leathery brown skin. His strong feet were fastened in sandals and Butler recognised the man's white jacket as tropical kit that used to be issued to the Army.

'Look at that,' said Paget in disgust. 'You call them twice and all they do is shuffle.'

The man halted in front of them.

'Well?' demanded Paget. 'Did you find it?'

'I look very carefully–' the man began. 'The book say–'

'I'm not asking you what the book says, Changarai,' roared Paget. 'I know damned well what's in the book and it doesn't tally with what's in the store. Where's the missing coffee?'

'I look carefully in the store,' said Changarai. 'All coffee bags are correct.'

'Say "sir" when you speak to me! I know where that damned coffee is: you've stolen it – you and those other thieving scoundrels.'

'I have not taken–'

'Don't answer me back, you stinking coolie!' and Paget lashed out with the riding crop. Changarai instinctively recoiled and the tip of the crop only skimmed his cheek, but the blow still had force enough to cut the skin. Paget swung again and Changarai ducked and put up his arm, but another vicious slash laid the skin open on the man's head, spattering blood on the white jacket.

'Damned little thief,' and Paget laid the crop on again. 'I'll teach you not to steal from me.'

The next blow thudded onto Changarai's shoulders and Butler stepped forward. 'I say, that's enough.'

'He won't have had enough till I've flayed his thieving black skin off him,' and Paget swung at Changarai again.

'Enough, I said,' and Butler caught Paget's upraised arm.

Paget shook himself free. 'What the hell do you think you're doing?' he demanded angrily.

'Leave him alone,' said Butler. 'He's had enough,' and he stepped between Paget and Changarai. The movement was a red rag to a bull.

'Get out of my way,' roared Paget, 'or by heaven I'll thrash you next.'

'You're welcome to try,' said Butler coolly, and without hesitation Paget took him up on the offer.

The braided leather hissed and cracked on Butler's quickly upflung arm. The blow stung red-hot and Butler wrenched the crop away. He gripped the stock in both hands and brought it down on his knee, snapping the crop in two, and flung the pieces into the trees.

Paget seemed about to have a fit. He went red in the face and his lips twitched and worked as words fought to come out.

'Get off my estate,' he snarled, and flecks of foam spotted his lips. He pointed a shaking finger at Changarai. 'And you're fired, you thieving swine. Set foot on my land again and I'll shoot you on sight.'

The native ducked his head and made a nervous attempt at a bow to Butler. Paget's foot shot out and Changarai sprawled in the dust.

'Get out!'

Changarai scrambled to his feet and hurried away and Paget turned as Butler took a step forward, his fists clenched.

'I said get off my estate, Butler, or I'll shoot you as a suspected thief.'

They glared at each other for a moment and Paget's square meaty face, with its veins standing out and the hard bone bridging the eyes, put Butler in mind of a leather bag that hadn't been packed properly.

'I'm going,' said Butler slowly. 'But I'll remember you, Paget.'

Paget's laugh was contemptuous. 'Remember me if you like, but I've already forgotten *you*. Now get out.'

Butler put his hands in his pockets and sauntered away, but his heart was beating fast and his fists remained clenched.

At the end of the track he stopped and mopped

at the inside band of his hat, already damp with sweat.

Twenty miles, Paget had said.

The prospect of a long hike in the foul heat held no attraction but there was no point wasting any more time around Tondipgiri. Perhaps at the Planters' Club he could lay his hands on transport of some kind – a horse, a cart – and then go back to Colombo and a decent hotel.

He started walking as strands of cloud crept furtively overhead.

'This is more like it,' said Butler to himself.

The building baked in the sweltering heat of the noonday sun, but apart from that he could easily have been back in England. Bay windows with leaded panes were set into whitewashed walls, a tiled roof with tall chimneys formed precise gable ends over the right and left wings and a long terrace led to a well-tended garden. Bright blooms sported in thick clumps and there was even a privet hedge.

He followed the curve of the drive round to the front door and went inside. The entrance hall, panelled in dark wood, was dim and quiet and deliciously cool after the heat, and the clack of billiard balls from somewhere down a corridor made him think of England and home comforts. The clink of glasses and the murmur of voices from one of the rooms announced that it was occupied, so he went in.

A dozen men were seated around small tables and all either held a glass or had a glass in front of them.

71

'...And if we're going to stop it what we need to do is to get–'

The speaker stopped upon seeing Butler.

'Hello, here's a new face,' and the other men turned and stared.

'My name's John Butler. I've inherited the Tondipgiri plantation.'

'Thin pickings there, I've heard,' said the man. 'I'm Donald Eliot. Sit down, old man, have a drink,' and he called a white-jacketed waiter over.

'Been here long?' asked another man with a heavy Scots accent.

Butler shook his head. 'Arrived yesterday. I came here to find some transport.'

'How did you get up here?'

'I walked.'

'That's a good sign,' said Eliot, nodding approvingly. 'You have to be fit to survive in this country. You'll need all the energy you've got if we're going to stop this damned blight.'

The Scot stabbed his finger at the table. 'I've told you, Eliot – there's only one way: if you want to get rid of the blight you have to keep your trees free of leaves.'

'You'll need a lot more workers for that,' commented one man.

'Aye, you need to double your workforce,' agreed the Scot. 'But that's what I've done; and I'm telling you – it's the only way.'

'There are other ways,' said Eliot. 'I think the answer's something to do with shade.'

'Och, you're talking nonsense, man,' commented the Scot dismissively.

'It isn't nonsense,' insisted Eliot. 'I've seen

72

coffee trees deep in the jungle, huge things – they must be a hundred years old – and *they* haven't got the blight.'

'Well, either we find a solution or it'll be the end of coffee in this island,' said another man. 'We'll all end up planting tea,' and the planters laughed.

'That'd suit Taylor,' chortled one man.

'It'll end in tears,' declared the Scot with a ponderous air of authority. 'There's no future in tea.'

'There'll be no future in coffee unless we get the damn blight under control,' said Eliot, 'Now, what I think–'

'Never mind what you think, Eliot, let's ask this young fellow. He might have some new ideas,' and they all looked at Butler. 'Well?' asked the Scot. 'What are you going to do? Your estate's got the blight, I've heard; badly too.'

Butler nodded and almost began to explain that he was planning to sell the place as quickly as he could and return to England, but he paused. There was something about these men – these tough, leathery, sun-burned planters, wrestling with the blight on their plantations but refusing to admit defeat – that made him feel uncomfortable at the thought of making such an admission. He felt that if he did tell them they would regard him as a quitter, and somehow that was a prospect he didn't relish.

'I'm not quite sure what to do next,' he said carefully. 'I came up here to see if anyone's got any ideas.'

'Is it bad?'

Butler nodded. 'Yes. Very.'

'Get into tea,' called one man.

'You've been spending too long with Taylor,' called back Eliot. 'There's nothing wrong with coffee that plenty of shade won't cure.'

'Who's Taylor?' asked Butler.

'James Taylor,' said the Scot. 'A good man. He's from near Aberdeen, like me, but he's got some strange ideas – he's only interested in tea.'

'Taylor's convinced himself that tea's the crop of the future,' explained Eliot.

'It might be if we can't get rid of the blight,' said one of the other planters and they turned back to their discussion.

Butler listened to them and everything they said confirmed his belief that selling and getting out was the only sensible thing to do. If these men – men who'd been running their plantations for years, men who knew everything there was to know – couldn't overcome their problems, what chance did a beginner have? He didn't want to confess to them that he was going to sell though, so he finished his drink and left. He had reached the steps outside before he remembered he still had no transport. Back inside he encountered a dark-skinned steward crossing the hall.

'I say, do you think you could help me? I'm looking for something to get around on. Any ideas?'

Four

Bicycles, in Butler's opinion, were definitely at their best when going downhill, but going down usually has to be preceded by going up and the abandoned machine he had eventually been directed to, located in a dusty shed behind the Planters' Club, didn't seem quite so enthusiastic on that point. Something was impeding the action of the pedals and the unhealthy grinding coming from the crank suggested that all was not well. He didn't try pedalling up hills for long before getting off and pushing. The exercise was made even more uncomfortable by the heat pressing down under the heavy clouds building up overhead.

Butler gave thanks.

There'll be rain soon, he thought; now this is more like England.

Three hours later he crested the rise near Tondipgiri and the wind struck him full in the face, and made him gasp. He freewheeled down the road, his legs out in front, and as he crossed the stone bridge the angry black clouds opened.

The bicycle wobbled and he nearly fell off. The bullets of rain didn't simply land on him, they *hit* him. Gasping, drenched within seconds, he forced the pedals round and aimed for the bungalow. There he shot through the open door with the precision of an arrow and ran straight into the wall. He disentangled himself and stood in the doorway, wiping the rain from his face and staring at the trees lashed by the wind. A world of insects – hornets, butterflies, sandflies – was shaken out and they wheeled and darted in mad confusion in the steam rising from the hot earth.

The wind and rain doubled then redoubled in strength, the insects were driven away and Butler began to feel nervous. He had vaguely expected that this would be much like an English storm: an hour or two of heavy rain, then the worst would ease off. But it didn't, and as evening drew on even the bungalow didn't seem a safe refuge any more. He wedged the door shut but it seemed a real possibility that the wind, howling around the walls, would get its fingers under the roof and tear it away. Already it was ripping at the existing holes and pulling out the thatch and Butler huddled against the wall as flies and fleas and ticks deserted their homes in the roof and dropped around him. He stared up at the holes and a brilliant flash of lightning lit the inside of the bungalow and illuminated the puddles spreading on the packed earth floor.

The door burst open, tearing out one of its hinges, and it swung despairingly for a moment before being snatched away into the darkness. The wind drove through, scouring the inside of the bungalow, upending the table and over-turning the chairs, and Butler retreated until his back was against the inner wall.

Tondipgiri seemed to be at the very centre of the storm and a stunning crack of thunder confirmed his suspicions; no mere rumble this but a crash all around as if the very air and sky were being ripped open. The remaining shutters were torn away, the rain drove in hunting for him, and in another eye-searing flash he saw the shaking trees outside twisting in torment, water streaming from their leaves, then the night reclaimed them and another crash of thunder drowned out the rain.

Rivers formed in the dirt, then streams of water running down the hill escaped the silted-up drainage channels and found a way in at the back of the bungalow. Soon a constant flow of water was running across the floor and out of the doorway at the front. At one point a rat was borne through on the tide, and it paused for a moment, staring at Butler, then rejoined the flow and vanished through the door. Other small animals followed: lizards, land-leeches and giant millipedes, disgusting things six inches long with bloated bodies and scores of legs that waved and paddled futilely as they swept by.

Leaves and branches swirled outside and Butler felt the impact as they struck the bungalow's walls. An entire section of thatch broke free, taking the wooden beam with it, and even above the din of the storm Butler heard the rip as it was wrenched away. The wind screamed its frustration around the bungalow and Butler pressed against the wall. There seemed to be something very wrong with this storm; this wasn't just bad weather, this was violence, anger, weather that wanted to get hold of him and do to him what it was doing to the rapidly fraying roof. Another clap of thunder made him crouch lower, and the wind and rain raged outside, waiting for the moment when the bungalow would be torn apart at last and their prey exposed.

All night the storm battered the bungalow. More of the roof came away, the floor was awash, and Butler sat shivering on the wooden bed in the back room, legs drawn up, pressed into a corner. Sleep was an impossibility.

With the coming of dawn the storm finally, reluctantly, abandoned the struggle and started to subside. The wind and rain made a few more half-hearted attempts to drive him out, then abated, taking the dark clouds with them. Butler ventured to the door, unable to avoid stepping in the miniature river now flowing through the bungalow.

Tondipgiri had taken a savage beating. Bushes had been flattened, large puddles covered the ground and flowed and emptied into one another as they trickled down to join the overflowing stream. The bridge lay a foot under water, jammed with saplings and splintered branches. Still stunned from the night's violence Butler stared for a few minutes, then went round to the back of the bungalow and looked up at the slopes.

The hillside was a shambles. All over it were splintered stumps and toppled trunks. Livid gashes on the handful of trees still standing showed where branches had been ripped away and there wasn't a single tree with leaves remaining.

Slowly Butler walked forward and began to climb the hill. He didn't know why he did it – if these gentle and sheltered slopes had been so blasted it was unlikely that there would be anything left on the steeper, more exposed eastern slope. Even so, it was still his inheritance, and he couldn't help hoping that there was at least something of it left.

Often his feet slipped and his boots and trousers were soon liberally caked with red mud, but he persevered and eventually stumbled onto the ridge.

He stared, numb.

The long eastern slope of Tondipgiri was entirely stripped of coffee trees. Not even the stumps remained; the trees had been plucked out by the roots like so many rotting teeth. All that was left, clinging tenaciously to the earth, were dense stubby bushes, stunted and short, their shiny green leaves glistening wetly. The river far below, swollen to twice its size, flowed heavy and grey carrying uprooted trees and branches.

Butler stood for a long time looking over the devastated slopes of Tondipgiri, then he went back down the hillside and slipped and slid to the bungalow. He picked up the dripping bicycle and wheeled it out.

The estate was a ruin and he knew exactly what he was going to do about it. He would go to the Planters' Club, offer the place to any planter he found there and take whatever price he could get; he no longer cared what they might think of him. If none of them wanted the place he'd go to Colombo and find an agent – even Compton –

whom he could turn the whole thing over to and instruct to arrange a buyer, then he'd take a room in a hotel and wait until the ship returned. There was nothing left here – no crops, no trees, just two sides of a hill, the stumps and some bushes; no one could blame him for getting out.

He pedalled to the bridge and lifted his feet as the wheels splashed through the flood. Some of the plantation workers were standing under the trees watching him go but he ignored them. He'd had enough; soon they would be someone else's problem.

Eliot and several other planters from the previous day were in the Planters' Club when Butler entered and they looked at him with interest.

'I say, Butler,' declared Eliot. 'You look a bit of a mess. Did you get caught in the storm?'

Butler, sweaty from the long cycle ride, glanced down at himself and realised what they meant. He hadn't shaved for three days, his once pristine white summer jacket was stained and damp and splattered with mud, and his trousers and boots were heavy with red earth.

He nodded. 'Yes, I got caught in it all right. Look, I'm selling Tondipgiri. Do any of you want to buy it?'

There was silence and the planters exchanged doubtful looks.

'Before the storm I heard it was in a bad way,' said Eliot. 'What's it like now?'

Butler hesitated, then decided to be frank.

'It was hit pretty hard,' he admitted. 'There's a few trees left, not much else; I just want to sell up and go home.'

A snort issued from the occupant of a wing chair, its back to Butler, and a sneering voice followed.

'I could tell that you haven't got what it takes.'

The chair's occupant stood up. It was Paget.

He stared distastefully at Butler's dishevelled appearance and wrinkled his nose in disgust. 'You stink, man,' and he looked Butler up and down. 'We don't want your sort here, Butler.'

Butler opened his mouth to reply but Eliot interrupted.

'I say, Paget, do you two know each other?'

'I had the misfortune to meet him yesterday,' admitted Paget sniffily. 'He was trespassing on my estate.'

'You mean I stopped you thrashing a native,' retorted Butler. 'Careful to pick on someone who couldn't fight back, weren't you?'

Paget reddened.

'You're a fool, Butler,' and his voice lashed. 'What in God's name possessed you to come out here? Did you really think, for even one minute, that you could make the grade as a planter?' and Paget gave a short derisive laugh. 'You'll never understand the coffee business, Butler. You're soft, through and through. You're no use out here and you never will be. Be a good little boy instead and run away home to England – where it's safe,' and he turned away dismissively.

'I'll go to England when I'm good and ready,' said Butler angrily, 'and that's *if* I go.'

Paget turned back and the other men stared at Butler. 'Does that mean you're staying?' asked

Eliot. 'You've changed your mind?'

'He won't last the month,' said Paget contemptuously. 'Look at him. He stinks of mud; he hasn't even got the sense to come in out of the rain. And look at that lily-white skin – a day's hard work would flay it off. You've got the hands of a milksop, baby Butler; they're soft, like you. I take back what I said about you not lasting the month; you won't even last a week.'

'Would you put money on that, Paget?' demanded Butler. 'I'm staying,' and he blinked – he didn't know where the impulse to say *that* had come from. But there was no going back now.

Paget simply snorted again and returned to his wing chair. Butler watched him sit down, then gave a short nod to the other planters and strode from the room, his head high. He shut the door emphatically behind him and the slam woke echoes throughout the building, then he subsided on a chair in the hall and dropped his forehead into one hand, his eyes squeezed tight shut, unable to believe what he had just done.

You bloody fool, Butler, he scolded himself. You stupid, stupid, brainless idiot. Have you got no damned sense? What on earth possessed you to say such a mutton-headed thing?

Impulsiveness, that's what it was. Bravado all over again. It had been the cause of that fiasco at the Boom Boom Club, had driven him to abandon all caution against The Fidget, and now it had dropped him in the soup once more; he had opened his big mouth and look at the mess it had got him into this time.

He smacked his thigh with his fist.

Stupid, idiot, crazy, fool – how could he have been so senseless as to say he was going to remain in Ceylon? It was a stinking, filthy hot country with bloody Devil birds squawking half the night and death drums beating through the other half and he, like the worst kind of imbecile, had nailed his colours to the mast and now was stuck with that poxy flyblown estate.

He clenched his fists tight, his nails dug into his palms and a tempting voice inside piped up and reminded him that he didn't *have* to stick with it; he could quite easily cut and run if he chose.

His head came up. Gad, that was appealing.

No, dammit, no one was going to be able to say that John Butler wasn't a man of his word. He had said he was staying, bloody fool that he was, and he was going to keep his promise. He'd damn well prove that vile brute Paget wrong.

But what was he going to do with the wretched estate? All that remained on it were a few useless coffee trees and some bushes. He smacked his fist on his thigh again. Perhaps if he could just find some use for it for a while, just long enough for all those tough planters to agree he wasn't a quitter after all, and then he could sell it on some pretext or other.

He brightened. Yes, there were possibilities there. It shouldn't be too difficult; he could get the natives to do all the work, then he could invent some elderly relative in England and pretend they were ill and knocking on death's door. That would justify him selling up and getting out.

But what could he do with the place until then? For ten futile minutes he stared blankly across the hall at his reflection in the mirror, racking his brains for some solution, anything, then he heard footsteps outside. The Scot who had been in the club the previous day was coming up the steps and an idea suddenly clicked into Butler's mind. He stood up and greeted the man as he entered.

'I say, old chap, you know that fellow you were talking about yesterday – Taylor? Where can I find him?'

Five

'Well, laddy, I reckon you'll be wanting something, coming all the way up here.'

Fierce blue eyes glared at Butler from under bushy eyebrows and Butler wondered if he was doing the right thing after all; the appearance of the giant he was speaking to didn't inspire confidence.

James Taylor looked like a country bumpkin. The man was about forty or so with hands like shovels and a beard like an untamed thicket. His clothes were simple and shabby and he spoke around a white clay pipe clamped firmly in his mouth.

'Well? What is it? Speak, man.'

'Er ... I heard you're something of an expert.'

'Expert?'

'About tea,' said Butler. 'I thought I might give it a go,' he added airily.

'Give it a go?' echoed Taylor. He glared at

84

Butler and sucked violently on his pipe. Butler found himself unsure of what to say next.

Taylor stared at Butler for a long moment, so long indeed that Butler began to feel uncomfortable.

'I started with twenty acres eight years ago,' declared Taylor eventually. 'Now I'm putting the whole one hundred under tea.'

'So you don't think there's any future in coffee?' asked Butler.

'Not any more, laddy, not out here.'

'There are men in the Planters' Club who still think there's a future for it,' said Butler, and Taylor snorted.

'They'll need more than shade to save their trees; aye, and stripping the leaves won't do any good. The only thing left in coffee out here is wretchedness and bankruptcy. But that's their choice; they can do what they want.'

He studied Butler again. 'So you want to know how to grow tea?'

Butler nodded. 'All my coffee trees had the blight and then the storm blew them down. There are stumps and tree trunks all over the place. I want to try something else.'

Taylor leaned forward, his eyes bright, and Butler had to make an effort to stop himself leaning away from the pungent tobacco reek of his breath.

'Don't think that you can just "try" planting tea, laddy. When you put tea bushes in the ground you put something in your soul. They get their roots into the earth and they get them into you as well.'

Butler assumed a serious expression and nodded, thinking it best to humour this wild-looking figure, and Taylor leaned back.

'I can see through you like I see through that window,' he declared. 'You think I'm mad. Well, there's plenty thinks the same, but you'll find out what I mean. Right now, you're walking away from your coffee trees, but you'll never walk away from your tea bushes.'

'All right, so how do I get started?'

'You're serious about it?'

Just for long enough for people to say I'm not a quitter, thought Butler.

'I'm serious.'

'Right.' Taylor stood up and loomed over Butler. 'No time like the present. We'll go and look at your Tondipgiri and see what can be done with it.'

Taylor's wagon creaked to a halt and he sat for a moment, surveying the remains of the plantation. Then he got down and Butler joined him.

Rubbish carried down by the storm still choked the stream under the bridge and the open ground in front of the bungalow was strewn with branches. The holes in the bungalow roof gaped and Butler shifted awkwardly. There was nothing left on the estate to be proud of but, surprising himself, he found that he didn't want Taylor to have a low opinion of it.

'The storm did a lot of damage,' he said defensively and pointed. 'There were trees all over that slope and down the other side as well.'

Taylor nodded.

'Right, let's have a look,' and he set off at a fast stride. The slope of the hill didn't slow his pace at all and Butler was hard pressed to keep up with him as he pushed through the sorry mess towards the top. They reached the ridge and Taylor glanced down the eastern slope and was suddenly very still. He turned and looked at Butler and his expression took Butler back to when Flogger Noakes had called him out in front of the entire school. Six of the best for stuffing old birds' nests down the headmaster's chimney and dislodging clouds of soot over the visiting Bishop.

'Why didn't you tell me?' said Taylor.

Butler was blank. 'Why didn't I tell you what?'

Taylor pointed to the slope. 'You came asking me about tea and all the time you're growing it yourself.'

'What?'

Taylor crossed to one of the stunted bushes. 'You're growing tea here.'

Butler went over and stared at the bush. 'Is that tea? I didn't know.'

'You didn't know?' echoed Taylor.

'No,' said Butler, 'I don't know what it looks like.'

Taylor stared at him suspiciously. 'Then where did this come from?'

Butler couldn't imagine and he shrugged his shoulders. 'I don't know; it must grow wild or something.'

'Tea doesn't grow here naturally, laddy; someone's brought it and planted it.'

'Well I can't imagine who.'

'Do you have no records of the place?'

Butler was about to shrug again, then remembered the file of papers Compton had given him.

Butler brought the file out and Taylor studied the contents, muttering to himself.

'Ah ha!' he declared after a minute. 'Just as I thought,' and he brandished a letter. 'Here we are,' and he looked at the name at the bottom. 'From someone called Edward Butler.'

Butler nodded, 'My father.'

'It's dated six years ago,' said Taylor. 'Your father writes, "Dear Mr Compton, Thank you for your hospitality on the occasion of my recent visit to Ceylon. On my return to England I gave much consideration to the conversation we had with Mr Thwaites on 10th February last, regarding the experimental planting of tea. I have decided that the eastern slope of Tondipgiri should be planted with tea seed and I would be grateful if you would visit Mr Thwaites and make arrangements to expedite this matter. Please include a report on the growth of the tea in your annual report."

'Well, well, well,' and Taylor gave Butler the letter. 'So your father obtained tea seed from George, did he?'

Butler was completely lost.

'I don't know what you're talking about,' he said. 'Who's George?'

'George Thwaites,' said Taylor. 'The director of the Royal Botanic Gardens right here in Ceylon. There's nobody knows more about tea than him; he's the fellow who started me off with seed ten years ago.'

Taylor dug his fingers into the ground and investigated a handful of wet soil. 'This place has possibilities, laddy. You've got rich ground here.'

Butler wished he would stop calling him 'laddy'.

'And you're off to a good start,' Taylor went on. 'You've already got bushes that you can crop. They're well established; in need of pruning, mind, but well established.'

'So I suppose I have to go and see this Thwaites fellow and get seed from him to plant on this slope,' and Butler gestured to the devastated hill.

'No need to,' declared Taylor. 'You can propagate,' and when Butler looked at him blankly Taylor expounded. 'Take a piece of tea-bush root, strip the bark from one side and bury it a hand's width in the ground. It'll throw shoots out from every eye and you'll have a full bush in less than three years.'

Butler didn't like the sound of that last part. All he wanted to do was run Tondipgiri just long enough to not lose face when he got out; he hadn't expected that this tea-growing stuff was going to take three years.

Noticing the lack of an enthusiastic response to his directions on propagating, Taylor frowned. 'Well? What's the matter, laddy?'

Butler brought his attention back to what Taylor had been saying.

'Three years to get a full bush?'

'Aye, what of it? Come on, man, what's eating you?'

Butler took the plunge. 'Look, I've got no experience with this sort of thing. I want to learn,' he added hastily, seeing Taylor's expression, 'but I don't know anything about planting. I mean, what do I live on?'

From the look on Taylor's face Butler thought that the tea expert was going to walk away in disgust, but Butler held his ground and stared right back.

Taylor sniffed and scuffed his boots in the ground, surveyed the devastated slopes, sniffed again then fixed his piercing eyes on Butler.

'Very well, Mr Butler,' and Butler noticed that he had dropped the 'laddy'. 'You're keen and I'll help you get started, but it'll be hard work; are you up to it?'

'I'm up to it,' said Butler.

Taylor didn't look convinced.

'You'll work harder than you've ever worked before,' he said. 'Don't think it's going to be easy.'

'I'm up to it,' repeated Butler stubbornly and held Taylor's level stare.

'All right,' said Taylor abruptly and turned to survey the estate.

'You can grow vegetables down here,' he said firmly, 'and you can get some livestock – goats, chickens. You need to pull those stumps out and clear the slopes, then you can propagate from your bushes on the other side. Aye, you've got a good position here. You can do a lot with this place. You'll have a lot to learn, though.'

'I'll learn it,' declared Butler.

Taylor cast a weighing-up eye at him.

'You can't learn it all,' he said. 'Nobody can. I've been out here twenty-three years and I'm

90

still learning. And now I think I'll take a closer look at that slope,' and Taylor wandered away along the base of the hill, stopping now and then to pick up a handful of soil, testing its texture, even smelling it.

Butler watched him, then noticed a man standing by the bridge over the swollen stream. He was waiting respectfully and Butler recognised him at once. He went down to the bridge.

'It's Mr Changarai isn't it? What can I do for you?' asked Butler, and the man made a small bow.

'I am Changarai,' he said, and there was a musical singsong lilt to his voice. 'Thank you for your kindness yesterday,' and he bowed again.

'That's all right,' said Butler, uncertain of what else to say. 'Don't mention it. What was the problem, anyway?'

The man ducked his head. 'Mr Paget said coffee bags were missing from store. Mr Paget said workers steal coffee. I say No. Workers are good workers. They work hard. They not steal coffee. Store was not wrong; book was wrong. Mr Paget writes book.'

'What was your job?' asked Butler.

'I was *Kangany*,' said Changarai, with a note of pride in his voice, and he straightened as he said it.

'*Kangany?*' asked Butler blankly.

Changarai hesitated and looked for the right word, then his face lit up.

'Foreman,' he declared.

Butler nodded, and it suddenly struck him that without a foreman there was no possibility of making the Tondipgiri estate work; he needed someone who could give orders to the workers, someone who spoke their language. But ... and he looked at Changarai doubtfully.

The native held himself with dignity, standing patiently, and Butler felt momentarily lost. He had no experience in judging whether a man would be a good worker or not and he realised that there was a vast gap in his experience somewhere.

Stop feeling sorry for yourself, Butler! he told himself fiercely. Up until a couple of months ago you made a living out of weighing up other card-players, making an assessment of what kind of men they were, how they would play, how they would gamble, and usually you were right. You did well at the races too because you had an edge: you'd realised you need to study more than just form – you need to study the owners, the trainers, the jockeys, the things they do and say that give themselves away, what they're up to. You're as good at judging character as anyone.

'Mr Changarai, my name's Butler. Would you like to work for me as *Kangany?*' and the man bowed.

'It is my honour, sir,' and he fixed bright eyes on Butler. 'Very much would I like to work for you.'

Butler nodded. 'All right. You've got the job.'

'I will serve you faithfully, Butler-Sir,' and when he bowed again Butler involuntarily made a similar bowing motion. He straightened, embarrassed, and cleared his throat.

'Right,' he said. 'First thing is to get everyone

on the estate together. There's work to do.'

Changarai repeated his bow and hurried away in the direction of the workers' shacks. Butler watched Taylor pottering about amongst the stumps and found himself quite looking forward to the rebuilding of Tondipgiri.

He saw himself sitting on his verandah, supervising Taylor and Changarai and watching the native workers bringing order out of the chaos left by the storm. He would, he decided, adopt a suitably serious air; probably nod judiciously a few times as if weighing up progress and finding it satisfactory. He might even take a turn or two round the estate, examining the work and letting the workers know he was in control of things. He savoured the word Compton had used to describe him: *Durai*. He, John Butler, was the *Durai*, the man in charge. The word had a good feel. He would be the *Durai* on the verandah, keeping an eye on what was going on. And cool drinks would be nice, he thought. It would be pleasant to sit in the shade with a refreshing drink in his hand. Perhaps he could get something brought over from the Planters' Club.

Then the big Scot ceased his pottering and Butler's pleasant musings were cut short.

Taylor, he quickly discovered, regarded Changarai as Butler's man and liked to preserve the proprieties. He gave his instructions only to Butler and it was for Butler to then instruct Changarai. Consequently, instead of lounging on the verandah, Butler was out on the estate all day accompanying Taylor and passing directions to

93

Changarai. There was very little sitting down to be had and Butler consoled himself with the thought that he had absolutely no intention of seeing out the three years that Taylor had stated would be needed to establish the new bushes. The moment, the very *second* he reckoned he had stuck at it long enough for no one to call him a quitter he would announce the imminent demise of the fictitious relative in England and then that would be that; they wouldn't see him for dust.

Six

Taylor was a hard taskmaster.

'Clear all this,' he announced, indicating the storm-blasted slope. 'If any of the tree trunks are good for timber get them sawn up. If they're only good for fuel cut them into logs and store them under cover. Dig those stumps out by the roots. Clear that undergrowth. Cut those weeds. Spread it all in the sun to dry, then burn it,' and he prowled round Tondipgiri, muttering under his breath and growling at things and people in equal measure.

Butler returned from passing on yet another instruction to Changarai and found Taylor investigating a patch of undergrowth. The man was shabby and looked like a buffoon, yet it began to dawn on Butler that he might possibly have made a misjudgement. Taylor's appearance suggested nothing of the expert, yet everything he said about tea and propagation and cultivation had the solid ring of authority. The man was a complete contrast to Paget, who had been conspicuously well turned out on the two occasions Butler had met him, yet was a complete oaf. Butler recalled the tough and leathery men in the Planters' Club and found the thought unsettling that perhaps finery and elegance might not be the measure of a man after all.

He had little leisure to ponder the thought further, for there was always more work to be done. The absence of large areas of roof on the bungalow meant that every day he was woken at first light and would crawl bleary-eyed from the wooden boards of his bed and stagger to the doorway. Invariably a welcome bowl of food would be waiting and he would consume it ravenously, then minutes later Taylor would arrive – the Scot seemed tireless; he must have risen before dawn to get there at that time – and it would be out onto the slopes once more to implement the relentless directions. On Butler's arrival Changarai would marshal the patiently waiting workers and they would attack the slopes again.

Immense bonfires of weeds and grasses and tree trunks built up and were finally set alight. The flames crackled and popped and dense clouds of insects rose up, escaping from the fires only to provide a feast for hundreds and hundreds of birds circling and diving overhead. The estate workers gathered round the roaring fires, waiting with forked sticks and looks of eager anticipation, and Butler didn't understand why until dozens of indignant evicted snakes came gliding out, heads erect, ready to strike. The natives jumped forward, pinning the snakes with the sticks and ruthlessly battering at the heads with rough clubs, then pounced on the carcasses. The meat was a great delicacy, explained Taylor, and there was much cheering every time another snake was killed.

'Right,' declared Butler, turning away from the final bonfire. 'That's nearly all of it. There's just those now.'

'Those' were stubborn old stumps, too deeply rooted for the natives to dig or pull out.

'How do we get those out?' and he looked at Taylor.

Taylor was sucking on his pipe.

'*We* don't,' he said, around the stem. '*They* do,' and he nodded past Butler.

Butler glanced round and gave a start.

'Good God!' and he took a hurried step back, oblivious to the exclamation of pain from Taylor as he trod on his foot. How they had come so close without making a noise Butler couldn't imagine but there, barely three yards away, stood three elephants.

He watched them nervously and eyes of dark honey stared back with mild curiosity.

In England he had once seen a drawing of an elephant and had supposed that they were about the size of large dray horses, but the reality of an animal nearly twice his height jolted him. It was a mystery how they had approached without making a sound; how could something so vast, with such huge legs – thicker than the stumps they had come to uproot – and those massive feet, sidle up to within a few feet of him without the sound of a single footfall or a snort or even a rustle?

He was just musing on the fact that these elephants were the same reddish brown as the earth rather than the grey he had been told that they were, when he realised that a crowd had gathered. They were all there – every field worker off the hill, all the children, older men and women that he had never seen before. They were congregating at a distance and standing very still, watching the elephants.

'They have great respect for them,' explained Taylor, 'and they never use the word "elephant", or the equivalent in their language, just in case one of the beasts hears them and takes offence.'

'Superstitious are they?' asked Butler.

Taylor shrugged. 'Perhaps. They think if you say its name you'll meet one – and an angry elephant can flatten an entire village. It's not something you'd want to see. So they don't dare do anything that might offend them.'

On each elephant sat a young boy, equipped only with a long thin stick, and one of them said something. Butler thought the boy was speaking to him, then he realised Changarai was standing at his shoulder and Changarai chattered back. The elephant flapped ears the size of blankets and the trunk curled and uncurled then stretched out towards Butler. Butler leaned back quickly.

'She likes you,' said Changarai, stepping forward and putting his hand out. The tip of the trunk brushed over Changarai's hand, then extended forwards again to Butler. 'She wants grass.'

Butler looked doubtfully at Changarai, then pulled up a handful of grass and offered it hesitantly, his hand spread wide. The trunk came up and the end snuffled drily over his hand, then curled around the grass and wafted it away into the elephant's mouth. The other elephants shuffled and their trunks stretched out to Butler. The workers nudged each other and muttered excitedly and Butler held out handfuls of grass and grinned.

Changarai said something to the boys and they jabbered at the elephants and guided them towards the slope, keeping up a constant stream of directions. At least, Butler assumed they were directions – the three boys could have been talking among themselves for all he knew. The first elephant waited patiently as a chain was tied loosely about its massive neck, and then, while the other two were having chains fitted, Changarai guided her to the nearest stump. He expertly wrapped the end of the chain around it and as much of the roots as had been exposed, then the boy, with much chatter and tapping with his stick, guided the elephant away.

She moved, the chain came up tight and she leaned into the pull, the great feet pushing and pressing into the earth. The stump creaked, the elephant moved and shifted again, then took the strain once more and a fan of fine cracks radiated outwards from around the stump. Another pull and this time the earth around the base of the stump creaked and sucked, then the roots tore and snapped and the stump came out and rolled to a rest. The elephant clearly knew that she had done what was expected of her, for she threw back her trunk and trumpeted in satisfaction and her rider guided her to the next one.

The elephants worked their way up and along the hill, repeated trumpetings signalling that yet another stump had been pulled successfully out of the red earth, and the estate workers followed, throwing their ropes around the uprooted stumps and dragging them down the slope. The stumps piled up at the base of the hill and another bonfire was soon smoking. Taylor regarded the scene with satisfaction.

Stumps, grass, loose undergrowth, all had gone, leaving an expanse of broken red earth sloping up to the crest of the hill.

He nodded.

'That's a good job done,' he declared and turned to Butler. 'And now I think it's time you met George Thwaites.'

Despite the heat Thwaites arrived wearing a dark suit with waistcoat and stiff collar, a small ribbon bow tie knotted tight and not a single grey hair out of place. Deep-set dark eyes weighed Butler up as they shook hands, and Butler found himself wondering again what it was about these men that unsettled him so.

All the ones who seemed to know what they were about, the ones who had made anything of themselves, seemed possessed of a quite extraordinary degree of inner confidence, at odds with anything Butler had encountered back in

England. All the swanks and rakes he used to associate with had appeared cool and sure of themselves, but compared to these tanned, sun-baked men he realised that what he had taken for confidence in his companions of old had been nothing more than bluster. The thought pulled him up short and, in a moment of crystal clarity, Butler realised that of all things in the world what he wanted most was to be as self-confident as these men. He didn't want to simply act it or pretend it, nor possess it as a sop to some self-conceit or as something to brag about; he wanted the real thing, that unshakeable self-assurance and composure, and he wanted it because, he admitted to himself somewhat shamefacedly, this at last was something he recognised as being truly worth having.

Exhibiting that same relentlessly tireless stride as Taylor, Thwaites climbed the slope to the top of the hill, the freshly turned earth bothering him not at all. Butler and Taylor accompanied him and watched as Thwaites examined the tea bushes, moving eagerly from one to the next, scraping at the earth around the base of the bushes. He came back, nodding approvingly.

'Very fine bushes,' he commented. 'Very fine bushes indeed. I would put it down to the soil – some of the best I've ever seen – combined with the exposed position on this slope,' and he pointed to the east. 'The wind comes from that direction and this ridge is the first thing that offers any real resistance. These bushes have dug in well; they've had to – it's been either that or be blown out of the ground. They're well rooted; stunted, mind you, but they're vigorous growers,' and he looked at Butler.

'You're going to have a quite excellent tea estate here, Mr Butler. These are all good healthy bushes; you'll be able to propagate quite extensively from their root systems. If you don't mind I'd like to come back here from time to time, just to see how they adapt to the other slope.'

Butler quickly nodded agreement. He was beginning to realise that the advice and expertise of Taylor and Thwaites was going to be invaluable. They went back down the hill and Taylor pointed out work that had to be done.

'It's been well cleared, but before you do any planting you need to put your paths and drains in. Be careful with the drainage: you don't want to lose all this good top-soil. You'll need silt-pits there, there and there,' and he pointed at spots along the slope. 'Build a system of side-drains, they can drain into leading drains and run off into the stream down there. You'll need a good system of paths too; you can't start planting until you've got your paths and drains laid out.'

Butler listened carefully and concentrated on what Taylor was saying. It was all rather interesting.

He caught himself and issued a stern reminder that he wasn't staying a moment longer than necessary, he was absolutely adamant about that. Until then, though, all this work and the improvements were no bad thing – they meant he'd get an even better price for the place when he finally sold it.

The system of drains and paths took shape and Butler, studying it from the vantage point of the top of the ridge, declared himself well satisfied.

'Jolly good,' he said aloud and a giggle made him turn.

From amongst the stubby bushes, barely ten feet away, a girl was watching him. She was perhaps fourteen or fifteen years old, her dress simple, and one hand was toying with the coloured stones of her necklace. When she saw him notice her she tipped her head to one side and twisted her fingers in the tangle of blue-black hair piled on top of her head. Butler grinned and winked at her and her eyes, deep and brown, widened, then the glowing honey-brown skin creased showing healthy white teeth in a smile that pushed her cheeks upwards and outwards. She giggled deep in her throat and ducked her head and ran away down the eastern slope. She stopped, peered over the bush tops at him, saw him still looking at her and bobbed down again. He kept watching and after a moment her head appeared over the bushes. She smiled shyly, then beckoned him. He smiled and shook his head, but she repeated the gesture, more insistent this time, then she did it again.

All right, he thought and went down the steep slope after her. She kept bobbing away ahead of him then ducking down amongst the bushes, and several times he thought he had lost her. He stared round and spotted her again – now she was at the bottom, standing by the rope bridge. He descended the rest of the slope and by the time he reached the bridge she was already halfway over, watching him.

The bridge was longer than it had first appeared when viewed from the top of the hill; there was at least a hundred yards of it and it trembled and swung as Butler, praying that all the boards were secure, started to cross. Holding on to the ropes that served as handrails he followed the girl, treading cautiously in case any of the boards slipped or were rotten. He was sweating by the time he climbed the gradient of the bridge on the far side and stood on solid ground.

The girl darted forward, clutched his hand in her small brown one and pulled him with her. She led him along a pathway heavily overhung with creepers and branches, and even though he had to duck and push them aside she didn't let go of his hand. Bushes encroached from the side as the track began to climb and Butler was concluding that they were entering the jungle proper when suddenly the girl stopped and dropped to the ground, pulling him down beside her. She held a finger to her lips that he should be quiet and beckoned him closer and Butler inched forward a little. Her hand on his shoulder made him stop, then she turned and very slowly, very carefully, pulled some of the branches aside. She peered through the opening for a moment, then turned to Butler and with a nod of her head indicated that he should look. He inched forward a little more.

They were crouching by the side of a track about twenty feet wide. Very few branches overhung it and the packed earth showed it was well used, but nothing was moving there and he couldn't imagine what he was supposed to be looking at. He turned and opened his mouth to ask and a hand that was warm with a hint of something vaguely spicy pressed against his lips, then the girl took her hand away and turned to watch the track.

Butler shifted restlessly and sniffed and the girl frowned at him. She was obviously waiting for something, so he shrugged and waited too. After a couple of minutes she clutched his shoulder and very slowly pointed a little way up the track. Butler looked to where she was pointing but saw nothing, only thick green jungle.

He began to shake his head, then he froze. An elephant was standing at the edge of the track.

'It is Him,' breathed the girl and Butler could barely hear her, so quiet was her voice. He stared at the elephant and couldn't believe what had just happened: he had seen nothing, had heard nothing, he was staring at exactly the same patch of tangled jungle as before, but the confluence of light and shadow had subtly altered and where there had previously been bushes and branches was now this huge beast. What he had thought was a branch was, he now realised, the curve of an ivory tusk. What he had thought were the trunks of trees were the animal's massive legs. And somehow the small movements of the elephant – the slight curling and twitching of the trunk, the slow flapping of the ears – matched the movement of the forest, preventing the elephant being revealed by too rigid a stillness. It blended into the jungle perfectly.

Butler and the girl were motionless. The elephant stood for a full five minutes, then stepped onto the track. It looked both ways, still making no sound, then its ears flapped and it began walking down the track towards them. Three more elephants emerged from the same spot and all moved as silently as their leader. Trunks swinging they advanced and Butler tensed, ready to run, but the girl next to him was absolutely still and it occurred to him that as she seemed to know exactly what she was doing then perhaps it was best if he copied her.

The leading elephant came abreast of them and halted. The trunk waved and the massive head moved slowly from side to side, as if puzzled by the presence of something it sensed was there but which couldn't be seen or smelt, and the following elephants stopped. All four were wary and alert, heavily scarred, sharply different from their smaller and more docile cousins who had pulled out the tree stumps. Butler held his breath, not even daring to blink, and the elephant's huge ears flapped again and it marched on. The others followed, and as each massive foot came down Butler marvelled that he could hear only the faintest sound of dust being crushed underfoot as they went past.

The elephants went down the track and were lost to sight round a bend. Butler let out his breath in an explosive gust. It was the girl's turn to grin.

'It was Him,' she said.

'Him?'

'Him,' she repeated and lowered her voice. 'It was the Old One,' and Butler remembered what Taylor had said: the natives always used other words for elephants, never daring to name them directly.

'Very impressive,' he said, not knowing what else to say, still feeling relief that they hadn't been spotted. She grinned again, then led him back along the overgrown track to the bridge, and once across she let go of his hand and ran off.

'Hey!' he called, but she took no notice and disappeared amongst the bushes. She didn't reappear and he thought he could hear girlish laughter. He couldn't imagine why she had wanted to show him the elephants and it was a mystery how she even knew they would be there, but his spirits felt somehow uplifted.

Seven

Butler toiled back up the steep eastern slope and was glad to sit down at the top. On the crest of the ridge he inhaled deeply of the breeze rustling the tea bushes and ruffling his hair, and he contemplated the hills and peaks and river and jungle surrounding the estate. His estate.

It really was very satisfying to see the progress being made. His eyes lit on the just visible shape of buildings through the thick stand of trees to the north of the estate, and he supposed that must be where the little girl had come from. It struck him that he hadn't yet been over there; not once since arriving had he taken a look at where the estate workers lived. It was an omission he might as well rectify now, he concluded. There was nothing pressing that needed taking care of and he wandered down the slope.

There was a well-worn path through the trees to where the workers lived – their daily route to the planting slopes, he deduced – and he followed it. He rounded some bushes and a thick tree, pushed a hanging branch aside and a group of children playing in the dirt jumped up, startled, and ran off.

Butler didn't move. He didn't know quite what he had expected to find, but it wasn't this. He swallowed.

In two lines, facing each other across a narrow strip of broken ground, was a pair of long low buildings. Large patches of stone and plaster had fallen away from their filthy walls and some of the resulting jagged holes were crudely plugged with mud and grass, but most simply gaped. The thatch of the roofs was threadbare and the gaps exceeded any in Butler's bungalow. Each wretched building had a dozen doorways, presumably indicating a dozen separate dwellings, and not one doorway had a door to it. Rubbish lay heaped against the walls and in piles on the ground and some of the scrawniest chickens he had ever seen scratched at it.

So this was where they lived, the men and women who even now were labouring and sweating for him: two sorry lines of tumbledown shacks, and the absence of sound and movement struck him. A place where people lived should be alive and buzzing with activity, it shouldn't be like this. Apart from the dejected clucking of the chickens he could hear children playing a game somewhere beyond the lines, but that was all, and it just served to emphasise the desolation.

It felt strange to be in such an uncared-for mess after watching the orderly construction of paths and drains on the planting slopes. It was like nothing he had ever encountered before. The stillness was oppressive and he began to feel uncomfortable. He was sure he was being watched. He took a step forward but felt at once as if he was intruding. God knew, being a planter was as far away from his previous life as it was possible to get, but this was beyond even that. This wasn't his world, he didn't belong here.

He backed away into the trees and turned and hurried along the path. When it emerged from the trees he was astonished at how reassuring he found the sight of his own rundown bungalow with its missing shutters and torn roof. The work steadily progressing on the hill was comforting too. He found he had been holding his breath and he let it out. He paused for a moment, then cleared his throat, adjusted his collar and strode towards the hill, suddenly very much looking forward to examining the neat and orderly and normal and safe activities up there.

His determined step petered out after three yards and he hesitated, then glanced round. The path was there, beckoning him back through the trees, but he didn't want to go. The memory of those mean hovels with their black doorways gaping wide like some sinister invitation unnerved him. But the path was still there, it was there to be walked, and he found himself returning to it, then walking along it, his steps slowing. He rounded the thick tree and with an arm that suddenly seemed to be made of lead he pushed the overhanging branch aside.

The scene hadn't changed. The chickens still scratched in the rubbish, the children beyond the lines were still playing their game and the black doorways still waited for him.

His throat was dry and his collar felt tight. Pots clanked somewhere and a wisp of smoke drifted across the lines. The smell of something cooking, something cloying and sweet, drifted after it. Slowly he walked down the strip of dusty ground, more sure than ever that he was being watched, and he stopped. One of the doorways was just a few yards away and Butler hesitated. He really didn't want to go in there but something inside him insisted that he take a look. At first his feet wouldn't move but eventually he approached. There was another moment of hesitation in front of the open doorway but the impetus to enter was too strong to be gainsaid. He bent his head to avoid striking it on the frame and went in.

His eyes took a moment to adjust from the blazing sunlight outside to the darkness within, then the pathetic contents became clear.

A hearth and a pitiful huddle of pots occupied one side of the packed-earth floor, there was some bedding made of rushes and grass, and against a wall lay what was either a pile of clothing or a pile of rags due to be discarded. The place smelt damp and stale.

The pile of rags moved, Butler's heart skipped a beat and he realised that underneath was an old woman with an impossibly wrinkled face, watching him with beady black eyes. He took a quick step backwards.

'I'm sorry,' he muttered. 'I beg your pardon; I didn't mean to intrude.'

He backed another step, knocked his head against the lintel, ducked and retreated outside. The voice of the woman followed him, creaking and uneven, and then it gave vent to a laugh like fingernails drawn across a blackboard and Butler found himself back on the path through the trees before he knew how he got there. When he reached the hill he was breathing heavily, not only from the exertion.

Taylor was standing there, studying the layout of pathways, and he turned as Butler approached.

'These paths are good, they–' and he frowned. 'Are you all right? You look pale.'

'I'm fine,' lied Butler. 'Fine. Just fine. No, really, I'm fine. What were you saying about the paths?'

Butler was up, ready and waiting before Taylor arrived the following morning. He had barely slept, and on each occasion that he had fallen asleep he had woken sweating and gasping from a dream that was the same each time, and yet he could remember nothing of it, save that it had involved cavernous black doorways. He was glad to get out onto the slopes and divert his thoughts to the routine work of preparing the paths and drains. He paid an extra degree of attention to what Taylor was saying and kept his gaze away from the northern end of the estate.

At mid-morning Taylor had to leave on some business of his own, and it wasn't long before Butler found himself glancing towards that stand of trees, the start of the pathway through them just visible. He remembered again what he had seen when he had reached the end of that path, and he straightened.

For God's sake pull yourself together, man, he scolded himself. The place had been deserted because everyone was on the slopes, that was all and, yes, the huts didn't have doors but what was wrong with that? He turned his face to the sun and shut his eyes, letting the heat bathe his face.

He glanced at the trees again. That was all they were – trees. He recalled the speed with which he had fled that hut, and admitted that he had acted rather foolishly. That woman had probably been asleep and he had startled her, that was all. He laughed a short, embarrassed laugh.

There was nothing wrong, he told himself, nothing wrong at all. Why, he could go over there now if he wanted to. It was his estate, he owned it, he could go anywhere he liked. Standing on the neat slope in the bright sunshine he felt silly to have acted as he had.

Go on, go and have another look, a voice said inside, and although he experienced a moment of doubt he went down the hill and crossed to the trees.

The path was quiet and Butler slowed as he

reached the end of it.

It's because I don't want to disturb anyone, he told himself, and stopped there. He didn't lift the branch but peered through the leaves.

Someone coughed right behind him and he jumped and spun round. It was Changarai.

'Thank God,' exclaimed Butler. 'I mean – I didn't know you were there.'

The old man stared at him, an expression of gentle curiosity on his face, and Butler felt compelled to give some explanation.

'I just thought I'd come and have a look,' he said with studied nonchalance. 'I stopped here because I didn't want to intrude on anyone.'

Changarai nodded politely.

'All at work,' he said. 'Come and see,' and he passed Butler and held the branch aside for him.

Butler felt he could hardly refuse, so he followed Changarai and they walked across the broken ground between the lines. It felt good to have Changarai at his side, and immediately after having that thought Butler berated himself for his cowardice. Grow up Butler! he commanded. You're the *Durai,* remember? Start acting like it.

They stopped and Butler looked at the huts. They were more like squalid sheds than places people could live in. Shadows shifted inside both lines and a handful of old men and women emerged, cautious and wary, to watch him. He attempted an encouraging grin and nodded to them but their expressions didn't change.

Something rustled behind him and he turned quickly.

Emerging from the trees were the estate

workers. They stood in silence and Butler faced them. Then he heard more movement on the other side and turned again and this time found a score of children watching him from the far end of the lines. He was surrounded.

The estate workers must have seen him coming over and had drifted down from the slopes to follow him. He stared at their faces and saw no threat, no resentment of his presence there, nothing to suggest he was an unwelcome intruder. If anything he thought they looked defeated.

'They don't look happy,' he muttered to Changarai.

'They worry,' said Changarai. '*Durai* is a father to them. *Durai* tells them what to do. *Durai* looks after them. For long time they have no *Durai*. Now they have, but they worry you will go soon.'

Butler felt distinctly uncomfortable. This was becoming too much.

'People come and go,' he said lamely. 'It happens.'

Changarai made no comment and the people stared, motionless, waiting for Butler to do or say something.

He looked at the dilapidated lines again.

'Why is everything so bad?' he asked quietly.

Changarai looked at him blankly and Butler tried again.

'Why haven't these huts been repaired?'

'No *Durai*,' said Changarai, as if that explained everything. 'Everyone works on the hill. Huts are always this way.'

Butler looked at him in disbelief. 'You mean it was like this before I came?'

Changarai turned and spoke to one of the workers, then turned back to Butler. 'He says it has been like this for many years.'

'Years?' and Butler turned on the spot, staring at the huts and wishing that he was somewhere else, somewhere miles away rather than under the gaze of all those people. He suddenly felt acutely ashamed, and the reason quickly followed: Tondipgiri was, for him, merely something to pass the time with until he could get out of Ceylon without the loss of face that quitting would attract; to these people, though, the estate was their livelihood, these shacks were their homes. They were unable to pack up and run because, unlike him, they had nowhere else to go.

Being *Durai* didn't seem quite such fun any more.

He shot another glance at the huts and looked away. Something should be done about them, he supposed.

'Er, Changarai, tell them they've got the rest of today and tomorrow off. Tell them they can use it to get these places fixed up.'

Changarai told them and it produced a few looks between the workers but nothing else.

'What's the matter?' asked Butler. 'What's wrong?'

'They are waiting for you,' explained Changarai. 'They wait for *Durai* to tell them what to do.'

Butler was taken aback.

'They want *me* to tell them what to do?' and he shrugged a helpless shrug and spread his arms. 'How can I tell them? I don't know how to...' and his voice trailed off.

Changarai was looking at him expectantly, so were the workers from the slopes, so were the old men and women from the huts, so were the children and so, he noticed, was the little girl who had taken him to see the elephants and who was now standing near Changarai. She was looking at him with an eager, hopeful, *trusting* look, as if she had no doubt of his ability to make everything right.

He looked at the huts again and ran his hand over his chin.

'What do you thatch roofs with, Changarai? Grass?'

'Thatching grass, Butler-Sir. It grows wild, but people have no time to look for it.'

'Right,' declared Butler. 'We'll soon change that. Send everyone out to find it and bring back as much as they need,' and he looked round. 'You see that lot?' He pointed to the stands of bushes that grew on his side of the road and which didn't form part of the planting ground. 'Clear that, clear all of it. I want that planted with thatching grass for the future.'

Changarai nodded. 'Yes Butler-Sir.'

'And while they're at it they might as well clear those,' and he pointed to the fouled watercourses that ran by the huts. Grass and rubbish, the evidence of past overflows, were washed up against the walls, and an idea occurred to him. 'They've been cutting drains on the hill; now that they know what to do they can cut some proper drains for these huts.'

Changarai gave instructions to the people and

they chattered and exclaimed and hurried around.

'It is done, Butler-Sir,' reported Changarai, but Butler hadn't finished. This wasn't as hard as he'd expected, he found he was quite enjoying himself. He went round to the back of one of the lines and Changarai followed.

Half a dozen skeletal goats stared at them from haphazard patches of vegetables growing amongst piles of rubbish.

'Put proper fences up for those animals,' ordered Butler, modelling himself on Taylor and giving instructions in the same way. 'Clear all that rubbish and burn it, then clear all this land and mark out a space for each hut to grow its own vegetables,' and he walked to the other line and repeated his orders.

He found himself quite satisfied. When the day came for him to leave Ceylon at least his workers would be living in better conditions than when he had arrived.

Butler was impressed with the speed at which his people worked. Now that they had clear directions for what to do they got on with it enthusiastically and the rubbish and rough ground were cleared quicker than Butler expected. The livestock was penned properly and Butler, feeling rather like a gentleman-farmer, supervised the marking-out of vegetable plots. Work started on the roofs and processions of workers returned from expeditions laden with tied bundles of thatching grass which gathered in piles until taken to thatch the next roof.

Butler nodded approvingly at his workers as they dragged the bundles along the lines, but frowned when he saw the girl who had taken him to see the elephants. She was panting, struggling to drag a bundle of grass that was bigger than she was. He went over.

'Here, I'll do that,' and he pulled on the string securing the grass, thinking it would be a small matter to pick up the bundle. Its weight surprised him but he heaved it up, disinclined to appear a weakling. He carried the bundle over to the main pile and gladly dropped it. The girl was beside him and she took his hand.

'We get more,' she said happily and Butler, taken by surprise, found himself going with the girl before he could say no. Somehow, without meaning to, he found himself part of a line of workers, picking up bundles and taking them back to the lines. Grass tickled his face and worked its way down his neck and the girl skipped happily beside him, singing a song. At first the workers looked at him with surprise – clearly they had never seen an owner helping with the hard manual work before – and each time a worker passed him Butler received a broad smile and a bob of the head. He returned each smile with a polite one of his own and the girl chattered and sang all the way. Returning from one trip Butler saw Changarai staring at him, mouth open in surprise; it was the first time Butler had seen him lose his customary composure.

'Come on, Changarai,' Butler couldn't resist saying. 'There's work to be done,' and he dumped the bundle and went for another.

It was dusty work, and by the time the last bundle was brought Butler's throat was dry and rasping. Without thinking he accepted a proffered bowl of water and gulped gratefully. He stood, breathing heavily, lips wet, a trickle of water sliding down his chin, and suddenly realised that he was standing in the centre of a group of native workers, his clothes covered in grass strands and dust. His hair was plastered damply to his head, his neck was itching, he must have looked anything but the picture of a sober, respectable plantation owner, but he had to admit he'd found the last few hours to be rather fun.

Enough was enough though, he decided; he was the *Durai*, not a menial, and when the workers began cutting open the bundles he made to leave, intending to go and clean himself up, but a knife was held out to him. He looked at it, then at the native who offered it. The man smiled and nodded and held the knife out again and it didn't seem right to refuse it. The man lifted a bundle over and set it down before him and Butler hesitated a moment, then copied the other workers and cut the securing string.

He'd had no intention of doing any more work, and as he cut more strings he asked himself what he was doing and why. Before he could arrive at an answer he found he had cut a dozen bundles and it seemed everyone on the estate was around him, gathering and sorting the grass and putting it into sheaves, each one tied with long grasses. He finished the bundle he was working on and stood in the middle of the crowd of kneeling people, uncertain of what to do next.

The little girl took his hand, indicating he should kneel down with her to cut some more bundles, and for a moment everything swung in the balance. For one brief instant he had the option to back away. He'd done some manual work, yes, but he could finish right there and leave his workers to it and he could stay the John Butler he'd always been. After all, if he joined those busy people there was no telling what might happen. It was a moment to make a choice, but he hesitated just a fraction too long, the little girl was tugging insistently on his hand, and a second later she had pulled him across the gulf of his indecision and he was kneeling down next to her, the moment gone. He knelt in the dust, trying to copy the deft movements of the people around him and wondering at the same time how he would ever get the knees of his trousers clean.

The workers accepted his participation more readily than he did and seemed to assume that he had joined them for the duration of the job. They included him in every task, with great respect certainly but never for a moment seeming to doubt that he would help. Butler was bemused to find himself given bundles of sheaves to carry to the huts for passing up and at one point he caught himself grinning at his involvement. He really didn't know what to make of it when he was assisted to clamber up onto the roof to help an old native who was busily putting the sheaves in place. The man's fingers moved faster than

Butler could follow and Butler was impressed with the speed with which the new thatch spread over the roof, packed and layered and tied.

Butler decided to have a go at securing one of the sheaves – it seemed easy enough, if others could do it so could he – and tried to duplicate the movements of the man on the roof beside him. That was the moment when he stopped enjoying himself.

The grass around the sheaf came away and the sheaf disintegrated. Butler tried another one, then another but to his frustration they fell to pieces in his hands. He was on the verge of angrily dashing the entire pile of sheaves to the ground, but the old man was suddenly beside him, strong brown hands on his, and in the same moment as Butler was framing a retort to the man's outrageous impertinence and presumption he found himself completing the tying of a sheaf into place. Then another sheaf was in his hands and he was making those same movements again and before he knew it that sheaf too was in place. The man took his hands away, grinned hugely at Butler and nodded with pleasure. He said something Butler couldn't understand and grinned again and Butler couldn't help but grin back. He looked at the two neat sheaves, then took another sheaf and found his hands could repeat those skilful movements. The sheer delight of not being defeated by a simple bundle of grass made him laugh aloud and he gleefully fastened another in place. He took another and worked through the pile of sheaves beside him, then gestured to the people on the ground to pass more up. The little girl was down there and she caught his eye. She jumped up and down and clapped her hands and Butler grinned back at her.

He slept like a dead man that night, sprawled on his bed and totally exhausted. When he woke it was painful and slow and when he sat up he grunted at the ache in his stiffened muscles. Feeling marginally better after flexing his shoulders and rinsing his face, he put on his shirt and inserted a collar stud, but exclaimed sharply when he pulled the ends of the collar together – the skin of his neck was raw. Tenderly he put his hand on the back of his neck and realised what had happened. Yesterday he had been sweating profusely and the combination of the damp collar chafing his neck and the sun beating on the rubbed skin had burnt it painfully.

He removed the collar and held it in his hand. He'd have to do without it until his neck had recovered. He was about to put it away safely, but stopped himself and looked at the stiff, starched fabric. Without a shadow of a doubt it was the most useless, pointless piece of clothing imaginable. There was absolutely nothing to be gained in wearing such a ridiculous thing in the relentless Ceylon heat.

It joined his other collars in the trunk and Butler resolved not to wear any of the damn silly things again until he was on his way home to England. He removed the collar stud from his shirt and pulled the neck apart.

Walking across to the lines he relished the absence of the collar and the feeling of freedom it gave him and he found further satisfaction when he looked up at the thatch he had put in the previous day.

'Long after I've gone those sheaves will still be there,' he said to himself, and couldn't understand why his cheerful mood abruptly lost some of its brightness. He shook his head to clear the thought and went to meet Changarai as planned.

After his success with the thatching Butler decided that in some form or other he could ensure he took a part in every job. He watched the estate workers closely and helped to make bricks, repair walls, even dig new drains: the latter was something he found he knew the rudiments of from watching the cutting of drainage channels on the hillside. His hands, previously used only to handling playing cards, quickly blistered through contact with bricks and rough old tools, and the disdainful pride of the Butler of old would have made him curse petulantly, but now his pride made it a point of honour that he stifle his groans and not let the natives around him know how much his hands were stinging. To this new Butler the voicing of complaints whilst his workers said nothing seemed as much of an infringement of right and proper behaviour as using the wrong knife for fish or passing port to the right. He pressed his torn hands against his thighs then carried on without a word.

One afternoon he was tying thatching grass into sheaves for his own bungalow's ruined roof and thinking about replacements for the missing door and shutters when he noticed the girl watching him again. He knew her name now, he had heard Changarai speaking to her. She was called Mirissa. He smiled and waved and she put her hand to her mouth, then she waved shyly and ran away to the lines. He waited but she didn't reappear.

Eight

Once the lines were repaired it was time to return to the slopes to complete the work on the paths and drainage channels and to prepare the ground for planting. The days were the hardest Butler had ever experienced, and every night he staggered to his bungalow and collapsed on the bed, convinced that he would be unable to rise tomorrow. But, somehow, he managed to drag himself out into the burning sun of each following morning to begin yet another day.

And then the day came when Butler went to bed not much more tired than when he had risen; after that he found it becoming ever so slightly easier to get up in the mornings. His muscles ceased to be sore, his hands ceased to bleed and he began to wake up refreshed instead of still being exhausted from yesterday's labours.

Taylor and Thwaites dropped by at regular intervals, casting judicious eyes over the work on the slopes, making a suggestion here, a correction to something there, and once or twice Butler caught the two men staring approvingly at the task he was currently engaged in. He took encouragement from that look and returned each time with new vigour to the work.

One day, in a drizzle that had persisted for the past week, he stood at the bottom of the hill, Taylor on one side of him, Thwaites on the other, and they stared up the slope to the top, taking in the neat lines and rows of gleaming whitewashed pegs stuck into the red-brown soil. The pegs ran in neat formation lines around the contours of the hill.

'Good work,' nodded Taylor approvingly. 'Contour planting's best; it stops the paths turning into drains and having all your top-soil washed away.' Thwaites murmured agreement.

'Now do I plant?' asked Butler, and Taylor surveyed the slope once more.

'Aye,' he said shortly. 'Now you plant.'

Thwaites scraped away at the base of the bush, putting handfuls of soil to one side until he had exposed the roots. He severed a length and pulled it from the ground, then he meticulously repacked the earth around the bush and picked up the cut root.

'Watch this carefully,' Taylor told Butler.

'Cut this into pieces about two or three inches long,' said Thwaites. 'Then take one of the pieces, cut away the bark on one side, like so, then plant this in the ground about a hand's width deep.'

He stood and surveyed the bushes. 'You're very fortunate, Mr Butler – I estimate that if you take a length of root from each one of these you should be able to cut enough pieces to plant all of the new area.'

Butler looked across the slope to where the ever-faithful, ever-reliable Changarai was waiting and he summoned him over.

'Watch this,' said Butler. 'Everyone must do this. One root from each bush. One root only,' and under Thwaites's careful eye Butler dug for a root, cut it into small lengths and trimmed the bark off one side of each length. Changarai watched closely and nodded, then hurried down the hill and fired out a stream of instructions to the workers. They picked up baskets, filed up the slopes, over the ridge and fanned out amongst the tea bushes on the far side.

Butler wandered up and down the rows of busy workers, concerned that they would be cutting too much or not enough, but Changarai had them under control; the roots were being cut as ordered, no one was making an error and the baskets of cut roots began to accumulate.

Butler was first onto the slopes the following morning. The estate workers assembled and gathered round to watch.

'I'll do the first one,' he said, forgetting for a moment that only Changarai understood him, and he took one of the cut roots, bent down to one of the white pegs, pulled it out and scooped a shallow depression as deep as the width of his hand. He put the root in, then smoothed the soil over and packed it down. He stood and wiped the dirt from his hands, then turned and looked at his workers staring at him expectantly. He gave a sudden exultant grin and with a wave of his arm gave the order.

'Plant!'

Whether they understood the word was doubtful, but the intention of his order was clear and the men and women were soon working in a long line. Someone started a steady rhythmic chant and the others joined in and Butler caught himself humming along. He stopped, then thought 'Why not?' He began humming it again.

'Nearly done,' Butler announced when Taylor came to look over the work.

'Nearly,' agreed Taylor. 'Once this lot's in you'll need trees – eucalyptus and acacia – to give some shade to your bushes. They'll keep the sunlight from any weeds that try to grow and they'll break the force of the rain and keep some of the moisture in the ground.'

Butler had thought that the planting work would be over once the tea roots were in the ground; he hadn't expected that trees would have to be planted too, but if that was what it took ... well, he wasn't going to do half a job, not with this estate. It would be worth more when he came to sell it, he told himself again, but this time, strangely, he didn't get the feeling of glee that he usually experienced when contemplating his departure from Tondipgiri.

An hour after midnight Butler stirred and twisted on the rough bed. He lay half-awake for a moment, wondering what it was that had woken him, then began to drift back to sleep. A sudden twitching by his feet woke him again and he raised his head.

Sliding under the blanket and over his lower leg was the end of a long, narrow black shape and Butler could hear it brushing against the blanket as it coiled itself.

He froze and the sweat broke out on his body. The snake was somewhere about his feet, and in the dim light he saw and felt the blanket moving as the creature began to move up along his leg. The blanket was at Butler's waist and the edge of it suddenly shifted and moved till abruptly the head of the snake emerged. Its eyes caught a beam of moonlight and sparkled and Butler was rigid. Its tongue flickered out and it paused for a moment, then gathered its coils. It was all Butler could do not to scream and throw himself aside, but he had seen how fast snakes moved; he had no doubt that whatever he might attempt this one would move faster than he ever could. The sweat beaded on his forehead and ran down his face and his skin was cold, despite the heat of the night.

The snake still lay on his stomach, unmoving, and Butler found himself praying.

Oh God, Oh God, don't let it settle down, don't let it go to sleep there.

Its body twitched again and it began to slither onto Butler's chest. Butler's head was raised and he could see the flat head slowly gliding towards him. He wanted to close his eyes, dreading what was going to happen, but found himself unable to shut them. The snake stopped again, staring at Butler, and Butler hoped that it wouldn't see his

127

frozen stare as a challenge. He didn't dare to blink; he hardly dared even to breathe, conscious as he was of the weight on his chest. The black eyes studied him, the tongue flickered out again and Butler could feel a scream beginning inside him, all ready to come up his throat and burst, splitting the night in a cry of pure terror, but a strangler's hand couldn't have silenced him more effectively. The scream stayed where it was, building up inside him, right underneath the snake.

The snake's head swayed from side to side then slowly it moved forwards again. It seemed to be coming straight for him but instead it slid onto his shoulder and onto the rolled-up blanket he was using for a pillow. Butler's neck was rigid. He didn't dare turn his head as he watched the long black body slowly coil and slide over his chest and shoulder.

There seemed to be no end of it; how long was this snake? Then suddenly there was the tip of the tail sliding past and Butler heard it slip onto the pillow as the snake began trailing off the bed and onto the floor.

Butler moved. Every muscle in his body convulsed, the wild yell finally escaped his lips and he threw himself off the bed. His feet hit the floor, sprang him forwards, and he threw himself at the new door, no time to open it. His momentum carried the door off its hinges and he crashed into the yard outside, rolling away desperately before getting to his feet and coming to a crouch, staring back at the bungalow, watching intently to see if the snake was following.

He heard distant voices, then the sound of running feet, and people from the lines came hurrying up, some carrying burning torches. Changarai was with them.

'Butler-Sir, what is wrong?'

Butler swallowed.

'A snake,' he said. 'A damn big snake in there, right on top of me.'

Changarai motioned two of the men forwards and went into the hut with them. Changarai's light moved inside, then there was a shout and some thumping and a moment later the men came out with a long dark shape hanging limply from the forked end of a stick. There was much chatter from the watchers and some laughter and Butler suddenly realised he didn't have a stitch on.

'Very lucky man, Butler-Sir,' said Changarai. 'Very poisonous snake. Very nasty. But very good to eat,' and the people began to disperse, leaving Butler with Changarai. Butler was still breathing heavily.

'Thank you,' he said and held out his hand. Changarai was taken by surprise by the gesture and he blinked and hesitated, then slowly reached out and gripped Butler's hand firmly. Then he bowed and hurried away. Butler watched him go, then turned back to the bungalow. He doubted that he would be getting any more sleep that night.

The following morning Butler was outside the bungalow, weighing up the possibilities for making the place snake-proof, when he heard a respectful cough and looked round to see Changarai watching him.

'There'll be no more snakes getting in here,' declared Butler. 'Not when I've finished.'

'Snakes always get in, Butler-Sir,' said Changarai with the utmost politeness. 'No man can stop snakes. You need special animal.'

He turned and only then did Butler notice that someone was standing behind Changarai. It was the little girl – Mirissa. Changarai introduced her.

'Mirissa is my daughter's daughter,' he said. 'Mirissa, give present to Butler-Sir.'

The girl stepped forward with a furry bundle in her arms. She held it out to Butler and he was about to take it from her when it suddenly uncurled and wriggled and dropped to the ground. Butler took a hurried step back – his reactions had sharpened since his encounter with the snake – but the animal stayed on the ground, the string around its neck held firmly in Mirissa's hand.

'This animal very good for killing snakes,' said Changarai. 'No more trouble with him in house.'

The animal was a mongoose, about a foot and a half long with grey-brown fur and a pointed head. A long tail, the same length as its body, trailed behind it. The little animal sniffed the air and scratched at the ground, then looked at Butler. Butler stared back at it and felt oddly touched that someone's protective instinct had been aroused for him.

Changarai whispered something in the girl's ear and she stepped forward.

'This is present for you, Butler-Sir,' she said,

130

holding out the string, and her voice was high and musical. Hesitantly Butler took the string and Mirissa held out a small pot with some kind of paste inside. 'Put on his feet, he never run away.'

Butler took the pot and made a small bow. 'Thank you very much,' he said and the girl giggled and ducked her head and her brown eyes sparkled.

Changarai took her hand. 'Come, Mirissa,' and they left. Mirissa turned to look back at Butler and then they were lost to sight in the trees.

Butler looked down at the furry animal which at that moment was yawning and scratching itself.

'What am I going to call you?' he mused aloud, and the animal looked up at him. Its grey-brown fur and beady eyes reminded Butler of someone and he knew immediately what name to give to his new companion.

'From now on I'm going to call you Coutts,' he said, and took Coutts into the bungalow. The animal wasn't bothered at all as Butler smeared the paste on its paws but waited patiently, and when Butler had finished it sniffed the paws, then set about licking them in evident enjoyment.

Well, thought Butler, if you're going to run away now's the time to find out, and he slipped the string from Coutts's neck. The door was open and if Coutts decided to scuttle out he would be gone before Butler could catch him, but the mongoose was otherwise occupied: whatever was in the paste had captured his full and enthusiastic attention.

Butler had no problem with snakes that night.

Several times he heard shufflings and snortings but discovered on each occasion that it was Coutts sniffing around the bungalow and Butler eventually fell asleep.

He woke abruptly to the sounds of a squeal and something thrashing about violently and he quickly drew his legs up. He looked over the edge of the bed and saw the long dark body of a snake lying motionless on the floor. Coutts was chewing away happily and he looked up at Butler in query, then returned to his feast.

'Good boy,' said Butler, in the manner of praising a well-trained hound, and sank back onto the bed in relief. Coutts, it seemed, had the snake problem well under control.

Nine

Word quickly got around that the newcomer was changing Tondipgiri from coffee to tea, and a number of planters visited the estate. They did it at first for their amusement, and scoffed at Butler's efforts, treating it all as so much nonsense. But the coffee blight was spreading relentlessly, and gradually the visitors' attitudes changed. They began to ask sensible questions rather than making dismissive comments and they took an interest in how the bushes were grown and cultivated. One day a portly planter with a condescending air and an irritatingly slow cultured voice rolled up.

'The name's Cameron,' he drawled. 'I heard you were trying your hand at tea so I thought I'd tool up here and have a look; give you some advice. I plant tea in India,' he explained, as if growers anywhere else were merely rank amateurs. 'Assam,' he added in a superior tone, and seemed a shade put out by Butler's lack of reaction. 'It's where the *best* tea comes from,' said Cameron loftily and listened, smiling a very superior smile, as Butler gave an account of Thwaites's method for propagating bushes using root cuttings. He laughed quietly to himself until Butler asked him why.

'My dear fellow,' he said patronisingly. 'That's not the way to do it. You'll not get good tea going about things that way.'

Cameron spoke as if it were the most natural thing in the world for his audience to be enraptured with his every word; Butler wanted to kick him up the seat of his pants. When they stood on the ridge and Cameron stared down his long nose at the tea bushes on the other side of the hill it was all Butler could do not to make some sharp retort.

'As I suspected,' declared Cameron with supreme disdain, and sniffed. 'You're going about this in completely the wrong way, young man. Of course, that's to be expected with a beginner. These stunted little bushes are quite useless – you should dig them out and burn them. And you've planted far too much down there,' he said, turning and gesturing languidly at the long slope.

'Dig out one row in three and put wind-breaks in, then grub out those fiddling bits of roots and grow your bushes properly from seed – you'll find it's the only way. And between you and me, don't take any notice of Thwaites; he means well but these new ideas of his won't work. Believe me, young Butler, I know what I'm talking about – I've been growing tea for years. I've probably forgotten more than you'll ever know.'

That got right up Butler's nose.

'I'll take my chances the way I'm doing it,' he said tightly.

Cameron tutted. 'Suit yourself,' and he waved a hand dismissively. 'But you'll be out of business within twelve months. On the other hand, if you have the good sense to take my advice–'

'Thank you for your advice, Mr Cameron,' said Butler, endeavouring to stay polite. 'But I'll do this my way.'

Cameron gave him an icy stare and departed with his nose in the air, clearly of the opinion that Butler was a fool to ignore his advice.

There were only two tea experts that Butler was prepared to listen to: Taylor and Thwaites – and one day, sitting on the verandah of Taylor's bungalow, he gained an insight into why Taylor was giving him so much assistance. Taylor had brought out some bottles of beer and was perched on the edge of the verandah table, his right foot twined around the back of his left leg.

'Coffee's had its day here,' stated Taylor flatly. 'They'll not stop the coffee blight, not now; it's too well established. They'll have to plant tea if they want to survive. And a good thing too,' and he poured the first inch of beer on the ground and took a deep swig from the bottle.

He caught Butler's surprised look at the beer swilling on the ground and explained. 'I always say the top of a bottle of beer's no good. Get rid of it,' and he took another swig and glared at Butler. Butler hesitated then poured an inch of beer from his bottle and Taylor nodded approvingly.

'This is a good land,' he said. 'Good earth and good people. I don't want to see it ruined by merchants in London.' He spat in the dust. 'Merchants! Men who've never been out here, who know nothing about running an estate, men who care only about money. The best tea – and I know what I'm talking about – comes when you pick just the bud and the top two leaves. But once the money-men in big corporations get control, all they'll be concerned with is getting as much from a bush as possible. They'll buy an estate, get a good price for the tea and then they'll kill the goose that's laying the golden eggs: they'll order more leaf to be picked from each bush. Those damned idiots think that if a little's good then a lot is better. They won't understand that the tea's good because it's plucked fine rather than coarse.' He took a deep swig, finishing the bottle, and threw it on the ground. He opened another one, discarded the top inch of beer and warmed to his theme.

'The corporations will squeeze out the small estates and then there'll be just a few big ones left, all doing what merchants in London tell 'em.' He peered at Butler from under his bushy eyebrows and spoke as if imparting a secret. 'Do you know what the answer is?' He answered the question before Butler could speak. 'Lots of planters, not just one or two. There needs to be a lot of profitable tea estates, estates that can stand on their own two feet, that can produce enough tea – good-quality tea – to sustain a market for it. The only way to stop those greedy merchants is to have tea planters who know how to do the job properly. Men who can plant and grow and harvest enough good tea to give them independence, to enable them to make a fair living without needing to sell out to corporations run from London.

'That's why I'm helping you,' and he stared levelly at Butler. 'First time I met you I thought you were just another of those young lads with a past they're running away from. Either that or you were one of those swells wanting to make a quick fortune. But I watched you and I knew that you were genuine, I could see that you wanted to do the job properly. You've shown you're a man with a real feeling for the land, for running an estate, for growing tea. You're the sort of man this country needs, John Butler.'

Butler's thoughts went back to that last visit to the Boom Boom Club and the humiliating circumstances of his departure, but he said nothing.

'You've knuckled down,' Taylor was saying. 'You've got on with it. You work hard, the natives like you, the–'

'They like me?' asked Butler, surprised.

'Of course they do,' said Taylor. 'Ever since that

136

business with the thatching grass.'

Butler was surprised Taylor knew about that and he shrugged.

'It was nothing,' he said dismissively.

'It wasn't "nothing" to them,' said Taylor. 'You helped them repair their homes; I've heard they were talking about it for days afterwards. As far as they're concerned you're as good as being family to them now. You've won their respect. Oh, they'd be polite enough to whoever was in charge, they'd bow and be civil, but what they say privately tells the truth and privately they've got a high opinion of you.'

Butler grinned, pleased at this news, and Taylor nodded sagely.

'Aye, but don't take their respect for granted or you'll lose it. They're good people – by and large – and their trust is hard-won and worth keeping. 'Course there's one or two bad apples but generally they're good people, so treat 'em right,' and he chugged some more beer. 'And don't over-pluck those bushes or you'll spoil the final brew.'

'I won't,' Butler promised.

'When the time comes to start selling your tea make sure you invest the profits in your land. Don't line your pockets and don't sell out to big corporations. Invest in your land and it'll pay you back.'

Taylor finished the bottle and threw it away.

'Those are good bushes you've got growing on the other side of that hill of yours,' he said. 'You'll need good machinery to make finished tea from them. Come on,' and abruptly Taylor was on his feet and striding from the bungalow before Butler realised what was happening. He hurried to catch up.

A dusty road and a flight of steps brought them to a neatly whitewashed building and Taylor took him inside. 'It's taken me years to get this right, so pay attention.'

The warm breeze was channelling through a window and onto a framework of racks spread with tea-bush leaves.

'Withering the leaves,' explained Taylor shortly. 'That means getting the moisture out of them. Usually takes about a day. You'll need to set up something similar. And you'll need this as well; I'll help you make one.'

'This' was a tapering mesh cylinder, about five feet long with a handle at one end, turned by a native who nodded and grinned at Butler. Dried leaves were inside the rotating cylinder, rolling, tumbling and breaking, and when Taylor pulled away a mesh stopper at the narrow end some fell out. The pieces were curled and beginning to turn the colour of bright copper pennies and Taylor examined them critically.

'Good,' was his short verdict.

The next room was dim and cool and another framework of racks held trays spread with the coppery leaves.

'This is the fermenting stage; the longer the leaves are left here the stronger the flavour they get.' Taylor leaned over and smelt the trays like a dog getting a scent. 'You have to get everything just right,' he explained. 'Ferment too long and the tea's too strong; but if you don't leave them

138

long enough there's no flavour at all.' He took his guest through to the next room, where leaves were drying on trays in what Butler took to be giant ovens.

'They have to be dried in here for just long enough too,' said Taylor. 'Let them bake till they're dark brown. Remember, five simple stages: pick it, wither it, roll it, ferment it, dry it.'

'Where can I get these things from?' asked Butler.

'You make 'em,' said Taylor. 'I'll show you how. But I'll have a look at that old coffee-house of yours first.'

Taylor stooped to miss the low doorframe and surveyed the coffee-processing equipment. It had stood idle for months and the neglect showed.

'There's a lot of this you can use,' he declared, and pointed to the large sorting sieve. 'You can make the rolling cylinder from that mesh. And those racks will do quite well for withering and fermenting. Move that drying oven and you can adapt it for tea. Yes, you've got the makings of a good tea-house here.'

He sniffed.

'But ventilate it first. Clean it all out and wash everything. You don't want your tea smelling of coffee.'

After Taylor had gone Butler returned to the old coffee-house and stood at the door. Taylor's parting comment had been that Butler was fortunate to have so much that could be adapted to the processing of tea, but Butler wasn't feeling buoyed by the news.

He looked at the jumble of equipment, the old racks and the oven, and turned away. This was all getting too serious. He glanced up at the slopes and frowned, grudgingly acknowledging that if he had bothered to give the matter any thought he would have realised that sooner or later he would have to actually do something with the leaves from his tea bushes, but all this stuff about converting the coffee-house and making machinery for processing tea was unsettling. It smacked too much of staying at Tondipgiri, of being a serious planter.

He shook his head and crossed to the slopes. The fresh breeze at the top might blow his confusion away.

Perhaps it was time to go. Perhaps now was the time to leave, to pack up, to say that he'd had the letter concerning that fictitious elderly relative, and then he could get on the next boat out of Colombo and be gone before Taylor could pay him any more compliments.

That thought brought him up short.

Taylor had paid him a compliment. Taylor, that grizzled pioneer who let people know damned quickly if they didn't measure up, had told him, John Butler, that he had the aptitude to run an estate, to grow tea and to grow it well. Butler cast his mind back for the last time anyone of such stature had paid him a compliment of that magnitude and he couldn't recall any such occasion.

But – a planter?

He toiled on and reached the crest of the hill.

He had never expected to become accustomed to the conditions on the estate – the heat and the damned flies and the hard work – but he had done it. He found living in the bungalow quite satisfactory and, he acknowledged, he was fitter than he had been in years.

He looked down at his hands and turned them over. They were tanned and hardened and could handle a hoe or a knife or a spade, or indeed any tool on the estate. He could thatch, make bricks, he knew how to lay drainage on a hill, how to propagate tea bushes. And apparently, without realising it, he had also become the sort of man who inspired the trust of others, who could win respect from people who only bestowed it on someone truly worthy.

Against all his plans and expectations he had not only managed but had managed rather well. And, to add to it all, Taylor thought well of him.

He looked at the sturdy stunted bushes that had dug in on the steep eastern slope, resisting wind and storm, stubbornly clinging to the earth, and the question presented itself again: should he stick with it and be a proper planter – a serious planter – right here in Ceylon? Or should he chuck it and go home?

Home? To what? To his old life? Something in him rebelled violently.

'I'm staying,' he said, and as if the land itself needed to witness his vow he raised his voice and the breeze carried his words away.

'By God, I'm staying.'

If it wasn't for Changarai, admitted the newly

141

determined tea planter John Butler, there would be no tea estate on Tondipgiri, no matter what his own contribution might be.

The old man worked indefatigably, driving himself hard, his age seemingly no barrier. He never hesitated to tackle any task and quickly understood the alterations that had to be made to the old coffee-house, marshalling the workers accordingly and supervising all that needed to be done. His experienced hands could wield any tool with a craftsman's precision and were adept at transforming the old coffee equipment into the things that were needed to process the tea crop.

He had a degree of conscientiousness that wouldn't let him settle for anything less than his best, an attitude that even extended to his treatment of Butler. He was far too respectful and polite to ever suggest that pieces of equipment Butler had declared finished could have been done better, but occasionally Butler would catch a glance that as good as said, 'Well, if you're satisfied with that, Butler-Sir, but...' All that was missing was a shake of the head in reproof. It wasn't long before Butler found himself reviewing work he had thought completed and finding with embarrassment that there was indeed scope for improvement.

Changarai's resourcefulness extended beyond the use of tools. When repeated washings failed to rid the old building and its equipment of the strong aroma of coffee Butler despaired of what to do next, but Changarai disappeared into the forest and returned three hours later with a basket of tough-skinned berries the size of tennis balls. He cracked them open and mixed the gluey inner pulp with water, producing a sweet-smelling liquid. Butler, curious, followed Changarai's example in using it to scrub the coffee-house and everything inside it. Two hours later the smell of coffee was completely gone.

When they had finished Butler and Changarai stood back and looked at the finished tea-house. Both men nodded. Cleaned and aired, the new machinery ready and waiting. All it needed now was the raw leaf.

'Just the bud and the top two leaves,' Butler ordered, and Changarai translated the instruction to the workers spread out in a line on the crest of the ridge. They advanced amongst the bushes and Butler hovered about the slope, watching anxiously.

When the baskets of freshly picked leaves were brought down to the tea-house Butler took it upon himself to make the first batch of finished tea. He spread the leaves evenly on the withering racks and made a mental note that someone would need to be on hand to sort the baskets and remove unsuitable leaves. He left the leaves to wither in the warm air.

There was a distinctly fruity smell about the withered leaves when he returned the following morning and he sniffed in appreciation; it reminded him of apples. He directed the transfer of leaves from the racks to the cylinder and left one of the natives, a relaxed-looking fellow called Naga, rotating the handle, then pottered about the estate. Impatient to see what progress was being made, after a couple of hours he returned to the tea-house, eager to examine the leaves, but was puzzled to find that instead of breaking and curling and starting to change colour inside the cylinder, the leaves and buds were almost as they had been when he had poured them in. Naga was turning the cylinder steadily, so it couldn't be a problem there and Butler decided to wait a little longer.

He came back after another hour but found little change in the condition of the cylinder's contents. He checked the cylinder but there was nothing wrong with the mesh, nor with the mechanism. Perhaps it was some characteristic of the bushes that grew on the other side of the hill, he thought, perhaps their leaves were exceptionally tough. At this, he remembered his mental note that someone would be needed to sort the leaves on arrival at the tea-house and he went in search of Changarai to arrange someone suitable.

He found Changarai at the northern end of the ridge and explained what was required, then they both went down the hill to have a look at the progress of the tea. Because they were at the far end of Tondipgiri they approached the teahouse from the back rather than being in sight from the front. They rounded the corner and entered and Naga looked up guiltily from the corner where he was slouching. He jumped to his feet and hastily turned the handle.

'You lazy–' began Butler, but his *Kangany* was there before him. A stream of angry words issued from Changarai and Naga attempted to argue, but Changarai was having none of it. He said a lot more things, clearly abusive, then grabbed the man by the shoulder, spun him round and kicked him sprawling out of the doorway. Naga got up and hurried away to the lines, a parting insult from Changarai ringing in his ears.

Changarai was deeply embarrassed.

'I am very sorry, Butler-Sir. Very sorry,' he declared vigorously. 'Naga is lazy, useless man. Not reliable. Naga does not work well. Always slacking.'

'Give him some work where he can't do any harm,' said Butler, annoyed, and looked at the cylinder, the leaves barely altered since he had put them in. Clearly he was going to risk the same problem in the future – turning a handle for hours at a time was a boring job and shirking would be a constant risk. If only he could power it somehow. He stood thinking and realised he could see the stream from the door.

Three days later Butler declared himself satisfied.

The cylinder – now powered by ropes and pulleys from the very basic waterwheel they had built over the stream – had taken just two hours to break the leaves and they had curled and turned a bright copper colour. He spread them onto racks to ferment and kept returning to inspect them, conscious of Taylor's emphasis on getting this stage right. The fruity smell began to fade and a new smell, like almonds, took over. Hoping that he was timing it properly he moved the racks to the framework arrangement he and Changarai had built over the oven. The rumbling in his stomach reminded him that evening was

145

drawing on and he hadn't eaten, but Butler stayed in his new tea-house.

The broken leaves turned light brown, then deepened to dark brown, just as Taylor had said, and Butler doused the oven and removed the racks. He leaned over and sniffed and the smell reminded him equally of burnt toast and caramelised sugar. He poured the finished leaves, dark and curled and inscrutable, into a wooden box and closed the lid. A thrill of excitement ran through him. Tomorrow he would take the lot and visit Taylor for his opinion; this was Butler's first tea, the first tea from Tondipgiri, and he hoped it was good.

Taylor was enjoying a bottle with George Thwaites when Butler arrived and Butler was glad that both the 'experts' were there.

'The first tea from Tondipgiri,' he declared and set the box down. 'I'd be grateful for your opinion.'

Taylor put some water on to boil and leaned over the box. He paused for a moment, then opened the lid and inhaled. He stared at the contents, then reached in and his big, coarse, spade-like hand was gentle and delicate in its movements. He spread a handful of leaves on his palm and made a sound of approval.

'What are you looking for?' asked Butler. 'Is it good?'

'The leaves are all the same colour,' commented Taylor, 'and they're all about the same size. You've broken it well,' and he sniffed the handful, his nostrils dilating, then narrowing. He nodded and poured the leaves into Thwaites's hands. Thwaites sniffed them too.

'That's good,' he pronounced. 'Very good. A good fresh smell.'

The water came to the boil. Thwaites put the leaves in a cup and carefully poured the water over them to nearly three-quarters of a cup-full, then he checked the time on his watch and sat back. Butler wanted to ask questions but neither Taylor nor Thwaites was speaking; there was an air of paying a respectful silence to some profound ritual. Thwaites watched the hands of his pocket-watch and after four minutes declared: 'Right.'

The three men examined the contents of the cup and Taylor and Thwaites glanced at each other.

'What?' asked Butler, noticing the look. 'What is it? Is it all right? Is it good?'

'Very interesting,' commented Thwaites.

'Why?' asked Butler. 'Why is it interesting? Look, tell me what you've found. Is it good or not?'

'Look at the colour,' said Taylor and Butler looked into the cup. 'Poor tea has a dead colour but this is deep and rich; it's almost glowing. And look at the leaves: they've all opened out – and opened out well.'

Butler stared at the pieces of open leaf in the dark liquid and looked up. 'What now?'

'Do you want the honours, George?' asked Taylor, and Thwaites nodded. He picked up the cup as if it was made of the thinnest, most fragile china and shut his eyes. Making barely a sound

147

he sniffed the aroma, then sipped the tea and rolled it round his mouth in a manner that reminded Butler of wine-tasters. Thwaites made indistinct appreciative noises, then swallowed the tea and licked his lips.

'Try it, James,' he said and passed the cup over.

Taylor took a sip, repeating the mouth-rolling action, then swallowed the tea and put the cup down with as much care as if it risked exploding. He and Thwaites stared at each other without expression.

'Well?' asked Butler, unable to bear the tension. 'Is it good tea? For God's sake, tell me!'

'Mr Butler,' said Thwaites slowly. 'I don't know how you managed it, but make sure you don't alter a single thing in the way you took those leaves and made this. I've tasted teas from all over China and India, but you've got something quite unique. At first it reminded me of one of my favourite Darjeelings, then it seemed similar to an Assam that I'm fond of. For just a moment it seemed like a China tea I tried once, but then it became something else altogether. What do you think, James?'

'Aye,' agreed Taylor. 'That's a grand fine tea. I like it. It's different from all the others and I'd wager it's something to do with the height.'

'You mean the height of the bush?' asked Butler.

'No, I mean the height of your land. You're growing your tea way up in the hills. That makes a difference.'

'And it's something to do with growing your bushes on the other side of that hill,' added

Thwaites. 'They're on an exposed slope, the first slope that the north-east monsoon hits when it reaches Ceylon. Those bushes have dug deep into that good soil you've got there and grown strong.'

'What about the bushes I planted from root cuttings?'

'They'll have the same qualities,' said Thwaites. 'They'll all stand up well to the monsoon and they'll all produce this good tea. This *excellent* tea. You've got something very special there, Mr Butler.'

Ten

'My name's Murchison.' The tall, lean man shook Butler's hand.

'And I'm Gill,' said his equally tall and narrow colleague. 'What can we do for you?'

Even as he entered their office Butler's hopes had risen. Murchison and Gill seemed to be a very busy firm of merchants indeed. Bills of lading, loading manifests, catalogues, invoices – the piles of paper that covered the tables and desks gave every indication of a company with wide experience and varied interests. These merchants must surely be able to help him, they must know hundreds of people who would be interested in his tea.

He put the wooden box on the table.

'I want to export some tea,' he said simply.

'And this is...?' enquired Murchison.

149

'A sample,' said Butler and opened the lid. Murchison peered at the contents, his neck extending like a vulture. He sniffed the tea then shot a meaningful glance at Gill and returned to his chair and sat down.

'It's very difficult to export tea, Mr Butler,' he said. 'There's no call for it from this island.'

'You see, the estates in India and China have the market all sewn up between them,' added Gill, and Murchison nodded. 'Now if it were coffee you wanted to export we might be able to come to an arrangement.'

That was the fourth time that morning that Butler had heard that particular view.

'I haven't got any coffee,' he said tersely. 'I'm a tea planter. My coffee crop was wiped out and I planted the whole estate with tea.' He tapped the box. 'This is what I've got now and I'm looking for a buyer.'

Murchison leaned back and regarded Butler dubiously. 'Mr Butler, I hope you won't think this an impertinence, but do you really think it was wise to commit yourself to growing a crop for which there is no market?'

'Of course there's a market: the whole of Britain.'

'Which, as we have said, is fully accounted for by estates in India and China,' said Gill.

Butler was silent. He breathed deeply and stared out of the window at the shady, tree-lined street beyond.

'Look,' he said at last, 'are you saying you won't even attempt to sell this tea?'

Murchison gave a pained sigh and withdrew a

notebook from a drawer. He consulted it for a few minutes, peered doubtfully at the contents of the box once more, then put the notebook down. He jotted a figure on a piece of paper and showed it to Gill, who pulled a face then nodded reluctantly.

'The best we can offer is four shillings a pound.'

Butler couldn't believe his ears. 'You *must* be able to do better than that.'

Murchison shook his head firmly. 'It's the best we can do, Mr Butler.'

'I can't afford to sell at that price,' protested Butler.

'I can't imagine anyone will quote you a higher figure,' said Gill, 'and that's if they even quote a figure at all.'

Butler stood silent, disbelieving, and the two merchants stared at him.

'I'm sorry, Mr Butler,' said Murchison, 'but it's the best we can do. It's a good offer.'

'I can't accept it,' said Butler, picking up the box and making for the door.

'You may have no choice,' called Gill.

Butler turned, looked as if he was about to make a retort, but couldn't think of anything suitable.

'Good day, gentlemen,' he said finally and left. Outside he stood irresolute, the box weighing heavy under his arm, and wondered what to do next.

At least Murchison and Gill had offered something. None of the other merchants he had visited had been prepared to even consider a figure. But there were other merchants in town, he wasn't beaten yet, and he strode away up the street.

Taylor poured away the customary first inch of beer, then passed the bottle to Butler. 'You couldn't find anybody else?'

Butler shook his head.

'It's unbelievable,' he said. 'I've got good tea here but no one's interested. Murchison and Gill were the only ones to even quote a price,' and he took a drink from the bottle. 'Four shillings a pound was all they offered. I can't understand it – I thought selling tea would be straightforward.

'How do *you* manage to make a living at it?' he asked and Taylor laughed.

'I don't.'

Butler stared. 'What do you mean? You export it, don't you?'

Taylor shook his head. 'No point. Three years ago I sent twenty-three pounds of tea to the London tea auctions at Mincing Lane and all I got for it was three and ninepence a pound; nearly all of that was eaten up by the cost of sending it. I haven't sent any since.'

'So how do you make a living as a tea planter?'

'I don't,' said Taylor. 'I work for a firm of coffee growers. This is their estate. They put me in charge with instructions to try cultivating tea plants and I've been working on them ever since.'

'But why are you growing tea if it's not profitable?' persisted Butler.

'It's experimental,' said Taylor, surprised at Butler's indignation. 'There's only twenty acres with full-grown tea; that's nothing like a

152

commercial scale.'

Butler felt a bubble of anger growing inside him.

'Why didn't you tell me this when I started?' he demanded.

Taylor stared. 'I didn't think you'd be interested. Besides, everyone knows that India and China dominate the market. Aye, it's going to take time for Ceylon tea to get a foothold, but you're going about things the right way; tea's the crop of the future here and–'

'Damn the future!' shouted Butler. 'What about right now? I've got an estate full of tea bushes and you're telling me it's not commercial?'

Taylor was taken aback by Butler's vehemence and he knitted his eyebrows together and glared at the young planter.

'It'll be commercial one day, and on that day those merchants in Colombo will pay you whatever you ask.'

'What the hell use is that to me?' shouted Butler. 'You made me think I could do all this *now*. Not once did you say I wouldn't be able to sell it.'

'You're a grown man,' retorted Taylor. 'I'm not your wet-nurse.'

Butler couldn't contain his feelings any longer and he jumped to his feet.

'You bloody idiot, what do you think I wanted to grow tea for? As a hobby? Have you got no sense, you stupid Scottish pillock? You've got someone paying your wages; who the hell do you think's going to pay mine? Thanks for nothing, you silly old fool,' and Butler threw the half-empty bottle, beer spraying from its broken neck, into the corner and stormed out.

He raged all the way back to Tondipgiri and vented his anger by forcing the bicycle's stiff pedals round.

Bloody fool, he thought, and applied the epithet to himself and Taylor with equal venom.

How could he have let himself make such a mistake? How could he have allowed himself to so blindly follow the crass advice of that idiot Taylor? He felt betrayed, deceived and duped. Damn Taylor, he thought savagely. To have put in all that work, all that back-breaking effort, to have planted the whole Tondipgiri estate – a hundred hard-cultivated acres – with tea, only to find that no one was interested in buying it. He roared with rage as he pedalled.

'Daaammmn!'

He got off the bicycle, threw it on the ground, kicked the wheels then climbed the hill, muttering to himself.

The breeze blew in his face at the top and he looked down at the side he had just climbed, at the neat rows of marker pegs, then he turned and looked at the mass of mature bushes growing on the other side.

There was no reason why his tea shouldn't sell just as well as Indian and Chinese, no reason at all, and he cursed the merchants in Colombo who had no belief in it, nor even any wish to make an attempt to sell it. How much effort would it have cost them? And Tondipgiri tea was good tea – Taylor and Thwaites had said so. Why should

Indian and China teas dominate the market?

He shook his head.

I'd be better off selling it myself, he thought savagely, and the notion took him by surprise.

Him? A merchant? Ridiculous.

But the thought wouldn't go away. It put its roots down with as much tenacity as his bushes. Why shouldn't he sell his own tea? He had gone from being a young man who did very little except gamble to becoming a tea planter, hadn't he? If a man could do that he could certainly become a merchant for his own tea. He could pack chests of tea and take them to England and then he'd damn well show those Colombo merchants. A man who believed in himself could do anything – he'd learnt that and learnt it the hard way. He flinched a little at the thought that he would have to leave Tondipgiri – it hadn't been long since he'd vowed he was going to stay – but the estate's survival depended on him finding buyers for the tea. And, he consoled himself, at least everything would be left in the capable hands of Changarai.

There was no point in delaying matters any longer and Butler strode down the hill, his mind full of plans. He would get a passage on the next boat home and take as much tea with him as could be prepared. He reached the bottom and sang out, 'Changarai! We've got work to do.'

Butler pulled the final restraining strap tight.

'Look after the place for me,' he said and Changarai bobbed his head.

'You know what to do,' said Butler. 'And if

155

there are any problems ask Mr Taylor.'

Changarai nodded again and Butler racked his brains for anything he had forgotten to say, but could think of nothing.

'Well, I'll be off,' he said, looking round the plantation and staring up the slope. 'I don't know how long this will take. I don't know when I'll be back, but–'

He looked at Changarai and impulsively put out his hand.

'Thank you.'

The grip between the two men was firm and Changarai broke into a broad smile. He nodded vigorously.

'All will be well, Butler-Sir,' he declared. 'All will be well.'

Butler nodded and was about to climb onto the wagon but noticed Changarai's granddaughter, Mirissa, solemnly watching him. A thought occurred and he went to the bungalow, searched around then emerged with Coutts under his arm. He came over to Mirissa and handed the placid animal to her.

'Look after him for me,' he said, and Mirissa was wide-eyed. She held Coutts, not knowing what to say, and Butler got onto the wagon. The boy driving it jerked the reins and shouted and the bullock lumbered forward, the wagon jerking and tilting under the weight of the tea chests.

They left Tondipgiri behind, and as they approached the rise Butler couldn't resist a last glance. He twisted in the seat and looked back.

Standing in the middle of the road was Mirissa, still clutching Coutts. When she saw Butler looking back she dropped the startled animal onto the ground and waved wildly, jumping up and down. Butler hesitated a moment and waved back, then the wagon crested the rise and Mirissa and Tondipgiri were lost to sight. Butler faced front again.

He had one important visit to make on the way to Colombo, one very important detour.

'I shouldn't have said it,' said Butler. 'It was completely out of order and I apologise.'

Taylor shook his head.

'Think nothing of it,' he said and scratched his beard. 'So you're going to try your hand at exporting?'

Butler nodded. 'I've got good tea; you've said so, and so has George Thwaites. If anybody knows what they're talking about it's you two. So I'm going to England and I'll find buyers for it myself.'

'Then good luck to you,' said Taylor. 'You deserve it.'

'I've left my foreman – Changarai – in charge,' Butler explained. 'I've told him if he has any problems to ask for your advice. Is that all right?'

'Aye, that's fine,' and Taylor went with him to the door.

'You'll do well, John Butler,' stated the big Scot. 'You don't give in when things get difficult, you've an independent mind and best of all you're plain downright stubborn. Do you think you'll ever come back?' he asked as they shook hands. 'Ceylon needs men like you.'

Butler hesitated, then nodded.

'I'm sure I'll come back. Some day.'

Eleven

Butler couldn't remember England being so cold. He huddled in the corner of the draughty railway carriage, his overcoat – a hasty and necessary purchase when he had arrived – pulled tight about him. The damp London air had left him thoroughly chilled and the reception he had received in the many brokers' offices on Mincing Lane, the home of the famous tea auctions, had been equally icy.

Murchison and Gill in Colombo, who had rejected his tea with very little ceremony, had at least been civil – a stark contrast to the brokers and dealers he had encountered in London. He replayed each conversation in his mind and bristled at the way he had been looked up and down and dismissed as someone of no consequence and therefore not worth taking seriously.

The train rattled north to Manchester. Butler – an animal running to a familiar refuge where he could lick his wounds – watched the misty, rain-soaked countryside passing by and reflected that he had at least learnt something important, although the way he had learned it hadn't been pleasant.

He was, he had been told bluntly, just a small man at one end of an important chain; he was the merchant, the man with tea to sell, and if he wanted to 'do things the right way' he should first of all find a broker, an expert who, if he had sufficient confidence in the tea, would recommend it to a dealer. If the dealer could be persuaded to accept the recommendation then the dealer would buy the consignment. For this 'work' the broker would get one per cent of the price paid to the merchant – Butler – and another half of a per cent from the dealer. The dealer would then offer his purchase at the auction where wholesalers would, perhaps, bid for it. The wholesaler who got it would then try to secure the interest of retailers who would then attempt to sell it to the public.

And at each stage all those links in the chain – all those intermediaries and middlemen – would be creaming off their profit, albeit under other, more euphemistic names: 'commission', 'fees', 'brokerage'.

His tea had been rejected by every broker and dealer on Mincing Lane, a humiliating repeat of his experience with those agents in Ceylon, but Butler was damned if he was going to give up now. If he had listened to people who declared themselves expert on doing things 'the right way' he would have paid attention to that pompous ass Cameron and grubbed up all the bushes on the other side of Tondipgiri, and where would that have left him? The London 'experts' had treated his tea with contempt, but that didn't necessarily mean that no one else would be interested in it. No, he had faith in what he was doing and he had faith in his tea; he had come this far, there was no reason – no reason at all – why he couldn't do the job himself and approach retailers in person. Dammit all, never mind the 'right way'; he'd jolly well do it *his* way.

Butler had never paid much attention to the Manchester shops before. He knew which sold good collars and who stocked the best port but otherwise they had held no interest for him.

But that was some time ago. It was a very different Butler who now wandered through St Ann's Square and the Barton Arcade and up Victoria Street, then back down Corporation Street and St Mary's Gate, carrying the tea box in its leather sling and dodging the carriages and horse-trams. He was hunting a grocer's; not just any old corner shop where his tea would be shoved on a shelf with a dozen other things and attract no special attention, but rather a shop where his tea would be placed on prominent display in the company of all those fine Assams and Darjeelings and China teas. Such a shop had to be outstanding: it had to be in the right location, everything about it had to breathe quality, and it needed some additional indefinable something that placed it above all the others.

He browsed the wares of a few possible candidates, carefully assessed their clientele, then rejected them and wandered out again. This wasn't a job to be rushed. If a shop wasn't right, wasn't absolutely what he was looking for, he wouldn't bother with it. The shop that would eventually sell Tondipgiri tea had to be special.

The crush of people going about their business in shops and offices made progress slow up Market Street, and he had almost reached

160

Piccadilly when he noticed a smart and well-presented establishment on the other side of the road, a carefully enamelled sign proclaiming this to be 'Hutton's – Fine Groceries & Provisions'. A further notice beneath declared: 'Families waited on daily'.

He crossed Market Street, stepping carefully around the piles of horse dung in the road, and examined the window display. He studied it for several minutes and concluded that perhaps he had at last found what he was looking for.

There was something about that display. It was no mere jumble of goods; it had been laid out with care, it was pleasing to look at and the eye was led easily from one item to another. Every article was clean and free from dust, unlike the displays of some of the grocers he had seen. The shelves and cloths and supports were clean too and all bespoke a careful businessman, someone who knew what he was about. Butler made a small adjustment to his collar and tie, tightened his grip on the straps of the tea box and entered.

It was a sizeable shop and well stocked, and the same meticulous care in presentation was evident inside. Some of the shops he had visited seemed to regard themselves as little more than warehouses, their goods stacked up or crammed into lofty shelves, without even an attempt to attract the interest of the customer. Hutton's shelves – all free from dust, Butler noted approvingly – also reached to the ceiling, but their boxes and packets and tins were neatly arranged, and shown to their best advantage in colourful displays and tidy arrangements. Someone had given a lot of thought to those displays. Indeed, everything suggested this was a shop where all the goods had been carefully selected to offer the customer only the very best.

The display that interested Butler most was a very attractive composition of teas and coffees, all presented with the same care and attention to detail as everything else in the shop. The extensive choice invited further exploration and, coupled with the spotless floor and the highly polished long counter, was further confirmation that the man who ran this establishment was an experienced shopkeeper and a shrewd salesman.

Butler nodded. He had no doubt. This was the shop.

The young man who was serving finished with his customer and turned to Butler, the only other person in the shop at that moment.

'Yes sir, how can I help you?'

'I'd like to speak to Mr Hutton, please.'

'Certainly, sir,' and the young man looked worried. 'It's not a complaint is it?'

'Not at all,' said Butler. 'I'd just like to have a word with Mr Hutton.'

The young man hurried out and a few moments later a middle-aged man in a waistcoat and clean apron entered. The knot in his tie was precise and his hair was parted neatly.

'I'm Hutton,' he said. 'What can I do for you, sir?'

'My name's Butler; I'm a tea planter. I'd like to interest you in my tea.'

Hutton politely shook his head and indicated the boxes of tea on the display.

162

'I don't think I can help you, Mr Butler. I already stock the most extensive range in Manchester. These teas are the very best; they're well established, they have a high reputation. I'm afraid you'll have to try somewhere else.'

Butler had anticipated this.

'I notice you don't have any Ceylon tea,' he commented, and Hutton frowned.

'No,' he said. 'That's because tea isn't grown in Ceylon.'

'Yes it is,' said Butler firmly, and put the sample box on the counter. 'Mr Hutton, before all those teas on your display reached you, a line of brokers and merchants and dealers and wholesalers all took their percentage and pushed the price up. But there are no intermediaries with my tea; I own the plantation. I took over a ruined coffee estate and planted tea.' He tapped the box and added, with a burst of inspiration, 'This is a sample of "Butler's Original".'

Hutton was on the verge of dismissing Butler; he had heard plenty of exaggerated sales talk from pushy salesmen before and had sent them all packing. But there was something different about this sun-tanned young man and Hutton hesitated. The characteristic desperation that lay under the surface of so many salesmen was absent and in its place Hutton saw steadiness, a calm and quiet confidence.

Butler noticed the hesitation and played his trump card. 'You be the judge, Mr Hutton. Brew cups of tea from all those teas on your display and brew a cup from mine as well. Then compare them.'

Hutton laughed. 'No one's ever tried to sell tea to me in that way before, Mr Butler. You must be very sure of it.'

'I am,' said Butler simply. 'And after you've compared it with those others you'll know why.'

Hutton studied him a little longer.

'I can see you're a very determined man, Mr Butler. All right, I'll try it.'

The laying out of a dozen cups and the brewing of the tea caught the attention of several customers. Curious, they stayed to watch, and that was all to the good as far as Butler was concerned.

He timed four minutes on his pocket-watch.

'That's it. Now, try my tea, Mr Hutton.'

Hutton was entering into the spirit of it all and he grinned and tasted Butler's tea. The grin faded and he raised his eyebrows.

'That's good,' he conceded. 'That's very good.'

'Now try the others,' and Hutton went along the line sniffing and tasting. He came to the end, then returned and sampled Butler's tea again. He put the cup down.

'That's a fine tea you have there, Mr Butler, very fine indeed.'

Butler turned to the watching customers.

'Would you like to try it?' he invited. 'Please, be my guests.'

The customers looked self-conscious, but shuffled forward and were soon announcing their satisfaction, just as Butler had expected.

He murmured to Hutton.

'I think you have some converts to Ceylon tea

there, Mr Hutton. What do you think? Might we perhaps come to some agreement?'

Hutton watched his customers chattering excitedly about Butler's tea. It had been novel to have a tea-tasting in his shop and he had gone along with it more out of amusement than out of any serious expectation that the Ceylon tea would be any good. But it had been very good – very good indeed – and to judge by the way his customers were enthusing they had come to the same conclusion. 'Butler's Original' clearly had possibilities.

'I think we need to talk, Mr Butler,' and he lifted the counter flap. 'Come through to the back room.'

Within the week Butler's cargo of tea arrived from the London warehouse where it had been waiting. Butler rented warehouse space in Manchester and personally supervised the delivery of two chests to Hutton's, both prominently labelled 'Butler's Original'.

Hutton was not prepared for what Butler did next.

It was unprecedented for a supplier to stand in the shop, approaching likely customers, but that was exactly what Butler did. He seemed completely oblivious to the ordinary conventions of the supplier–retailer relationship and Hutton was uncertain of how to handle the situation. He had reservations, indeed resentment, about the man's continued presence but there was something so easy and good-natured about him that Hutton's resolve to order him off the premises was undermined. He watched from behind the counter, highly dubious about Butler being in the shop at all, but the customers didn't seem to mind. Butler's manners were exemplary and he was politeness itself when talking about 'Butler's Original'. Indeed, the presence of someone so sun-browned enhanced the credentials of the tea; he was a tangible link to the colony from whence it had come, and that seemed to actually help sales. Butler had to order the delivery of another half-dozen chests, and when Hutton counted his takings and discovered how much 'Butler's Original' was contributing to his profits his misgivings were finally dispersed.

'You look thoughtful,' commented Hutton one morning, and Butler nodded.

'I've noticed that most customers don't browse; they just come in and buy exactly what they want.'

Hutton agreed. 'The shopkeeper's eternal problem. How to get customers to buy more than they came in for.'

Butler was silent for a moment.

'I've got an idea,' he said.

It had always been a pleasure to shop at Hutton's. He and his staff were always so polite and the goods were always of such high quality, especially this new tea he was selling – 'Butler's Original'. Now a visit to Hutton's had an added attraction, an innovation that had become a talking point. Upon arrival at the shop a customer would be welcomed with the courtesy and respect that had always been a hallmark of Hutton's, but now

166

there was the offer of a complimentary cup of 'Butler's Original', an unheard-of idea in itself, but made especially novel as the offer included a complimentary biscuit.

Other traders sneered and dismissed it all as flim-flam, but it was only in Hutton's that customers, compelled to linger in order to drink the tea and eat the biscuit, would find their eyes wandering round the shop and alighting on this or that item they previously hadn't noticed. Hutton was always on hand to discuss a sale, and the ringing of his till announced the increase in his profits.

The man was standing outside when they first noticed him. He was a big fellow, filling out a brown check suit and sporting bushy side whiskers. He kept peering in through the window, but it wasn't until the shop was momentarily empty of customers that he came in.

'Are you Mr Hutton?' he asked gruffly and Hutton nodded.

'Then you'll be Mr Butler, I take it?'

'I'm Butler.'

'Aye, I was told I might find you here,' and the man straightened. 'Right, gentlemen, I'm a plain man and I'll come straight to the point. My name's Alsop. I run three grocery and provisions shops in Salford. That's far enough not to be a competitor to you, Mr Hutton, but it's not so far that I haven't heard things. And what I keep hearing is how good this "Butler's Original" tea is. Fact is, I keep having my customers asking me why I don't sell it. Seems they've tried it round at other houses – friends and families who won't touch anything else – and now they want it themselves. Now, I'm a sensible man, I've been in the retail trade long enough to know that what your customers want, you give 'em, and that's why I'm here,' and he faced Butler squarely.

'Mr Butler, I'd like to sell your tea in Salford. As I say, that's far enough away to be no threat to Mr Hutton's business, so how about it? I'm asking you to sell your tea to me at wholesale rates. What do you say?'

Butler looked to see whether Hutton was uneasy at the prospect of no longer being the sole supplier of 'Butler's Original', but Hutton was quite relaxed.

'All right,' said Butler, outwardly calm but inwardly cheering, and Alsop shook his hand in a good hard grip.

'Your tea's making a name for itself, Mr Butler and selling it more widely'll benefit all of us. The more people who drink it, the more there'll be to tell other folk. And that means folk all over Manchester and Salford – and beyond too. You're onto a goldmine there, Mr Butler.'

Part Three

1881–1882: GRINDING

'The leaf is rolled in order to break it down
and release its natural juices.'

One

John Butler, agreed the mothers of maiden daughters, was a most *eligible* man. He was thirty-two, unmarried, the owner of a large house on Wilbraham Road – *with servants*. There were connections with trade, true, but they were the natural and unavoidable consequence of being an owner of land in the colonies. He was a gentleman planter, and therefore eminently respectable. Most importantly, with his tea a household name, he was successful, and that made him a most suitable object for matrimony.

Butler, making his regular weekly visit to Hutton's, was not unaware of the interest of those mothers and was quite capable of appreciating, as he was doing now, the demure smile of an attractive daughter whose mother was taking rather longer than was strictly necessary to conclude a matter of business with Mr Hutton. It was a good opportunity to let her daughter attract the eye of the handsome gentleman planter, but eventually the matter of business could be drawn out no longer and with a polite inclination of the head to Butler the lady left the shop, her daughter casting a discreet look back and being rewarded with a courteous smile that would keep her in rapt daydreams for the rest of the week.

But finding a wife was at that moment the least

of Butler's concerns.

The door closed, leaving only Butler and Hutton in the shop, and Butler was all seriousness. Seriousness tinged with worry.

'Any more cancellations, George?'

'Another one this morning – a lady who's been buying "Butler's Original" for the last three years. That makes five orders cancelled this week already. They're buying other Ceylon teas instead: Empire Fine Leaf, Mountain Special Reserve, Premium Yield, Colonial Supreme.'

Butler was at a loss to understand it. 'Why? Why are they cancelling?'

'The lady this morning said something interesting; she said: "Butler's' isn't as good as it used to be. After a while it tastes bitter."'

'Bitter? That's impossible,' and Butler stared in disbelief at the rich dark tea in the open chest. Hutton came round the counter and joined him.

'That's the second chest I've had complaints about,' said Hutton. 'There are three more unopened chests in the storeroom.'

'There's only one thing to do,' said Butler. 'We've got to test them all.'

Butler put the last of the cups down and frowned. Three samples brewed from the three chests and none was right. He knew the flavour of his own tea and this wasn't how it should be.

'Something's getting in and spoiling the flavour,' he said, and they inspected Hutton's stock and storeroom minutely. Whatever the 'something' was it didn't come from there. The place was dry and clean, there was nothing

172

nearby that could have contaminated the tea, and the chests themselves were intact – no holes or splits. So if the tea in those chests wasn't being contaminated from something outside, it could mean only one thing – the tea was being contaminated at source.

A horrible remembered vision of coffee trees discoloured and decayed by coffee blight went, through Butler's mind, quickly followed by the worry that some new, equally damaging blight was affecting the tea bushes.

He must send a telegram to Changarai – at once.

'What about the tea?' Hutton asked, and Butler paused.

'Don't sell it,' he ordered. 'I'll reimburse you. Say you're sold out; people will accept that easier than they'll accept bad tea. We don't want its reputation damaged any further,' and he hurried out.

Butler fretted and fumed over the next four days, picturing every slow mile from the Colombo Telegraph Office over the hills to Tondipgiri.

Reports came in from other retailers citing daily complaints about the unwelcome new flavour in 'Butler's Original' and wholesalers who had previously grumbled about Butler's success now took the opportunity to aggressively promote other Ceylon teas newly arrived on the market. Grudgingly Butler tried them and had to concede that their flavour was good; not as good as his original, successful tea, but much better than the tainted one. He brewed samples of

173

'Original' taken from the stocks of all the other retailers and the bitterness was present in every one. He halted all sales of 'Original' and reimbursed the retailers for stocks already purchased, but this was only an emergency measure to stop his tea getting an even worse name.

When Changarai's reply arrived it left Butler even more confused.

No tea disease stop Taylor Thwaites confirm all good stop Tondipgiri tea good stop Changarai

Butler put the telegram down and stared moodily at the packet of 'Butler's Original'.

If the bushes weren't diseased – and Taylor and Thwaites could be relied on to be accurate about that – then the problem had to lie in the way the tea was being picked. Perhaps the Tondipgiri workers were over-picking, taking more than just the bud and top two leaves. Or perhaps they were picking from each bush more frequently, not giving the new buds and shoots time to develop properly.

And what about the soil? Something could have got into it and was attacking the bushes at the roots.

It might be none of these things. The fault might not lie with the bushes at all. Perhaps something had gone wrong with the machinery in the tea-house. Or perhaps the tea was being contaminated at the packing stage.

But whatever the cause, one thing was clear: the problem was in Ceylon, and if he didn't go out there immediately and solve it the damage to the

174

name of 'Butler's Original' would be irrevocable; the new Ceylon teas would push him aside and their position in the market would become unassailable.

He had to return to Tondipgiri. Fast.

Two

The next steamer bound for Ceylon wasn't due to leave London for two weeks and Butler fumed, and counted the days impatiently. He still wasn't satisfied even when he was aboard the steamer in the Channel with England falling steadily away behind. The thought that something was ruining his crop whilst he was ambling down to the Mediterranean and idly plodding through the Suez Canal was too much to bear and he swore and thumped his fist on the rail.

'Are we to expect this behaviour for the entire voyage?' enquired a cool clear voice, and Butler turned. A woman in her early twenties with a superciliously sweet smile was staring at him.

'I beg your pardon,' he said politely. 'I thought I was alone.'

'Obviously,' she commented. 'In future it might be wiser to check before displaying your temper,' and she turned and walked away.

Butler watched her go and shook his head. If only she had his troubles... The six weeks on board clearly weren't going to be pleasant if he had to depend on *her* for company and he hoped the other passengers turned out to be more congenial.

They were a varied collection.

In addition to the young woman and Butler the complement was made up of a young man being dispatched to Ceylon by his family to 'make something of himself', wryly reminding Butler of the circumstances of his initial voyage, two couples who frequently and loudly made reference to the fact that they were friends of the Governor, two elderly sisters travelling to visit a relative, a businessman of Butler's age who fancied himself something of a wit, a crusty retired general and his wife, and a very aloof couple who dedicatedly found fault with everything.

Mealtimes were the only occasions they were all together, and Butler found them tedious affairs. The young man was too unsure of himself to strike up a conversation with anybody, the sisters were too stern and severe to engage in pleasantries and the Governor's friends and the standoffish couple rarely strayed from their specialist subjects. The general turned every conversation to a ponderous declaration about the risk of war in the Sudan, his wife saying nothing, and after a very short time the wit of the other man became rather wearing. The young woman, whose name, Butler learnt, was Charlotte Noble, stated only that she was going to Ceylon to join her father, a businessman, and she rarely spoke to Butler except to request that he pass the salt.

The voyage, decided Butler, was going to seem a lot longer than six weeks.

The water hissed alongside and Butler was savouring the refreshing flurries of Mediterranean spray on his face when he realised that Charlotte Noble was standing nearby. She looked as solemn and austere as ever.

There was a long silence and Butler decided he should break the ice.

'Good morning,' he said pleasantly.

'Good morning.'

'A fine morning, isn't it?'

'Quite.'

'Rather fresh, though.'

She made no answer to that and Butler tried again.

'So, you're going to Ceylon,' he ventured as a conversation opener.

She turned frosty blue eyes on him.

'I presume that remark was either a statement or a question, Mr Butler. If it was the former it seems a somewhat obvious thing to say. If it was the latter it makes one wonder what else you might suppose people are doing on board a ship bound for Ceylon, other than travelling there.'

He was momentarily lost for words.

'I beg your pardon, I'm sure,' he began, with as much icy civility as he could muster, but she had already turned and was walking away. She was stiff and precise in a pristine cream dress, her back ramrod-straight, and Butler, with just a touch of malicious satisfaction, decided she would quickly find the tight bodice uncomfortable once they reached Egypt and began their passage of the Suez Canal. He hoped, for her sake, that she possessed something cooler to wear in the tropics.

One evening, two days from the Canal, the Captain came below and cast an amused eye over his passengers clinging nervously to the saloon rails.

'How long will the storm last?' asked Butler, and the Captain stared at him in surprise.

'Storm?' he echoed. 'Storm?' and he snorted. 'This isn't a storm, Mr Butler. Why, this is a piddling rain-shower by comparison. And if you take my advice you'll pray to God you never find yourself in a real storm; miles out from land, nothing but countless fathoms beneath your keel and old King Neptune trying to turn you over. Why, I remember once...' He launched into a vivid tale of fifty-foot waves and helpless crewmen washed overboard in icy seas and Butler could have sworn the Captain was enjoying his audience's discomfort as the ship rolled drunkenly and groaned deep in its ribs. His bass voice rumbled over the roaring and crashing outside, and the swinging lamp and crazily dancing shadows made a terror of it all.

Within five minutes of the end of the story and the Captain's chortling departure ('Storm? Ha!'), the other passengers, pale and frightened, had all retired unsteadily to their cabins.

'That seems like a good idea,' said Charlotte Noble from the other side of the saloon, and Butler agreed. They stood simultaneously and she gave him that icy stare again.

'I hope you're not going to offer to escort me to my cabin, Mr Butler,' she said, and Butler was amazed at her presumption.

'The very last thing on my mind,' he said with perfect truth.

She let go of the saloon rail and was taking a step towards the door, when the ship rolled violently and Charlotte Noble stumbled sideways and collided with Butler. She clutched at him and instinctively he gripped her waist to steady her. For the first time he noticed how compelling those clear blue eyes were and how her hair was the precise colour of roasted chestnuts. He was just registering how firm was everything under the dress, and realising that there was no stiff corseting to make it so, when the ship straightened and Charlotte stepped backwards. She was breathing quickly and she swallowed.

'Good evening, Mr Butler,' and she seemed unsure, as if about to say something else, before she turned, opened the door to the passage and hurried to her cabin. Butler stayed where he was a while longer, the blue of Charlotte Noble's eyes and the startlingly warm imprint of her body against him vivid in his memory, then he too left the saloon.

Two weeks out from London the steamer arrived at Suez and they had to wait their turn to enter the Canal. They baked offshore in the still, dry air, and Butler was taken by surprise by a sudden yearning to experience the tropical conditions of Ceylon again. Restlessly he wandered the narrow promenades that ran past both sides of the central cabin block and went up onto the deck above. He looked on as the crew went about their work, then he went to the starboard rail and leaned there, watching fishermen along the shore standing knee-deep in the water as they whirled their handnets above their heads before casting them to drop in neat circles into the water. They didn't have long to wait before hauling the nets in, silver fish flapping inside.

The Captain came along the deck and exchanged pleasantries with Butler, then left to give some shouted orders and Butler remained at the rail, the mid-morning sun throwing his shadow down onto the silt-swirled water. The heat was stifling and eventually drove Butler, fanning himself with his hat, for'ard in search of shade. His shadow on the water went with him.

From the small window of her cabin Charlotte Noble watched it go. She had heard the voices above her cabin and had blushed when she recognised John Butler's. She had avoided him since that night in the saloon, but in the last few moments he had been only a few feet away, the closest they had been since she had fallen into his arms.

Her cheeks burned again and she rehearsed the incident once more. She couldn't get it – and him – out of her mind. She had never known a memory to be so vivid and she recalled again the crash of the sea outside, the howl of the wind, the warmth inside the saloon, the swinging lamp, the shadows cast by it sliding around the walls, the tightness at the neck of the dress she had been wearing, the rustle of her skirt as she had got up. And then the thump of water against the side of the ship, the swooping feeling when she lost her balance and fell, the sudden arresting of that movement by the collision with John Butler, the way she had clutched at him, the feel of his strong hands on her waist, the momentary feel of the cloth of his jacket against her cheek, the steadiness of him against the rolling of the ship, the freshness of his shirt–

She was breathing quickly. The cabin was too hot, it was unbearable, intolerable, and she tore the pins from her hair and dashed them on the table. She shook her hair loose over her shoulders and sat for a moment, then lay down, not relishing the thought of how uncomfortable she would be at dinner, her hair bound up once more, her collar tight, all buttoned up and petticoated as a respectable lady should be.

Butler glanced across the dinner table at Charlotte Noble and wondered how she did it. How did she manage to look so relaxed in that close and stuffy saloon? Good heavens, she even seemed cool.

She was as distant as ever, though. Not one word did she speak to him. At one point he had the quite ridiculous impression that she glanced at him, but when he looked at her she was paying attention only to the meal. He noticed her cheeks had a touch more colour than previously and he concluded with satisfaction that perhaps she was feeling the heat after all. But she was still stand-offish; instead of participating in conversation afterwards, she retired early.

The steamer entered the Canal the following

morning and crawled along without the merest breath of a breeze to provide relief from the heat. The cabins were stuffy and suffocating, the air outside them dry and parched. Butler found the conditions highly uncomfortable, but at least his time in Ceylon meant that he wasn't entirely unprepared for them. His fellow passengers, however, were visibly wilting. The general seemed to cope with it best, and it set him off prating about the rigours of campaigning in the heat of India. The other passengers listened weakly to his accounts of the Mutiny, too drained by the heat to devise excuses to get away from him.

Charlotte Noble was conspicuous by her absence, appearing only at mealtimes, and it was incomprehensible to Butler how she could choose to remain in her cabin despite the soaring temperatures. It had to be something to do with her icy cold nature, he told himself. Her un-failingly frosty behaviour towards him must somehow provide her with the means of staying cool in hot weather. He sat under an awning on the deck and resigned himself to waiting out the slow passage down the Canal.

Her cabin door was firmly bolted and Charlotte Noble kept glancing at it to confirm that no movement of the ship had slipped the bolt. It would be most improper for her to receive anyone in her present state of dress – or rather, undress.

Her cabin, as Butler had deduced, was indeed extremely uncomfortable. At one point she had felt sure she was about to pass out, and to avoid that humiliating possibility had made the concession of unfastening a collar button. She had had no intention of loosening or removing anything else; it was, after all, impossible to know when one might be called upon to appear in public, but the discomfort was finally too much, and careful bolting of the door allowed her to remove the bodice. The intolerable heat had further prompted the removal of the overskirt and resulted in her current attempt to find relief by wearing only her chemise, open at the neck, and her ribbon-threaded pantaloons. Her hair was unbound.

She gave thanks that she had left off the petticoat before going in for dinner last night. She felt sure that if she had not she would have fainted. She had sat there, longing to shed that tight bodice, shake her hair loose once more and kick her legs free, but instead had been compelled to endure the dinner and the desultory conversation and ensure that at no point did she meet the eyes of John Butler. She had desperately wanted to look at him but every element of her upbringing forbade such forwardness. There was that one glance she had given, of course, but that had been all and she was sure she had been the very picture of correctness. Aunt Agatha, the maiden aunt who had been her moral touchstone ever since her mother had died, could have found no fault in her conduct last night.

But that august lady would certainly have had something to say were she aware of the thoughts and emotions which had been exercising Charlotte since that evening in the saloon. Her aunt's stern visage presented itself and reluctantly Charlotte bowed to the questions that she knew she should be asking herself.

Had she behaved properly when the rolling of the ship had thrown her across the deck and into that man's arms? Why hadn't she immediately delivered a stinging rebuke to put the man firmly in his place after his outrageous presumption, his over-familiarity in holding on to her?

She blushed. She blushed each time she thought of that event.

At least, she told herself, her aunt couldn't disapprove of her decision to keep to her cabin. That, at least, was behaviour that was entirely correct. A well-brought-up young lady should seek privacy and solitude in which to regain her self-control, her composure. In the seclusion of her cabin she could put the incident in its proper perspective and then discard it as having been correctly dealt with.

But Charlotte was a spirited woman and such strictures chafed.

She had enjoyed it, she admitted wildly; she had been in John Butler's arms and had enjoyed every second!

But she shouldn't have, ruled that unyielding inner voice; she should adopt a cold and distant manner and ruthlessly suppress any thought, any feeling, which couldn't be regarded as entirely seemly.

And she shouldn't think of him as 'John Butler' either – 'Mr Butler' would suffice. The use of a first name, even if only in one's thoughts, signified a degree of familiarity that certainly should not be extended to that particular passenger, given what had happened three days ago.

The facts of that incident were plain: the movement of the ship had upset her balance, had caused her to stumble, quite accidentally, and he had taken foul advantage of it. He had been familiar, had held on to her for too long, for much too long. His conduct had breached the most basic and fundamental rules of etiquette. From the very first his casual and easy demeanour had indicated someone who had no regard for the proprieties. His thumping of the rail and the appalling language he had used on the occasion of their first meeting were confirmation of that.

Such a man was no gentleman.

On the deck above, and not a dozen feet away, a steward brought Butler a scotch and soda and he sipped it gratefully. The ripples of the steamer's passing washed astern and Butler sighed. This crawl was as fast as they could go. There was nothing else to do but endure it.

His position when she had fallen, thought Charlotte, had been fortunate; it had saved her from possible injury. It had been a relief to find herself safe and unharmed and she recalled a pleasurable feeling of gratitude.

But that, warned the stern voice within, was all she should feel. It hadn't been a situation that a respectable young lady should derive anything from, other than a determination to maintain an icy reserve, both to conceal her own clumsiness and to discourage any misreading of the situation by the man in question.

She frowned.

In fairness, and she held fairness to be a virtue she should always seek to practise, he had saved her from injury and her subsequent conduct had not been exactly admirable. At the very least she had been ungrateful. Even if she did maintain the icy reserve her aunt demanded of her she should nevertheless thank him and make some sort of apology for her curtness.

The thought made her feel better. Yes, such a course of action would settle the matter. She would wait for an appropriate opportunity and then everything would be as it should be, the proprieties would have been observed and her thoughts and feelings, she hoped, would cease the violent gyrations they had been experiencing since those unsettling few seconds in the saloon on that stormy night.

Two days away from Ceylon Butler went on deck after dinner and was leaning against the rail, enjoying the evening, when he heard that clear voice speak from behind him.

'Mr Butler?'

She was standing a few feet away and looked determined.

'Miss Noble,' he acknowledged shortly. 'What can I do for you?'

She stepped to the rail and took a breath. 'I wish to thank you for catching me when I fell during the storm.'

Butler shrugged. 'I was glad to be of service.'

'Also, I feel I was rather uncivil to you afterwards. I wish to apologise. You see, I found it rather a shock to be so literally thrown into someone's arms.'

'A pleasant shock I hope?' asked Butler with a grin and Charlotte looked him in the eye. He could practically hear the sound of glaciers forming and he groaned and mentally kicked himself for being such an ass.

'I'm sorry, Miss Noble, that was an impertinent remark. I hope you'll forgive me.'

'So I wasn't mistaken,' she said after a moment, each word like an icicle snapping. 'My first impressions were quite correct after all. Good evening, Mr Butler,' and she walked away, once more stiff and rigid.

Thank God this voyage is nearly over, thought Butler.

Three

The port of Colombo was considerably busier than the first time he had arrived. A dozen ships jockeyed for space in the harbour and a waiting crowd clamoured on the jetty. There were twice as many barefoot children begging for pennies; they ran around, getting in the way of the men trying to land the cargo.

The boat from the steamer bumped against the bottom of the jetty and Butler climbed the ladder. He reached the top and his eyes came level with a pair of smart shoes topped by tropical whites.

'What are *you* doing back here?' demanded an angry voice, and Butler looked up.

Apart from a blotchier face and fat where there had once been muscle, Paget was exactly as Butler remembered him.

Butler stepped onto the jetty and bent to assist Charlotte Noble, who was coming up the ladder.

'Get your hands off,' snapped Paget and shoved Butler aside. Charlotte took Paget's hand and gave him a hug as soon as she was on the jetty.

Butler was unable to contain his surprise.

'This is your father?' he asked incredulously.

'Yes.'

'Your *father?*'

'Well, stepfather,' said Charlotte, squeezing Paget's arm. 'My real father died when I was very young,' and she stared at Butler. 'May I ask what business it is of yours, Mr Butler?'

'Has this man been harassing you, Charlotte?' demanded Paget.

'No, I have not,' interrupted Butler angrily, and Charlotte looked from one to the other.

'Do – do you two know each other?'

'We certainly do,' said Paget grimly, 'and it's an acquaintance I have no wish to renew. Come along, Charlotte,' and he whisked her away into the crowd.

Paget's stepdaughter.

It was unbelievable.

Charlotte Noble was *Paget's* stepdaughter. Never once on board had she mentioned his name; all she had said was that he was a business-man. But she might just as well be Paget's natural daughter, decided Butler, thinking back to her conduct on board ship – she was as rude and arrogant as he was.

The country had certainly changed since he had last been there. The frequent coffee plantations had given way to lush tea estates, but Butler was too preoccupied with his worries about Tondipgiri to pay them much attention. Two days of rough roads and tangled forest finally brought the wagon over the familiar rise and Butler told the driver to halt. He jumped down, recalling the moment when he had first arrived and had stopped on that very spot. He stood in the middle of the dusty road and suddenly found it unaccountably difficult to swallow.

When he had left, five years ago, the gently sloping western face of the hill had been sporting hundreds of white pegs, each one marking the place of a future bush, shoots already beginning to form in that rich red earth. Now the slope was a dense sheet of vivid green, delineated into neat squares by the network of paths that he remembered so laboriously marking out. Women in bright sarees moved amongst the thick bushes, picking the leaves and tossing them over their shoulders into baskets carried on their backs. They were singing and their cheerful song carried faintly up to him. There were other people visible too, moving busily amongst the lines where the workers lived.

It was all so different from that first view of the place when he had stood where he was standing now, sourly regarding his inheritance. Now it had revived and was bursting with life.

My God, thought Butler, I own all this, and the lump swelled in his throat.

Paget's land on the opposite side of the road was yet another estate where coffee-growing had been abandoned in favour of tea, and Butler recalled how the coffee planters had scoffed at the notion of tea-growing. Times had certainly changed, he mused, then he remembered why he was there: 'Butler's Original', his fine distinctive tea, had turned bitter.

Butler hadn't telegraphed that he was returning to Tondipgiri and the look of surprise on Changarai's face was comical.

His mouth dropped open, his eyes widened, he seemed completely flustered, then he rushed forward chattering excitedly, every other word 'Butler-Sir', all reserve about shaking Butler's hand now gone.

'Look at the tea plants, Butler-Sir, all growing very strong. All very happy here, Butler-Sir, everyone happy to see you. Everything very good,' and Butler was unable to get a word in edgeways.

'Come see, come see,' and Changarai shouted at some of the workers to unload Butler's bags. 'Come see,' and Changarai took him to the bungalow. Butler hesitated for a moment before entering, the old memories strong, then he firmly pushed the door open and stepped inside. It had happened, he had come back, just as he had told

James Taylor he would.

He looked round the bungalow and was pleasantly surprised. He had been expecting to find signs of neglect, but it was clear that somebody had been looking after the place. Everything was in good repair and the inside was clean and brushed. Changarai shooed the luggage-bearers out.

'Everything all nice. All looked after. Butler-Sir, there will be much happiness, much happiness now you are here. Very glad, Butler-Sir, very glad to see you again after many years,' and Changarai pumped his hand again.

'I'm glad to see you too, old friend,' said Butler. 'It's good to be back. But we've got a lot of work to do,' and he told Changarai about the problems that had arisen in England. Changarai was appalled that something might be wrong on the estate and Butler knew that the old foreman was worried that the fault reflected badly on his stewardship.

'But it's obviously something that no one could spot,' said Butler, hastening to reassure Changarai. 'If Mr Taylor and Mr Thwaites couldn't find anything wrong it's no wonder no one else has found anything.'

Changarai didn't seem at all comforted by that thought and protested long and volubly that the estate was running well. It was only after a lot more soothing words from Butler that he reluctantly left.

Butler was up with the sun the following morning and he and Changarai commenced their search for whatever it was that was blighting 'Butler's Original'. They began in the tea-house and examined every piece of machinery. The withering racks were all right, and a worry of Butler's that perhaps something was caught in the mesh of the rolling cylinder proved unfounded. They went over all the fermenting trays, even inspecting the undersides.

Nothing.

Nor was there anything wrong with the racks and trays above the ovens, and the dirty job of raking out the ovens themselves and inspecting the insides turned up nothing that could be affecting the tea.

The problem, whatever it was, didn't lie in the tea-house. It *had* to be something to do with the bushes.

'It's up there, Changarai,' said Butler, looking at the green slopes of Tondipgiri. 'Whatever it is that's spoiling the tea is up there.'

Five weary hours later, standing on the ridge and watching the women carrying their loaded baskets down to the teahouse, Butler was running out of options. His workers were doing their job properly; no one was plucking too much or plucking incorrectly.

'The problem must be in the roots,' said Butler, lost for any other ideas. 'There's nothing else it can be,' and they gathered a basket of root samples to take to Taylor and Thwaites for their opinion.

'I'll go and see them tomorrow,' he told Changarai, and they parted at the foot of the slope. Butler went back to the bungalow, torn between optimism that they had at last found the source of the problem and worry that it might still be something else. As he approached the bungalow he saw one of the women about to enter, a bundle in her arms. He frowned, wondering what she was up to, and he called out, 'Hey, what do you think you're doing?'

The woman stopped and waited for him to approach.

'Well?' he demanded as he came up.

'Butler-Sir does not like snakes,' said the woman in a dark mellow voice, and held out the bundle. A whiskered snout poked out, sniffing and twitching, and Butler grinned. It was Coutts, the determined little companion who had faithfully kept the bungalow free of snakes. Then Butler realised this animal was too dark to be Coutts, who would certainly be much older and greyer by now. The last time he had seen Coutts was when he had given him to Changarai's granddaughter to look after. What was her name?

'Where's Mirissa?' he asked and the young woman looked at him, a gentle, confident, *knowing* smile on her lips.

Butler was about to ask his question again, but hesitated.

Mirissa had been a shy little girl when he left Ceylon five years ago. She couldn't have grown up this much since then.

'Mirissa?' he said uncertainly.

'Butler-Sir remembers me,' and the woman bobbed her head and looked at him again, her dark eyes shining.

It was her.

Butler could hardly believe it.

She was about twenty now and had the same glowing skin, the same white teeth as that small, slight girl, but the childish roundness of her face had gone. Her nose, once cheekily tilted, was now more finely chiselled, and thick sable tresses, gathered at the back and hanging down at the neck, replaced the urchin tangle of black hair. The eyes were as brown and bright and sparkling as he remembered them, but now they had an additional quality – an awareness, a look of composure and self-assurance. Gone was the slight, straight form; her skirt hung on curving hips above which a strip of supple brown midriff showed, topped by a well-rounded and filled-out saree bodice.

She smiled more widely as she watched him appraising her and the smile was as warm and honest and genuine as Butler remembered.

'Mirissa,' he said simply, this time with no uncertainty, and when those deep brown eyes twinkled and sparkled and she threw back her head and a warm bubbling laugh of sheer happiness escaped her lips he knew he had truly come home.

The fruitless search for whatever-it-was had left him bone-weary and Butler expected to sleep soundly, but his mind wouldn't settle. It spun wildly with notions of things that might be at fault, things he had already ruled out, and the uncertainty frustrated him like nothing else he had known. If the problem was diseased roots it would be a disaster, but at least it would give him something specific to fight. It *had* to be a problem with the roots; they had checked everything else.

He lay sweating in the darkness and Mirissa wandered through his thoughts, a dark figure with warm, liquid eyes, inviting him and tangling his confusion even more.

A noise from outside startled him and he sat up. He listened for a while but it didn't come again and after a while he lay down, dismissing it as a night sound. An animal hunting, maybe.

He stared at the roof for a while longer, then turned on his side and tried once more to sleep.

Four

Changarai was waiting for him when he returned from visiting Taylor and Thwaites.

'It's not the roots,' said Butler flatly, and Changarai looked bewildered.

'I do not understand, Butler-Sir. Everything is well, but the tea is bitter. This is a great mystery.'

'Mm,' agreed Butler, not disposed to talk. The problem didn't lie with the roots, and that could only mean that he had overlooked something somewhere. The thought depressed him and he wanted to be on his own to think it through. He went into the bungalow.

This is no good at all, he decided later that night. Any more lost sleep and his head would be spinning. He took a chair out onto the verandah and sat for a while, watching bats flitting around and under the trees.

He was about to go back inside when he heard that noise again. In the stillness of the night it was clear and sharp, a snapping, cracking sound unlike any noise an animal would make, so Butler got a lamp and went to investigate. He crossed the yard, occasionally stopping to listen, and came level with the storehouse. On impulse he opened the door and went inside. The storehouse was warm, the air close and dense, unsurprising after such a hot day, and Butler supposed that the noise he had heard was the crack of wood fibres in the storehouse walls as they contracted in the cool of the night.

He stood in the doorway looking at the tea chests, all stacked neatly, all carefully stencilled 'Butler's Original', and he took out his knife. He levered one of the chests open, surprised that the lid should come away so easily, and made a mental note to tell Changarai that lids must be hammered down more securely in the future. The tea was black in the shadow of the chest and Butler balanced the lamp on a nearby stack and squatted down. He dug his hand in and lifted it, letting the leaves drop, and he sighed.

'Butler's Original' had been a splendid tea with a fine flavour. He was at a complete loss to understand what could have gone wrong and he folded his arms on the rim of the tea chest and rested his chin on them. The rich dark scent filled his nose and he stared moodily at the tea.

Suddenly he was very still. He had been selling

this tea for four years, he had demonstrated it, knew its taste, knew its very appearance, and *that*, he realised, was what was wrong with what he was looking at.

Most of the leaves had that distinctive curl that had been there right from the start, right from that first batch that he had prepared himself and which had won the approval of Taylor and Thwaites. But amongst those leaves he now noticed some that curled differently, twisted differently. He picked one out and examined it more closely and compared it to one of his familiar leaves.

The interloper was superficially similar, barely noticeable when in the chest and mixed with 'Butler's Original', but picked out for examination it was coarser, the curl not as regular. Could this be the source of the contamination?

Butler's lethargy left him and he went outside for a bucket. He filled it from the chest and took it back to the bungalow, then poured it onto the table and spread the leaves, painstakingly picking out all the coarse ones. He brewed them, tasted the resulting liquid and slapped his hand down on the table top.

Got it! This was the source of that bitterness. These coarser leaves with their bitter flavour were finding their way into the chests. Somehow they were infiltrating the consignments and ruining the flavour of the good Tondipgiri tea–

He paused.

There was no question of 'somehow'. These leaves hadn't simply appeared in the chests; someone must have put them there. Somebody was interfering with Tondipgiri tea.

Butler breathed heavily, anger rising, and another dark thought occurred. He studied the latest sheaf of production figures and the paper shook in his hand. Each consignment had a regulated weight, but the figures showed nothing unusual, there were no changes in volumes – so that meant that coarse leaves weren't merely being added; they were *replacing* Tondipgiri tea. Somewhere along the line, before the chests were sealed, a quantity of his tea was being taken out and substituted with the bitter leaves. And in that case what was happening to the extracted tea? Presumably the thief was selling it somewhere else.

Butler smacked the paper onto the table and crumpled it in his hand.

The thief had to be someone who worked for him. Only someone on the estate, someone who knew the routine well and who could work in the storehouse without their presence being questioned, could be behind this.

And whoever it was was doing it on a large scale – every single chest in that last consignment to England had been contaminated – so the culprit was someone with regular access to the store-house.

You've got away with it until now, thief, thought Butler. But I'm back, and you won't get away with it any more.

The following day Butler never let the storehouse out of his sight. Even when he was on the slopes he never went over the ridge; he kept to the western side, near enough to see who was going into the storehouse and how long they were in there. At the end of the day Butler watched the finished chests being carried in and he scowled. Nobody had been inside long enough to tamper with the tea chests; the thief must be staying away, aware that Butler was watching.

In the evening Butler sat on the verandah, thinking and planning. The thief clearly wasn't going to tamper with the chests whilst Butler was nearby, even if it meant losing a day's thieving. So tomorrow, decided Butler grimly, things were going to be different.

He would let it be known that he was going to be working on the other side of the hill all day, but would discreetly slip back and hide near the storehouse. Then he would catch the thief with his hands in the tea chests and God help the thieving swine.

A movement under the trees made Butler look up. Something was out there, approaching. The shape was indistinct at first, blending with the shadows, and he tensed, supposing it to be some wild animal on the prowl, then a figure emerged from the trees and his eyes widened. The unmistakable swing of those supple hips and the calm, assured walk told him exactly who it was.

Butler stood and she stepped onto the verandah.

'Good evening, Mirissa,' he said.

'Good evening, Butler-Sir,' she replied.

He broke from her level gaze and gestured round.

'It's a lovely evening,' he said, and Mirissa murmured agreement.

'I wanted to thank you,' he said, 'for keeping my house so clean. I suppose that was you, wasn't it?'

Mirissa nodded. 'I like to keep Butler-Sir's house clean. I come here every day. I like to look after Butler-Sir's house.'

'Thank you,' said Butler again and Mirissa took a step to one of the verandah posts, stretched one arm up it and turned and half-leaned against it.

'I am happy you are back,' she said simply in a voice of molasses and honey, and there was something in the way she said it that dried his mouth and dispatched a cold shiver down his spine and back up again.

He cleared his throat.

'I'm happy to be back,' he said. 'And I'm happy to see you, too.'

She arched her back against the post and he could have sworn she purred.

They stared at each other. Butler swallowed and Mirissa's eyes widened. A muscle tripped at the side of her throat and slowly she straightened.

They stepped towards each other simultaneously and both stopped, momentarily uncertain. Then Mirissa tilted her head slightly to one side and her lips parted. Butler took the final step that closed the gap between them and realised that she was quite a tall girl, only two inches shorter than him. She returned his gaze, bold and provocative, and Butler slowly reached out and put his hands on her shoulders.

She wasn't half so calm and assured as she appeared. The firm shoulders trembled under the thin material of her bodice and a breath escaped her. Hesitantly, he drew her towards him and she came willingly. Her eyes were wide and the muscle in her slender neck tripped again.

His head was moving ever so slightly toward hers, a movement she was mirroring, when a sudden sound from the darkness broke the moment and his attention snapped up.

It came again, that wooden, cracking, snapping sound, and Mirissa, sensing that she no longer had his attention, stepped back. Butler's hands fell and the sudden movement stirred him and he looked at her. She gazed back curiously.

'Sorry,' he said distractedly and stared out into the darkness again. Then he realised what the sound was and relaxed, dismissing it. It was only the wooden walls of the storehouse, contracting in the cool evening air. He turned back to Mirissa and her hands came up around his neck again–

The storehouse!

He left the verandah at a run, Mirissa completely forgotten, and tore towards the storehouse. He rounded the corner and the impact with the man standing there sent them both tumbling in the dust. Butler was the first to get to his feet and found that the other man was Changarai. His anger close to boiling, he pulled him up roughly.

'What's going on? What are you doing here?'

'There was a sound,' said Changarai, shaken but pointing to the storehouse. 'I heard a sound and came to see.'

Butler grunted, turning towards the storehouse, and he froze rigid as a new and horrible thought struck him.

The thief was an employee, someone who knew the routine well and who had regular access to the storehouse. That much he had already deduced. And there was one employee on Tondipgiri who had been overseeing the estate, unsupervised, for years – one employee in the perfect position to do something like this.

Butler didn't like the direction his thoughts were taking him.

But ... surely not. It couldn't be Changarai. Changarai's surprise at seeing him had been genuine. Hadn't it? It had been genuine, unexpected pleasure. But he had been flustered too, so what did that say about the man?

Perhaps the big welcome was just a clever act to conceal his shock. Shock that the Master was back and might discover the thieving. Butler shook his head, more confused than ever. What did he really know about Changarai?

'Butler-Sir?' asked Changarai. 'Is everything all right?'

Save the performance, Changarai, thought Butler savagely. 'I'm fine,' he said. 'I was just thinking of something,' and he opened the door for Changarai to enter the storehouse ahead of him. If Changarai was indeed the thief Butler wasn't going to give him the slightest chance of getting away.

A lamp was still burning and Changarai looked shocked as he surveyed a collection of rough tools strewn across the floor.

God, he was a cool one. He must have heard

Butler running across the yard, realised discovery was imminent and had gone outside, pretending to arrive just as Butler rounded the corner of the storehouse.

It was all clear to Butler now. The sounds he had heard in the night hadn't been the contracting of wood at all, it had been the sound of wooden tea-chest lids being hammered back into place.

He picked up the lamp and inspected the nearest chests. All were as they should be.

Except one.

A corner of the lid was slightly raised, not seated properly, and Butler seized on it. The lid was fastened tight but he was sure he had now found the evidence he needed. With a lever from the collection of tools he prised open the lid and bent down close to peer at the tea, then his hand snapped out and picked up a leaf. He examined it in the light of the lamp and his hand trembled.

It wasn't Tondipgiri tea.

He plunged his hand deeper, pulled out a handful of tea and found more of the intruder leaves. Slowly Butler stood, his lips tight and bloodless. The chest had been freshly packed that day; every leaf in it should have had the regular curl and twist that he knew so well. But in the last few hours someone had removed a good few pounds of prime Tondipgiri tea and substituted the coarse leaves in their stead, mixing them in with the good tea. Now Butler understood – the thief worked at night; no wonder nobody had suspected anything.

He turned to Changarai.

'I knew I'd find the answer here on the estate,' he said coldly, and Changarai stared at him, his face blank.

'I came in here last night and found coarse leaves in one of the chests,' said Butler, fighting to keep his anger under control. 'Leaves like these,' and he held out the handful. 'This is what's been doing the damage. Someone's been adding them and stealing Tondipgiri tea. I thought it was happening during the day and I've been watching the storehouse. But nobody was in here long enough and I had no idea who the thief was. But I know now.'

'Who is it, Butler-Sir?' asked Changarai, wide-eyed, and Butler dashed the leaves in the man's face.

'God damn you, you lying thief! I trusted you, left you in charge and you've been tampering with the tea. Where's the stuff you took out? Been selling it, hey? Been making a nice profit, you bloody swine?'

Changarai blinked as if bewildered and Butler's rage boiled over. His fist shot out and Changarai sprawled on the floor. Butler stood over him, fists balled and breathing hard.

'Get off my estate,' he snarled. 'Get off it and if I find you here again you'll wish you'd never met me.'

He glared at Changarai, 'You nearly managed it, didn't you? Changing the tea over at night when there was no one to see or hear; thought you were safe, didn't you? Well, not tonight, you damned little thief. I heard you, I—' and he stopped as he remembered Mirissa.

So that was their plan; the devious pair were in it together.

She had been sent to distract him, to keep him occupied while her grandfather tampered with the tea. She had emerged from the darkness and so enchanted him that his attention had been solely on her. She had been in his arms, another few minutes and ... well, he knew right enough. If it hadn't been for that giveaway crack of wood he would have taken her inside the bungalow and then would have heard nothing outside. She was involved right up to her pretty little neck, curse her.

'And you can take that damned little seductress of a granddaughter with you. Get her and get the hell off my estate.' Changarai scuttled out.

Butler turned to survey the evidence of the deception and savagely kicked at the tools. Blind with anger he stalked back to the bungalow.

She wasn't there.

Of course she wasn't. The minute he had run over to the store she would have known that the game was up and had fled. He ground his teeth and slammed the door in a fury of rage and betrayal.

Sleep was impossible after what he had discovered and he lay for hours, sweating and cursing and staring up at the roof in the darkness, listening to Coutts's successor shuffling around the bungalow. Butler couldn't settle and he went out onto the verandah. Some animal was snuffling and honking in the undergrowth and he listened for a while then turned to go inside, wondering whether Changarai and Mirissa had left yet. He glanced towards the storehouse, and if he had been only idly enjoying the night and if the storehouse hadn't figured so prominently during the last few hours he would have missed it. A momentary flicker of light escaping the storehouse shutters.

Unbelievable!

That damn thief Changarai was at it again, doubtless assisted by that devious granddaughter of his. Talk about coolness of nerve. The arrogance of the man.

Well, not this time. His ex-foreman was going to be black-and-blue by the time he had finished with him.

He dressed hurriedly and crossed to the storehouse. Stepping lightly he drew close to the wall and ghosted up to the shutters. This time he would catch Changarai red-handed, and Butler had to grant that the man had colossal cheek and nerve: to have been caught and dismissed, yet still having another go at the tea before he left. Unless of course he was attempting a more serious kind of sabotage, and Butler's fists tightened.

Slowly, with infinite care, he raised his head to peer through the slats.

There he was, the damned thief, on his own, bent over one of the chests, the lamp held low and shielded. Of course, he didn't really need the light – he had done this a good many times already. Right Changarai, thought Butler, now I've got you. Then he froze.

The figure bent over the tea chest had moved,

and with a shock Butler realised that it wasn't Changarai after all. Nor was it Mirissa – the shape and movements were those of a young man. The face was in shadow but what he was doing was clear enough: he was busily scooping tea from the chest and filling a sack which, to judge by its shape, was nearly full, doubtless with good tea taken from the other chests.

The man added the contents of a black sack to the chest, then plunged his hands in, mixing it up with the Tondipgiri tea. Then he picked up the chest lid, careful to muffle it before he banged it into place, and Butler nodded to himself. It must have been the man's clumsiness at this stage that had alerted him before.

But ... that had been Changarai hadn't it?

The possibility that he had perhaps made a mistake flitted across his mind, but he quickly dismissed it, rationalising that this was probably some confederate of Changarai, sent to finish the job.

I'm going to follow you, thief, thought Butler and restrained the urge to rush in and collar the man.

The mystery figure put the now empty black sack inside the full one and with a grunt swung the full sack onto his shoulder. He extinguished the lamp and moved to the door and Butler kept back in the shadows as the man emerged.

Now he saw who it was and he remembered the man well. It was Naga, the lazy fellow who had been shirking the turning of the withering cylinder when Butler had made his first batch of tea. He looked leaner and moved more sinuously than Butler remembered, and was quietness itself as he crossed down to the road. If Butler hadn't known exactly where Naga was moving in the shadows he would have missed him completely.

Over the bridge and onto the road Naga hurried, padding silently on the dusty ground. Butler was equally quiet as he trailed behind. He was expecting him to make for somewhere well away from the scene of the crime, but Naga hadn't gone far when he turned off onto Paget's estate.

Was Paget connected in some way then? Butler kept well back and trailed Naga up the track. The native crossed the open space in front of the plantation bungalow and entered a long, low, windowless building. No sooner was he inside with the door closed behind him than Butler was running low and silent across the yard. He halted by the wall, waited a moment, then eased the door open a fraction and peered through the crack.

It was a storehouse. Stacks of tea chests met his view and somewhere beyond was the glow of a light and the sound of voices. He dropped to his knees and crawled into the shadows behind a pile of chests. He listened, trying to hear what was being said, but the voices were muffled. He turned his head, turning his ear to the voices and noticed the name stencilled on a tea chest less than a foot from his face: 'Empire Fine Leaf'.

He didn't comprehend for a moment, then realised that it was the name of one of the teas that were taking sales from 'Butler's Original' in England. God, that was galling; to be losing sales to Paget of all people. He shook his head in disgust, turned again to catch what was being said, and saw the name on another chest. This one was 'Mountain Special Reserve'.

Butler leaned back. That was the second of those new teas. Paget was growing both of them. He looked to his left and saw 'Premium Yield'. To his right was 'Colonial Supreme'.

He couldn't believe it.

The four new teas that had come onto the market and displaced 'Butler's Original' were being produced by Paget. Butler didn't know what to make of it all but was determined to find out what Paget was up to. He stayed on his knees and threaded his way through the stacks to within one stack of the voices. He kept low and in shadow and slowly peered round.

This was much more than just a storehouse. This was the scene of some careful and systematic operation. Full sacks like the one Naga had carried from Tondipgiri lay in front of a line of four long tables and on each table was a set of scales and various scoops and measuring pans. Behind the tables were four separate stacks of tea chests, each stack distinguished by the names stencilled on the wood: 'Empire Fine Leaf', 'Mountain Special Reserve', 'Premium Yield' and 'Colonial Supreme'.

A number of old chests stood nearby, marked 'Bad. For mixing only', and a bare yard away from them was Paget. Naga was in front of him, opening the sack and displaying its contents.

'You should have been here hours ago,' Paget was saying. 'I've been waiting for you.'

'Small problem, sir,' said Naga obsequiously.

'What problem?' demanded Paget.

'Butler-Sir came to the storehouse—'

'You damn fool, did he see you?'

'I hid in bushes. Butler-Sir and Changarai came. Butler-Sir say he knew about tea. Butler-Sir very angry at Changarai. He think Changarai is changing tea. He call Changarai damned little thief. Tell him to get off estate.'

'But he didn't see you?'

'No sir, he not see me.'

Paget snorted.

'The damn fool,' he said contemptuously. 'Blamed his foreman and got rid of him, did he? Excellent,' and he chuckled. 'Right, add the tea and get the measures right. And get a move on – it's late.'

'Too late for you, Paget,' and Butler stepped from behind the pile of tea chests.

Naga froze, guiltily clutching the sack of Tondipgiri tea, and for a moment Paget's cheeks were red with fury. It was for only a moment though, and he quickly recovered his composure. He laughed.

'Well, this is a surprise. What are you doing here, Butler? Something I can help you with?'

'Drop the act, Paget, I've caught you red-handed.'

'Caught me? Caught me at what? You've got no proof, Butler. I'll deny everything. And don't think anybody will believe a word this lazy rogue says – everyone knows he's dishonest,' and Paget was smug. 'It's your word against mine.'

'You're fired, Naga,' said Butler. 'If you ever come onto my land again I'll shoot you on sight. Get out.'

Naga dropped the sack and ran.

'So this is what you've been up to, Paget,' said Butler. 'Stealing my tea to improve the flavour of your own and then using that muck,' and he pointed to the old chests, 'to ruin mine.'

Paget hitched up an elegant trouser leg and sat on the edge of the nearest table.

'I'll say this much for you, Butler,' he drawled. 'You're growing good tea on those slopes of yours. That fellow Changarai's done more work for you than he ever did for me,' and he shrugged. 'Of course I took your tea. I'm not a fool, I could see how good it is; it was just a simple matter of finding a suitable thief. It wasn't easy to get the blend right – I had to experiment. But then I hit on the idea of making several different ones and now I'm doing very nicely out of it. My tea's established and yours is on the wane.'

Butler couldn't believe the man's effrontery.

'You admit it? You can sit there and baldly admit what you've done?'

'Why shouldn't I admit it?' scoffed Paget. 'What are you going to do, Butler? Take me to court?' and Paget gave a short laugh. 'You'd be wasting your time; you can't prove anything against me. I said years ago that you were soft, that you couldn't make the grade as a planter, so you might as well give it all up now. If you like, I'll buy your estate off you. I'll give you a good price,' and his smile was cool and insolent.

Butler breathed deeply, but he had a card to

211

play that Paget in his arrogance had overlooked.

'You're right, Paget,' he admitted. 'I can't bring a case against you. But I don't need to.'

Paget's eyes narrowed. 'What do you mean?'

'There's a much simpler solution,' said Butler, 'The only reason your tea's done so well is because Tondipgiri tea was mixed in with it. But that's over now. Without my tea to make your foul brew taste better you'll lose your buyers and you'll lose their orders. I don't have to take you to court, Paget – you're going to be wiped out, and it's your own tea that's going to do the wiping.'

A sudden noise from behind made Butler turn quickly, thinking that perhaps Naga had come back.

It was Charlotte Noble.

She was dressed in a thin white shift and her chestnut hair was unbound and floating loosely about her shoulders. She was staring at Paget with something rather less than admiration in her eyes.

'How *could* you?' she said slowly.

'You heard?' asked Butler, and Charlotte nodded.

'I saw you running across the yard so I came to see what was happening. I heard everything,' and she looked at Paget again, horrified. 'How could you do such a thing?'

'Go to your room,' snapped Paget, and Charlotte flushed. 'Get out, Butler.'

'I'm going,' said Butler and he inclined his head slightly to Charlotte.

'Good night, Miss Noble. My commiserations on finding out what your stepfather is really like

– *I've* known for some time.'

He left and strode down the track, his satisfaction at simultaneously having solved the problem of the bad tea *and* having thwarted Paget blotted out by one single, sobering thought: he had been wrong – terribly, terribly wrong – about Changarai, and he felt a hot blush of shame. God grant that he hadn't left the estate already, and Butler hurried along the road.

And if Changarai wasn't involved that meant that Mirissa wasn't involved either. Butler started to run.

The hut that Changarai shared with Mirissa was the one at the end of the lines nearest to Butler's bungalow, signifying a hierarchy of place. There was light within and Butler hurried up. The door was open and he realised that if he had been just a minute or two longer it would have been too late – they would have gone.

A small pile of belongings lay on the floor near the door and Changarai and Mirissa stood as Butler appeared in the doorway. They stared at him silently, Changarai sad, Mirissa tight-lipped, and Butler wondered where to start. How to apologise to this man to whom he owed so much? He cleared his throat.

'I've come to ask you not to go,' he said. 'I made a mistake, a bad mistake, and I got it all terribly, horribly, wrong. I jumped to conclusions – and they were all the wrong conclusions. I'm sorry. Don't go.'

They stared at him, not speaking, and Butler knew that what he had done to Changarai was a terrible thing. He had struck him, knocked him to the floor, insulted him, he had hurt the man's pride. Changarai had every right to ignore Butler and walk off the estate.

The worst thing is to trample on a man's pride, Butler reflected, and he tried again.

'I can't run this place without you,' he said, and Changarai looked at him expressionlessly. 'Tondipgiri means so much to me and when I found out somebody was tampering with the tea I just didn't think straight. I saw you near the storehouse and assumed that you were to blame. But I was wrong, Changarai, terribly wrong, and I'm apologising – to both of you. I'm asking you to stay. Please.'

Changarai stared back coldly, and with a sick and hollow feeling Butler knew that it was no use – he'd lost him, all his pleas had been in vain.

'I need you, old friend,' he said softly.

Changarai stared at him and looked at Mirissa.

'I found out who was responsible,' said Butler. 'It was Naga. I caught him passing the tea to Paget. I fired him. He won't be coming back; there'll be no more trouble.'

'Naga,' said Changarai, and nodded to himself as if in confirmation of some private suspicion.

There was silence.

'Will you stay?' said Butler, wishing there was some expression that he could read on that lined, brown face and in those dark unfathomable eyes.

After a moment Mirissa reached out a hand to her grandfather and her look was one of pleading. She squeezed his hand and Changarai stared at her, then looked at Butler. Butler held out his hand, Changarai looked at it, looked at Butler, then looked at Mirissa. Mirissa gave a small encouraging nod and Changarai slowly put out his hand and grasped Butler's.

The grip was firm and Butler was flooded with relief. He had meant it when he said he couldn't run the estate without Changarai and he knew what a narrow escape he'd had.

'Thank you,' said Butler, and Changarai gave a slight, pained smile, perhaps not entirely mollified but resigned to staying after all. Mirissa looked at Butler and his heart leapt at the expression in her eyes. He wanted to hold that gaze but knew that this wasn't the moment, so he simply said 'Thank you' again and walked out into the stifling night.

Five

Butler resolved to tread very carefully as far as Changarai was concerned. He didn't want to chance rubbing any raw nerves, so in the morning when he greeted Changarai he tried to do so with the same ease as had always existed between them. He made sure he worked nearby during the day, making no mention of the previous night's events, and he made a point of saying, 'It's good to work with you again, Changarai.' Changarai was civil, almost as friendly as before, but there was a stiffness in his attitude and he wasn't as talkative as usual. He seemed to thaw as

215

the day wore on, however, appearing to recover some of his customary cheerfulness, and Butler gave inward thanks.

The next day he was up early and went with Changarai to check the cropping of the bushes on the other side of the hill. They worked for a few hours, ensuring that all the pickers were consistently selecting only the bud and top two leaves, then he left Changarai working his way along the slope and climbed to the top of the ridge.

He hadn't realised how much he had missed all this: the muted thunder of the cascades rumbling up from below, the hills in the west stretching away to the far mountains, the sheer expanse of blue sky, even the tangle of jungle beyond the river. Below him the women pickers in their bright and colourful sarees worked their way steadily across the slope, and standing there with the breeze on his face and the sun on his back he felt strong, vital, *alive*, and he inhaled deeply. He stared down at the lines, the factory, the store and his bungalow, and he stiffened.

A few yards from the bungalow, a hand shading her eyes, was a figure in a bright red saree.

Mirissa.

Changarai seemed willing to let bygones be bygones, but what about his granddaughter?

Charlotte Noble adjusted her collar, tucked a stray tendril of chestnut hair behind her ear and studied her reflection in the mirror. She frowned. She was prevaricating and she knew why she was prevaricating.

John Butler.

She was going to visit him, knew she *had* to visit him – after all, *someone* had to apologise for what had happened, the thefts, the deception – and as her stepfather had laughed in her face at the very idea of apologising it was up to her to attempt to make amends.

Her opinion of John Butler had been completely revised.

When she saw him flitting across the yard to the storehouse she had been sure he was about some furtive business, and that was consistent with the black picture her stepfather had painted of him. But the admissions she had heard and the evidence of the appalling fraud lying all about the storehouse had undermined everything he had told her. John Butler was the wronged party in all this and now, for a second time, she was in the position of having to make an apology to him.

The prospect made her rather nervous.

She realised, and felt a pleasant tremble in her body, that she very much wanted to see him. She had lain awake long into the night recalling all the moments they had been in each other's company aboard the ship and she regretted every uncivil word she had uttered. He had always been courteous and polite to her; apart, of course, from that rather poor attempt at wit during their final meeting on board. Even his conduct at the ship's rail when she had first encountered him could be excused; he hadn't known she was standing there, men doubtless behaved differently when not in the presence of ladies, she had been wrong to judge him so.

She could picture his face clearly, those compelling blue-green eyes, the thick dark hair. She could remember every look he had ever given her, and the line between her eyebrows creased at the thought that so many of those occasions had been cold and stiffly formal. In conversation with others he had been unfailingly polite and good-natured and she wished she had enjoyed equally polite and good-natured conversations with him.

She put on her hat, checked it in the mirror and left the bungalow. There was no point in telling her stepfather where she was going; it would only generate further acrimony. She had decided what she was going to do and was adamant that she would do it.

After making the apology it was possible that further conversation might follow, and she smiled to herself. In due course, perhaps they would even be able to talk as friends. As for any more than that ... well, being only across a road from each other they were bound to meet from time to time and she reddened and felt that pleasant tremble again.

Butler paused on the ridge, uncertain, then strode down the slope. As he descended he saw Mirissa straighten and he knew she had seen him. He half expected her to walk away but she didn't move. He crossed to her and stopped.

She regarded him steadily, her weight to one side, the hip thrust out, her face expressionless. Then she smiled.

'Good morning, Mirissa,' he said and her smile widened. She stepped onto the verandah and looked at him, raised an eyebrow and tilted her

218

head, then went inside. Butler followed, and this time when he put his hands on her shoulders and drew her towards him there were no intrusive noises from outside to interrupt the movement, nor its completion.

Charlotte came to the end of the Paget plantation track. It had startled her to find out that John Butler owned the plantation opposite. To judge by the neat squares of luxuriant greenery that blanketed his tea slopes he must have put in a lot of work – and, in that heat, it must have been hard and hot work – to produce those well-ordered rows and obviously healthy bushes. Much character and determination would have been needed to carve out that plantation and then establish the tea in England.

That loose curl escaped again and she tucked it back, then told herself off for hesitating.

She altered her hat a fraction, glanced down at herself, approving again of the dress and straightening a fold, then determinedly walked up the road to the entrance to Butler's estate. Once off the road she paused on the little stone bridge, the stream bubbling coolly beneath, and took her bearings before crossing to the whitewashed bungalow.

The door was ajar and she hesitated, then slowly she pushed it wider.

'Mr Butler?' she called softly and, receiving no answer, stepped inside. The room was empty and she took off her hat, intending to wait for him, then it occurred to her that that might not be such a good idea – it might be hours before he returned from wherever he was. She moved to leave but a muffled noise from the back room made her pause.

'Mr Butler?' she called outside the door, then knocked lightly and entered.

The room was dim, but not so dim that her eyes didn't adjust quickly and her hand automatically flew to her mouth.

Wearing only trousers, his back to her, John Butler twisted round on the bed at the change of light in the room and froze in surprise. The figure next to him rose on one elbow and Charlotte had a glimpse of smooth brown skin before the girl pulled a tangle of red cloth up to her throat.

The girl was very beautiful.

For a moment Charlotte and the two figures on the bed stared at each other, then Charlotte recovered her composure.

'I'm sorry to have interrupted you at your work, Mr Butler,' she declared coldly. 'Good day,' and she turned and swept out.

He called out to her to wait but she ignored him, stepping off the verandah and struggling with the stupid hat as she went towards the road. The sound of running feet in the dust made her quicken her step, but he was in front of her, blocking her way, before she reached the bridge.

'It's all right, Miss Noble, don't go.'

She fixed her eyes rigidly on his, very aware that he had not stopped to put on a shirt.

'I'm sure we have nothing to say, Mr Butler. Please don't concern yourself on my account; I'm sure the young lady is missing you,' and she glared at him. He looked as if he were hunting for something to say but Charlotte wasn't inclined to wait.

'Excuse me, Mr Butler, you seem to be in my way,' and Butler could do nothing but step aside. Walking as quickly as she could she crossed the bridge over the stream and hurried along the road, her cheeks burning with an embarrassment caused by three things: first, the event she had interrupted; second, her conviction that, by going there at all, she had made a complete fool of herself; and, third, an image she just couldn't dispel of a bare-chested, sun-tanned John Butler.

Dumbfounded he watched her go. Why on earth had she come in the first place?

Whatever the reason it certainly couldn't have been anything of a pleasant nature – her curt behaviour on board the ship had demonstrated she was incapable of that – so the reason could only be connected with what she had witnessed in Paget's storehouse. Doubtless she had taken Paget's side and had called with the intention of venting yet more icy criticism upon him.

He shook his head; she was unbelievable. Apart from that one flippant and ill-judged comment during the voyage, which he had immediately regretted, he had endeavoured to be polite to her at all times but she had consistently treated him as being beneath contempt. On the very few occasions when she had come down from the ivory pedestal on which she clearly felt she belonged and had deigned to speak to him her every word had been a calculated snub. The only possible reason for someone so proud and

221

haughty to call on him was an intention to be even more caustic.

Well, he could do without that. Paget was certainly the right person to be her stepfather; they were both as unpleasant as each other. Good riddance to her. He turned and went back to the bungalow.

Six

It was a surprise to Butler that Mirissa's subsequent continued presence in the bungalow didn't seem to bother her grandfather. She was quite open about moving her belongings over from the lines and Butler expected some reaction from Changarai, but the old man seemed quite unmoved by it. He was no less civil, no less cooperative, as ready as always to work side by side with Butler on anything that the estate needed, and gradually Butler relaxed.

One day, agreeably surprised at the absence of snakes around the bungalow, he asked Mirissa what had happened to Coutts.

She was immediately serious.

'Coutts dead many years,' she said solemnly. 'Coutts good friend to Butler-Sir,' and Butler nodded.

'I like this little fellow,' he said, watching Coutts's successor rooting in the corners, 'but when I first arrived it was Coutts who lived here with me. I don't think I'd have slept a single night if it hadn't been for him dealing with the snakes.'

'Coutts is in special place,' said Mirissa.

'Where?'

Mirissa took his hand. 'Come. I show you.'

She took him up over the ridge and down the eastern slope to the river. The bridge was still the same narrow affair of rough boards and rope rails and it swayed and bounced as they crossed. As they went up the rough path on the far side Butler recalled the occasion when that small shy girl had taken him this way to see the elephants, and he squeezed Mirissa's hand. She grinned at him and together they pushed through the bushes to the elephant track.

It was wider than it had been; frequent use had eroded the track and pushed back the vegetation on each side. Butler hesitated, fearing the presence of another elephant hidden in camouflage like the last time, but Mirissa confidently led him out onto the track and they walked up it.

'Changarai's a good man,' said Butler suddenly, and Mirissa nodded.

'My grandfather,' she said. 'Very wise. Very special,' and Butler agreed.

'Where do your parents live?' he asked, and she shook her head.

'Parents dead long time.' She lowered her voice. 'He came from forest very angry. Knock houses down. Many died. Parents died.'

'"He"?' repeated Butler. 'Who's "He"?'

She put her finger to her lips that he should be quiet.

'The Old One,' she said and looked round.

'The Old One,' said Butler blankly, then

realised. 'You mean–' but her hand was over his mouth before he could say it. She shook her head urgently.

'Do not say His name, Butler-Sir. He may be near. May be angry to hear you,' and slowly she took her hand away. 'Come quickly.'

She hurried their pace along the track and didn't begin to relax until they had left it and had gone at least half a mile into the forest.

'Once, Mirissa, you took me to see, er, "Him". Do you remember?' and she nodded. 'How could you bear to do that, knowing that "He" killed your parents?'

She looked blank.

'It is the way,' she said.

'What way?'

'It is the way of life. He comes, people die. It is the way.'

'But don't you hate Him for what He did?'

She frowned and tried to explain it in a way he would understand. She pointed to the sun beating down through the branches.

'Sun is hot, yes?'

He nodded. 'Yes, it's hot.'

'Do you hate sun?'

He shrugged. 'It's just there,' he said. 'There all the time. You can't hate it.'

She waved her hand at the forest around them.

'He is there,' she said. 'There all the time. So no hate.'

She looked at him hopefully, wondering whether he understood, and was relieved when he nodded.

'I see what you mean,' he said slowly. 'I think I understand.'

She smiled and took his hand again.

'Now I show you Coutts.'

They walked another mile in forest so dense that it seemed to Butler that the air itself was green. He was just beginning to wonder whether Mirissa was lost, when abruptly they stepped out of dense undergrowth into a broad clearing and Butler halted, rigid.

'My God!' he exclaimed.

On the far side of the clearing was a cliff, at least fifty feet high, and carved into it almost to the top was a standing Buddha. Its hands were raised to its mossy shoulders, palm-outwards, and it stared at them impassively. Mirissa knelt respectfully and after a moment of indecision Butler copied her.

Mirissa bowed her head briefly, then stood. Butler got up and Mirissa took his hand.

'Coutts is here,' and she led him across the clearing, through the thick grass and wild flowers to a small patch of cleared ground. In the centre was a colourful bush, and Butler could smell a gentle and peaceful scent.

'Coutts is here,' said Mirissa. 'Under little bush.'

Butler began to say something but the words caught in his throat. Coutts, that small animal, his companion all those years ago, had died and instead of being tossed on a rubbish heap to be scavenged by vermin he had been carried here and Mirissa had buried him beneath a fragrant bush under the eternal eyes of the ancient stone Buddha. Butler stood quietly for a while, not trusting himself to speak, then bent and placed his hand on the ground beneath the bush.

'Good boy, Coutts. Good old boy,' and he stayed that way for a moment, then stood and sniffed and rubbed the corners of his eyes with the heel of his hand.

'You picked a nice spot,' he said to Mirissa and she was pleased.

'Very nice place for Coutts,' she said proudly and Butler held out his hand for hers.

The burial of Coutts like a family pet, with a fragrant bush above his little grave, seemed somehow a peculiarly *English* thing to do, and the thought made him suddenly intensely homesick; yet simultaneously he felt he was already where he belonged, was already where he was meant to be, and the disparity between his feelings confused him and he didn't know what to say.

Mirissa was smiling at him, her eyes bright, and he smiled too.

He looked at Coutts's grave once more then turned to that wonderful, sensitive, surprising and sensuous woman at his side.

'Thank you, Mirissa,' he said and squeezed her hand. 'Let's go home.'

Seven

'Furthermore, Mr Paget, the bank has learnt that you mistreat your workers.'

'That's none of your business, Dunlop,' growled Paget.

'But it is our business,' insisted the banker, not at all put off by Paget's surly response. 'Anything that affects or may affect your ability to repay the sum you owe is our business.' He fingered his beard and consulted the sheet of paper again. 'We also have it on good authority–'

'What "good authority"? Tell me the swine's name. He won't be a "good authority" on anything by the time I've finished with him.'

Dunlop was unruffled.

'We also have it on good authority,' he repeated, 'that your methods of harvesting leave much to be desired.'

'What do you mean?'

'It is standard practice to pluck only the bud and top two leaves from each bush. Yet you pluck the bud and top two leaves and *more*.'

'So? I get a better yield.'

'But it affects the quality of the finished product, Mr Paget, and it reduces the ability of the bush to produce good tea in the future. In short – to use what I understand is the correct term – you are distressing your bushes.'

'Now see here, Dunlop, how I run my estate has nothing to do with you.'

Dunlop continued as if he hadn't heard.

'The quality of your bushes is declining and that fact is reflected in these business figures.' The banker opened the file on his desk and withdrew a sheet of figures arranged in neat columns. 'Sales of your tea have been declining steadily for nearly a year now.'

'Look at that damn paper – I'm producing more than ever before.'

'Yes, Mr Paget, but your *revenues* have declined. You are getting considerably less per pound of tea than you were a year ago.' Dunlop tilted his head slightly to one side and looked enquiringly at Paget. 'Was there any material change in your estate, your methods or your resources a year ago? Was there anything you altered that may have affected the quality of your tea?'

Paget was silent and Dunlop leaned forward. 'We are very concerned.'

Paget's lips thinned. 'Aye, concerned for your damned money.'

Dunlop regarded Paget solemnly for a moment, then leaned back, all pretence of concern for Paget now gone.

'Very well, Mr Paget, if you wish me to be blunt I will be. Yes, the bank is concerned about its money. You have borrowed a considerable sum and on several occasions we agreed to extend the repayment period. But that arrangement cannot continue.'

Paget frowned. 'Of course it can; all you have to do is extend the repayments again.'

Dunlop steepled his fingers and gave a pained sigh. 'I can see I'm not making myself entirely clear. In the simplest possible terms, Mr Paget, the situation is this: the bank will not extend any more credit to you. Furthermore, you have thirty days from today to repay the money you owe, in full with interest, or we will seize your estate–'

'Seize my estate?!'

'And seize whatever other personal assets may be necessary in order to satisfy the debt.'

'Why you jumped-up little–'

'I would further remind you, Mr Paget, that you have funds on deposit with this bank–'

'Yes,' interrupted Paget. 'I'll take that money now.'

'I'm afraid not. We are holding those funds against any non-payment of the money owed.'

Paget's face reddened and his meaty shoulders bulged as he clenched his fists. Dunlop wasn't put off though.

'You have thirty days from today, Mr Paget. Failure to pay by that date will, I strongly suspect, result in you being declared bankrupt.'

Paget breathed heavily, an undecided bull debating whether to attack, and Dunlop regarded him calmly. At last Paget spoke.

'What the hell do you expect me to do?' he said sullenly.

'Candidly, I see no prospect of you deriving sufficient revenue from sales of your tea to pay off the debt. The only option remaining is to find a buyer for your estate.'

'What? Sell it?' asked Paget, unbelieving.

'Sell it,' repeated Dunlop. 'Do you have any dependants?'

'Dependants?'

'Family.'

'I have a stepdaughter.'

'Ah yes, I recall she visited for a short while last year. She left rather abruptly.'

'She said it didn't suit her,' said Paget sourly.

'And she's living in England now?'

Paget grunted.

'Then there is nothing to stop you. Find a buyer and sell the estate at a price that will enable you to pay off your debt.' Dunlop pushed the sheet of paper across the table. 'The exact amount you owe is detailed there.'

'I know how much I owe, damn you,' said Paget, sweeping the paper to the floor, and he stood up.

Dunlop rose.

'Thirty days, Mr Paget. I trust that when we meet again the result will be to our mutual satisfaction.'

Paget sneered and left. Dunlop, expressionless, watched him go, then recovered the paper and wrote a careful note of their meeting. He placed the documents in the file and closed the cover.

'A thousand acres,' declared Paget expansively. 'A thousand acres of prime land and there's not a better position in the whole of Ceylon. Why else do you think my teas are so successful? I tell you, whichever lucky fellow buys it will be making the best investment he could wish for,' and he looked round the lounge of the Planters' Club. 'So, who's going to make the first offer?'

The dozen or so planters who were listening to Paget exchanged glances. There were some shakes of heads and a couple of the men turned back to the bar.

'Why are you selling?' asked one of the planters.

'It's because of my stepdaughter,' said Paget. 'She's back home in England, an impressionable girl, and she needs me there to stop the damned young gold-diggers who keep trying to catch her eye. Of course I'd prefer to stay here and keep my estate running as successfully as it has been, but she needs me in England. I need the quick sale so I can leave as soon as possible. Are you interested?'

The man gave a small shake of his head and turned away, raising his eyebrows as he looked at the man next to him. That man turned away also.

Paget was silent for a moment, looking at their backs, then he turned to the others.

'What about anyone else?'

Butler was watching from across the room and Paget scowled and ignored him.

'Well? Anybody?'

The other planters were carefully avoiding his eye and Paget frowned.

'Of course, you need time to consider,' he said. 'It's a big decision. So give it some thought. You know where to find me,' and he walked out.

Nobody spoke for several minutes.

'It's no good for me,' said one man at last. 'It's too far away – I'd have to travel fifty miles to farm it. What about you, Wilson? You're nearer.'

'Aye, I'm nearer, but the place'd take a lot of work, getting the bushes up to a good yield.'

'So you've heard too?'

Wilson nodded. 'Distressed bushes take time to recover.' There were murmurs of agreement from the other planters. 'And I'm still paying off the bank. I can't afford to buy something I'll get no return on for months.'

There were nods of sympathy. They had all taken out loans to enable them to make the original conversion from coffee to tea and some had needed to borrow more than others to develop their tea estates. None of them could afford to buy Paget's estate and the discussion soon turned to other subjects. Butler didn't join in the conversation but wandered out onto the terrace deep in thought.

That evening, Mirissa came out of the bungalow and stopped in the doorway. She cocked her head to one side and studied Butler sitting in one of the chairs, his feet stretched out on the verandah rail. He was staring at the setting sun.

She sat nearby, her hands folded demurely and waited. At length Butler stirred and looked across at her. He smiled and her face lit up, relieved that she wasn't the cause of his frowns.

She looked at him enquiringly.

'The land?' she asked, and indicated Paget's estate across the road.

Butler nodded.

'I could do something with that place, Mirissa. Other men could too, of course. They know all about his bushes and what he's been doing to them. They know his workers are none too happy either and that affects how much tea gets picked. But I could change all that. I could add those thousand acres to Tondipgiri and it would be easy to run the lot together, but...' and he stared moodily at Paget's estate.

Mirissa put a hand on his arm.

'But?' she asked.

Butler sighed.

'Money, Mirissa. It all comes down to money. All those other fellows have taken out loans and they won't borrow any more. They don't want to take on more debts. Now me – I've been lucky; I

232

got into tea early and built this up and I didn't need to go to the bank for anything. But I haven't got enough to make an offer for that land. I'd have to borrow the money and I don't fancy the thought of doing that.'

'Then do not borrow money.'

Butler nodded.

'That's the sensible thing to do, of course,' and he looked at Paget's estate and frowned again.

'He's ruining that land, Mirissa. His problem is he doesn't know how to get the best out of his ground. Look at his drainage – it's all wrong: instead of following the contours of the hills it's been laid running straight down; he's losing good top-soil. He's got no shade trees and he doesn't know how to crop his bushes properly. No wonder he had to add my tea to his to get decent sales. But we could re-lay the drains and dig out the bushes he's ruined and if we manured the ground well and planted root cuttings from our bushes we could build Tondipgiri up from a hundred acres into an eleven-hundred-acre estate.'

Mirissa stood, came round the back of the chair and put her arms round him, caught up in his enthusiasm and happy to see him so animated. Butler held her hands.

'But it all comes back to the money. Should I borrow it?'

Mirissa nuzzled his ear and he laughed and swung her round and onto his lap.

'Are you listening to a word I'm saying?' and he buried his face in her neck. She squealed in delight and jumped up and Butler chased her inside, both laughing.

Eight

'I need to borrow some money.'

R.V. Dunlop, Assistant Manager of the Oriental Bank, nodded. 'How much are you wishing to borrow?'

'How much will you lend me?'

'That depends on what you want it for, Mr Butler,' commented Dunlop. 'Is it for improvements to your estate?'

'You could say that,' said Butler. 'I want to extend it. A planter nearby is selling up. I want to buy his land and join it to mine.'

'I see.' Dunlop took up his pen and started to write. 'And which estate is that?'

'It's run by William Paget.'

For the merest fraction of a moment the smooth movement of Dunlop's pen halted, then continued.

'Yes, I think I've heard of him. So he's selling, is he?'

'That's right,' said Butler. 'It'll be easy to combine the two estates and run them together. There's a lot I can do to improve that land. It'll be successful, I assure you.'

Dunlop smiled and put down his pen.

'I'm sure it will, Mr Butler. Everyone knows how well your Tondipgiri estate is doing.'

Butler nodded.

'However,' and Dunlop gently scratched the

corner of his right eyebrow, 'even the best-run estate can meet with difficulties – trading conditions, problems with the crop, you know the sort of thing I mean. In case, Heaven forbid, you became unable to repay the loan the bank must have some protection for its investment, some security.'

'What sort of security?'

'Well it's usual in these cases for the bank to hold the deeds to the estate against any unfortunate inability to repay the money. Which of course we all hope won't happen,' added Dunlop smoothly. 'You pass to us the deeds to Tondipgiri' – the banker's eyes gleamed like hard coal chips and he almost rubbed his hands together, but arrested the movement just in time – 'and we will be happy to lend you the money. All we have to do now is agree upon a figure. Plus a suitable rate of interest, of course.'

An hour later Dunlop escorted Butler to the door and shook hands with him.

'A pleasure to do business with you, Mr Butler,' and Dunlop smiled and showed Butler out. Then he came back to his desk and this time he allowed himself that pleasure of rubbing his hands together and the tip of his tongue darted out and moistened his lips.

A most satisfactory piece of business. The sum that he and Butler had eventually settled on had included – and Butler was unaware of this – an amount equal to the loan and interest still outstanding on Paget's account. Butler was, in effect, taking on Paget's debt.

Dunlop moistened his lips again. He was a winner in every way: Paget would accept Butler's offer and use some of the money to pay off what he owed, thus wiping that troublesome loan from the books – and Dunlop would get all the credit. The interest rate he had compelled Butler to accept would make repayment of the loan highly profitable for the bank and if Butler failed to repay, then the bank would keep the deeds to Tondipgiri.

Tondipgiri! The banker shivered with delight. Butler's estate enjoyed outstanding success and many envious eyes had turned towards it. Dunlop could almost wish for Butler to fail to make the repayments.

Butler found Paget drinking alone in the Planters' Club. Paget glanced up and the look he gave Butler was hostile.

'Can I buy you a drink?' asked Butler, determined to be civil. Not so Paget.

'What do you want, Butler? I've no business with you.'

'You may have soon,' said Butler, and Paget stared at him.

'And what does that mean?'

'Have you found a buyer for your estate?'

'None of your business,' and Paget knocked his drink back.

'I'd like to buy it.'

'Never,' and Paget poured another drink.

Butler paused. He had expected Paget to be difficult but he hadn't been prepared for such an abrupt rejection. He tried again. 'I'll give you a good price. Fifty thousand.'

'I'm not selling to you.'

'Look, Paget, I know we've had difficulties in the past–'

Paget snorted.

'Keep your damned money, Butler, I'm not selling to you,' and Paget knocked the glass back again and stalked out.

'Look here, Dunlop, I need more time to find a buyer.'

'I'm afraid there can be no more time, Mr Paget,' said Dunlop with insincere sympathy. 'There are five days left and then, regrettably, the bank must take possession of your estate. I'm very sorry.'

Paget scowled and prepared to depart, but Dunlop wasn't going to let him go so easily.

'Have you had no offers at all?' he asked innocently. 'Has no one made you any kind of an offer?'

Paget's forehead creased and his brows knitted together.

'Just one,' he admitted sullenly. 'But I can do better than that.'

'And who was that offer from?' enquired Dunlop casually.

'Fellow opposite. Butler.' Paget spat the name out.

'How much did he offer?' asked Dunlop.

'Fifty thousand,' muttered Paget.

'There are only five days left,' repeated Dunlop. 'It doesn't seem likely that you can "do better" than the offer from this fellow, what did you say his name was? Butler? It might be wisest to accept,' and Paget ground his teeth together.

There was a long silence in the banker's office and Dunlop studied Paget carefully.

'Bankruptcy can be a painful business,' commented Dunlop, shaking his head sadly. Paget looked up and glared, then stared out of the window.

'Only five days,' started Dunlop.

'Yes, I heard you,' snapped Paget and the banker subsided and waited. Paget had no other options and Dunlop knew it.

'All right, blast you, I'll sell it to Butler.'

'It's for the best,' said Dunlop smoothly, a doctor convincing his patient to take some unwanted medicine. Paget snorted.

'If you wish,' ventured Dunlop, 'I'll let Mr Butler know, shall I? I can arrange a date for the sale.'

Paget, breathing heavily, gave a short nod and looked away. His knuckles were white.

Butler tried to reassure his foreman as they walked up the dusty track.

'There'll be no problems, Changarai. I hand over this bankers' draft for the money, he gives me the deeds and we all sign the bill of sale. That's why I asked you to come with me – to witness it all. You've practised your signature and when everything's been done we'll leave. Don't worry about Paget – he can't do anything to you. You're not his foreman any more.'

Changarai wasn't happy but he kept pace with Butler.

When they arrived at the bungalow Butler didn't need to knock. He barely had one foot on the verandah when the door opened and Paget stepped out.

'That's far enough, Butler, I don't want you in my house,' and he glared at Changarai. 'What's that little rat doing here? Get him off my land.'

'He's here to witness the signatures,' said Butler, and twisted the knife a little more. 'It's this way or no way, Paget. If you can find another buyer go ahead.'

Paget looked as if nothing would have given him greater satisfaction at that moment than taking Butler apart, limb by painful limb, but he screwed the lid down on his anger.

'Where's your money?'

Butler took the draft from his pocket. 'Where are the deeds?'

Paget took them from the inside of his jacket and threw them onto the verandah table.

'There, damn you. Now give me that draft.'

'There's the small matter of the bill of sale,' said Butler, and unfolded a sheet of paper, 'Have you a pen?'

Paget looked fit to burst but went inside and returned with pen and ink.

'I'll sign first,' said Butler, and bent over the table. 'Now you, Paget.'

Paget snatched the pen from Butler and scribbled, 'Received under duress from J. Butler the sum of £50,000'.

'Now you, Changarai,' said Butler, and added softly, 'As you practised it.'

Changarai slowly wrote his name and carefully

put down the pen.

'All legal and above board.' Butler held out the bankers' draft. Paget snatched it.

'Now get off my land,' he growled.

'Mine now, I think you'll find,' Butler corrected, holding up the deeds. 'Make sure you've gone by sundown,' and he turned on his heel and left, Changarai quickly following.

Nine

The months that followed were the happiest Butler could remember.

They were hard-working months though, and the amount of work to be done was immense, for Paget had distressed his bushes to a critical point, picking far more from them than he should. He'd taken no care about pruning, nor about manuring and weeding. The estate had been declining rapidly and Butler estimated – and Taylor and Thwaites agreed – that the estate would soon no longer have been viable.

Butler knew that without a happy and contented work-force he would achieve nothing, and on his first day as owner he made a point of taking Changarai with him to speak to the workers. Previously they had known only Paget and his brutal ways but they had heard good things about the Tondipgiri *Durai* and had long envied their cousins working across the road. Daily the contrast between the new owner and his predecessor was clear to see. They were treated better, Butler-Sir always had a cheery word for them, and soon their singing voices accompanied their labours in the fields.

Butler didn't neglect their accommodation either. One of his first jobs was to examine the lines, and they were as bad as he feared, worse even than the neglected Tondipgiri lines when he had first arrived. Ventilation, sanitation, all were in a grievous state, and Butler cursed Paget and his slipshod ways. He directed the rethatching of the roofs and the clearance of rubbish and ensured that new sanitation drains were dug.

On the slopes and in the fields new irrigation channels were cut and old growth pruned from the existing bushes. Root cuttings were carefully taken from the Tondipgiri stock, and with the planting of the first of those cuttings Butler ceased to think of the new acreage as being formerly Paget's land.

He estimated the future yield of the enlarged Tondipgiri estate and quickly concluded that his existing tea factory would be inadequate. Larger facilities were needed, so he completely gutted what had previously been Paget's bungalow and extended it to become the new factory. In went building materials, in went new machinery – bought or built – and Paget's old factory became the new storehouse.

He intended to pull down the old Tondipgiri factory, but a suggestion from Mirissa stopped him. He had the old building cleaned out and it became a sort of school where the not in-considerable numbers of children from the extended workforce could stay during the day. The children were kept busy, they were happy and their parents were happy too. The happier workforce worked harder on the estate and the new, larger Tondipgiri flourished beyond Butler's dreams.

And throughout it all, never far away from him during the day and always beside him at night in the bungalow, was Mirissa. Her smiles and laughter and sheer zest for life were a source of inspiration and energy and her constant support and presence made it all worthwhile. Sometimes he would stop in the middle of some task and look at the estate flourishing around him and doubt whether he would be achieving any of it were it not for the vigour she inspired in him.

On the day that Butler was finally satisfied that the additional land had been properly in-corporated, that everything was running well, that the two former estates were truly working as one, he stood on the top of the Tondipgiri ridge and held Mirissa's hand. The breeze moulded her saree to her body and ruffled his hair and Butler, looking at the vast estate stretched out below him, remembered a day years earlier when he had held a letter in his hand and had read his father's hope that either the estate would be the making of Butler or that Butler might make something of the estate.

Both had happened, he reckoned, and laughed, surprised at himself.

In England, before he had inherited Tondipgiri, he had been a young man with no proper job, living on his gambling wits and reduced to the ownership of some clothes, some luggage and a few other small effects; a member of a number of seedy gaming clubs and possessed of a vague sense of restless dissatisfaction with it all.

And now look at him. If it hadn't been for his father... Butler shook his head. The Old Man had known what he was doing all right.

Not such a bad old stick after all.

He caught Mirissa looking at him questioningly and he smiled and shook his head again.

'Just something I remembered,' he said and they went down the hill, their joined hands swinging between them.

Part Four

1884: FERMENTATION

'A critical stage. The longer the tea is allowed
to ferment, the stronger the flavour will be;
but be warned: if left too long,
the flavour will be lost.'

One

5th May, 1884

'Hello, who's this?' said Ferguson, a planter who worked an estate not far from Tondipgiri. Butler turned from the bar. Entering the Planters' Club lounge was Eliot and with him was another man, clearly not a planter.

The man was about fifty and bearded, a clear six feet tall, and whereas Butler and the other planters were tanned and lean from hard work in the blazing sun, this man's skin had been beaten dark by hard weather. He was broad and solid in a dark jacket and crows' feet were sharply etched in the lines around his piercing blue eyes. They could smell the sea off him.

'This is Captain Bentinck,' said Eliot introducing his guest. 'He has a proposition to put to you gentlemen.'

There was a stir of interest at this and the other planters shifted round to be more comfortable.

'What's your proposition, sir?' asked one, and Captain Bentinck leaned on the bar.

'I'm Master of the *Elizabeth Miller* – a clipper ship in Colombo harbour. The owner of a steamer that's docked there has bet me that he can get a cargo home to England before me. I say he can't.'

'You'll lose your bet then,' interrupted one of the planters. 'He'll be going through the Suez

Canal while you're sailing round the Cape of Africa. He'll be in England weeks before you.'

The Captain turned hard blue eyes on the planter and the man faltered.

'That's just how it is,' he finished lamely.

The Captain turned his attention back to the rest of the assembly.

'The owner of this steamer reckons he's faster than me, even in a straight race. He reckons he can race me on the one route – Colombo to the Cape, round the tip of Africa – and still beat me home to England.'

He looked round at the company. 'I say he can't. In a straight race my clipper's faster than that dirty steamer and I'm going to prove it. But I'm not about to waste a voyage without a cargo aboard. And that's where you gentlemen come in: do you want to back me with a cargo of your tea? What do you say?'

Eliot looked at his fellow planters. 'How about that for a wager? It'll capture the imagination back home – it'll be like the old clipper races of twenty years ago. And it'll be profitable too: there'll be a lot of betting and there'll be a premium price for the winning cargo. How many tons do you carry, Captain?'

'Near enough nine hundred,' said the Captain. 'My rate's seven pounds a ton,' and his eyes narrowed and studied the plantation men. 'Any takers?'

The planters exchanged glances.

'There used to be a lot of publicity on those old races,' commented Ferguson. 'The winner would get as much as three or even four shillings a pound extra at auction,' and he warmed to the theme. 'And you say it's a straight race? Both ships on the same route?'

The Captain nodded.

'Well there you are then,' declared Ferguson. 'A clipper could never beat a steamer if the steamer's cutting through at Suez, but a race together ... that would really be something,' and the other men agreed.

'What about you, Butler?' sang out Eliot. 'You're game for it, aren't you?'

Butler stirred from the bar.

'I might have been – once,' he said, 'but I've got a big loan to pay back. I'm right at the limit – a few pounds the wrong way and I've got problems. I can't afford to take the risk. You'll have to get someone else for your wager.'

'What about you fellows?' asked Eliot and drew interested murmurs from the planters. They gathered in a group, talking, and Bentinck watched them.

The door to the lounge opened and a planter, Wilson, came in. His face was tight and pale, and when he spoke his voice was sharp and it cut through the discussion.

'Gentlemen, can I have your attention?' Wilson didn't mince his words. 'The Oriental Bank has gone bust.'

There was a stunned silence.

'When?' asked one of the planters.

'Two days ago,' said Wilson. 'Fortunately, the Governor himself has stepped in to guarantee the bank's notes.' Here there was a relieved murmur, but it subsided as Wilson spoke again. 'But we've all borrowed from that bank; some of us owe more than others,' and Wilson looked directly at Butler.

When he came over the ridge and saw Mirissa's white-sareed figure waiting by the road Butler knew something was up, and when he got closer he understood. A wagon with a bored-looking driver was in front of the bungalow and a neatly suited man was waiting on the verandah. He stood as Butler approached.

'Mr Butler?'

Butler nodded.

'Good afternoon, Mr Butler, my name's Jessell. I'm with the Oriental Bank.'

'I heard the news,' said Butler. 'I didn't expect you here so soon though.'

'I like to expedite matters,' said Jessell smoothly and nodded at the wagon, 'The transportation is rather rudimentary, but important issues need early resolution, don't they? Shall we sit down?'

They sat and Mirissa stood behind Butler's shoulder.

'The bank,' said Jessell, 'is, I am happy to say, now on a level footing once more. The Governor of Ceylon has stepped in to make a personal guarantee.'

'So I heard,' said Butler. 'That's very good news.'

'Indeed,' agreed Jessell with a small smile. 'Now we come to the question of your loan.'

'That's all right, isn't it? Everything was agreed with Mr Dunlop.'

Jessell looked slightly uncomfortable. 'Mr

Dunlop is no longer in a position to make loan agreements. He has been – erm – assigned to other duties.'

'Why is that?'

'Unfortunately, Mr Dunlop extended the bank's lending position further than he should have.'

Butler stared at Jessell. 'You mean he lent too much and broke the bank?'

Jessell held Butler's gaze for a moment, then smiled that small smile again.

'Let's deal with the business in hand, shall we? Suffice it to say that the bank requires the prompt repayment of its money. In your case, Mr Butler,' and Jessell consulted a sheet of paper, 'the sum outstanding is a shade over thirty thousand pounds; thirty thousand and eighty-seven pounds, seventeen shillings and sixpence to be precise. That includes the interest.'

Butler nodded. 'Yes, I'm making the repayments.'

'The bank requires prompt repayment in full, I'm afraid.'

Butler's jaw dropped. 'What do you mean?'

'I mean that you have four months to make full repayment.'

'Four months! I can't repay all that in four months.'

'I'm afraid we must insist.'

'You can't do that,' exploded Butler indignantly. 'You've got to give me time to repay it.'

'If you look at the details of the agreement you signed, Mr Butler, you will see that the bank can call in the loan – in full and with interest – at any time, giving four months' notice.'

'I can't do it,' said Butler.

Jessell gave a small shrug and stood up. 'If you can't repay the money, Mr Butler, the bank is holding the deeds to this estate and will take the land in lieu of payment.'

'Look, hold on,' said Butler, standing. 'I don't mean I won't pay it; I'm just saying I can't find that much money all at once. Everything's been invested in this,' and he gestured to the estate around them.

'The terms of the loan are quite clear, Mr Butler. The amount you owe, plus interest, must be repaid in four months or the bank will seize the estate. I really don't think there's a great deal more for us to say, do you? I'll leave you to make arrangements for repayment. Four months, Mr Butler,' and Jessell left.

Stunned, Butler watched him go. He stood frozen to the spot, one thought driving everything else from his brain: non-payment meant the loss of the estate and non-payment was exactly what was going to happen, for if one thing in the world was certain it was that there was no possibility of getting thirty thousand pounds together in four months.

A hand slipped into his and Butler looked at Mirissa. A worried frown creased her face as she saw the shock and disbelief in his eyes.

'I don't know what's going to happen, Mirissa. I just don't know,' and Mirissa, with no idea of what else to do, squeezed his hand.

A leaf blew in Butler's face and he looked up at the darkening afternoon sky. Despite his mind whirling with the bombshell Jessell had just delivered, he registered that the sky was darkening too early; it could mean only one thing – an approaching storm. Butler stepped off the verandah and hurried up the hill. They reached the crest together and halted.

God, this was going to be a bad one.

The normally intense green of the jungle to the east had taken on a sickly yellow tinge under a vast wall of dense blue-black cloud that filled the sky. Dirty grey clouds, the forerunners of the storm, boiled overhead and fine drops of rain fell on his face. The storm would be upon them very soon and Butler gave silent thanks for the fact that at least the storm was hitting at the end of the day. He had no idea what he was going to do to pay off the loan but he knew he couldn't afford to lose any cropping time.

He felt Mirissa turn at his side and then her hand abruptly clutched his arm. He glanced at her, then followed her shocked gaze.

'Bloody hell,' and he plunged down the hill, his shouts echoing across the valley. 'Fire! Everyone out!'

Two

Flames were already flickering under the eaves of the storehouse and escaping through the thatch and Butler ran for the door. He jerked it open and recoiled as flames billowed out, scorching his face. The new source of air fed the flames and

253

tongues of fire licked the door and snaked upwards. Butler went to the side of the storehouse, looking for a way in, but the fire was everywhere. He went back to the front and shouted frantically at the people hurrying up.

'Get water from the stream. Come on!'

Mirissa pulled at his sleeve and opened her mouth to speak but an electric-blue flash lit up the estate and the very air seemed to crack as thunder crashed around them. She was pointing towards the Tondipgiri slopes and shouting but the sudden collapse of part of the roof drowned her words. A cloud of sparks shot into the air and the thatch crackled as the fire seized it. Flames shot up the walls, cracking and snapping, and the sudden hiss of pouring rain was added to the noise as the storm clouds humped over the ridge of Tondipgiri and emptied themselves.

Thank God, thought Butler, perhaps the rain would put out the fire, but the fire was well established and wasn't going to release its grip on the storehouse that easily. Mirissa pointed to the slopes again and mouthed something, then she ran off into the storm darkness.

'Mirissa!' he shouted, but she couldn't hear him. People carrying buckets came hurrying up from the stream and Butler directed them to throw the water on the fire.

'Get rakes,' he shouted. 'Pull the walls away.'

Changarai ran up and saw Butler yelling furiously, illuminated by the fierce glow of the burning storehouse.

'Butler-Sir! Butler-Sir!'

A tremendous bang of thunder made them

both duck instinctively and Changarai gripped Butler's arm.

'It was Naga,' shouted Changarai wildly.

'What!'

'Mirissa saw him. He ran up the hill.'

Butler stared at Changarai in horror then ran around the store and looked towards the slopes. The bushes were glowing red from the fire raging below them, then another brilliant flash of lightning lit the entire slope revealing a figure in a white dress scrambling near the top.

'Mirissa,' yelled Butler fruitlessly, then she was over the ridge and gone and the dark of the storm was on them again. Butler squinted at the roaring fire, the flames writhing wildly in the pouring rain.

'Save it, Changarai, save as much as you can. Get the tea out,' and he turned and ran for the slopes, the rain driving into his face.

He reached the slope and tried to run up it but the ground was streaming and his booted feet slipped in the mud. He bent and dug his hands in, clutching handfuls of earth to help him climb, and he slipped and sprawled several times, but he reached the ridge at last, then was nearly blown back off it by the force of the wind.

'Mirissa!'

There was no sign of her but there was only one way she could have gone and that was down to the rope bridge. He stumbled down, lost his footing and slid in the mud, rose to his feet and stumbled again. He came to the bottom of the slope, and the roar of the river, already swollen over its banks, added to the din of the wind and rain. He staggered to the bridge, head bent as the rain burst on him and around him, and he grabbed at the hand-ropes. Nearly halfway over the relentless needles of rain forced him to stop and shield his head. He felt a new motion added to the swaying of the bridge and he looked up. Someone was crossing from the other side.

'Mirissa!' he shouted and lurched forward again. The approaching figure stopped, and a lightning flash showed Butler it wasn't Mirissa at all.

The man was streaked with mud and looked wild. Even in the poor light Butler could see the feral gleam of teeth as Naga drew back his lips in a snarl. His hand moved at his waist and Butler saw the glint of a knife.

'Where's Mirissa?' demanded Butler, roaring above the storm. Naga's answer was to charge at Butler, knife swinging.

Butler stepped back, the bridge rocking and twisting crazily, and then Naga was upon him. The knife hissed past his face and Butler lashed out, sending Naga stumbling against the ropes, but the man was as quick as a cat and he bounced back, swinging the knife again.

It felt to Butler as if a white-hot razor had sliced across his chest, then Naga was on him and Butler had no time to consider the wound. He grabbed Naga's knife-arm and Naga shouted something above the roar of the storm and tried to bite Butler's hand. Butler elbowed him in the face and punched him in the stomach and Naga rolled away. Butler scrambled to his feet but missed his footing on the soaking planks and was tangled in the side-ropes. Naga saw Butler's predicament and jumped forward. The impact of his body knocked Butler's legs from under him and he swung out over the river, only his desperate grip on the soaking ropes preventing him from falling.

The momentum of the attack carried Naga off the bridge also and in clutching at the ropes to save himself he dropped the knife into the river. Both men were now at full stretch and Naga jackknifed his body up and kicked and kneed Butler, who twisted frantically and lashed out with his own booted foot. Naga gasped, but his knee smacked hard into Butler's thigh and he felt his leg go numb. The leg hung limp and numb, and Naga, seeing his enemy at his mercy, kicked out viciously again. The blows rained in, and Butler knew that if he didn't do something and do it damned quick he would be kicked off the ropes.

Naga swung in closer, kneeing and kicking, but his rush of confidence betrayed him. Butler took a knee in the ribs to lure him closer and then, dreading that his grip would fail him, he clung to the rope with one hand and swung his fist, praying that his aim was good.

The blow landed solidly in the middle of Naga's face and something caved in underneath with a crunch of bone and gristle. Naga gurgled horribly and lost his grip on the ropes. He fell, arms and legs thrashing madly, and the river swallowed him.

Butler hung one-handed from the rope, gasping, then threw his other hand up to get a grip. He took a ragged breath and tried to swing back up onto the bridge. On the fourth attempt he made it and lay clutching the planks, lashed by the rain and whooping for breath. He got to his feet, his numb leg wanting to buckle under him, and staggered across the bridge. He stumbled up the path through the storm-tossed bushes and fell out onto the track.

'Mirissa! Mirissa!'

He looked both ways, then a movement a hundred yards up caught his eye. A figure in what might have once been a white dress but which was now muddy and torn was struggling to rise to its feet.

'Mirissa!' shouted Butler and her head came up. He started towards her but stopped as he felt vibration through the muddied earth. He turned and his blood ran cold.

A dozen elephants, crazed by the storm, were stampeding along the track. They would reach Mirissa long before he could. Waving his arms, yelling like a crazy man, he stood his ground in the middle of the track and swore and shouted at the charging herd. Jumping up and down, windmilling his arms, he bellowed curses and made himself as frantic a figure as he could.

He must have succeeded because the leading elephants slowed uncertainly, then stopped, and the others milled around behind them.

'Get up, Mirissa!' he shouted over his shoulder. 'Get off the track!'

Whether she heard him Butler didn't know. His attention was fixed on the elephants. They were starting to retreat, but another brilliant flash of lightning and a simultaneous crack of shattering thunder panicked the ones at the back. They squealed and pushed and the pressure from behind forced the elephants at the front to shed their uncertainty at the sight of the wild man capering in front of them. They trumpeted and started forward again.

'No!' yelled Butler desperately. 'Go back!' and he stood his ground, but the shoulder of the leading elephant effortlessly lifted him off his feet and threw him sideways into the undergrowth.

The bushes exploded beneath him and he burst through, expecting to fall onto flat ground, but he landed on a slope and rolled down in a mass of mud, branches and rotting vegetation. Spinning, battered by rain, he slipped and slid until, completely disoriented, he flung out his arms to stop his slide and collided painfully with the trunk of a tree. Uprooted bushes and loose branches rained down on him and Butler fought to get to his feet. Filthy and plastered with decaying leaves he scrambled back up the slope and burst onto the track.

The elephants had gone and there was no sign of Mirissa.

Thank God, she had made it.

He stumbled along the track, his boots slipping in the mud, and came to where he had seen her. She must have crawled to safety amongst the bushes and he drew breath to shout for her, but the shout died in his throat. In the middle of the track, in the middle of the oozing red mud, lay a crumpled figure. Butler threw himself down next to her and stared, numb.

She had been trodden into the ground. Whilst he was rolling down that slope she had fallen under the feet of the elephants, the animals she'd never dared to name in case it provoked their anger. She had avoided that anger but not their panic, and now she lay in a shapeless huddle, half-submerged in the sludge of the track. Her limbs were awry and her dress was a muddy rag but somehow, by some blessing, Mirissa's lovely face was untouched and the rain was washing the mud splashes from it.

Butler's throat seized, words he wanted to say strangled and he knelt in the mud, the rain slashing at him and drenching the crushed body of the woman he loved.

He didn't know how long he knelt there – the elephants could have come back and trampled him but he wouldn't have cared. Oblivious to the storm, the thunder, the lightning, he kept a vigil at her side until, at length, some impulse made him stir. He was about to lift her but couldn't bear the thought that she might be so crushed that pulling her from the mud might disturb her broken body any further. He dug his hands down deep into the mud and pushed them under her, then forced himself up and stood in the middle of the track, rain pouring down on him and mud dripping from him and from the figure in his arms.

Changarai stood at the front of the despondent knot of workers standing silently in the pouring rain and stared at the burnt-out wreck of the storehouse. The rain had finally conquered the fire, but Butler-Sir wasn't going to be happy when he saw the twelve tea chests which were all they had been able to save and which now lay around in the mud.

There was movement as people turned to look at the slopes, and through the rain and dimness a figure appeared, carrying something. As it came closer Changarai saw it was Butler-Sir, a ragged bundle in his arms.

'We saved some tea, Butler-Sir,' began Changarai, then stopped as he realised what Butler was carrying. Changarai stared at Mirissa's face, her head thrown back, then looked in horror at Butler. Butler's face was hollow and expressionless and his eyes were the eyes of a man who had seen hell and must now live with the knowledge of what he had seen.

Butler walked slowly towards the bungalow, taking Mirissa home, and Changarai walked with him. After a moment the stunned estate workers followed.

A couple of men slipped away, back to the lines, and a minute later a slow and rhythmical drumming began. It continued, measured and monotonous, until dawn.

Three

'Seen Butler recently?' asked Eliot, as he approached the bar in the Planters' Club.

'Not for the last two weeks,' said Wilson. 'Not since the fire.'

'Pretty bad I've been told,' said Eliot.

'Burnt his storehouse out. Lost the lot.'

Eliot whistled softly. 'Owes a fair bit, doesn't he?'

'A good few thousand.'

'I heard he lost his woman as well.'

'Mm, native girl. Got trampled by elephants. Apparently she–' The planters halted their conversation.

Butler was in the doorway. He spotted Eliot at the bar and crossed to him.

'Eliot,' he said by way of greeting.

'Butler,' Eliot acknowledged, and was shocked at the man's pallor. The colour had been leached from the tightly drawn skin and livid dark rings underlined his eyes.

'That race,' said Butler. 'I want to be in on it.'

Eliot and Wilson exchanged a look.

'Slight difficulty there, old man,' said Eliot. 'Everyone fancied it, everyone wanted to put up a cargo, but the problem was they all backed the steamer. No one wanted to put a cargo on the clipper. Not easy to make a race of it when there's only one side. Seems no one thinks Bentinck can do it. So we called it off.'

For a moment there was confusion and doubt in Butler's eyes, then his jaw firmed and he gave a small nod.

'Right,' and he turned and went out.

There was only one clipper in Colombo harbour, a long black-hulled vessel moored fast to the harbour wall, and Butler made straight for her. Gilt-yellow lettering on a long nameboard proclaimed her as the *Elizabeth Miller* and Butler halted at the foot of the gangway. A seaman with a tarry pigtail and arms like tattooed hams was swabbing the deck. Butler hailed him.

'Is Captain Bentinck aboard?'

The man straightened and came to the rail. Very deliberately he looked Butler up and down and spat in the water.

'Who wants him?'

'I do,' said Butler grimly and he too spat in the water. 'Well?'

The man regarded Butler silently for a moment, then grunted, 'I'll get him,' and went aft.

Butler waited, his thoughts somewhere else, until interrupted by a voice.

'You want to speak to me?'

Captain Bentinck descended the gangway and Butler came straight to the point.

'Captain Bentinck, my name's Butler. I'm a tea planter. I want to take you up on that wager to race a steamer to England. How long will it take?'

'With good winds about sixty days,' said Bentinck, and grinned. 'So you and your friends are game for the race after all.'

'That's right.'

'Plenty of 'em backing the steamer?'

'Yes.'

'How many of 'em are backing me?'

'One,' said Butler. 'I am.'

Bentinck's grin faded. 'You mean you're going to make up a full cargo?'

'Some of it.'

The Captain stared at Butler suspiciously. 'What do you mean, "some of it"?'

'I calculate I can crop about twenty-five tons.'

Bentinck snorted in disgust.

'I need a damned sight more than a poxy twenty-five tons before I race anybody. Let me tell you something about running this ship, *Mr* Butler: I have to pay for victualling, for stores, repairs, wages; every ton I carry pays its way – or I don't carry it. Nine hundred tons at seven pounds a ton; that's six thousand, three hundred pounds to make a voyage worthwhile. And all you've got is twenty-five tons? Well I'll tell you what you can do with your twenty-five tons: you can–'

Butler cut in angrily.

'Let me tell *you* something, Captain Bentinck. I'll lose my plantation and everything I've got if I don't raise enough money to pay off what I owe. I can make up twenty-five tons but if I send it by regular steamer I'll get only a regular price – ten shillings a pound. That's no good to me. I need a premium price and the only way I'll get it is if my tea gets home first in a big race.' He stabbed a finger at Bentinck. 'So don't quote calculations at me, Captain, I know damned well what your rate is. If we win and I get at least thirteen shillings a pound I can pay off my loan and I can pay off your freight charge as well.'

Bentinck stared at him.

'All of it?'

'All of it,' said Butler.

Bentinck took a good long look at Butler. He looked him straight in the eye and Butler stared right back.

Then the Captain put out his hand.

'Very well, Mr Butler, you've got yourself a ship. But if you don't pay off my charge–'

'If I don't pay off your charge, Captain

Bentinck, it'll be because I'm dead. That's the only thing that can stop me.'

'They're to be in the fields at first light, Changarai. They're to be picking tea as the sun comes up. No late afternoon finishing either. Picking goes on till dusk.'
'But the dark, Butler-Sir—'
'Light torches at dusk and then bring the tea down,' directed Butler coldly. 'The factory's to work all night. And if anybody doesn't like it you can tell them that they either do it this way or when I lose this estate they'll lose their job. Understand?'
Changarai blinked at Butler's brutal words. He nodded. Butler gestured to the fields and slopes. 'We've been cropping every bush once every two weeks. Not any more – we're going to crop each bush every week. Double the yield,' and Butler tramped over to the storehouse.
'Get this rebuilt. Today. Work into the night if necessary.'
'Yes, Butler-Sir, but—'
'Get on with it,' snapped Butler and Changarai nodded hastily. Butler, his lips tight, stared at the rolling green folds of the estate then turned on his heel and stalked into the bungalow.

When there were moments for conversation – and there were very few – the estate workers talked about Butler.
For the last month he had been driving them relentlessly, and it was disconcerting whenever Butler-Sir suddenly appeared and watched what

265

they were doing. Up until these last weeks they had never heard him shout at anyone, but now nearly all had felt the lash of his tongue. He was always hovering around somewhere on the estate – in the factory, on the slopes, in the storehouse – checking and chivvying. They much preferred the Butler-Sir of old, the one they had known before Mirissa had been trampled by the elephants. This *Durai* never smiled.

Butler finished a calculation and scribbled some figures.

'A shade over twenty-five tons,' he declared. 'Get those chests loaded. And if anyone drops one or spills any I'll have their hide. Get them working.'

Changarai acknowledged Butler's order and turned to direct the men loading the convoy of wagons. The last chest had just been secured when Butler emerged from the bungalow carrying a couple of large leather bags. He threw them on the leading wagon.

'You're in charge,' he said to Changarai, and climbed up onto the leading wagon. 'I'll be sixty days at sea, then I've got two weeks in England to arrange the sale at auction and to telegraph the money.'

'When will we know if you have won, Butler-Sir?' asked Changarai.

Butler knew the date as if it were engraved on his soul.

'Fifth of September,' he said curtly. 'If I haven't sold this lot by then you can say hello for me to the man from the bank when he comes to seize the estate,' and he turned to the driver.

'Go,' and Butler faced front. He was pale and stern and didn't spare another glance for Changarai, nor for Tondipgiri. The wagons jerked and swayed and then began their rattling journey to Colombo.

'Twenty-five tons,' repeated Captain Bentinck in disgust and shook his head. 'We've taken on the ballast already. All eight hundred and seventy-five tons of it,' he added sarcastically. He turned and shouted up to the Mate, an ox of a man working on the deck.

'Mr Webb, take the cargo on board. Twenty-five tons. As soon as you can, if you please,' and the Captain stared along the quay to where a squat black steamer with a single tall funnel was belching dirty smoke. The name *Dragon* was painted on her bows.

'Damned greasebucket,' he scowled. 'He won't forget this race in a hurry,' and he turned to Butler. 'Your cargo'll be in England in sixty days. That's my promise. I'll let you know by telegraph as soon as we reach Liverpool.'

'There'll be no need for that, Captain.'

Bentinck nodded. 'You're going through Suez, eh? You'll be home ahead of us all right.'

'I'm not going through Suez,' said Butler. 'I'm coming with you.'

'Not on my boat, you're not,' said Bentinck violently. 'I'm having no lubbers aboard.'

'That's my cargo, Captain Bentinck,' started Butler and the Captain cut in.

'Aye, and this is my ship. With a working crew

aboard. Twenty-eight souls and every man has his job – they're not there to be nursemaiding landsmen who come along for a ride. You cut along through Suez and wait for us in Liverpool; you're not sailing on my boat,' and Bentinck turned away in dismissal. Butler's grip on his arm arrested the move though, a grip so tight that Bentinck blinked. Butler stepped closer and his voice was hard and strong and left Bentinck in no doubt as to the determination of the man.

'You listen to me, Captain Bentinck. Everything I own is riding on that cargo. I'm going with it every step of the way and I'll be working as hard as anybody. Those men of yours are going to do their jobs and if anyone doesn't then God help him, because he'll wish he'd never met me. I'm going to get that cargo to England in sixty days and nothing's going to stop me, not you, not the sea, nothing.'

Butler stared into the Captain's face a moment longer, then released his grip. Bentinck's face was stony.

'How big's your estate, Mr Butler?'

'Over a thousand acres,' said Butler.

Bentinck pointed across the harbour to the open sea.

'That's my estate – thousands and thousands of *miles*. There's none of your comfortable Planters' Clubs out there, just a lot of water and a lot of hard work. And you're coming along? I don't think so.'

'I'm coming with you,' said Butler, 'and you'd better resign yourself to that fact. Nothing's going to stop me, so start the damned race, man.'

Four

The first seven days were uneventful and Butler congratulated himself on picking what he was convinced was the faster of the two ships. At this rate they might even be in England *before* the sixty days were up. It had been his firm intention to be on deck at all times to make sure Bentinck's sailors weren't slacking, but they all seemed busy enough and Butler was reduced to pacing the deck and watching the sea streaming past. With nothing to do he had leisure to look about the *Elizabeth Miller* and observe what manner of ship he was entrusting his cargo to.

There were three islands of accommodation along her length: the stern block held Bentinck's cabin, the saloon, the pantry and accommodation for the Mate, Second Mate and Steward. Butler was sharing with the Second Mate, a thin man called Fox.

Forward of this block and down a ladder to the main deck were the other two blocks of accommodation: the forward one comprised the galley and carpenter's workshop and a cramped bunkroom holding twelve seamen; the middle block housed the carpenter, sailmaker, bo'sun, cook and eight apprentices. Chicken coops were outside the latter's door and in the bows were pigs, penned amongst ropes and nets and other tackle.

The ship herself was long and slim and cut the

water with a hiss, a far different proposition to the plodding steamers that had previously taken Butler to and from Ceylon. She was clean, her decks were orderly and well laid out and there was no loose gear rolling about, nothing to impede the sailors in their work. She was braced up tight and running fast.

The only jarring note was the crew. Whenever they spared him a glance, which was seldom, he felt acutely out of place. He could sense them weighing him up, all those solid quiet men in caps and jerseys and coarse flannel shirts, with their thick trousers and thick belts and leathery skin the colour of old bronze. Without saying a single word the sailors, the apprentices, even the steward all let him know that out here he was a novice and they were the masters.

Every day Butler scanned the horizon for a sign of the *Dragon,* searching for that plume of smoke, but he saw only the empty expanse of rolling sea.

'He'll be well behind us,' scoffed Bentinck one evening as they ate in the saloon, and Webb and Fox, who dined there also, grunted in agreement.

Butler chewed the meat in silence and frowned. 'Then what's his edge?'

'His what?'

'His edge. If he's already fallen so far behind what makes him think he can win this race? What advantage has he got?'

Bentinck wiped his mouth.

'He's got an engine,' he said, through a mouthful of bread. 'We need the winds to get us home, but he doesn't. He knows that once we're round the Cape and heading up north by Africa we'll run into the doldrums. He's expecting to pass us there.'

'Doldrums?' asked Butler.

'Educate the man, Mr Webb, if you please.'

'The doldrums,' said Webb, 'are miles of open sea where you might get no winds, not for days. Or weeks even.'

'What will you do when we reach them?'

'We'll wait,' said Webb shortly.

'Wait?'

'There bain't nothing else to do,' and Webb attacked his dinner again.

'That's what that steamer's counting on,' said Bentinck. 'He reckons to find us becalmed and then steam right on past. That's his "edge".'

'And what's your edge, Captain?' asked Butler softly. 'You wouldn't have taken this race on unless you believed you could win it. You've known about these doldrums and about him planning to steam past us. So how are you going to win?'

Bentinck leaned back and looked at Butler with a knowing smile.

'Have you ever asked yourself why we're racing to Liverpool and not London?'

Butler confessed he hadn't.

'The problem with London,' explained Bentinck, 'is that there's no winds to carry us up the Thames. We'd need a tug to take us to the finish. But what if there's no tug on hand? Or what if that greasy steamer gets there ahead of us and bribes the tugs to give us a miss? Without a tug we can't win, can't even finish. But Liver-

271

pool, now that's a different matter. With a good wind and a good tide I can sail this lady up the Mersey and put her right against the dock wall. I'm not losing a race to any damned steamer just for want of a tug.'

'But what if there isn't a good wind? Or a good tide?'

'You'd better pray that there will be, Mr Butler,' declared Bentinck grimly. 'Otherwise the bet's lost,' and he got up from the table and went into his cabin, shutting the door behind him.

Butler stared after him, open-mouthed, then turned to the other men.

'Is that it? Is that our only edge? Praying for a good wind and tide?'

Webb chewed on a piece of bread. 'Twenty years ago there was a ship – *Lightning,* damned fast she was,' and Fox nodded in agreement. 'Raced from Melbourne to Liverpool. Did it in sixty-three days and ran up the Mersey and docked without any tugs,' and Webb nodded his head towards Bentinck's cabin. 'He was Second Mate on that ship. There isn't another Captain at sea that could win this race, but he can. He's the best edge we've got, right there. Don't bother praying for good winds and tides, Mr Butler, pray that nothing happens to the Captain.'

The air began to get distinctly cooler and the sea seemed much more restless. Butler didn't understand what the sailors were doing but he could see they were doing a lot more of it. They were up in the rigging more frequently and a gang of them rigged ropes about the decks, just

272

above head-height, and strung nets along the sides. He couldn't imagine what they might be for, until one day the tilting deck made him lose his footing and throw his hands out. He clung to one of the ropes and didn't let go until he heard Webb guffawing.

'Well done, Mr Butler, that's how you use a lifeline. Didn't expect to see you hanging onto it so soon though,' and the watching sailors laughed.

One bitterly chill morning Butler emerged from the accommodation block and started down the ladder to the deck. The breeze cut at his cheeks and at first he thought the sound he was hearing was the cry of a seagull. He looked up and realised it wasn't.

Two sailors were high in the rigging, more than a hundred feet up. One had fallen and the other was desperately holding onto him. Other sailors on deck stopped and looked up and several dashed to the rigging and started climbing.

'He's slipping. For God's sake help me!'

The fallen man screamed and kicked wildly, then flung up his free hand and grabbed in panic at his saviour's collar. The weight round the man's neck pulled him forwards, he lost his grip on the ropes and with terrified yells both men fell. Butler felt the vibration through the deck as the bodies landed.

He was about to rush forward but none of the other sailors were moving. After a moment several of the men went to the bodies and untangled them but made no attempt to see if they were still alive.

'Over thirty, forty feet it don't make no difference.' Butler found Fox standing next to him. 'The fall'll kill you. Only difference is – the higher you are, the longer you can enjoy the view on the way down,' and Fox turned away.

Butler looked at him, stunned at the callous indifference, then looked at the two bodies. Bentinck was on deck now and he crossed and stared down at them.

'Over the side,' he ordered and looked round at the crew. 'You all know what this means,' and he walked past Butler, his face grim, and went aft. The sailors picked up the limp forms without ceremony and heaved them over the side. There was a faint splash as the sea swallowed them and Butler stepped to the rail. He stared in horror at the featureless patch of water, quickly left astern, and he turned.

'Don't you have a burial at sea, or something?'

One of the sailors hawked in the back of his throat and spat over the side. 'Damn 'em,' he said shortly. 'Rot 'em in hell, I says.'

Butler looked at him.

'What do you mean? Weren't they good sailors?'

'Doesn't bloody matter now, does it?' said the man in disgust. 'Two men gone. That means more work for the rest of us,' and he spat again then turned his back and went for'ard.

Butler watched him go then glanced again at the grey sea sucking and washing alongside them. He stared up at the mast from where the men had fallen and saw two sailors there, presumably finishing whatever task the dead men had been about. He looked aft and saw Bentinck standing near the ship's wheel; the Captain gave an order to the man working it then went below.

Butler stayed on deck for a long while and the cold he felt wasn't entirely due to the chill wind. He had been – still was – obstinately determined to complete this voyage, to get his tea to England and win the race, but he hadn't been prepared to find quite such a degree of disdain for life aboard the ship. A voice inside protested at such a casual attitude to death, then something else ruthlessly smothered it; if the men aboard this ship weren't going to let the deaths of others get in their way then neither was he. It was a damn good thing – it meant they were as determined as he was to win this race. Nothing would stop them.

Five

'I hope you've found your sea-legs, Mr Butler,' said Captain Bentinck with rough cheerfulness as they sat at the table. 'You're going to need them.'

'What do you mean?'

'I mean we're approaching the Cape. You've had it easy these last few days but you're going to have to work a bit now. You ever been round it before?'

Butler shook his head. 'I've always travelled through the Canal.'

'Well you're in for a treat,' said Bentinck. 'Now's your chance to do some proper sailing. I hope you've had plenty of sleep too, because you're not going to get much when we're rounding the Cape.'

'Is the sea bad there?'

'Only the Horn is worse,' said Bentinck, referring to the stormy Cape at the foot of South America. 'A piece of advice, Mr Butler: keep one hand for yourself and one hand for the ship, because if you go overboard we aren't turning back for you,' and the Captain went out on deck.

Butler turned to Webb for explanation.

'Whatever work you're doing keep one hand free for holding on to the ship,' said the Mate. 'Take both hands off and you'll probably be washed over the side,' and he looked at Butler's hands.

'Short nails,' he commented, 'but not short enough. Get a knife and cut 'em or the ropes'll tear 'em out.'

Butler was at a loss to understand why they were giving him such advice. 'The ropes' he presumed was a reference to the lifelines, but as he had no intention of venturing outside if they encountered heavy seas the warnings about preventing himself being washed overboard were unnecessary.

Seventeen hours later the *Elizabeth Miller* was in the grip of those heavy seas and Butler had wedged himself firmly into a corner of the saloon. It was clearly the safest place to be and he was just bracing himself more securely when the door slid open and a bundle of sopping oilskins flew in, showering him with water. A pair of heavy sea-boots followed.

276

'Put 'em on, Mr Butler, and come outside,' and the Mate slammed the door shut. Butler hesitated, then donned the black waterproof jacket and trousers, put on the sea-boots and climbed cautiously out of the saloon. He slid the door open and was nearly blown back inside. He clutched at the sides, struggled out and slid the door shut, then clutched at the deckhouse frame and stared around him at a world gone mad.

There was no longer a horizon, just a crazily shifting and twisting sea, the crests ripping off in wind-driven fury. The *Elizabeth Miller*, struggling in the middle of it all, slid down a wave and there was a great *crump* as a solid mass of water ruptured and exploded over the decks. A cloud of spray blew back, taking Butler's breath from him, and the smoking white spume streamed across the deck as the ship twisted to free herself from her predicament. Another wave hit her and the sailors on deck bent their backs as the sea rained down around them.

It was grim to look at but it was the appalling sound that Butler couldn't accept. The wind was shrieking through the ropes and rigging, the acres of sails were flapping and cracking and the gale whistled hoarsely around them, all the noises competing with the roar of the sea as thousands of tons of ocean heaved and surged and advanced on the *Elizabeth Miller*. The First Mate, Webb, shouted something and Butler couldn't hear a single word. He cupped a hand behind his ear and the Mate bellowed again.

'I said get down on the deck and haul on that

line, blast you!'

Butler looked for'ard and saw men hauling on ropes. Automatically he moved forward and got a foot on the top step of the ladder, then the *Elizabeth Miller* shuddered and twisted again, trying to escape the sea coming in on her starboard side. The ship tipped over at least forty-five degrees and Butler's hands slipped off the soaking rail. He tumbled onto the deck, the sea washed him against the base of the mast and the sheer weight of water running off the deck pinned him there, finding its way up and under his waterproofs. He gasped and shuddered with the cold, everything he was wearing completely soaked. He clutched at the mast and got to his feet, then staggered back to the ladder. He got one foot on the bottom rung and looked up. Webb was standing at the top.

'Where the hell do you think you're going? I said haul on that rope.'

'I need to change,' yelled back Butler. 'I'm drenched.'

'Get your blasted hands on that rope,' roared the Mate. 'You'll get a damned sight wetter before we're out of this. Get to it you lazy–'

Butler never found out what sort of lazy thing the Mate was comparing him to, for another wall of water exploded around them. There was no mistaking the Mate's angry gesture though, and Butler stepped back and clung to the lifelines as he made his way for'ard.

'Pull on this,' shouted one of the men, holding out a rope. Butler had no idea what he was hauling or why, but at that moment it was clearly

278

the most important thing he could do. He clamped numb and icy hands around the two-inch-thick rope and heaved.

The sea came over the side, green and grey and hungry, and knocked them off their feet. Butler remembered Bentinck's advice and despite his legs being washed from under him he clung desperately to the rope and twisted in the water, then got to his feet as the ship wearily righted herself yet again and the sea streamed off her. He steadied himself and hauled on the rope once more.

He lost track of the hours he was on deck. Somewhere in it all he became reduced to a cold and frozen body, a mere lump of meat that existed only to add weight to the pull on the ropes or the holding of gear in place. At one point something hit him with stunning force, completely disorienting him, and he had no idea where he was as he felt himself manhandled and lifted and swung, then dumped onto something hard. Gasping, his head spinning, the first thing he realised was that water wasn't raining about him any more. Hands were at the tie-string of the sou'wester hood, then it came off and the rim of a bottle was between his lips. Fiery liquid burnt its way down his throat, setting his insides on fire, and he choked and spluttered and the burning liquid bubbled out of his mouth and ran down the oilskins.

'Get it down, you swab,' and more of the liquid scoured his insides. He coughed and his vision swam back into focus.

He was in the saloon, sprawled on the bench,

and Bentinck was standing over him, eyes wild, beard and whiskers and oilskins streaming icy water.

'Better now?' enquired the Captain roughly.

Butler nodded. 'Is the storm nearly over?' he asked hoarsely.

'Over?' echoed the Captain, and Butler grabbed the edge of the bench as the ship heeled violently. 'It's barely started. On deck if you please, Mr Butler, there's work to be done.'

A massive hand hauled Butler to his feet and he lurched towards the steps. A push from the Captain sent him up and out and he plunged once more into that world of wind and racing water.

Time became a blur of storm and cold and pain. The gale drove a thick blizzard of snow across the sea, freezing the water on the deck, and Butler's brain refused to accept that they were working up to their waists in icy waves for ten hours at a stretch; he couldn't accept that there could be weather of such violence, nor that it could continue for so long. Then somewhere along the way his battered brain gave up the contest and resigned itself to accepting that this was how it was, this was the world they were enduring and there was nothing else to be done except work and keep working, sleep if possible, then work some more. Afterwards Butler tried to reckon how long they had endured the gale and he refused to believe it when his calculations told him it had been at least three days.

He became a tool to be directed by others. How the sailors managed to concentrate on their work, to think consciously about what they were doing, he never knew. A shouted command would direct him to some task and he would bend himself to it until ordered to the next one. Breaking waves as high as a house enveloped the ship, burying her in a wall of water that drove Butler and the sailors, battered and bruised and bloody, against the masts and rails, and then they would pick themselves up and carry on.

In the depth of one impossibly violent night, when the storm was shrieking and howling at the ship, Butler in a rare moment of lucidity told himself that at least things couldn't get any worse.

He was wrong.

'Get up. Get up, damn you,' a voice roared through the storm, shredding the fog of sleep enveloping Butler's mind. He felt himself dragged from his bunk and thrown to the floor where he sprawled in the wet like a man in a drunken stupor. 'All hands on deck.'

He staggered outside, his clammy wet oilskins freezing on him, and squinted into the tearing wind. Bentinck was by the wheel, shouting some order to the Mate, and Butler dragged himself over.

'What's happening?' he croaked, and his throat cracked as he shouted his question again.

'We're losing sail,' bellowed the Captain and pointed.

Butler followed the pointing finger and looked up. The sails which had brought them this far and stood up to so much were starting to shred as the horizontally-driven ice splinters bit at the canvas. The wind picked at the rips and Butler watched in horror as one of the sails tore apart, the pieces whirling away into the grey confusion of foam and spray that blurred any distinction of where the sea ended and the sky began. The air about them was a driving mist of water and Butler had to turn his face aside and shield his mouth in order to breathe.

'What's to be done?'

'We're taking it down. If we lose it all now we'll never win the race.'

Butler had quite forgotten the race; his world had closed down to the single task of fighting the gale.

'The steamer won't be making any distance in this, will it?' he shouted, and couldn't tell whether the Captain was snarling or grinning when he answered – the lips were parted and the teeth were bared.

'He'll be hugging the shore. He'll be cutting inside us.'

Butler could have raged at this but his anger was nipped in the bud by the Captain.

'Four men have gone overboard. The sails have to come down and I can't spare anyone else to help. Get on the yards.'

Butler opened his mouth to speak, but had to turn away as spray blew in his face. He gasped then tried again.

'What do you mean, "yards"? Where are they?'

Bentinck looked as if he was about to burst a blood vessel at Butler's ignorance of things nautical.

'Where? They're up the masts, blast you. Those damned long pieces of wood that the sails hang off. Now get aloft.'

Butler looked up at the remaining unfurled sails flapping with gunshot-like cracks in the wind. The ship canted wildly to one side, bringing the tips of 'those damned long pieces of wood' down towards the freezing sea, and Butler clutched at one of the lifelines.

'Up there?' he shouted to Bentinck. 'I don't know anything about sails.'

'Then damn well learn, Butler,' and Bentinck thrust him against the rail and leaned into him, the rough bearded face up close, eyes red and raw from the stinging salt spray and the icy sea.

'You said you wanted to win this race, didn't you?' he bellowed. 'You said you'd work as hard as anybody, didn't you? Well now's the time to prove it,' and he gripped Butler's coat front. 'Get your blasted hide up that mast and get that sail down. If you can't do it you're no use to me and you're no use to anyone. I can throw you over right now and lighten the ship,' and he shouted violently into Butler's face. 'Get up there and get that sail down!'

He threw Butler from him and Butler grabbed at the rail. He looked at Bentinck and the Captain glared back, an unholy mad gleam in his eyes. Butler looked for'ard at the half-dozen men staggering around the base of the mainmast and hanging onto the rigging and he made his way to them. They clutched the ice-encrusted ropes on the starboard side and began to climb.

He quickly understood why the men had chosen to climb on this side of the ship. The *Elizabeth Miller* was being beaten down on her starboard side and was rolling wickedly away to port. Every time she rolled and the mast tipped to port the men could climb; when she rolled back and over to starboard they all hung grimly to the rigging until she righted herself again. Butler entwined himself in the rigging and the oilskins flapped around him and the wind tore at his body. The spray and flying ice splintered on his face and his cheeks were quickly numb.

Fifty freezing feet up the rigging and they reached the main yard. Without hesitation the sailors edged out on the foot-ropes, clinging grimly to the yard lines, and Butler with no other option copied them. He inched along the ropes, swinging sideways and back and forth as the ship swung underneath him. At one point he made the mistake of looking down and realised he was so far out on the yard that he was over the sea itself. It was no longer recognisable as water but was a churning devil's brew of froth and foam like boiling milk. He shuddered and shut his eyes and only an oath from one of the sailors made him open them and move further out. He joined the other men and copied them, holding on with one hand while pulling at the sail with the other. Yards and yards of stiff, frozen canvas flayed his finger-ends raw, but Butler felt nothing.

Blinded by the vicious snow and scything wind they wrestled for two hours to gather the sail, and Butler never understood how it was that he was able to hang on, his body numb with cold and soaked with icy water. Finally, agonisingly, the sail was tied up, and slowly they began to retrace their steps along the yard.

The *Elizabeth Miller* suddenly corkscrewed and the men were thrown against the ropes. One man lost his grip and his scream was smothered as he plunged into the broth of sea below, but no one spared him a thought, his shipmates were too busy hanging on as the ship began to buck and twist.

'The wheel's gone over the side,' someone yelled and Butler looked down. The Captain and Mate and some other men were working feverishly where the wheel should have been and the Captain was screaming orders at them.

There was a sudden whip-like *crack* and every man on the yard looked up. The remaining sail above them had filled out with the wind and they all heard the creaking and straining of the mast as the sail stretched and pulled. The new force acting on the *Elizabeth Miller* swung her round and plunged her bows into the sea, shipping tons of water along her decks.

Even above the storm the men heard the bellow of Captain Bentinck as he yelled at them to gather the sail.

They edged to the mast and began to climb and for some horrible reason that Butler couldn't comprehend his fogged and numbed brain chose that moment to clear. He realised in a drench of cold horror that he was over a hundred feet above the deck and climbing frozen rigging. His horrified brain was too stunned to send any message to his hands and feet to tell them to stop working, and mechanically he climbed upwards, fighting to hang on as the wild yawing of the *Elizabeth Miller* translated up here to wicked swayings and swoopings, swinging first one way then violently changing direction and pulling in another. Another faint cry made Butler look about him; of the six men he had followed up the mast there now remained just four.

They reached the top yard and three men went out to starboard while Butler and another man went out on the port side. The arc that the top of the mast was tracing plunged them in gut-wrenching swoops towards the water below and Butler felt his feet sliding from under him. He locked his arms around the yard and dangled over the sea, sure that this was the moment when he too must lose his grip. His arms might even have been slipping, but he was too numb to be sure when the ship righted herself once more and his feet paddled desperately for the foot-rope.

He kept one hand twisted in the yard line and pawed at the sail billowing below them. The canvas filled and shook and ice flew up and thrashed at his face. Huge seas slid down upon the *Elizabeth Miller* and the never-ending fog of driving ice and snow forced Butler to turn his head away and bury his chin in his shoulder to catch a breath. In this position he was first to see the menace about to assail them.

From the top yard it was like staring into a huge valley as the sea parted, a great trough dropping away. *Elizabeth Miller* was on the crest of the slope and even as Butler yelled in warning the ship teetered on the edge, then slid sideways down the face of the water. As the ship tipped to the side so the mast swung with it, swinging the men out over the water. *Elizabeth Miller* hit the trough of the valley with sickening force and reeled violently in he opposite direction as she careered sideways up he far wall. The sea subsided under the ship and she dropped and met a wall of icy white-flecked ocean advancing upon her.

She shuddered in every spar and the creaking of her timbers was audible despite the terrible noise of the gale. Then the huge wave hit her. The impact rocked the ship like a boxer taking a roundhouse blow square on the chin and she reeled under it, whipping the masts back.

Every man on that top yard felt and heard the crack of splintering wood that followed.

The whole yard twisted and strained, then the starboard arm broke and fell away in a tangle of rope and flapping sail. The three men working on the yard shrieked and screamed and slid downwards, scrabbling for the ropes but falling too fast to get a grip. One was swallowed by the sea, the others were snuffed out on the deck and the water enveloped them and snatched them over the side. Then the port arm of the yard twisted and jerked, dropped and fetched up abruptly. Butler fell forward, knocked his jaw on the wood with sickening force and tasted blood in his mouth. Ropes whipped about him and the sail flapped hysterically, but the yard didn't tilt any further. Butler looked up, dazed, and saw the other man tangled in rope at the junction of the yard and the mainmast. The man's right leg hung at an impossible angle and he was screaming at Butler.

'Cut the ropes, man, cut the sail.'

Butler looked at the mess of ropes around him and looked at the sailor in bewilderment. The sailor fumbled and held out his knife.

'Cut them,' he screamed again.

Butler swung and inched to the trapped man and took the knife.

'Which ropes?' he yelled into the man's face. 'I don't know what I'm doing.'

The shrieking wind tore the sailor's oath away and Butler shook his head.

'What?'

The sailor pointed. 'That one!'

Butler followed the pointing finger and gingerly edged back along the tilted yard. He sawed at the rope and the fibres tore, then the weight of the sail snapped the rope and the ends flew apart slashing Butler in the face, but his skin was too numb from the flying ice to feel anything. He looked at the sailor and the man pointed frantically at another rope, then the yard jerked and slipped once more. Butler grabbed wildly at the yard to keep himself from falling and looked to the sailor again but the man had gone. The yard was scraping against the mast and momentarily Butler saw a red smear, then the snow and ice and spray washed it away and Butler realised in horror that he was alone. He looked down at the pitching deck, over a hundred feet below, and squinted through the blizzard at the wrecked yard he was clinging to.

It was bucking and swinging and the maniac canvas sail that was still attached to it was filling out with the wind, flapping and snapping and Butler didn't know what to do. He hugged the yard, his hands twisted into the confusion of ropes, his numb feet similarly wedged, and the world spun around him.

Another lucid moment occurred and now he understood why the sailor had been telling him to cut the ropes: the rogue sail was just the lever the gale needed to take the ship and shake her and torment her and drive her into the sea. The sail was the storm's best chance of killing them all. If he severed it they might survive. He gripped the knife and started along the yard. Then he remembered Bentinck shouting that they would need all the canvas they could muster if they were to win the race.

The race, the damned race. That was why all this had come about, that was what had put him up here, and now his words came back to haunt him. He had boasted that nothing would stop him, not even the sea, but now the sea and the wind and the snow and the ice had united, tormenting him, ripping the ship apart, the elements having the last laugh after all.

He cursed his grandstand performance on the dock at Colombo, the arrogant words that had led him out here to perch at the top of a mast in a freezing gale, the lives of many men already lost and leaving him now facing a choice he could never have dreamed of. Yes, to cut away the sail might save the ship and save his cargo, but he'd lose the race if he did and that meant no more Tondipgiri. But if he didn't cut the sail the chances were good that he would lose ship and cargo both. And his life.

He screwed his eyes shut, striving to squeeze the thoughts from his brain, but the sail bucked and billowed again and loose ropes lashed him, making him open his eyes, demanding that he confront the situation, insisting he must make the decision. The spicules of ice tore at his face and the wind battered the breath from him and Butler screamed into the storm. He shouted mindlessly, wordlessly, a primitive yell of rage and fury and frustration, and he slashed at the few ropes left tight about him.

The ropes were dense with water and frozen solid but there wasn't a force on earth that was going to stop Butler now. He sawed at the fibres, blind with anger, cursing a world that had taken Mirissa from him and was now going to take his plantation, but he was damned if it was going to take his life. Screaming in physical, mental and emotional agony, he cut and cut, roaring his pain and hurt into the gale, the tears freezing on his lacerated cheeks.

Tons of soaked, frozen sail abruptly snapped the rope he was hacking at and whirled away into the storm. Free at last of the mocking sail that had been the torment of her, the *Elizabeth Miller* threw up her head and swung around. Butler dropped the knife and scrabbled at the yard but his frozen fingers could no longer grip. His body fell back, tangled hip and thigh in the mess of ropes, and he dropped. He had only time to register that he had started to fall when the fall was arrested with a sickening jerk. The ropes tightened about him with cruel force and he cried out. Everything spun crazily, and his final thought before passing out was that cutting the sail free had been pointless. The ship had lost its wheel. He had failed.

Six

Butler was at the bottom of the ocean and slowly floating back to the surface, because it seemed his mind was coming up from somewhere very far below. He felt himself rolling and swaying and supposed the current had got him, but he was too tired to fight it. My body will end up on a beach somewhere he thought dreamily, then he heard the creaking of timbers and realised he was in his bunk and that the rolling and swaying motion was the ship's.

I can't face the storm any more, he told himself wearily, then it dawned on him that he couldn't hear the storm. He could hear the sea sluicing past the ship, but gone was that wild drunken motion that he had fought against at the top of the mast.

He must have dozed off because he found himself waking a second time and this time he could hear a voice. He opened his eyes and found Captain Bentinck standing over him.

'So you're alive,' said the Captain. 'Thought we'd have to tip you over before long.'

Butler managed a weak smile and gave a small shake of his head. He tried to speak, but needed to wet his cracked lips first.

'What happened?' he croaked.

'We're still afloat,' said the Captain. 'But it was a damned close thing. We finished rigging the spare wheel just as you cut that sail. Without that lump of canvas hindering us we managed to get some steerage way.'

'Sorry about that,' said Butler weakly. 'Sorry about cutting the sail.'

Bentinck shook his head.

'Enough. The fact is, if you hadn't cut it we'd be food for the fishes by now.'

'I need to apologise for some of the things I've said,' said Butler, endeavouring to raise his head, determined to say this one thing, his mind clearer and calmer and somehow more at peace than it had been for weeks. 'You're the Captain, you're in charge; not me. You know what you're doing,' and he sank back on the bunk. 'It was a good try,' he added tiredly.

'What do you mean, a good try?' asked Bentinck.

'The race,' said Butler. 'We tried, but the sail's gone, those men died–' and he shook his head.

'It isn't over yet, Mr Butler,' growled Bentinck, and Butler stared.

'What do you mean?'

'I'm not beaten. *We're* not beaten. I lost twelve men out of twenty-eight in that storm but I'm not admitting defeat until I see that steamer tied up ahead of us at Liverpool.'

Butler was dazed.

'But the sails–' he began.

'Every man aboard is on deck sewing up all the canvas we can scrape together. That's why I'm here now, Mr Butler: you're about to learn how to use a sailmaker's needle. Get out of that bunk.'

Something had happened to Butler.

When he stepped on board the *Elizabeth Miller* he had no other thought, no other goal, no regard for anything, bar one thing: winning the race. Everything and everyone had been subordinate to that. Now, under the critical eye of the sail-maker – a dark man the other sailors called The Swede – he forced a needle through tough canvas and his thoughts went back to the moment when he left Tondipgiri. He shook his head remembering his curt treatment of Changarai.

Butler sighed.

He had loved Mirissa and lost her and he knew he had been so wrapped up in his grief that he had given no thought to the fact that Changarai had lost his beloved granddaughter. That was the second time he had treated Changarai badly – the first time he had jumped to all the wrong conclusions and accused him of doctoring the Tondipgiri tea; then after Mirissa's death he had been offhand and rude and had driven Changarai hard. He didn't deserve the man, he really didn't. But, thank God, Changarai had stayed, he hadn't taken offence or left. In the middle of the vast ocean Butler thought of Tondipgiri and mentally apologised to Changarai.

He made the same heartfelt silent apology to the crew also, as yet another repaired or patched or jury-rigged sail was hauled aloft to billow and fill and give more speed to the *Elizabeth Miller*. He felt heartily ashamed at his cavalier treatment of so many good people, all the men and women who worked on the estate, all the sailors on the ship. All of them were people he depended on, people whose labours were, God willing, going to result in the saving of Tondipgiri.

As the *Elizabeth Miller* sliced her way northwards Butler applied himself with a new attitude. He got on with whatever he was required to do, no matter how hard or tiring, nor how menial, and perhaps, just perhaps, they would reach Liverpool before the *Dragon*, of which so far they had seen nothing. One evening Butler raised this with the Captain.

'Not surprised we ain't seen him,' snorted Bentinck. 'He won't be going too far from land – he needs coal. Besides, with a bit of luck he may have sunk already,' and he knocked back a stiff tot of rum. 'I'll be frank, Mr Butler – I wouldn't race at any other time of year. This is when we get the best winds. Otherwise there's no way we could finish ahead of that steamer.'

The candid admission startled Butler.

'But you said you're faster in a straight race.'

'Aye,' acknowledged Bentinck. 'Provided I've got good winds at my back. And provided I'm not shipping to a port where I need to wait for a tug,' and he downed another tot. 'I tell you, this here's going to be a close race. Damned close. We might not see him until we're in the Channel. Or even off Wales. All we can do is run as fast as we can and hope. With twelve men lost out of twenty-eight and patched-up sails aloft we'd all better start hoping,' and Bentinck stood up.

'Try praying as well,' he added. 'We're going to need it when we reach the doldrums.'

Butler had forgotten about those.

'A hundred miles of sea and no wind,' said

Bentinck. 'Not even a breeze. Nothing to do 'cept sit and wait and drift until we're out of it,' and he went out on deck.

Four thousand miles from the Cape of Good Hope the wind that had been driving them northwards began to drop. Knot after knot fell off the *Elizabeth Miller*'s pace, despite the wealth of sail aloft, and within the hour all forward movement had gone. The sea was a glassy calm and the ship as still as a rock.

The doldrums had claimed them.

Seven

Butler grimaced and turned away from the rail. His eyes ached and swam from the steely sunlight glitter on the surface of the sea and he blew out his breath in a long sigh. This was the third day of motionless floating that they had endured, not even the smallest of breezes to give some relief, and the ship so still that there wasn't a single creak from her. The patched sails hung tiredly from the masts and *Elizabeth Miller* baked in the heat.

The sailors sprawled on her decks. On the first day of their enforced idleness they had occupied themselves with lesser tasks of painting or greasing or splicing ropes, jobs that got done only when there was nothing more pressing to tackle. Everything had been done in a slow and laboured way, for the men saw no point in haste, but on a ship run as tightly as Bentinck ran the *Elizabeth Miller* there was very little that got neglected and now there was nothing left to do. It was too stuffy and suffocating to stay below and all the crew were on deck, lolling in any spot that afforded shade; even the effort to talk was too much. Someone had begun singing a shanty earlier but had soon given up; the heat weighed them down and they lay as if drugged.

Only Butler was on his feet, chafing at the stillness of the ship. He rubbed his tired eyes again and caught Webb staring at him.

'How much longer is this going to last?' asked Butler.

The Mate shrugged and didn't hurry himself to give an answer.

'Mebbe a week. Mebbe more,' and his voice was slow and dreary. 'I was stuck here once for two weeks. Two weeks solid. Nothing to do for days and days and days 'cept sit around and sleep,' and his eyes closed and a snore followed in short order.

Butler shook his head in exasperation and looked aft. The Captain was by the wheel, staring at the sea, and he made no movement as Butler came up to him.

'Is there nothing that can be done?'

Bentinck seemed not to have heard at first, then with the air of a man making an immense effort he turned his head. He stared at Butler without expression, then looked at the sea again.

'Nothing,' he said.

'For God's sake, there must be something.'

Again the Captain took his time answering.

'When we've drifted a bit more, perhaps I'll put the boats over and we'll pull the ship.'

'Why not do it now?'

Bentinck shook his head. 'A bit more drifting and we may pick up a breeze.'

Butler stared at the flat sea mocking them, then turned to the Captain again.

'Look, if this race is going to be as close as you say then even a minute could make all the difference. We need to make every effort.'

Bentinck dragged his eyes from the sea and gave Butler a long stare from under heavy eyebrows, and for a moment Butler wondered if he had pushed the Captain too far.

Bentinck spoke softly but his voice was hard.

'Mr Butler, every man aboard wants this ship to be first home. No one wants that damned greasy steamer beating us to Liverpool. But I'd remind you of one thing,' and his eyes bored into Butler's. 'I've got barely half a crew. If I break their backs pulling on oars when there's nothing to be got for it there'll be no fit men to run the ship when we find a wind. When there's good reason for putting the boats over I'll put 'em over. Not before,' and the Captain turned away dismissively.

On the fourth and fifth days occasional rain squalls hit them, preceded by short breezes that had the crew moving and the Mate barking orders, and then the *Elizabeth Miller* would start to move. But each time, after about twenty minutes the wind and rain were gone and the ship would drift slowly again.

The heat was the only feature of their situation that Butler endured with any equanimity. Ceylon had accustomed him to constant oppressive sunshine and the lack of any sort of cooling breeze, and he gave thanks that this at least he could endure with as much patience as anyone.

By noon of every day each man's water ration was gone and all went thirsty until the following morning. By the sixth day of desultory drifting some of the crew were becoming surly and received their orders with scowls and dark mutterings. Webb used his fists with good effect to quell one man's reluctance to do as he was told and at midday Bentinck decided to put up with their situation no longer.

'Run the boats out, Mr Webb, if you please. Lines from the bow and every man on an oar. That includes you, Mr Butler.'

The two boats were lowered and with the exception of Bentinck – who stayed at the wheel – every man aboard took an oar. Even the cook had to join them.

Webb was at the tiller of Butler's boat. 'Right lads, bend your backs,' and they dipped their oars in.

For five solid minutes they pulled, and only then did *Elizabeth Miller* begin to move, like a sulky dog at the end of a leash. She came reluctantly at barely one knot and they could get her to move no faster. The sailors were already weary, each man having had to do the work of two to run the ship, but they gripped their oars and pulled and sweated and roasted in the heat and dragged the ship, foot by sluggish foot, across the water.

The Captain gave them no respite even when the sun went down. They were allowed to come alongside for food and within the hour they were back at their oars. Then the whole process of coaxing *Elizabeth Miller* to move had to begin once more.

After twelve hours in the boats the Captain ordered them aboard and they fell into their bunks like dead men. The muscles in Butler's arms and shoulders and back burned and screamed for release and he lay tight and cramped, enduring the agony until sheer fatigue gave him that release.

Back on their oars at dawn Butler could see that they weren't making even the speed of yesterday. The relentless effort was sapping the men, they couldn't last much longer and the Captain, scowling viciously on station at the wheel, realised it.

'Bring them aboard, Mr Webb,' he ordered at last, and the boats crawled slowly, tiredly, back to the ship. It took an eternity to climb the sides and once over the rail they fell on the deck and lay there, too exhausted even to find shade. The Captain surveyed them, frowning.

'Mr Butler,' he barked finally, and Butler blinked and forced himself to his knees. 'A job for you. The moment we get some wind these men are going to have to work hard, damned hard, but right now they need to rest. While they're doing it you get yourself up there,' and the Captain pointed to the top of the mainmast, 'and sing out the minute you see any water that's being stirred. If there's a breeze anywhere on this blasted ocean we'll row for it. Aloft now, if you please,' and the Captain added sardonically, 'I think you know the way.'

Butler nodded wearily and stumbled to the rigging. He paused for a moment to gather his breath, then started to climb and the rope stung his blistered and aching hands. After climbing for what didn't seem much more than a mile he reached the top yard and slumped against the mast.

'Stay awake, dammit!' a voice roared from below and Butler stirred himself and peered round. The sea was smooth, devoid of so much as a ripple, the only movement the long oily swell that barely rocked the *Elizabeth Miller*. He wanted sleep with a desperation he couldn't believe, but he forced himself to sit straighter, determined to stay awake.

Three hours later Butler was nodding drowsily. His head fell forward and he woke with a start. He blinked and sat up, grimacing as he realised how foul and dry his mouth was, and he cleared his throat and shook his head to wake himself. He looked down at the sailors dozing on deck and decided they might all be dead, judging by the positions they were in. For all he knew the ship could have been boarded by pirates whilst he was asleep and every man murdered. He wondered if the Captain was also asleep, then spotted him near the stern. He was awake, staring moodily at the water around them.

Butler returned to his survey of the sea and stared off to port, scanning the ocean, the lowering sun reflecting and glaring in his eyes. He blinked and squinted and continued the circuit, now staring forwards, now moving towards starboard and–

He straightened so suddenly he nearly fell off the yard and had to grab at the mast.

'There!' he yelled and had to cough and clear his throat again. 'There's a breeze!'

The men stirred below and Bentinck came running from the stern. He followed Butler's pointing finger.

Somewhere between half a mile and a mile away the smooth surface of the sea was broken into moving ripples.

'Are you sure, Mr Butler?' the Captain bellowed.

'Damned sure,' answered Butler, and the Captain glared, but it was for only a moment.

'Get the men in the boats, Mr Webb. Come on, get up, you lazy bunch of barge-arses; you've had it easy up to now. This is where those lily-white hands of yours are going to do some real work for a change. Up I said, damn you!'

The boats were afloat and rowing to the full length of their cables before Butler had reached the bottom of the rigging. He joined Bentinck in the bows and the cables came up taut. The bronzed figures in the boats heaved and pulled and grudgingly the bows of the *Elizabeth Miller* began to come round to starboard. She crawled forwards and Butler gripped the rail.

'Come on,' he muttered. 'Come on.'

Bentinck looked at him.

301

'Still game for the race then, Mr Butler?'

Butler nodded. 'Still game.'

Elizabeth Miller inched her way across the sea, Butler urging her on, and Bentinck stared up at the sails.

'At last,' snarled the Captain, and his voice rang across the water. 'Bring them back, Mr Webb. At once, if you please.'

Butler shielded his eyes and looked up.

The sails, previously limp and lifeless, were slowly shifting and swaying. Then they began to fill and Butler heard the familiar creak of rope. He felt the ship stir under him, a sensation he hadn't experienced for days, the motion of a ship with wind in her sails, not the pedestrian crawling of a ship towed humiliatingly behind rowing boats.

The men lost no time in pulling the boats aboard. Webb and Fox bellowed at them to trim the sails to best take the wind and now they heard the masts creak. Every man shared one thought but no one dared voice it: let this be a wind that lasts, not another cat's breath of a breeze that peters out.

And the wind didn't fail them.

The breeze strengthened and water swirled around *Elizabeth Miller*'s bow. Butler stared at the flat featureless sea of the doldrums falling behind them and his spirits lifted. Neither thousands of miles of sea, nor a gale, nor the dreary doldrums had managed to stop them, and he began to believe, with a determination like nothing he had ever felt before, that they were going to make it to Liverpool after all. Nothing could stop them now.

Eight

All the men felt it – the sense of excitement, the knowledge that the worst was behind them. Every day was taking them closer to home. The ship was undermanned but a full crew could not have worked harder than these men did. They were within sniffing distance of the prize now and they were fiercely determined that that prize was going to be theirs.

Bentinck spoke for them all one day as he stood at the wheel, finely judging the *Elizabeth Miller*'s course. Butler was at his side.

'We've come too far and lost too much to lose this race now,' he said intensely. 'We'll take the money, by damn, and thank you for it, but this goes beyond coin. This is a fight we're going to win, and God help anyone who gets in our way.

'I can't spare men for lookouts,' he added, 'so from now on that's your job, Mr Butler. At first light every morning take your food and water ration and go aloft. You're up there to find that steamer. Sing out if you see his smoke, then you can come down. Otherwise you stay up there till the light's too bad to see. Understand?'

Butler nodded and Bentinck muttered something Butler couldn't catch.

'I beg your pardon?'

'I said, by the Grace of God we're going to win this,' and the Captain looked embarrassed to admit that there might be another agency they depended on, something other than muscle, sweat and sheer unrelenting guts.

'Well, what are you standing there for?' he demanded abruptly. 'Up that mast, Mr Butler, if you please,' and Butler went hastily for'ard.

Blazing sun, icy rain and whipping winds couldn't dislodge Butler from his post at the top of the mast. After the second day of gripping the yard he devised a better method of ensuring he wasn't shaken loose; he went aloft with a length of rope and tied himself to the mast. The *Elizabeth Miller* dipped and rolled and plunged into heavy seas as she beat her way northwards, but Butler was secure. He whipped about, one hundred feet above the deck, and refused to be beaten. It was a matter of sheer endurance now; he was no sailor and he knew it, but if the saving of Tondipgiri was to be achieved by a stubborn refusal to admit defeat, by the application of sheer damn-cussed obstinacy, then Butler was the man to do it.

Every day at dawn he climbed to the top of the mast and stayed there until dusk, when he would come down and join the Captain and First Mate in the Captain's saloon. He never complained, never objected, he just stuck at it. One evening he came into the saloon, his hair salt-caked from the spray, his clothes wet through, and dropped his coat in the corner. He sat down and the two men stared at him. He started to eat, but glanced up and caught the Captain and the Mate nodding in approval. Butler returned his attention to his meal. The food was hot but his acceptance by these two leathery men of the sea warmed him as the food never could. He finished the meal, shared a tot of rum with them then went to his bunk.

Butler spotted plenty of ships as they approached the English Channel but none had the *Dragon*'s distinctively tall centre funnel.

He looked back but saw nothing.

Elizabeth Miller kept on her northward passage and entered the St George's Channel, the stretch of water that would take them up to Anglesey and the Irish Sea, where they would make their turn for the River Mersey and Liverpool. The spray burst over her bows as the wind freshened and it seemed to Butler that the excitement of the men had communicated itself to the ship and now she too was straining ahead, refusing to be beaten by the dirty black steamer. She scudded on northwards, the sea creaming under her bows, the Welsh coast away to her right.

'That's Anglesey, Mr Butler,' boomed Bentinck from below, and even as Butler looked he saw a flash and heard the distant *boom* of a cannon.

'Signal gun,' shouted Bentinck. 'They know we're coming. They'll be letting them know in Liverpool.' The cannon fired again as the ship began to alter her course to round the headland, and Butler felt a momentary qualm, then dismissed it. Bentinck and his crew hadn't raced thousands of miles just to lose it all now by carelessly piling up on the rocks.

And if Butler hadn't been roped to the mast he

would have jumped up.

'There it is!' he yelled, pointing wildly.

A dozen miles ahead of them, thick smoke boiling from the single funnel, was the *Dragon*. She was running straight as an arrow across Liverpool Bay, Mersey-bound.

Butler heard Bentinck and the Mate yelling orders, but all he could do was stare at the *Dragon*. He knew nothing of that ship, nor of her crew, yet at that moment he found he could almost hate them, for they were ahead of the *Elizabeth Miller* and if the steamer reached the dock first then Tondipgiri would be lost. Years of work and back-breaking toil would have been for nothing.

'Mr Butler! Are you deaf, man? Get down here!'

Butler broke from his focus on the steamer and untied himself. He slithered down the rigging and jumped to the deck and joined Bentinck at the rail. The Captain had a telescope to his eye.

'Blast his arrogance,' he muttered. 'Thinks he's safe home already, damn him – there's no one on stern-watch.'

He lowered the telescope.

'Well done, Mr Butler,' he said grimly. 'We're matching him knot for knot, but the minute some lazy swab looks over the stern and sees us on his tail he'll go a damned sight faster. And if this wind drops any more–' He left the sentence unfinished. Butler looked at the sails and realised that the wind was falling away as they left the Irish Sea behind.

'Get every scrap of cloth you can find,' ordered

Bentinck. 'Blankets, anything. Go on, man!' he roared as Butler stood irresolute, not knowing what the Captain meant. 'Get on with it.'

Bentinck returned to his telescope and Butler ran to the cabins at the stern. He heard Bentinck's roar that the steamer had now seen them and Butler ripped the blankets from the bunks, then went for'ard into the seamen's quarters and emerged with all their blankets too. He dropped them on the deck and went below, searching for anything that might satisfy the Captain's demand. He found a few square yards of sail canvas that had been shredded from one of the sails and heaved it outside. The blankets he had brought out were already spread on the deck, and when the sailmaker saw the canvas his face lit up. He added it to the blankets and with a dexterity that Butler marvelled at he began joining the pieces of cloth together. The needle flashed and stabbed as The Swede made broad stitches and tight little knots and Butler looked impatiently from the man to the steamer ploughing ahead of them. Fox and two other men helped but it seemed an age before the sailmaker abruptly announced:

'She's ready.'

Now the sailors set about the expanse of canvas and blankets, fastening ropes to it, hauling other ropes down from somewhere else, then they hauled powerfully and shot the strange sheet aloft to join the rest of the sails. She billowed and filled, then Webb barked some more orders and the men pulled on other lines.

Butler got out of their way and went to the

stern where the Captain was directing the man at the wheel. Bentinck's face was tight and set and Butler thought better of speaking. Spray flew over the rail and pattered on the deck and seagulls cried overhead, joining in the excitement, and some of the sailors began shouting.

'Keep those men in order, Mr Webb,' bellowed Bentinck, adding in a lower voice, 'Good lads, those. Watch the wheel, dammit!' – this last to the man at his side.

Bentinck exchanged a look with Butler. This was it. They were down to the last few miles. It was all or nothing now.

'The pilot!' a sailor shouted. 'He's stopping for the pilot.'

Bentinck yelled exultantly and smacked a thick fist into a meaty palm.

'We're in with a chance yet, Mr Butler,' and he roared a wild laugh. 'We've got the bastard now. Work those men, Mr Webb!'

'What's happened? What's the pilot?' asked Butler, not understanding but caught up in the exhilaration.

'The swab needs a pilot to navigate the Mersey,' and Bentinck laughed that crazy laugh again. 'Now we've got him!'

'What do you mean? What pilot?' and Bentinck calmed down enough to explain.

'Mersey's full of shoals and currents. Easy to go aground unless you've got a local waterman aboard who knows the river. We'll catch him now.'

Elizabeth Miller made ground while the *Dragon* took the pilot aboard, but then a small boat cast off from the steamer's side, the water churned under the steamer's counter and it began to gather way again. *Elizabeth Miller* strained to catch up and Butler saw pale faces at the stern of the steamer and frantic activity on deck.

Bentinck suddenly cursed and swore. The small boat that had been alongside the *Dragon* was steering into their path and a man was shouting to them.

'He's asking to come aboard,' called Fox. 'He's coming under the bows.'

Bentinck roared in anger and ran to the bows, Butler at his side. They leaned over and Bentinck shook his fist at the small boat bobbing towards them.

'Wait for the pilot,' a man called from the boat.

'Don't need one,' shouted back Bentinck.

'You must have a pilot,' the voice called back.

'Get out of my damn way!' but the boat clung doggedly to its course, cutting across *Elizabeth Miller*'s bows.

Bentinck snarled and ran back to the stern, Butler hurrying to keep up.

'What about the pilot?' asked Fox as Bentinck climbed the ladder.

'I know these waters better than any damned pilot, Mr Fox. Get off that wheel, you,' and Bentinck pushed the startled seaman aside. Bentinck took the wheel, spun it to starboard and *Elizabeth Miller* veered away. The little boat scraped down *Elizabeth Miller*'s side, bobbing and rocking in the wash, and the men aboard her cursed the clipper as they slid past, clutching at the sides of their boat to prevent themselves being thrown overboard. The boat was barely

clear of the clipper's stern when Bentinck swung
the wheel again, this time to port, and put
Elizabeth Miller back on her course.

A billow of wind made the sails flap and fill and
the clipper crept up on her rival. They were well
into the Mersey now, the river was narrowing and
the clipper was gaining. Half a mile, then a
quarter of a mile, then a bare hundred yards lay
between them. A few minutes more and *Elizabeth
Miller*'s bows started to overtake on the steamer's
starboard side. *Elizabeth Miller*'s sailors cheered
as the clipper slowly drew level.

The Captain on the steamer's bridge stared at
them angrily, then appeared to give an order to
the man at the wheel and the *Dragon* abruptly
slewed to starboard. The gap between the two
ships quickly narrowed and Bentinck swore and
pulled on the wheel but the ships were too close
and the side of the steamer hit them. It crunched
against *Elizabeth Miller*'s hull and the steamer
held to the new course, crowding the clipper,
pushing her across the channel, and Butler could
see that unless something changed and damn
quickly the *Elizabeth Miller* was going to be
forced aground on the far shore.

No option was open to them as far as Butler
could see. *Elizabeth Miller* couldn't go faster and
cut in front of the steamer, so the only thing she
could do to save herself would be to slacken sail
and fall away, which doubtless was the steamer's
intention.

Butler raged impotently and smacked his fist
on the rail. Bentinck, though, was equal to the
challenge. He spun the wheel and *Elizabeth Miller*

veered even further to starboard. The gap between the ships opened and sailors aboard the steamer jeered, then stopped in mid-laugh as Bentinck swung the wheel hard to port, cutting *Elizabeth Miller* back across the froth. Butler had a glimpse of the *Dragon*'s Captain staring openmouthed and men running along the steamer's decks, then the ships collided. *Elizabeth Miller* shuddered with the impact and her timbers hummed, but the jolt must have been greater for the man at the *Dragon*'s wheel, for the steamer yawed suddenly to port and *Elizabeth Miller* knifed ahead.

The steamer's whistle blew angrily as she straightened her course but the clipper was in front now. The docks were coming up on the left and only now did Butler notice a vast cheering crowd lining the dockside. *Elizabeth Miller* left the main channel and the wind slackened. Her sails began to droop, allowing the steamer to gain a few more yards, but the clipper wasn't going to be caught. Both ships aimed for the dock wall and the *Dragon* was closing fast, but *Elizabeth Miller* closed faster. In fact she was closing too fast, for the wall was nearly upon them and there was no time to take down her sails. The seamen threw rope fenders over the side, Bentinck heaved on the wheel and turned the clipper's head but *Elizabeth Miller* still crashed against the dock, throwing Butler to his knees, and she rasped along the wall with a terrific grinding of wood and stone. Butler scrambled up and hurried to the side and could only presume that what happened next had been done many times before, so precise was its execution.

Sailors jumped from *Elizabeth Miller* to the quayside and Butler thought they were trying to escape the collision, but they got to their feet and ran along the quay, chasing ropes that other men aboard threw after them. The ropes slithered along the quayside as the clipper continued her slide, but working feverishly the sailors wrapped them round cast-iron mooring bollards and the ropes came up taut. There was a great creaking of rope and timber, then something splintered and tore somewhere up near the bows, but it didn't matter any more because all forward movement had ceased and the ship lay still.

The crowd pushed forward, shouting wildly, the slowing steamer came to the dock wall and she too scraped along it, her fenders bumping and groaning. A chorus of cheers greeted her, but that didn't matter to Butler. *Elizabeth Miller* was first home. He had won, and in just over a week his tea would be fetching the premium price at auction. Tondipgiri was safe.

He stared about him – at the exultant crew, at Webb and Fox slapping each other on the back, even Bentinck was grinning from ear to ear. They had put thousands of sea-miles behind them, they had won through against storm and wind and calm. They had made it.

Butler crossed to where the gangway was being run out and the roar from the crowd startled him. A brass band began playing and gaily-coloured banners dipped and waved. One man threw his hat in the air and dozens of people copied his example. Butler swallowed and

312

couldn't help grinning. He stood at the rail and self-consciously raised a hand in acknowledgement and the roar redoubled. It seemed as if the cheers and waves from that sea of colour were for him and him alone. His chest swelled and he grinned some more, then the crowd parted and what was obviously the official welcoming committee came forward. There was one central figure that the others moved around and the man nodded at something said by one of his aides, then looked up at the *Elizabeth Miller*. His gaze met Butler's and their eyes locked.

Prickly greying hair and the unkind effects of the intervening years made Paget look a harder brute than ever.

Bentinck propelled Butler ahead of him down the gangway. The crowd cheered again, pushing forwards, and Butler received his second shock.

Charlotte Noble was at Paget's side.

It had been three years since their last meeting in the bungalow and her eyes were more vividly blue than Butler remembered. She stared at him, expressionless, as he stepped onto the quay and Butler ventured a smile. She didn't respond.

The Captain and some of the crew of the *Dragon* shouldered through the crowd and Paget said something to the Captain. The Captain looked startled then spoke urgently to the crewman at his side. The man hurried back to the steamer and Paget held up his hands. The band stopped playing.

'Gentlemen, gentlemen.' The cheering subsided. 'And ladies of course.' There were good-

natured murmurs and the crowd fell silent again
'This has been an epic race. These two fine ships
have raced over twelve thousand miles in the bes
tradition of the great clipper races of twenty years
ago. Gentlemen, I bid you remember the grea
race between *Ariel* and *Taeping* in sixty-six.' (A
cheer) 'The race between *Thermopylae* and *Cutty
Sark* in seventy-two.' (Another cheer) 'Race
between strong ships crewed by strong men, and
now these ships and these men have arrived
safely home, by the Grace of God and their
Captains,' and the crowd murmured agreement.

'This day,' continued Paget, 'recalls those
famous races. The same dangers have been faced
the same obstacles overcome. Also,' and his voice
took on a new tone, 'it has been run under the
same rules. Ladies and gentlemen, under those
rules we do not yet have a winner. The race is no
yet over!'

A great roar went up, and it was a minute
before the crowd were quiet enough for Paget to
continue. Butler was rigid, staring at Paget
wondering what he was up to.

'As I say, the race is not over. Under the rule
of the clipper races the winner is *not* the first ship
to tie up at the quay; the winner is, and always
has been, the first ship to land some of its cargo.'

Paget gestured to the expanse of quayside with
a look of mock surprise.

'Nobody has yet brought any cargo ashore
Until someone does the race isn't over.'

There was a moment's silence, Butler and
Bentinck looked at each other and both understood at the same instant. They turned and ran

up the gangway and the crowd roared.

'Covers off the hatches,' bellowed Bentinck. 'Loose those battens.'

The sailors rushed to the hatches, but even as they knocked away the securing battens a great cheer went up from the crowd. Butler rushed to the side and stared along the quay. Two men carrying a tea chest were hurrying down the steamer's gangway. A yard from the bottom one man stumbled and slipped, the chest fell onto the quayside and split. Rich, dark tea spilled out and the cheer doubled.

Paget was shouting again and pointing and the noise subsided enough for Butler to hear what he was saying.

'The first cargo ashore is that of the steamer *Dragon*. Gentlemen, I give you the winner of this race!' and the roar went up again. Paget shot a triumphant sneer at Butler, then was swept away with the crowd as it surged towards the steamer.

Butler felt sick.

He gripped the rail with both hands – his sudden dizziness would have caused him to fall otherwise – and his head swam. He clung to the rail, fighting down the nausea, and his vision cleared. One person remained on the quay looking up at him.

Charlotte.

Her eyes were wide, her mouth was open and she seemed genuinely shocked. Butler, unshaven and sunburnt, stared at her and she looked at him helplessly. She mouthed something, then turned away and hurried after the crowd.

Butler, his knuckles white on the rail, understood it all now. That whispered exchange between Paget and the *Dragon*'s Captain, then the crewman hurrying back to the steamer; with just a few quiet words Paget had snatched away Butler's victory.

Butler stared unseeing at the dock warehouses, the blood rushing in his ears and throbbing in his head.

He had lost.

He had lost the race and Tondipgiri would surely go next, for there would be no premium price for a tea that had come second. A swirl of images blurred before him: Tondipgiri; the vicious gale and men dying around him; Mirissa – dark and smiling; *Elizabeth Miller* becalmed in the doldrums; the race for home. Charlotte Noble, standing cool and composed on the dockside. That crowing look of victory on Paget's fat face.

Butler couldn't control the heaving in his stomach any longer. He leaned over the rail and was violently sick.

Nine

The Commercial Sale Rooms in Mincing Lane had been the venue of the London tea auctions for fifty years. Custom and tradition were its watchwords and the routines and practices were so well-established and of such long standing that they had almost attained the status of rules.

316

One such tradition, which it was unthinkable might be broken, was that no woman would ever presume to enter this exclusively male preserve. That was how it had been for half a century, and the gentlemen associated with the Commercial Sale Rooms fully expected that arrangement to continue.

The shock to the brokers and dealers who happened to be in the entrance hall for Monday's business on the morning of 1st September 1884 was therefore considerable when a young woman came through the doors, stood and surveyed her surroundings, oblivious to the dropped jaws of the men standing nearby, spotted her quarry and walked confidently across the floor. Some were torn between, on the one hand, covert appreciation of her trim figure and, on the other, startled outrage that a woman – *a woman* – had dared to enter the building. The like had never been heard of before. A few – a very few – of the goggle-eyed men had the manners to doff their silk top hats, but most were too stunned to do anything other than watch as she approached the deeply tanned planter pacing restlessly on the far side of the hall, a leather case in his hand.

He stiffened when he saw her. She came up to him and there was silence.

'Miss Noble,' he acknowledged finally.

'Mr Butler.'

'I presume your stepfather's with you?' He could barely bring himself to be civil to her.

She shook her head. 'I haven't seen him for several days.'

Butler didn't believe her for a minute.

'Is there something I can do for you, Miss Noble?' he said with cold formality, wishing she would go. 'Perhaps you are unfamiliar with the rules of this institution.'

She bit her lip. 'I just came to wish you luck.'

'To wish me luck?' and Butler stared at her.

She nodded. 'I hope you get a good price at the auction.'

Her audacity took Butler's breath away. After what she had done...

'I lost any chance of a good price when the other ship landed their tea first,' he said stiffly. 'You were there, Miss Noble, you saw it. You were standing by your stepfather when he spoke to the steamer's Captain.'

'I didn't hear what he said,' protested Charlotte. 'I didn't know he was going to do that.'

'And the joke's certainly on me, isn't it?' continued Butler sourly, as if she hadn't spoken. 'If I don't get the price I need – and that seems likely – you and your stepfather can have a good laugh at my expense when the bank seizes my estate.'

Charlotte's lips tightened. When she spoke it was with spirit.

'I bear you no ill will, Mr Butler. I came here to wish you good luck and that's the truth. And I won't be having a good laugh at your expense; if you lose your estate I will feel deeply for you. Remember, I saw it; I know how beautiful it is and I could see how much work you must have done to it. No one should have something they've worked so hard for taken from them by means of a rotten trick. I knew nothing of what my

318

stepfather was going to do at Liverpool and it came as much of a shock to me as it did to you. It was outrageous and I told him so. That's the reason I haven't seen him for several days: the argument we subsequently had about what he did led to me moving out of his house and going to live with my aunt. I have no particular wish to see him or speak to him again. Your anger about what happened is entirely justified, Mr Butler, but I'm not the one who deserves your censure.'

She drew herself up.

'I came to give you my support and to wish you luck. I've done that, and now I'll take my leave of you. Good day, Mr Butler.'

She turned and would have marched away with as much head-high determination as she had entered with, but Butler stopped her.

'Miss Noble?' and she halted, then turned.

'Yes, Mr Butler,' and the ice was there again but Butler pushed on.

'I owe you an apology. Obviously I knew nothing about the circumstances you've described. I'm sorry for jumping to conclusions. And I apologise for being so short-tempered. I've ... had rather a lot on my mind.'

Her expression softened.

'We do seem to have a talent for annoying one another, don't we?'

Butler grinned. 'I'm sure it doesn't always have to be that way,' he said. 'I'm sure that if we both – er – tread carefully, we can have an entirely cordial conversation.'

Charlotte's eyes twinkled. 'I feel that's a distinct possibility, Mr Butler,' she said.

Butler noticed the stares from the score of me
in the entrance hall.

'Let's go outside,' he said, and Charlott
promptly took his arm.

'Where are we going?' she asked. 'Don't you hav
to be inside for the auction?'

Butler shook his head. 'It doesn't start unt
noon. Shall we walk?'

At the end of Mincing Lane they turne
towards London Bridge and walked in silence fo
several minutes.

'I still can't believe it,' said Butler suddenly
'The race was ours; we had it won, and then t
have it stolen from us like that...'

'Will it affect the auction?' asked Charlotte a
they turned onto the bridge.

'My tea came second,' said Butler simply. 'I
didn't win and that's that.'

'You'll get a good price though, won't you?'

Butler breathed deeply. 'I don't know.'

'You're not hopeful,' she concluded, and Butle
stopped. He stared away downriver, then looke
at Charlotte. She studied his face and noticed th
deep-worn creases. He shook his head.

'No,' he said, 'I'm not hopeful. It's a specia
auction today – something of an occasion,
understand. It's everything I'd hoped for: a rac
to catch the public imagination and push up th
price – but now?' and he shrugged. 'I used to ge
ten shillings a pound in the general auction bu
my tea's the loser and if I get ten shillings
pound today I'll consider myself lucky.' He shoo
his head again. 'I can't tell what's going to hap

320

pen,' and after a moment they continued walking.

'I understand that the race was quite dangerous,' said Charlotte.

'I've never seen a sea like it before,' said Butler. 'When I left Ceylon I thought everything would be straightforward – down to the Cape with all sails flying, then north to England. But it was hard, a lot harder than I expected.'

'Do you miss Ceylon?'

Butler recalled his departure from Tondipgiri and coloured with embarrassment at the memory.

'I treated some people rather badly,' he said slowly. 'People who work for me. I shouldn't have done that.'

They came off the bridge and walked in the direction of the railway station. There was one question Charlotte particularly wanted to know the answer to.

'Was there anyone special you left behind?' she asked with studied casualness.

'Special?' asked Butler.

Charlotte hesitated, looking for the right words. 'The last time we met, in Ceylon, I remember there was a woman...'

'Yes,' said Butler. 'Her name was Mirissa,' and he paused. 'She's dead.'

'Oh,' said Charlotte and, after a moment, 'I'm sorry.'

'She was trampled by elephants,' said Butler, and was surprised to find he could speak of Mirissa without feeling that terrible pain. He recalled the moment of rage and fury at the top of the mast, the moment he cried all the agony he had felt since her death into the storm. He had reached rock-bottom at that point.

Charlotte was looking at him with concern and he gave a small smile and shrugged.

'Sorry,' he said. 'Just a memory.'

Charlotte, aware that she had ventured onto sensitive ground, sought to change the subject and was relieved to notice a shop with bread and cakes in the window. The sign above proclaimed it to be one of the shops of the Aerated Bread Company.

'Do you mind if we look in there? I'd like to buy something for my aunt.'

Butler nodded and they crossed to the shop.

He stood to one side, his thoughts on the forthcoming auction, whilst Charlotte made her purchases. The manageress noticed him and as she handed the change to Charlotte she asked in a low voice:

'Is the gentleman all right, Miss?'

Charlotte glanced at Butler. 'He's ... preoccupied.'

'Well, I know what you need,' said the manageress and came round from behind the counter. 'Why don't you both come through here and have a nice cuppa tea?'

Butler blinked and looked at Charlotte, undecided, then looked at his pocket watch.

'Why not?' he said and they followed the woman through to the back of the shop. They found themselves in a parlour where four tables with chairs were set out. It seemed particularly arranged so and the manageress noticed their looks.

'For people off the trains,' she explained. 'Friends of mine. I've been managing this shop for nearly thirty years and I've got to know some of the regulars. They're always either arriving from long journeys or going on one; either way they appreciate a nice cuppa tea. So I decided to set these tables out a bit. I provide the tea myself and sometimes they buy a cake to have with it. It's a nice thing to do for your friends, isn't it? Now, you sit down and I'll put the kettle on.'

The woman disappeared through another door and Butler and Charlotte sat down hesitantly.

'It's certainly very nice of her,' commented Charlotte.

Butler agreed. 'Very kind.'

He looked round the parlour, noticing photographs on the walls – relatives of the manageress presumably – and half a dozen small paintings of different thatched cottages. A spotless white lace curtain hung at the window.

He was silent and Charlotte tried to draw him out.

'Tell me about your plantation.'

Butler glanced at her.

'Well, you saw it, of course,' he said. 'It's on the west and east slopes of a hill. They call it Tondipgiri.'

'What does that mean?'

'In the native language it means King Tondip's Hill. Presumably there was a king of that name once, though why the hill was named after him I don't know.'

She seemed genuinely interested and Butler mentioned the difficulties of the early days, the coffee blight, the struggle to establish his tea on the Tondipgiri slopes. It felt good to be thinking about Tondipgiri again and he found himself telling her about the country and the people who worked for him. He spoke with enthusiasm and Charlotte noticed how his eyes shone.

'When your stepfather left Ceylon I bought his estate.'

Charlotte was surprised. 'He never told me that.'

Butler nodded. 'I borrowed the money from the bank and bought it off him. I built it up, replanted it, improved the land. Got some good results too. But then the bank collapsed and called in the loan. I lost all my tea in a fire – set by the same man who helped your stepfather steal my tea – and the only way I could repay the bank was to win that race and get the winner's premium.'

He gave a wry smile. 'Perhaps there's still a chance; coming second may still count for something.'

'How much do you need?'

'Thirteen shillings a pound – and I need it this week. After that it'll be too late. If I can't telegraph the bank by Friday that I've got the money they'll seize Tondipgiri and I'll be bankrupt. I'll lose everything.'

Charlotte was concerned. 'Nothing left at all?'

'Nothing,' said Butler tightly. 'Ah, this looks good,' and he brightened as the manageress brought a tray to their table. She set down a brown earthenware teapot and two cups and a small jug of milk.

'This is very good of you, Mrs...?' enquired Butler.

'Carey, love.'

'Mrs Carey. How much do we owe you?' and Butler reached into his pocket.

'Put your money away, love,' said Mrs Carey. 'You just enjoy your tea,' and she disappeared into the shop before Butler could say another word.

'Is the tea as good as yours?' asked Charlotte with a smile.

Butler grinned. 'Let's see.'

He lifted the lid of the teapot and studied the contents carefully, then grunted and poured.

'The colour's all right,' and he picked up his cup, gently breathing in the scent, then he sniffed it and took a sip. He savoured the taste and nodded.

'Not bad,' he commented. 'A little bitter, but it's all right. It's a blend. There's some good tea in there – you can see the leaves have opened nicely – but it's been mixed with inferior tea. Old tea.'

'You sound like a wine connoisseur,' said Charlotte.

Butler smiled. 'Just things I've learned over the years,' he said. 'At this particular moment it is very acceptable.'

'Half-past eleven,' said Butler, consulting his watch. 'We'd better get back,' and they went into the shop.

'Thank you, Mrs Carey,' said Butler. 'That was very kind of you. I appreciated it.'

325

'That's all right, dear,' said Mrs Carey. 'I hope everything goes well for you.'

'Thanks,' he said and they turned to the door. Butler hesitated, then opened the leather case he was carrying and took out one of the bags from inside.

'Would you accept this with my compliments, Mrs Carey?'

The manageress was surprised. 'Oh, I don't want paying.'

Butler nodded.

'It's just a token of appreciation,' and he explained. 'I'm a tea planter, Mrs Carey. I have an estate in Ceylon; this is some of my tea. I'd like you to have it,' and he handed the bag over the counter. Mrs Carey took it uncertainly.

'Well, it's very kind of you,' she said.

'My pleasure,' said Butler, and left with Charlotte before Mrs Carey could make any other protest.

'That was a nice gesture,' said Charlotte as they walked towards the bridge.

'In an hour or so I won't need that tea sample. Either I'll have my estate or I'll have nothing.'

Charlotte pressed his arm in encouragement but both wore worried frowns as they crossed the bridge.

'You won't be allowed in the Sale Room,' said Butler when they arrived back.

'That's all right,' said Charlotte. 'I'll wait in the entrance hall.'

'They might not allow that either.'

'Just let them try and stop me,' and she thrust

out her chin and sat on one of the benches, ignoring disapproving looks. 'Good luck,' and she squeezed his hand.

Butler nodded, gave a small smile and went through the Sale Room door.

Ten

One minute before midday the chairman and his two assistants entered the Sale Room. They carefully hung their silk top hats on pegs on the wall behind their table, then sat down. Precisely on the stroke of midday the chairman's gavel rapped on the block.

'Thank you, gentlemen,' and the excited buzz of conversation subsided.

'Our business today concerns the teas that were the subject of the race which concluded in Liverpool just over a week ago, on Friday, twenty-second of August.

'Gentlemen, we followed the reports in *The Times* with keen interest, but in case anybody is unaware—' and a buzz of laughter ran round the room. Even the chairman permitted himself a small smile. 'This was a race between the steamer *Dragon* and the clipper *Elizabeth Miller*. The two ships raced each other home to England from Ceylon, via the Indian Ocean, the Cape of Good Hope and north by Africa and the race was completed in exactly sixty days. A considerable achievement. The race was very close in the final stages and the *Elizabeth Miller* was the first of the two ships to tie up at the quay.

'However,' and Butler could guess what was coming next, 'this race was run specifically under the arrangements of the memorable clipper races of twenty years ago; races which, as you are all aware, generated unusual excitement in these Rooms. Accordingly, although the clipper arrived first, the winner was not confirmed until the first cargo of tea was unloaded on the quayside. That consignment of tea was unloaded from the *Dragon* and the *Dragon* was, therefore, declared the winner. It is that consignment which is the first item on today's list.'

The chairman consulted a paper in front of him.

'Several estates contributed teas to the final cargo; these represent the individual Lots on your order papers. Sampling and inspection have taken place. Gentlemen, let business begin.'

The excited murmur returned and quickly faded.

'Lot number one: from the estate of D. Collins – the Cobo Valley plantation – a break of ten thousand pounds in seventy chests and fifty half-chests. What am I bid per pound? Am I bid nine shillings? Thank you, nine shillings. Nine and six? I have nine and six. Will anyone bid ten? Thank you. I now have ten shillings.'

'Eleven,' a voice called out.

'I now have eleven shillings. Do I hear twelve? Twelve is bid. Will anyone go thirteen? Thirteen shillings. The bid stands at thirteen shillings. Will anyone go higher? Fourteen. I am bid fourteen shillings. Fifteen, thank you. Any advance on fifteen? Gentlemen, I have fifteen shillings per pound on Lot number one; do I have any advance on fifteen? Going once at fifteen. Going twice at fifteen.'

The gavel rapped on the block.

'Sold at fifteen shillings to Wilkinson's Teas. Lot number two on the order paper is from–'

The chairman read out the details of Lot number two but Butler didn't hear them. He trembled and the order paper shook in his hand. If the winning teas were commanding fifteen shillings it meant that there was still a chance, a real chance, that even though his tea had come second it might attract high bids; perhaps as high as thirteen shillings a pound. He prayed that it would be so. He wasn't beaten yet; Tondipgiri might still be his, and he counted again the Lots on the order paper that preceded Item Two – his Tondipgiri consignment.

Standing to the right and slightly behind Butler was a man of about Butler's age, also studying the order paper. The man's name was Richard Kent and he worked for a firm of tea wholesalers. Part of his job was to buy teas at auction and the sale of Lot number one for fifteen shillings hadn't pleased him as much as it had Butler; if the teas were going to go for those sorts of prices, he reflected, he might just as well not have bothered coming. In fact he might as well get back on the train right now.

He had told them this would happen; he had told his bosses that these teas would sell for

329

premium prices. The novelty of the race, the way it had fired the public imagination, was bound to drive the prices up, he had told them, but still they had given him specific instructions that his bid limit on this occasion was no more than twelve shillings a pound; that should be enough, they had said, he had no authority to go above it.

It rankled. He had fifteen years' experience with teas, knew all the nuts and bolts of running a tea wholesale company, but still they had limited him to twelve shillings. What had they thought he was going to do, for God's sake? Blow the Company's budget? Auctions required quick-thinking, decisiveness, but never once could anyone have accused him of recklessness. The limiting of his bidding authority was just one more instance of – he looked for the word – *ossifying*, yes, that was it, that was what was happening to his Board: they were ossifying. They were sticking rigidly to old ways, but these weren't the times for that; there was too much going on in the world, too much that was new and advancing. Some people, he mused, still had ambition and aspirations, still had the capacity to conceive of great ventures and, more important, to bring those ventures to fruition. It was a time for vision, not timidity, and he admired people like that fellow, Butler, standing just over there, who had the courage to try something new and the determination to make it work.

The Lot currently under consideration reached twelve shillings and Kent raised his paper. The chairman acknowledged it but the bid was quickly overtaken by others and Kent was disgusted. Yes, there was no doubt; he was working for small-minded, stale businessmen and if he didn't do something about it soon ... well, he *had* to do something about it soon. Meanwhile he consoled himself with the thought that he might be in with a chance when Butler's tea came up. It probably wouldn't reach a high price but it would still have the distinctive cachet of having been involved in the Great Race. It was a tea that would sell well, and Kent resigned himself to waiting until that item was reached.

Bidding was brisk and each sale of winning Lots brought the auction closer to the moment when Butler's tea would be offered. Teas were selling to various wholesalers but mostly the gavel came down on bids from Wilkinson's. Butler couldn't see who their man was – the Sale Room was crowded and the mystery bidder was on the other side of the room.

By the time bidding had commenced on the final Lot in the winning consignment Butler was sweating. He rubbed his palms on his jacket and waited.

'...Sold at fifteen shillings to Wilkinson's Teas. Now, gentlemen, the second item on today's list is the consignment of tea from the *Elizabeth Miller*, which tied up first but unloaded second.'

There was a murmur at that but the chairman continued.

'Despite coming second this consignment does nevertheless have the distinction of competing in a race between sailing ship and steamer. Very unusual, very distinctive, and which, to judge by letters to the newspapers, has vividly captured the nation's imagination. You may choose to reflect that fact in today's bids.'

The chairman consulted his paper.

'There is one Lot: from the estate of J. Butler – the Tondipgiri plantation – a break of fifty-six thousand, two hundred and fifty pounds of "Butler's Original" in four hundred and forty-one chests and two hundred half-chests. What am I bid per pound?'

Butler stared at the floor.

'Am I bid eight shillings?'

Butler's head came up. Eight shillings? Why wasn't he starting at nine, as he had for all the other Lots?

'I have eight shillings. Do I have eight and six? Eight and six I am bid. Will anyone bid nine? Thank you, nine shillings is bid. Nine and six. Any advance on nine and six? Ten shillings, thank you. Ten shillings, any advance on ten? Gentlemen, I have ten shillings, is there any advance on ten?'

To Butler the pause seemed endless.

'Eleven shillings, thank you. Eleven shillings, the bidding is at eleven shillings. Will anyone go higher?'

'Come on,' muttered Butler under his breath. 'Somebody, come on.'

He was aware of a movement to his right and the chairman acknowledged it.

'Twelve shillings. I am bid twelve shillings. Do I hear thirteen? Gentlemen, the bid stands at twelve shillings, do I hear thirteen?'

The chairman looked round the Sale Room.

'Gentlemen, I have twelve shillings. Do I have any advance on twelve shillings?' and the Sale Room was silent.

'Going once.'

'No,' screamed Butler, but the scream was in his mind only.

'Going twice.'

Not twelve, prayed Butler; please, not twelve, and he looked round the room. It couldn't be over yet. Surely someone else would bid.

An order paper waved but through the crowd of top hats Butler couldn't see the bidder's face, only a grey-gloved hand holding the order paper.

'Thirteen,' announced the Chairman. 'I have thirteen. Is there any advance on thirteen?'

Thirteen! Golden Thirteen! He had done it! He had got it! Tondipgiri was safe! He realised he had been holding his breath and he let it out.

'Gentlemen, I have thirteen shillings. Will anyone go higher?'

Butler couldn't care, not now. He had his thirteen shillings per pound. He had done it! *He had done it!*

'Is there any advance on thirteen?'

Butler looked across the room again but still couldn't see who had made the bid.

'Thirteen shillings from Wilkinson's Teas. Will anyone go higher?'

The Sale Room was silent. The assembly of dealers and wholesalers shifted restlessly, the owner of the top hat that was obstructing the face of the grey-gloved man moved away and Butler saw his benefactor from Wilkinson's Teas.

Paget.

'Going once.'

Paget was going to get the cream of Butler's crop; tea that Butler had driven his people to pick, tea he had nearly killed himself for in bringing it home to England, tea he had worked and laboured and sweated for. And now all of it was about to belong to that sneering slug.

'Going twice.'

There were no more bids, it was going to be Paget who got it. Paget, now wearing a self-satisfied smirk, a smile of conceited, arrogant triumph, the smile of a man who had bested his opponent and who had no qualms about the fact that he had connived and twisted, right from the quayside in Liverpool, in order to win.

It seemed to Butler that a balloon was inflating in his head, his collar felt tight and the Sale Room was spinning. He heard a voice shouting and although the voice was loud it seemed to be coming from far away. The voice was familiar and he wondered where he had heard it before.

'No Sale!' the voice was shouting repeatedly, and with horror Butler suddenly realised the voice was his own. The Sale Room was in uproar and the crush of bodies swirled around him, heads turning and staring. Then the hubbub quietened and the Chairman was looking at him.

'Mr Butler? Did you say–?'

Butler swallowed.

'I said "No Sale". It's my tea and I'm withdrawing it. No Sale.' He turned and walked towards the door and the voice in his head was insistent and demanding.

'What have you done? What *have* you done?'

334

Eleven

The tan couldn't hide the draining of colour from Butler's face and Charlotte hurried to him, concerned.

'What's happened? Did you get it?'

Butler swallowed and stood very still, waiting for the entrance hall to stop revolving around him.

'I've just done a very stupid thing.'

Charlotte grasped the hand he put out to steady himself. 'What? What is it?'

She saw the looks on the faces of men streaming out of the Sale Room and she stared worriedly at Butler.

'I've just turned down an offer of thirteen shillings a pound,' he said slowly and distinctly, and Charlotte was speechless. She stared at him, disbelieving, then a voice hateful to them both spoke.

'Most spectacular, Butler, most spectacular.'

They turned to look at Paget.

'Commercial suicide is, I think, the term. You'll get no other offers after this; you won't even get ten shillings a pound.'

Paget regarded Charlotte with a barely concealed look of contempt.

'You're very foolish to associate yourself with this—' and he waved a dismissive hand at Butler 'this second-rater. Don't come crying to me

335

when you finally see him for the fool he is.'

Paget started to go, but turned. 'And Butler, when you've tried to sell your tea – and failed – I'm still prepared to give you a good price; say, four shillings a pound,' and Paget guffawed and walked away.

'Tell me what happened.'

Butler explained as they walked. 'I don't know what happened to me. When I saw it was him I found myself shouting "No Sale" and before I knew what I was doing I'd withdrawn from the auction.'

He looked at her. 'I've lost it. I've lost Tondipgiri.'

Charlotte bit her lip and looked around. They were on London Bridge but neither of them remembered walking there.

'How about a cup of tea?' she asked softly. Butler gave a faint smile and they continued across the river.

Mrs Carey looked up as they entered the shop.

'Hello, I wasn't expecting to see you again so soon. Did everything go all right?

'I can see it didn't,' she added as she studied their sombre faces.

'Could we impose on you for another cup of tea?' asked Charlotte and Mrs Carey wiped her hands on a towel.

'Of course you can, dearie. Go straight through.'

They went into the back parlour and a couple at one of the tables nodded politely to them.

336

They sat at the same table they had used before and Mrs Carey brought the tray through. She hesitated, was about to say something, but decided not to and went back into the shop. The couple at the other table resumed their conversation and Butler sat in silence, staring unseeing at the teapot. Charlotte watched him.

'What are you thinking?' she asked eventually. Butler looked up.

'Nothing very much,' he said wearily. 'I'm just wondering what to do with twenty-five tons of tea.'

'You can still sell it, can't you?'

Butler gave a short laugh. 'Yes, probably, but I won't get thirteen shillings a pound. Paget was right – after what happened today I shouldn't think I'll even get ten. But anything's better than nothing. At least I should get enough to pay off the Captain of the clipper,' and he fell silent again.

'Have you had anything to eat?' asked Charlotte suddenly, determined to cheer him up, and Butler shook his head.

'Well you're in for a treat,' said Charlotte. 'Try the Madeira cake; it's delicious,' and she went through to the shop.

The couple at the other table got up and left and Butler absently watched them go. A man carrying a newspaper came in and sat down and a minute later Charlotte returned. Mrs Carey went over to the man, spoke to him, then went through to the other room.

'This is my treat,' said Charlotte. 'Try that,' and she set down two slices of golden-yellow cake.

'Thank you,' acknowledged Butler, but was too absorbed with his thoughts to pick his slice up. Charlotte poured the tea and smiled at Mrs Carey as she served the man and cleared the other table.

'What do you do to see if it's a good tea?' asked Charlotte brightly, as much to take Butler's mind off his troubles as to actually learn something. He straightened.

'Breathe in the aroma,' he said and took the lid off the pot. He inhaled and Charlotte was relieved to see signs of interest starting in his face.

'Now *that is* a good tea,' he said. 'I don't even need to test it.' Charlotte picked up her cup and sipped it.

'You're right; that's good,' she said. 'Could you tell just by the scent?'

'With that tea I could,' said Butler. 'It's from Tondipgiri. Mrs Carey's brewed it from that sample I gave her.'

Two men came in and sat down and started discussing something to do with railway shares. Mrs Carey went through again and Charlotte picked up the cake.

'Of all cakes this is my favourite,' she declared. 'But it's not possible to eat such a delicious cake in a ladylike fashion, so you'll have to forgive me,' and she took a big bite and murmured with pleasure. 'That's so good,' she said through a mouthful. 'Tondipgiri tea and Madeira cake – marvellous.'

Butler nodded and smiled, surprised at the contrast between Charlotte's usual refined behaviour and manners and her enthusiastic enjoyment of the Madeira. He tried his own slice and nodded in agreement.

'Mm, very nice.'

He looked at her over the slice of golden-yellow Madeira and grinned. Looking back at him over her own slice she smiled and her eyes softened. Her smile widened and she put the cake down and laughed, a lovely warm bubbling of amusement, and Butler laughed too. He put his slice on the plate and looked at her again. For some reason he couldn't stop smiling.

She had lovely eyes, the sort a man could look at for a lifetime and never get tired of. The deep yet translucent blue reminded him of a loch he had once seen when somebody had invited him up to Scotland for a week's shooting. The loch had held the reflection of the clear blue sky overhead and its shimmering surface had deepened the blue and somehow warmed it, catching soft diamonds of sunlight. He remembered how he had sat there, with no inclination to move, content to just be amongst the heather and watch the surface of the loch.

He realised she was returning his stare, yet there was no unseemly boldness in her look. It was a look of honesty and interest; she was as content to look at him as he was to look at her. There was a crumb of golden cake just to the side of her mouth and she must have realised it for she raised her hand, folded her fingers slightly and extended her little finger to her cheek. The fluffy cake crumb transferred itself to the slender fingertip and her coral-pink lips parted. They closed around finger and crumb and when she drew the finger away the tip of her tongue followed coyly and moistened her upper lip. She never took her eyes from his and Butler suddenly found himself wanting nothing more than to take Charlotte to Scotland and show her the blue water of that loch.

The man on his own at the other table scraped his chair back and left the parlour. Charlotte blinked and for a moment seemed unsure what to do next. She sipped her tea and picked up the Madeira slice again.

'The good thing about this cake,' she said quickly, after she had taken another bite, 'is that you can buy it everywhere. There are ABCs – Aerated Bread Company shops – all over London. There's one near my aunt's; it does marvellous scones. In fact they all do. I remember once–' and Charlotte began an account of an occasion when she had visited that particular shop. As she did so a young couple entered, the girl obviously nervous but happy, and when they sat down it was only a moment before the young man was discreetly holding her hand. Charlotte continued with her tale and Mrs Carey came through, greeted the couple cheerfully and brought their tea. As she went back to the shop she raised her eyebrows at Butler in amusement.

'A busy day, isn't it, love?'

'In fact,' Charlotte was saying, 'I told so many people that the next time I went in–'

Mrs Carey had said it was a busy day, and as Charlotte talked Butler recalled the busy days at Hutton's. Sometimes it had been so busy that the kettle was never off the boil. He remembered how it had struck him that so very many people were ready to drink tea at any time of day, even whilst out shopping.

He glanced at Charlotte. She had lovely hair as well as beautiful eyes.

The two men took their discussion of railway shares and left and from the corner of his eye Butler saw the young man lean over and whisper something in the girl's ear. She suppressed a giggle. Absently Butler sipped his tea and ate the cake, returning the polite nod of a well-dressed man who entered and sat down.

'Well of course, that made all the difference, so next time—' Charlotte was saying, and suddenly, with absolute clarity, Butler realised what he was seeing.

'What did you say?'

Charlotte paused. 'I beg your pardon?'

'A minute ago; what were you saying?'

'It was about my aunt, she—'

'No, before that. Something about ABCs.'

'I said that they're all over London; you can get this nice Madeira cake at all of them...' and she stared at Butler. 'What? What is it?'

Butler was staring at her, all trace of his lethargy and dejection gone, his eyes bright and shining.

'Mrs Carey's busier in here than in the shop,' he said excitedly. 'There've been half a dozen people just while we've been sitting here.'

'Yes,' said Charlotte uncertainly, agreeing with what Butler was saying but unable to understand why it was making him so animated. He leaned

341

closer to her.

'Imagine,' he said, trembling with excitement. 'Imagine if *all* the ABCs were like this one, if they *each* had a room with tables and chairs and someone to serve tea and cakes; not just someone doing it from the goodness of their heart like Mrs Carey, but someone actually *selling* the tea to them. Just imagine what that would be like.'

'Well, it would certainly be very convenient. It would mean–'

'It would mean that all over London there would be places like this where people could go and have tea and Madeira cake. Or scones. Or buns, or sandwiches or whatever they wanted.'

'Yes, I suppose they could,' said Charlotte, still not comprehending.

'And tea,' said Butler intensely, willing her to realise the significance of what he was telling her. 'They could buy tea to drink with whatever they were eating. *Tea*, Charlotte! Tondipgiri tea!'

It was the first time he had used her name and both were aware of it. Their eyes locked and although Charlotte wanted to prolong the moment, the significance of what he was saying suddenly struck her and her eyes widened.

'Of course! And with all those shops all over London they'll–'

'They'll need lots of tea,' finished Butler, barely able to sit still. 'I still have a chance. If I can persuade them to buy my tea I could still save Tondipgiri. I'll go and speak to them right now. All I need to know is where their offices are... Ah, Mrs Carey,' and he stood up, hardly able to contain himself. 'Might I have a word?'

The manageress came over, curious at Butler's obvious excitement, and Butler sat her down.

'Mrs Carey, I've been sitting here, watching the people coming and going – and drinking tea – and I can tell you that right here, in this very room, you have the basis of something new, something really wonderful. This could be a tea shop, a shop where you can charge for the tea you give people and where they can choose sandwiches and cakes from a proper menu. I've got all the tea the Company would need; all I need to do is speak to them if you'll tell me where their offices are...' and his voice trailed off. Mrs Carey was slowly shaking her head and smiling a sad smile.

'It's a nice idea, love. I know what you're talking about but you'd be wasting your time. I've tried it already, you see.'

'You've tried it?'

'I had the same idea about six months ago and I told the supervisor about it when he was round. We had a chat about it and he told one of the managers, but it turned out they weren't interested. Too risky, they said. So that was that.'

The disappointment on Butler's face, his enthusiasm wiped away, touched Mrs Carey and she tried to console him.

'Never mind, dear. It was a nice thought though,' and she smiled that sad smile again and went back into the shop.

Butler, totally deflated, glanced at Charlotte and shrugged. He attempted a grin.

'Well, I tried,' he said and Charlotte nodded, not fooled for a moment by his attempt to appear unconcerned. She wanted desperately to cheer him up but couldn't think of a single suitable thing to say.

Sitting in gloomy silence neither of them noticed a man of about Butler's age enter from the shop. He crossed to one of the tables, was about to sit down, then noticed Butler and started. He hesitated a moment, then came over.

'Excuse me, it's Mr Butler, isn't it?'

Butler looked up, then stood. 'Yes, I'm John Butler.'

'My name's Kent,' said the man. 'Richard Kent. I was at the auction just now.'

'Mr Kent,' acknowledged Butler and they shook hands. 'This is Miss Noble.'

Kent made a small bow of his head to Charlotte.

'Were you bidding?' asked Butler.

'Yes,' said Kent. 'In fact I nearly bought your consignment. I bid twelve shillings and thought it was the top bid, then Paget topped it with his thirteen. And then of course you, er...'

'I withdrew it,' said Butler flatly.

'Yes,' agreed Kent and there was an awkward silence. He gestured to the table he had nearly sat at.

'I thought I'd have some tea before my train leaves.'

'Would you like to join us?' asked Butler.

'Thank you,' said Kent and they sat down. Mrs Carey brought another cup and was about to return to the shop when Kent stopped her.

'Mrs Carey, I don't suppose Miss Elizabeth...?'

344

Mrs Carey shook her head and gave him a sympathetic smile.

'I'm sorry, love. No, she hasn't.'

Kent nodded and Mrs Carey went out. Charlotte poured the tea, Kent tasted it and he looked up in surprise.

'That's "Butler's Original",' and Butler nodded, pleased at the recognition.

'Excellent tea,' said Kent. 'Are you going to enter it at next week's auction?'

Butler shook his head. 'I can't wait that long. I need to sell it by Friday. At thirteen shillings a pound.'

Kent sipped his tea for a moment, then put the cup down. 'I hope you won't consider it an impertinence for me to offer my opinion, Mr Butler, but I suspect such a sale will be rather difficult to achieve.'

'Oh?'

'All the major wholesalers were there today,' explained Kent. 'A lot of the lesser ones too. They made their bids for your tea and dropped out. I was the last in at twelve shillings. I fear you won't find any wholesaler interested at thirteen shillings a pound.'

'You seem very sure,' commented Charlotte.

'I am,' said Kent simply. 'I've been in the business a long time. I know people in all the major companies – dealers, brokers, wholesalers, retailers. If they wouldn't go to thirteen at auction they certainly won't go to thirteen anywhere else. Sorry.'

Butler nodded and stared at the teapot.

'I should have accepted Paget's thirteen,' he

said at last and looked at Kent. 'Do you know him, too?'

Kent was silent for a moment, looking for the right words.

'Our paths have crossed a few times,' he conceded eventually.

Butler grunted.

'Did you buy any teas today?' asked Charlotte brightly, trying to lighten the atmosphere.

Kent shook his head. 'No, they all went for more than twelve shillings a pound and I had no authority to go above that. Most unfortunate. That race generated a lot of interest; the teas that took part have sold for better than average prices and they'll all do well in the shops. Even yours, Mr Butler, went above the average.'

The young couple in the corner went out and Kent glanced at them.

'It's very popular here,' he commented. 'Mrs Carey's arrangements are becoming quite well known. She's always busy; whenever I come in there're always plenty of people at the tables.'

'The same thought struck me,' said Butler. 'This could be made into a proper business. I was even going to approach Aerated Bread and suggest it, but apparently Mrs Carey's already tried. The managers turned her down.'

Kent looked sour.

'Managers,' he muttered, and looked as if he had a lot more to say on that subject, but refrained.

'It's a pity,' said Butler, 'because all this isn't unusual, you know; the shop I first sold my tea through – in Manchester – offered tea and biscuits to customers and there was never any shortage of takers. No matter what time of day, people are always ready for a cup of tea.'

'Some people have no vision,' agreed Kent. 'A new venture always carries some risk, but if there were no people prepared to take a chance where would we be? Look at Trevithick, Stephenson, Brunel; without them what would we do for trains and bridges? And that French chap, De Lesseps; there'd be no Suez Canal without him.'

Butler was mildly amused at the notion of tea shops being classed as the equal of projects of heavy engineering, and Kent looked sheepish and held up his hands in acknowledgement.

'Yes, I know; rather a difference, but the principle's the same,' and he leaned forward, warming to his theme. 'The point is we'll always need people with new ideas. And we'll always need people to back them, people who are prepared to invest–

'You need Pickering,' he said suddenly and his eyes were wide.

'I need what?' asked Butler, startled.

'Sir Henry Pickering,' said Kent excitedly. 'He's a venture capitalist. *And* he's the majority shareholder in Aerated Bread. Mr Butler, take my advice: don't waste your time putting your idea to the Company's managers and having them refuse it. Put it to someone they *can't* refuse. Put it to Pickering himself.'

'Er, right,' said Butler uncertainly.

'Do it now,' urged Kent. 'Go and see him, convince him to support you. In fact I'll come with you,' and he stood up. 'Let's see him together and not leave until he's said yes. He lives in Kensington somewhere; I know someone who'll know the exact address – we can call on him on the way. Come on, we'll go there now.'

Caught up by Kent's enthusiasm, they stood, then Butler paused.

'Mr Kent, I'm not ungrateful, but why are you doing this? Believe me, I appreciate your advice but you know nothing about me. Tell me frankly: why are you being so helpful?'

Kent looked directly at Butler and spoke with feeling. 'Mr Butler, everyone in the tea business knows about you. We all know how you risked everything on being the only backer of that clipper and you damn nearly won.'

Immediately he looked at Charlotte. 'I'm sorry, Miss Noble. Forgive me for the use of that word.'

Charlotte smiled and shook her head and Kent turned back to face Butler.

'I work for a company that's standing still. They won't attempt anything new, they daren't take even the smallest risk and our conversation has made me realise what I should have realised months ago: they're stagnating and I've been stagnating with them. But not any more. You've got a bold idea, an idea with vision, and quite frankly I want to be part of making it a success.'

He tapped his chest.

'Mr Butler, I'm a businessman, not just an auction bidder, and I can tell you that supplying tea to Aerated Bread's shops all over London will be a vast undertaking – you'll need offices, warehouses, you'll need to employ people, pay them, manage, them. That's *my* expertise. That's

348

what I can contribute. We could really build something if we work together, between us we could build something with a real future. We could take your idea and make it work. There'd be no timid managers holding us back. What do you say?'

Butler hesitated.

It all seemed too good to be true. He was like a punch-drunk boxer, reeling from blow after blow – the setback on the quay at Liverpool, the setback in the auction room when he saw Paget, the setback when Mrs Carey told him she had already proposed his tea shop idea and had it turned down. His world was due to cave in on him on Friday when the bank in Ceylon didn't get its money and now out of the blue someone was throwing him the lifeline he needed.

He felt tired and drained. There were no other options left; he had used them all up. He might as well go along with Kent's idea, he had nothing to lose that wasn't already going to be taken from him on Friday.

But still...

Kent nodded as if he could read Butler's thoughts.

'You know nothing about me, Mr Butler,' he acknowledged. 'This is all very sudden. I'm proposing a business partnership and I could be anybody. But, whatever you think of me, don't let your idea slip away. It's worth fighting for. So fight for it. At least see Sir Henry Pickering and get him to support you. And if you're uncertain about having me as a business partner you can simply employ me instead. Then you can fire me if you're not satisfied.'

Butler looked at the eager and enthusiastic Kent and a memory returned, a scene from a time long ago when he had stood on the bridge over the stream at Tondipgiri, speaking to a native he had seen only once before and about whom he knew nothing. There had been no one to tell him what to do, there had been nothing else upon which to base his decision except his own judgement, his intuition, his gut instincts. He had trusted those instincts on that occasion; he had employed the man as his foreman and Changarai had never let him down. This was a similar moment; there were no guarantees, no certainties, and Butler trusted his instincts again.

'Mr Kent, let's go and see Pickering.'

Outside, Kent hailed a hansom and the cab took the three of them first to see Kent's business friend and then, armed with the address, to an impressive house in Kensington. The manservant who answered the bell was polite, but distant.

'I'm sorry sir, you've just missed Sir Henry. He left ten minutes ago.'

'Where's he gone?'

The man regarded them coldly and said nothing.

'Look,' said Butler, 'this is very important. There's a great deal of money at stake. It's vital that Sir Henry knows.'

The cryptic words were enough to sow a seed of doubt in the servant's mind and he blinked uncertainly.

'It's very urgent,' added Kent.

'There may not be enough time,' put in Charlotte, compounding the man's confusion.

He hesitated, then, 'Sir Henry has gone to London Bridge station.'

'The station?!'

'The four o'clock train for Folkestone, sir. Sir Henry is leaving for Paris.'

'When will he be back?'

'In three weeks, sir. He–' and found himself addressing empty air. The two men and the woman were hurrying down the steps and the un-tanned one was yelling wildly to the cabby to come back.

'We'll never get there in time,' said Kent.

'We'll get there,' said Butler, and called up to the cabby.

'Can't you go any faster?'

'I'm going as fast as I can, sir.'

'You're barely trotting, man.'

'This is a good speed, sir and if–'

'A guinea if you get us to London Bridge station in fifteen minutes.'

'A guinea? Why didn't you say?' The cabby's whip cracked loudly and Butler fell back into the seat as the cab shot forward.

Porters jumped out of the way as the cab clattered up the approach and it jerked to a halt, the horse sweating and lathered. Butler threw the guinea at the cabby and they ran into the station.

'The Folkestone train?' Kent asked a porter breathlessly.

'Over there, sir,' and they hurried in the

direction of the pointing finger.

'That's him,' said Kent.

Beyond the barrier a stout man in a dove-gre
overcoat and silk top hat was climbing into one o
the carriages of a waiting train. A burly railwa
official was standing by the barrier, inspectin
tickets.

'We'll need a ticket,' said Kent and looke
towards the office. There was a long queue and i
wasn't moving.

Butler shook his head. 'We'll never make it. B
the time we get a ticket the train will be ready t
leave. We need time to convince him to suppor
us.'

'When the man steps aside, you two go throug
the barrier,' said Charlotte suddenly.

'What?'

But Charlotte was already walking to th
barrier.

'What's she up to?' said Butler, astounded.

'Your ticket please, Miss.'

'Of course,' and she fumbled in her purse, the
hesitated and put her hand to her head.

'Are you all right, Miss?'

'Yes. Thank you,' and she fumbled in her ba
again.

'Oh dear,' and her hand went to her head agai
and the purse fell to the ground, 'I don't think
– oh,' and she swayed. Automatically the officia
put out his hand as she staggered, seemingly o
the verge of collapse.

'If I might sit down,' she mumbled. 'The benc
over there, if you would be so kind,' and th

official picked up her purse and gave her his arm to lean on. She walked unsteadily and Butler was already coming over, concerned, but Charlotte dropped her purse again and as the official was bending to pick it up she gave an urgent jerk of her head at Butler and nodded towards the now unattended barrier. Butler and Kent caught on at once and were through the barrier before the official straightened.

'Is that better, Miss?'

'Much better, thank you. A momentary dizziness. It will pass, I think. I will sit here for a moment. Thank you for your help; you're very kind.'

The official touched his cap, pleased to help such an attractive lady, and returned to his position at the barrier.

'What the deuce!'

Pickering jumped as the door of his carriage burst open and two men plunged in.

'Who the devil are you? Is this a robbery? Are you after money? By gad, sir, I'll call for the guard.'

Pickering raised his ivory-handled cane, prepared to strike out with it, and Butler hastened to explain.

'It's not a robbery, Sir Henry. I hope you'll forgive the intrusion when you've heard what I've got to say, but this is a matter of the utmost urgency.'

'It had better be of the utmost urgency, young man. What is it you're after? Hey?'

'We'd like to interest you in a business

proposition, Sir Henry,' said Kent.

'And bursting into carriages is how you go about business, is it? Well, let me tell you, sir–'

'Sir Henry,' Butler broke in, and his voice was calmer, 'Sir Henry, I apologise again for intruding on you but we found out that you're going to France and not returning for three weeks. What I need to discuss with you cannot wait. Literally cannot wait. If I can't persuade you to support our proposal then by this Friday I will have nothing.'

Pickering stared at him. 'Your name, sir?'

'Butler. John Butler. This is my associate, Richard Kent.'

'Mr Butler, I have all manner of men trying to get money from me for crackpot schemes: inventions, expeditions. I ignore them. Why should I treat you any differently?'

Butler picked his words carefully. 'Sir Henry, I own a tea plantation in Ceylon. At this very moment I have twenty-five tons of the finest tea sitting in a warehouse and with your help it can all come together in a new venture that will excite people right across London. It needs your support, Sir Henry. Not your money, but you're the only one who can ensure its success.'

Pickering looked perplexed. 'You don't need my money?'

'No.'

'But it won't succeed without me?'

'Correct.'

Pickering looked at Butler, then at Kent, then at Butler again. He took out his pocket watch.

'Mr Butler, my train leaves in twenty minutes

and I will be expecting to enjoy this compartment in peace. If you're going to convince me to support your scheme I suggest you start now,' and he looked at Butler expectantly.

Butler was about to relate his observations on the readiness of so many people to drink tea and to tell Pickering about the possibilities for the Aerated Bread Company, but the man's air of impatience made him dispense with that approach. He had a better plan.

'Sir Henry, I'd like you to have a cup of tea.'

Charlotte leaned over to Butler.

'Are you sure this is a good idea?' she whispered.

'Trust me,' he muttered, but he couldn't help feeling a small doubt as they waited for Mrs Carey to bring the tea service. Pickering was frowning, clearly of the opinion that exchanging his comfortable compartment for a shop that sold cakes was a complete waste of his time. Even Kent seemed tense.

Mrs Carey put the tray on the table, wondering what was happening, but she said nothing. Butler had specifically requested that no tea should be put in the pot and that the boiling water should be in a separate jug. Now he opened his case and withdrew one of the sample bags.

'I'd like you to try this, Sir Henry,' he said, loosening the drawstrings. 'Tea from my own plantation,' and he measured the tea into the pot and added the water. Pickering watched and lost his air of impatience. He leaned forward, clearly intrigued, and watched Butler's actions closely.

Butler timed the tea, then poured it and presented the cup to Pickering.

'With my compliments,' he said.

Pickering sipped the tea and looked startled. He savoured the brew, then very carefully put his cup on the tray. He stared at it for some moments, then looked first at Butler, then at Kent, then at Butler again.

'I'm impressed, gentlemen; that's a very fine cup of tea. But what does it have to do with your business proposition?'

Butler explained what he had in mind.

'With my tea and the Company's bread and cakes the shops would be hugely popular. You could open one near every railway station in London. People like to drink tea – that's an absolute fact – and if they have somewhere to go, somewhere where they can sit down with their friends and enjoy good tea and good food, those places will be popular, I guarantee it.'

Pickering looked at Butler levelly.

'If I may say so, Mr Butler, that's either an extremely confident statement or an extremely reckless one. May I ask how you can justify it?'

Butler looked him in the eye.

'I have confidence in my tea, Sir Henry. You've tasted it, so you know what I'm talking about. You have confidence in the quality of the bread and cakes that Aerated Bread sell–'

'Otherwise you wouldn't be their principal shareholder,' put in Kent and Butler nodded.

'Put the two things together, Sir Henry and those tea shops will be busy all day.'

'I see,' said Pickering. He stood up. 'Would you

excuse me for a moment? I'd like to speak to the manageress. Excuse me Miss Noble, Mr Kent,' and he left the parlour.

'What do you think?' asked Charlotte anxiously.

'Well at least he hasn't dismissed us out of hand,' said Butler. 'But I thought there'd have been more reaction. I couldn't tell if he liked the idea or not,' and he looked worried. 'Perhaps we've wasted our time after all.'

Pickering paused before returning to the parlour. The tea shop idea certainly had merit. Mrs Carey had confirmed how she had decided to set out tables and provide tea for her friends from the trains and it was a mystery to Pickering why such an outstanding idea hadn't been tried before. And Butler's tea was certainly good, the best he'd ever tasted, but it could still be nothing more than an attempt, a very clever attempt, by this young man to simply get his hands on some money. For a confidence trickster to succeed he had to be plausible, and this fellow Butler was very plausible indeed.

But he might be entirely honest.

The only way to find out for sure was to test him, to knock him off balance, to catch him out, and Pickering knew exactly how to do that.

They all stood as Pickering came back into the room. He looked squarely at Butler.

'I like your idea, Mr Butler,' he declared. 'I'll support it.'

Butler blinked, not sure that he was hearing properly.

'You'll support it?'

'I'll support it. Twenty-five tons of tea, I think you said?'

'Er, yes. That's right.'

'What's your price?'

'I need to sell at thirteen shillings a pound.'

Pickering considered for a moment.

'A shade under thirty-six and a half thousand sterling,' he commented. 'Consider me in, Mr Butler. I'll make an immediate recommendation to the Board,' and as a tide of relief crossed Butler's face, Pickering delivered the underhand blow. His manner was casual but he watched Butler closely as he spoke: 'Not for the full amount of course, but I'll recommend they invest five thousand pounds.'

Butler shook his head at once. 'That's no good to me. I can't do anything with that.'

'It's that or nothing,' said Pickering.

Again Butler shook his head. 'I need the full amount. If you won't go above five thousand, Sir Henry, it means we've wasted our time and wasted yours too. I'm sorry,' and he gave a bitter laugh. 'You might as well keep that tea sample.'

Pickering wasn't finished yet. Butler's response could be just another ploy. Pickering held up his hand.

'Very well, Mr Butler, you've convinced me. I'll recommend ten thousand – and that's my last word.'

'It's no good,' said Butler. 'To pay off the bank and pay off the clipper captain I need exactly thirty-six thousand, three hundred and eighty-seven pounds, seventeen shillings and sixpence. I can't accept anything less.'

Pickering leaned back. He held Butler's gaze for a long while, his face expressionless but his mind racing ahead, calculating, weighing up, assessing. He was satisfied. His test had worked.

'I needed to know, Mr Butler,' he said at last. 'I needed to know if you were genuine. Someone simply after fast money would have jumped at the offer of five thousand, and someone holding out for a bit more would never have let the ten thousand escape them. But you turned down both offers – turned them down flat. You said you had until Friday?'

'That's right,' said Butler. 'If I don't repay what I owe by then the bank will seize the estate.'

'Then we'll have to move quickly,' said Pickering decisively. 'I suggest you telegraph your bankers in Ceylon, inform them that you have the necessary funds and that they will be transferred within seventy-two hours. A meeting of the ABC Board must be called – and at short notice.'

'What about your train?' asked Charlotte.

'The meeting I'm attending in Paris isn't until Monday. I can alter my arrangements; this matter requires my immediate attention.'

'Are you sure the Board will agree to it?' asked Butler.

Pickering nodded. 'As principal shareholder I don't expect to encounter serious opposition. I will speak to some people in advance of the meeting but I'm quite confident that the Company will want to take you up on your proposal. And,' he added, 'against any possibility that they might not, I give you my personal guarantee: if the Company should go against my recommendation – and I don't think they will – I will buy the entire consignment myself. For the full amount,' and he smiled a quiet smile, 'including the seventeen shillings and sixpence. Like you, Mr Butler, I too have confidence in Tondipgiri tea. Do we have an agreement?'

Butler, feeling slightly dizzy and hardly daring to believe he had succeeded in persuading Pickering, nodded.

'We do indeed, Sir Henry,' and he gripped Pickering's outstretched hand. 'We do indeed.'

'Come for dinner tonight,' said Pickering in a voice that suggested a refusal was unthinkable. 'All of you.'

'That's very kind–' began Butler, but Pickering waved his thanks aside.

'That's quite unnecessary. Miss Noble? Mr Kent?'

Kent nodded eagerly and Charlotte laughed. 'We'd love to.'

'Good,' declared Pickering. 'After all, there's much to discuss.'

Dinner at Pickering's Kensington home was lavish. The wine and food were excellent, the courses were punctuated by much conversation and laughter, and Butler was still in a whirl. Events had moved so fast – eight hours ago his rejection of Paget's thirteen-shilling bid had, he had thought, brought certain ruin. It still seemed incredible that the utterly bleak depression he had felt could be replaced with such optimism and relief. A new door had opened, he had a new opportunity. And he still had Tondipgiri.

At one point they were all enjoying a tale told by Richard Kent and Butler looked across the table at Charlotte. The candlelight was picking out highlights in her chestnut hair and her eyes sparkled. She met his gaze and smiled and they raised their glasses to each other.

Kent noticed and grinned. Butler grinned back.

'Still hard to believe isn't it?' said Kent.

Butler nodded. 'After what happened at the auction this seems like a dream.'

'And what a dream!' said Kent, raising his glass to Butler and Charlotte.

'Will your wife not be wondering where you are?' asked Charlotte, and Kent shook his head.

'I'm not married, Miss Noble. I almost was, but...' his voice trailed away, his thoughts somewhere else, then he remembered where he was and, with mock poetic tragedy, said, 'But, alas, 'twas not to be.'

He turned to Pickering. 'This is an exceptionally fine wine, Sir Henry.'

'I didn't expect I would be enjoying French wine in England this evening,' commented Pickering jovially from the head of the table. 'I had rather expected to be enjoying French wine in France.'

His guests laughed and then Pickering had a question for Butler.

'Tell me, what's the name of your company?'

'Just "Butler and Company",' said Butler.

Pickering nodded and leaned back. 'May I offer

a suggestion?'

'Of course.'

'I think now's the time to change its name. To something a little more evocative, to something a little more redolent of its Ceylon connection. What do you think?'

Butler was thoughtful.

'Something Ceylonese,' he mused to himself.

There was a long silence.

'Are there any words in the native language you could use?' asked Pickering at last.

'Tondipgiri means King Tondip's Hill,' said Charlotte suddenly. 'So why not use that? "King Tondip's Tea"?'

'"King Tondip's Tea",' repeated Butler thoughtfully, rolling it on his tongue. '"Tondip's",' he announced decisively, 'The Tondip's Tea Company". That's what we'll call it.'

'I like that,' said Charlotte, and Pickering and Kent agreed.

'I suggest we raise our glasses,' said Pickering. 'A toast – to the new name and the new venture.'

'Tondip's Tea!'

Part Five

1886: DRYING

'The fermentation process is stopped, the leaf stabilises and the flavour is locked in.'

One

London

The man in the anonymous dark suit entered Butler's office on the fourth floor of the Tondip's Building unannounced.

Somehow, unnoticed, he had come up past three floors of busy clerks, secretaries and supervisors all going about Tondip's Tea Company business. At the top of the stairs he had bypassed the main entrance to the fourth-floor offices, through which lay general access to Butler's office, and with unerring accuracy had made straight for the little-used corridor which held Butler's private door. He knocked once, then quickly entered.

'Mr Butler?' he asked, and Butler later reflected that the question had been totally unnecessary; the man was clearly well prepared and very well informed.

'Yes,' acknowledged Butler and stood. 'Can I help you, Mr...?'

'Brand,' said the man. 'I wonder if I might have a quiet word?' and he stood expectantly.

'Sit down, Mr Brand,' said Butler after a moment, and Brand sat precisely, his fingers laced.

'What can I do for you?' asked Butler.

'It may be more a case of what I can do for *you*,' said Brand. 'I'm here on behalf of a group of businessmen who wish you to consider a financial proposal.'

'Who are they?'

Brand gave a small shake of his head.

'At this stage I am not permitted to reveal their names. Suffice to say they are several very discreet gentlemen, known for the wisdom and soundness of their judgement and aware also of the importance of not letting their identities be revealed too early in business negotiations. If it were to become known that they were making representations to you there might be considerable – premature – interest from other parties. At this stage they wish merely to establish whether you are prepared, in principle, to give consideration to their proposal.'

Butler regarded Brand carefully. Clearly this surprise visitor wasn't going to reveal who had sent him, so Butler leaned back and nodded.

'Very well, Mr Brand, I'll listen to what you have to say.'

'Of course,' said Brand smoothly, as if no other response had been possible. 'There are two types of tea companies; there are those like your own – Tondip's Tea, a company confining itself to selling the produce of a single estate; and then there are companies that incorporate a number of different estates – in India and Ceylon – and the teas they sell are very carefully formulated *blends* of those different teas. The gentlemen I represent are from one of the latter companies.'

Brand paused.

'Go on,' said Butler.

'They wish to make an offer for the Tondip's

Tea Company,' said Brand. 'They are well aware of your success; after all, who wouldn't be? Tondip's is the confirmed favourite of customers of the Aerated Bread Company's expanding chain of tea shops; it enjoys considerable success in stores and groceries the length of the country and, indeed, the very existence of this building is a testament to Tondip's popularity. The people I represent wish to apply their not inconsiderable expertise and resources and enhance Tondip's good name even more. They have a reputation for shrewd investments, hence their interest in the Tondip's Tea Company.'

'If they sell blends,' asked Butler, 'what do they want with Tondip's Tea?'

'They wish to incorporate it in new blends that they are planning,' said Brand. 'The results will, they feel, be of quite exceptional quality,' and Brand looked calmly at Butler.

'Does this offer,' asked Butler deliberately, 'have anything to do with the fact that Tondip's Tea is one of the tea companies that have been invited to participate at the Colonial and Indian Exhibition next month?'

'Not at all,' said Brand smoothly.

Butler nodded. 'Then neither, I suppose, does it have anything to do with the fact, as is fairly well known, that three of those tea companies will subsequently be chosen to compete for a special award of the Royal Warrant?'

'Mr Butler,' said Brand. 'If you win the right to put "By Appointment to Her Majesty The Queen" on your tea you will deserve all the success and prosperity that the award will bring.

It will prove what those who instruct me have said: that Tondip's is of outstanding quality and a favourite of a great many people.'

Brand, it seemed, wasn't going to be put off.

'All right,' said Butler. 'What's the proposal?'

'An offer for the Company in its entirety,' said Brand. 'The purchase of the estate in Ceylon, the people you employ, all the Company's land, buildings, assets, liabilities and current business contracts.'

Butler shook his head. 'I'm sorry, Mr Brand, but Tondip's Tea isn't for sale.'

Brand wasn't at all disconcerted by this.

'Those who instruct me have considered the possibility that that might be your answer,' he said. 'I am authorised to reveal to you that the sum they are prepared to pay for the entire Tondip's Tea Company is five hundred thousand pounds.'

The amount jolted Butler. He swallowed.

'That's a considerable sum,' he ventured at last; at least it was something to say whilst he recovered his composure.

'An entirely appropriate one, given the success of your Company.'

'I can't give you a decision immediately,' said Butler. 'I need to speak to my business partner.'

Brand gave a small nod. 'Of course, I quite understand. When should I call again? Shall we say the day after tomorrow? At noon?'

Butler thought for a moment, then nodded.

'Excellent,' said Brand. 'Thank you, Mr Butler,' and he was gone, again through the private door, before Butler could rise to show him out.

Butler sat for a long while, the letter he had been writing quite forgotten. Never had he dreamed – or even dared to dream – that he would ever be within reach of such a sum as half a million pounds.

He frowned. Tondipgiri wasn't just a piece of land bought speculatively one year and sold the next for a profit. He had, quite literally, put his blood into the place.

He needed to talk to someone.

'And that's for everything,' said Butler. 'Estate, warehouses, offices, the lot. When he said half a million pounds I nearly fell off the chair. It's a mad sum of money, crazy,' and he shook his head, still bemused. 'What do you think?'

Richard Kent was as stunned as Butler. 'They must want it pretty badly. They must be really impressed with our success.'

Butler agreed and Kent had another thought.

'Do you think they'll go higher? Could this be just an opening bid?'

'God knows,' said Butler. 'If it is, what resources must they have to be able to offer *more* than five hundred thousand?' He shook his head incredulously and walked to the window. He stared across the road at Hyde Park, not really seeing what he was looking at, and spoke without turning.

'You're my business partner, Richard. What do you think? Should we sell?'

'You're the majority shareholder, John,' said Kent. 'Ultimately it's your decision.'

Butler grunted.

'But it's a hell of a lot of money,' continued Kent. 'I can't imagine we'd ever get another offer of that size.'

'Who are they?' mused Butler. 'Have they got half a million in hard cash, or will they need to borrow it? They must have rich backers.'

'Does it matter?' asked Kent. 'Once we're half a million better off will it matter to us whether they had to borrow it?'

Butler shrugged. 'No, I don't suppose it would,' and he fell silent. Kent watched him and waited.

'It's not like simply selling a piece of land,' said Butler, frowning, his forehead pressed against the glass. 'I lived there. It was my home. I have ... *friends* there. It isn't just another commodity to buy and sell. Tondipgiri–' and he stopped.

He turned.

'I don't know what to do,' he said frankly. 'I need to give it further consideration,' he looked at his watch, 'and it'll have to wait until this afternoon. I'm lunching with Charlotte.'

Kent raised an eyebrow.

'What?' asked Butler.

'Why don't you marry the girl?' said Kent. 'She won't wait for ever, you know.'

Butler coloured. He cleared his throat and fingered his collar. 'I – I don't know what the devil you mean.'

Kent laughed and when Butler glared at him Kent laughed even louder. He was still laughing even after Butler shut the door and strode away along the corridor. He went to the window and waited, then watched as Butler left the Tondip's Building and strode across the road.

'She won't wait for ever, John,' he said again after a moment and, as he turned away, added wistfully, 'My girl didn't.'

Butler didn't say a great deal through lunch and Charlotte could tell he was preoccupied with thoughts of something. He barely grunted when she reminded him they had tickets for the theatre that evening and he had no eyes at all for the spring flowers she pointed out as they walked back through the Park. She was quiet, and when they reached the lake and walked the pathway around it she tried again.

'That was a nice lunch,' and Butler merely nodded. A few steps further on and he stopped.

'I've had an offer for the Company. For everything.'

Charlotte didn't say anything at first.

'Will you accept?' she asked eventually.

'I don't know,' said Butler, and watched as several hungry ducks paddled towards them expectantly. 'They've offered half a million pounds,' and Charlotte gasped.

He glanced at her and nodded. 'A lot of money. More money than I could ever imagine. A fortune.'

Charlotte studied him closely. 'But you're uncertain, aren't you? Even for half a million pounds?'

'Even for half a million,' Butler agreed. 'I'd be stupid to turn it down though, that's certain. I might never get an offer like that again, not even one close to it. But,' and he shook his head, 'I don't know.'

The ducks quacked at them impatiently for several fruitless minutes, then gave up and floated away.

'Can you bring yourself to sell Tondipgiri?' she asked suddenly.

Butler frowned and they started walking again.

'A man in Ceylon once told me something,' said Butler. 'He said "When you put tea bushes in the ground you put something in your soul." Now I know what he meant. When I first went out there all I wanted was to get my hands on the deeds so that I could sell Tondipgiri and go home again. But something made me stay,' and he laughed self-consciously. 'It's got its roots into me now; I don't know if I can bring myself to sell it. But half a million pounds? How can I turn that down?'

'There are the people to consider,' said Charlotte. 'The people who work for you.'

She'd done it again. Put her finger right on the critical issue.

'What's the name of that man who runs the estate for you?'

'Changarai,' said Butler, and pictured the bright-eyed, leathery-skinned man who had stood by him and worked so dependably for him for so long. It had been two years since he had last seen him, but the estate was running well and Butler knew he owed Changarai a lot; there would be no Tondipgiri estate at all if it hadn't been for the work he and Changarai had put in together. How could he sell the place and thereby sever his friendship with the man?

'Charlotte,' he said, 'I'm not selling.'

'Not even for half a million pounds?'

Butler shook his head.

'No. Not even for half a million pounds.'

'That's my decision, Mr Brand.'

Brand nodded. If he was disappointed he didn't show it.

'Was the proposed payment a factor in your decision? Was it insufficient?'

Butler shook his head. 'The money had nothing to do with it, Mr Brand. Over the years I've put a great deal of myself into both the estate and the Company; too much to let me sell them now.'

He returned Brand's steady gaze and Brand must have realised that further discussion would be fruitless.

'I understand perfectly,' and he stood. 'Thank you for your time, Mr Butler.'

'One moment,' said Butler, also standing. 'Now that we've settled everything there's no reason for you not to tell me whom you represent.'

Now it was Brand's turn to shake his head.

'I'm afraid I still can't tell you, Mr Butler. I bid you good day, sir,' and in one smooth and swift motion he was through the door and into the corridor.

Butler was about to sit but a suspicion occurred to him. His face tightened and he went out into the corridor. Brand had gone, but when Butler hurried to the top of the stairs and listened he could hear the man's footsteps descending. Butler followed, treading lightly and keeping to the outside edge so that he wouldn't be seen if Brand looked up the stairwell.

Brand's footsteps echoed as they crossed the

tiled entrance hall and Butler hurried the last couple of flights. He sprinted across the hall startling the doorman, and ran outside. He looked both ways and spotted Brand, already on the other side of the road and moving very quickly. Butler ran across, dodging a hansom and attracting a string of curses from the driver, and followed Brand, staying about a hundred yards behind him.

Brand turned onto one of the paths cutting across Hyde Park and Butler cursed and dropped back. A hundred yards was too near should Brand happen to look behind him, but once over the Park he would be amongst the streets and squares of Mayfair, and if Butler didn't catch up smartly the man would be quickly lost.

Out of the Park and Brand trotted straight across Park Lane and down one of the streets. Butler sprinted the rest of the path, leaping over a dog on a long lead whose owner wasn't paying attention to it, and reached Park Lane. A four-horse carriage was making its stately way, but it was too stately for Butler. He ran across almost under the noses of the front pair of horses startling them and making them rear. The driver swore at him but then Butler was over and catching up on Brand.

Brand rounded a corner and when Butler reached it he thought he was too late, but no, there he was, the black-hatted figure moving quickly across Grosvenor Square. Butler was torn between staying far enough behind not to be noticed should Brand look back, or getting close enough so as not to lose him, no matter where he went. For Brand was making a number of quick turnings now. Down an alley and through Three Kings Yard, then past Claridge's Hotel and through another yard, then down a gloomy passage. Brand would be certain to hear anyone following in the close and narrow passage and Butler kept near to the wall, praying that Brand would be too intent on reaching his destination to waste time on looking round.

At the end of the passage Brand turned right and Butler put a spurt on. He reached the road and for a moment he panicked. He couldn't see Brand anywhere. He hurried along the pavement and breathed easier when he spotted him moving briskly on the other side. Brand suddenly turned left and Butler had to brave the cabs and carriages again.

On the other side Butler buffeted an old gentleman who spluttered and lost his monocle and Butler started running to catch Brand. The old fellow shouted after Butler, brandishing his fist, and Butler hoped that Brand didn't hear and turn to see what the fuss was about. At the end of the road Brand turned right, and when Butler reached the corner he found he was on Regent Street. Determined not to lose his quarry he drew closer. If Brand turned now he would surely see Butler following him, but Brand had been so intent on reaching his destination that Butler was sure he wouldn't look back now.

Another hundred yards and Brand went up a flight of steps into an ornate-fronted building. Butler ran to it and stared at the name cut into the masonry. The elegantly chiselled lettering proclaimed this to be the offices of The Great

Eastern Tea Company and Butler felt a momentary relief – he had suspected that Brand was working on behalf of Paget and Wilkinson's Teas.

He still wanted to know more about who had sent Brand, and he ran up the steps. Opening the frosted-glass door he found himself in a columned hall where a man wearing maroon livery was speaking to two top-hatted gentlemen.

Ahead was a staircase and Brand was rounding the corner of the stairs.

Butler didn't wait.

He walked across the hall as if he had every right to be there, hoping that the two men would obstruct the view of the liveried attendant. He got to the stairs without challenge, hurried up them and paused on the first floor. The footsteps were going higher and Butler followed the sound up two more floors, then heard the steps receding along a corridor. He went up the remaining steps two at a time and peered round the corner.

Brand had stopped at a door. He knocked, then entered. Butler hurried along the corridor and looked at the door. Solid wood, no nameplate.

Only one way to find out, he decided, and grasped the handle. He swung the door open.

'I might have known,' he said coldly.

'Thank you, Mr Brand, that will be all,' and Paget leaned back expansively. Brand nodded, nodded to Butler and left.

'Well, Butler, changed your mind? Decided to sell after all?'

'What are you doing here, Paget? You work for Wilkinson's.'

'Not any more,' said Paget. 'Great Eastern has recognised my talents. It's a company with plans and ideas, a company with a glowing future. You'd be wise to sell Tondip's to us.'

'I'll never sell to you,' said Butler.

'You might change your mind one day,' said Paget smugly.

Butler shook his head. 'You'll never get your hands on Tondip's. Never. There's no sum of money you could offer that would make me change my mind.'

'Hardly a sign of an intelligent businessman,' commented Paget.

'Your opinion is a matter of complete indifference to me, Paget,' said Butler. 'All that matters is that you'll never, ever, buy Tondip's,' and he turned on his heel, left the office and shut the door in a manner befitting the end of the discussion. The slam echoed down the corridor and a couple of heads popped out of offices to see what all the noise was about. Butler paid them no heed, walking straight to the stairs and then out of the building.

Two

A membership at Bramley's club for gentlemen, t was said, was harder to obtain than a knight-1ood and, in the eyes of many, was considerably nore useful. Being a member of Bramley's 1fforded access to some of the most influential people in England, and the promise of a discreet word with the Applications Committee had been the decisive factor in the deliberations of more than one Cabinet minister. Other clubs might jealously try to cultivate a reputation for exclusivity, even going so far on occasion as to refuse an application simply to demonstrate how difficult it was to be accepted, but Bramley's had no time for such games. Quite simply, if an applicant met all the criteria he was accepted. Unfortunately for most, very few met those criteria.

Not least was the requirement that three existing members should personally recommend the application. Paget, sitting with three well-dressed gentlemen in the Club's green buttoned-leather armchairs, had every hope that when he made his application it would have their endorsement. Because by then he would have joined them as a colleague – provided he could deliver on one particular promise.

'This is very disappointing,' said one of the men and his two associates murmured agreement. 'We made you the offer of a directorship on the basis of your claim that you could obtain Butler's agreement to sell. I hope we haven't misjudged you.'

'Merely a temporary setback,' Paget protested.

'But he has turned down a very generous offer,' said the man, 'and turned it down most emphatically I understand. I find it difficult to believe that he can still be persuaded.'

'He'll sell,' said Paget, but the man continued

as if Paget hadn't spoken.

'If the task is beyond you, William, there is no shame in admitting it. But in that case we would have to withdraw our offer of a directorship.'

'That won't be necessary,' said Paget. 'Butler just needs the right kind of persuasion. He turned down the offer because he let personal considerations get in the way of business. But there's more than one way of getting our hands on Tondip's. I know of a way that can't possibly fail.'

The man leaned back and contemplated Paget through half-closed lizard eyes.

'William, we have been very impressed with your work and our offer of a directorship was unanimous. But the offer was conditional on you making good on your claim that you could obtain the Tondip's Company for us. Your positive attitude is commendable but I must remind you that the reputation of Great Eastern Tea is paramount. Nothing and no one is permitted to tarnish that reputation. If you are contemplating an act of hard business in order to secure Tondip's I suggest you think very carefully before undertaking it. If you are unsuccessful or if you do anything that reflects badly on Great Eastern we would have to reconsider our offer. Reluctantly we would also be compelled to review your position within the Company. I hope you understand.'

Paget understood perfectly. If he succeeded and obtained the Tondip's Company for Great Eastern Tea the Board would welcome him with open arms. Membership of Bramley's would almost certainly follow. But if he failed, the Directors would wash their hands of him.

'I won't let you down.'

The man gave a small smile. 'I'm sure you won't. Thank you, William.'

Paget nodded but made no move to leave.

The man's smile disappeared. 'I'm sure you have much to attend to, William.'

It was an unmistakable dismissal and the colour rose in Paget's cheeks.

Outside Bramley's he ground his teeth and shoved a boy selling newspapers into the gutter. Damn them! Treating him like that. They thought themselves hard and manipulative, but just wait until he was on the Board; then they'd find themselves dealing with someone who could out-scheme all of them. He laughed – a short, sharp snort. He was going to obtain Tondip's – his plan for that was foolproof – and then they'd get a shock. It would belong to him, they would be expecting him to meekly hand it over but then they'd find out what sort of man they were dealing with. He'd extract the directorship *and* the membership of Bramley's *and* a few other things besides. And if they baulked and refused to honour their promises it wouldn't matter because he would be in possession of a Company worth at least half a million pounds. He could do a lot with that.

He laughed again.

Butler was going to get a shock he'd never recover from.

Three

4th May, 1886

South Kensington, London

'I hope this is going to be worth it, John Butler,' said Charlotte with mock severity.

'Trust me,' said Butler. 'Keep looking the other way.'

Charlotte shook her head in exasperation but kept her head turned. She held Butler's arm as they joined the throng of people invited to the Exhibition's opening, the gentlemen formal and smart with shining silk top hats, the ladies splendid in their brightly coloured spring finery and carrying elegant parasols. Butler suddenly stopped.

'All right, now close your eyes.'

'John–'

'Come on, close your eyes.'

Charlotte closed her eyes and Butler turned her on the spot.

'Now open them.'

She opened her eyes.

'If you think I–' she began, and stopped.

'Well?' asked Butler, grinning, and Charlotte could only nod.

The fifty-foot-high entrance to the Colonial and Indian Exhibition stood at the far end of the approach to the exhibition ground. Two giant half-globes crowned the high central arch, painted with a map of the world on which the colonies and dominions of the British Empire were picked out in bright scarlet. Above the globes four clocks proclaimed the time in Ottawa, Cape Town, Calcutta and Sydney. Another huge clock was above them, showing Greenwich time, and above that, on the pinnacle of the roof, was Britannia with shield and trident, looking nobly towards the sea. Behind Britannia rows of pendants and flags streamed in the breeze.

'Wait until you see inside,' said Butler. 'It has to be seen to be believed. It's also warmer,' he added in a lower voice, and Charlotte was relieved. The morning frost was still on the ground, even though it was nearly midday. 'Butler showed his Exhibitor's Pass and they went inside to take their seats for the Opening Ceremony.

A glass roof arched above them and ahead lay a red-carpeted platform, a golden throne placed in the middle of it. To one side was a military band, tuning up. Various sounds from trumpets and tubas added to the buzz of noise as the guests milled around, waiting for ushers to show them to their seats. On the other side of the platform was a one-hundred-voice choir, already in position, the conductor deep in conversation with the military bandmaster. Butler had hoped he and Charlotte would get good seats near the front, but those rows were taken by hundreds of officials, all of them clad either in smart coats and bright chains of office or in neat uniforms with gleaming buttons. Opposite them were guests from the four corners of Empire – maharajahs, nawabs, kings, prime ministers and princes. Everywhere there were busy equerries – some in blue tunics, some in scarlet, all of them immaculate with gleaming medals and pristine gold braid. Butler and Charlotte found themselves seated almost at the back.

'Are you nervous?' asked Charlotte as they waited.

'A little,' nodded Butler. 'But we've spent a lot of time on our booth; wait till you see it.'

Charlotte squeezed his hand and there was a stirring of interest as a column of English beefeaters and Indian troops entered in precise formation to take up positions on either side of the entrance, forming a bodyguard for the Queen to pass. Officials hurried about, whispering and conferring, then, as if a sign had been given – though Butler saw nothing – there was sudden movement amongst the equerries, all the guests and officials rose and the troops stood to attention. A trumpet fanfare rang out and Victoria, by the Grace of God of the United Kingdom of Great Britain and Ireland, Queen, Defender of the Faith and Empress of India, entered the vast exhibition hall.

She was momentarily lost to sight as she passed a troop of tall Sikh cavalry, without their horses but holding the long, gleaming-pointed lances, then they saw her again as she stepped up onto the platform. She stood in front of the throne and the national anthem began.

'Isn't she small?' Charlotte couldn't help

383

whispering as they sat down at the end of the anthem, and Butler grinned at the impropriety of her comment.

The Queen took her seat upon the throne and a bearded man resplendent in uniform stepped forward and spoke.

'The Prince of Wales,' said Butler and Charlotte nodded. Butler had trouble seeing what was happening as the lady in front was wearing a hat that seemed to consist solely of large feathers. He craned his neck to watch the Prince.

At the conclusion of the opening address the Prince passed an ornate scroll to an aide on the platform, who in turn presented it to the Queen. She opened it and began speaking.

Seated so far back Butler and Charlotte couldn't hear what was being said, but they knew when the opening proclamation was concluded amidst a deafening cheer the Queen rose stepped forward and acknowledged the acclaim of the gathered assembly with a series of slow and very dignified curtsies.

The trumpets sounded again and the choir lifted their voices in a hymn of praise for the Empire, declaring it victorious over all its foes.

Then the singing was over and the Queen moving with difficulty and assisted by the Prince of Wales, came down from the platform. A score of officials and aides gathered around her and the procession set off to inspect the first of the exhibits.

'Come and see what we've done,' said Butler and they left the Opening celebrations and went through to the Indian Court. Exhibitors were fussing over their displays, making last-minute adjustments in case Her Majesty should process through.

'The India and Ceylon section takes up about a third of the whole exhibition,' explained Butler. 'I'll show you round it all later. Some of the exhibits are quite extraordinary.'

They reached the Tondip's Tea booth in the Teas and Coffees hall and Kent greeted them proudly.

'There it is,' he said beaming. 'What do you think?'

Charlotte caught her breath. 'It's marvellous,' and Butler agreed.

Tables at either side were covered in white lace tablecloths; an ornate silver tea-service was on one and on the other was a simple tea-service of the sort Charlotte remembered from the ABC shop at London Bridge. In attendance, pink with embarrassment but looking exceedingly proud, was Mrs Carey herself, her apron smartly starched.

'Hello, dear,' she greeted Charlotte. 'My, but I never expected this. Whatever next?'

'By agreement with the Aerated Bread Company,' Butler explained, 'Mrs Carey's going to be here every day.'

A large table occupied the centre of the booth and hundreds of packets of Tondip's Tea formed a multi-tiered display upon it. An arch garlanded with white and yellow flowers framed the display, and assistants in white aprons stood by. The rear wall of the booth was taken up with various paintings and sketches.

Charlotte stepped closer.

'That's... Tondipgiri, isn't it?' she said. 'I remember the hill.'

Butler grinned, pleased that she recognised it.

'I commissioned those specially,' he said, 'and I did a couple of the sketches myself. The others I described and supervised.'

'So that's what you've been up to so secretively for so long,' said Charlotte. 'It all looks wonderful.'

Butler nodded.

'We've worked hard for this,' he said. 'It should make all the difference when they come to choose which three companies are going to compete for the Royal Warrant. We've got packets for sale here and Tondip's is available in the Colonial dining room. Just through the arch over there there's a special tea-room area and Tondip's is on sale there too.'

A sudden buzz of excitement further down the Teas and Coffees hall made Butler turn. A flustered man hurried past.

'She's coming,' he was saying excitedly. 'She's coming.'

'So soon?' exclaimed Kent, surprised, but the man was gone.

'I didn't think she'd be visiting this section so early,' said Butler, and he checked the display.

'Where should I go when she arrives?' asked Charlotte nervously. Butler glanced along the exhibition hall.

'Stand here,' he said decisively and pulled her to one end of the display.

'But I can't,' protested Charlotte, horrified. 'I

don't know what to do.'

'You'll be fine,' said Butler, taking position at the other end of the table. 'There's nothing to worry about.'

Privately Charlotte disagreed, but she stood as straight and composed as she could manage. She looked down at her blue tailored dress and waisted jacket and wondered whether the fringing that decorated the skirt made her appearance too frivolous for meeting the Queen. She wished she was dressed in something rather more austere.

'Here they come,' hissed Butler, and everyone in the booth straightened.

The group of top-hatted officials and aides in scarlet and blue uniforms was making its way along the hall. Of the small lady they were accompanying there was no sign but she would be in the centre. At one point the procession paused to inspect one of the exhibits and Butler sweated as he waited – they seemed to be taking an age. Suddenly the procession was moving again and approaching. Butler heard one of the aides, a tall man with impressive side-whiskers, making a comment about 'Various teas, Your Majesty', then the grouping parted and a woman of less than average height was looking at them. She was nearly seventy, rather plump, but holding herself with great dignity, despite having to use a walking stick. Her dress was black, a royal blue sash ran from shoulder to hip and a jewelled coronet topped the lace mantilla that hung from her head to her shoulders. At her throat diamonds sparkled and she was wearing earrings that held the largest pearls Butler had ever seen.

Butler bowed deeply.

'Your Majesty,' he said, and from the corner of his eye he was aware of Kent bowing and Charlotte and Mrs Carey and the assistants curtsying. He straightened.

'Which of Our dominions does this tea come from?' the Queen asked her entourage, and the man with the whiskers opened his mouth to speak.

'This tea is from Ceylon, Your Majesty,' broke in Butler and the Queen stared at him.

'Do you work for one of Our companies?' she enquired.

'I own an estate there, Ma'am,' and impulsively he picked up one of the packets from the stand. 'May I offer this as a gift to Your Majesty?'

The whiskered man reddened and compressed his lips but said nothing as the Queen inclined her head. An aide hurriedly stepped forward and took the packet.

'How very kind,' said the Queen. 'Your name, sir?'

'John Butler, Your Majesty.'

'Thank you, Mr Butler.'

With a gracious smile the Queen nodded and moved on. Everyone on the Tondip's stand hastily bowed or curtsied again, and when Butler straightened it was to see the whiskered man standing in front of him, glaring with ill-concealed fury.

'You insolent young pup,' snarled the man in a low voice, his eyes like chips of ice. 'How dare you have the effrontery to address Her Majesty without invitation. Speak only when you're spoken to,' and he turned away and rejoined the procession.

For several seconds Butler made no movement, then realised that he was trembling and he let out his breath. Everyone on the stand chattered excitedly.

'Well, that seemed to go all right,' he said at last, when he had recovered himself. 'I think a cup of tea's in order, don't you?'

In the afternoon Charlotte accompanied Butler through the crowded exhibition halls.

Examples of art, trade and architecture from every country in the Empire were on display, with exhibitors in national costume in attendance. An entire section was given over to gallery after gallery of the latest furnishings and devices for the modern home, ranging from ventilation and sanitation to heating and lighting. There were sound-proof shutters, indestructible locks, and there was much curiosity about an intriguing construction advertised as being simultaneously a secure means of escape from fire and a ladies' resting room, and which, the maker claimed, could be 'adapted as an approach to light foot bridges or dangerous crossings'.

The cultural wealth of the colonies was displayed by means of ornamental gateways which led to pavilions devoted to individual countries and three-dimensional, life-sized depictions of wilderness and village scenes. Carved screens guided visitors through arches and bays decorated with sculptures and curios and there was barely an inch of wall space that wasn't covered with paintings or drapes.

The centrepiece of the India and Ceylon section was a reconstruction of an Indian palace, built from pine wood and carved all over with stylised flower and leaf designs. It housed a collection of fabulous silks and Charlotte sighed as she examined them, feeling them slide over her hands.

In the middle of the vast Central Court Butler pointed out the intricate piers and pillars of the exhibition building itself.

'Do you know,' he said to Charlotte, and his voice was heavy with emotion, 'it was two years ago tomorrow when I was told the bank had collapsed and they were calling in the loan. If anyone had told me I would be exhibiting Tondipgiri tea here, with the finest of everything surrounding it, I would have said they were mad.'

Charlotte stopped to look at one of the exhibits and Butler stared up at the vaulted roof.

'Incredible,' he said.

'John Butler?'

'Yes, that's right,' and Butler turned. The owner of the voice, a short man with sharp features, held out an envelope. Automatically Butler took it and the man turned away and was swallowed up in the crowd. Butler looked down at the envelope. It was plain and marked only with his name. He slit it open and took out the single sheet of paper from inside, then unfolded it and Charlotte turned from the exhibit she was admiring.

'John–'

He looked up and at his worried expression she put her hand on his arm.

'John? What is it?'

For a moment Butler didn't know what to say. He looked at the paper then at Charlotte.

'It's a Writ of Summons,' he said slowly. 'I'm being taken to Court.'

Part Six

1886–1887: THE FINAL BREW

'Tasting – the ultimate test.
Has the effort been worthwhile or
must the process begin again?'

One

Late autumn, 1886
Temple Court Chambers, London

They waited patiently, Butler, Charlotte and Kent, and Butler looked doubtfully at the scratched old desks in the cramped office. The solicitor, Mr Newbery, hastened to reassure him.

'All barristers' chambers are like this, Mr Butler, it's done quite deliberately. If the chambers were more opulent it might make clients wonder about the fees they have to pay. But Mr Gunn is a QC; he's one of the very best.'

Butler grunted, about to say something, but the door opened and the barrister's clerk stepped through.

'Would you come this way, please?'

The room they entered was exceptionally neat. Tall bookcases filled with thick bound volumes of Law Reports lined the walls and the shiny leather of the books suggested they saw frequent use. A long table was covered with stacks and rolls of documents, all precisely arranged, and Butler had no doubt that someone knew exactly where to lay his hands on any particular document he might want.

That someone was a very composed man in his mid-forties sitting behind a desk in front of which were two chairs, and he got up and held out his hand.

'Mr Butler?'

Butler nodded.

'How do you do, sir. I'm Robert Gunn.'

Butler made the introductions and added, 'I should mention that Miss Noble is Paget's stepdaughter.'

'Indeed?' said Gunn. 'That's very interesting,' and he pulled up two more chairs for Charlotte and Kent, then sat down.

'I'll come straight to the point, Mr Butler,' he said. 'I suspect this case is going to be rather painful, for you personally.'

'Why do you say that?'

Gunn leaned back and chose his words carefully. 'Mr Paget has retained one of the very ablest of advocates – a man named Henning Marshall; does that name mean anything to you?'

Butler shook his head.

'Henning Marshall,' said Gunn, 'never takes on a case unless he's supremely confident he can win it. And he usually does win. So I find it very puzzling that he's taken on this case.'

There were many documents spread out on the desk and Gunn tapped them.

'I've studied Mr Paget's Statement of Claim, your Defence, his Counterclaim and your Reply, and their case comes down to two things: there is only one witness – Mr Paget – and only one piece of evidence,' and Gunn held out the receipt that Paget had given when he sold his estate to Butler.

'What's wrong with the receipt?' asked Butler. 'He can't dispute its authority, surely?' Butler read the receipt and handed it back to Gunn. 'It seems perfectly straightforward to me.'

'On the contrary, Mr Butler,' said Gunn, 'this is the central plank of his case,' and he read the receipt out loud:

'"Received under duress from J. Butler the sum of £50,000". What do you interpret that to mean, Mr Butler?'

'Well, it meant Paget's estate was in a bad way. It wasn't running very well, he needed the money, so he had to sell. I was the one he sold it to.'

Gunn nodded. 'That isn't how Mr Paget's representing it to the Court though; he's claiming that you were the source of that duress.'

Butler looked blank and Gunn explained.

'He's claiming that he had to come back to England to look after his stepdaughter's interests and therefore needed to sell his estate. Inexplicably, he claims, no one wanted to buy it. He was getting desperate, he says, then you turned up and made an offer. By that time he couldn't delay leaving any longer and so he sold to you at a price that he claims was far below the real value of the estate.'

'I don't see any problem with that,' said Butler. 'I made an offer; he accepted it.'

'Mr Paget implies that the lack of any offer from the other planters was due to your influence with them. The duress he claims he was under was therefore directly attributable to you.'

'That's absolute nonsense,' said Butler heatedly. 'His estate was doing badly and he *had* to sell. He won't get far in Court if that's what he's claiming.'

'I quite agree,' said Gunn smoothly. '*If* that's all he's relying on – an alternative interpretation of five words on a sale receipt. But Henning Marshall doesn't take on cases where all he's got is one witness and the only evidence is an ambiguously worded note. And that's why I made the comment that this case may turn out to be painful for you, Mr Butler. Putting myself in Marshall's shoes, I would conclude that the way to win the case is to make the claim of duress more credible. The only way to do that is to make a personal attack on you and persuade the Court that you are exactly the sort of person who would do what Paget is claiming.'

'And the Judge will believe him?' asked Butler incredulously. 'Just because he says that?'

'It wouldn't be anything so simple as saying, "Mr Butler, I suggest you're a bad chap." You'd deny it and the Judge would ignore him. So Marshall will have to do a lot more than that; he'll have to convince the Court that you are of bad character. He'll try to introduce details of your past that he can use to attack your reputation. So I have to ask,' and Gunn leaned forward, 'is there anything, anything at all, which Henning Marshall could use to imply that you're dishonourable?'

'There's nothing,' said Butler indignantly.

Gunn wasn't put off. 'Their only piece of evidence is the wording on that paper and I can assure you they can't win with that alone. To make the Judge believe you're the type of person who would apply the duress referred to they'll have to find things in your past that support their claim. It's the only way they can use that paper to their advantage. So think very carefully, Mr Butler; somewhere in your past is something they think they can use against you.'

Gunn's eyes flickered to Charlotte and Kent. They were listening intently, and Gunn looked at Butler and his tone softened.

'Recalling the events of one's past can be difficult. Recollections can be painful. Would you prefer that we discussed this privately?'

'No!' Butler was adamant. 'I've done nothing I'm ashamed of.'

Gunn nodded. 'Good. In that case I must ask you some very frank questions.'

'Ask them,' said Butler tersely.

'Have you led an entirely pure life, Mr Butler?' Butler was silent and Gunn noted Butler's hesitation. 'Mr Butler?'

'I gambled a bit,' he admitted finally.

'A bit,' repeated Gunn. 'How much?'

'When I was younger – a *lot* younger – I used to bet on cards and horses,' said Butler.

'Where did you play cards? The homes of respectable people?'

'No,' said Butler, 'It was a club in town – in Manchester. But it's shut down now; I heard that the police raided it.'

Butler felt Newbery stiffen next to him and began to realise what Gunn was getting at.

'A gambling den now shut down by the police,' said Gunn heavily. 'It may be that they've traced someone who saw you there. Did anything happen at this club that could be used against you?'

Butler remembered the night he went there after reading his father's letter. 'I was–' and he looked for the right word, '"invited" to leave; I didn't have enough money to match the pot.'

'Or,' said Gunn, 'to put it as crudely as Marshall undoubtedly will, you were thrown out because you had lost all your money. Is that correct?'

Butler closed his eyes, breathed deeply, then opened them again.

'Yes,' he admitted, his voice low. He didn't dare look at Charlotte. Or Kent.

Gunn rose and went to the window. He stood for a moment, deep in thought, his hands behind his back, then returned to the desk and sat down. He shook his head.

'It can't be that,' he said. 'You wouldn't be the first man to lose money at cards but who then went on to make something of himself. There must be something else, something that can be turned to make you appear dishonest.'

'There's nothing.'

'Are you sure?'

'Of course I'm sure!' and now it was Butler's turn to stand and pace. 'There's nothing they could use!' and he turned to face Gunn. 'They're not going to get my estate, Mr Gunn. When I went to Tondipgiri I found it blighted with coffee disease; I pulled weeds and bushes out with my bare hands and I planted tea bushes. I built the place up and I found buyers in England for my tea. I bought Paget's land – fair and square – and I went through a storm at sea to save it all.'

He slammed his hand down on the desk.

'That's *my* estate,' he shouted. 'It belongs to me and I'm not going to lose it. By God, I'm not!'

Gunn was not at all put out by Butler's outburst.

'Would you like to sit down, Mr Butler?' he invited. Butler glared at him, then complied.

'I'm learning a great deal,' commented Gunn. 'A great deal that's positive. You have commendable resolve, Mr Butler, and that will be a great asset in the days and weeks to come. Your determination to turn a blighted estate into a profitable concern speaks volumes for your character and I'm sure we can impress the Judge with that. But I have also now learned that you have a vulnerability, a vulnerability that Henning Marshall will exploit with absolute ruthlessness if he finds it.'

'What vulnerability?'

'Your temper, Mr Butler. The prospect of a threat to Tondipgiri aroused great passion in you and you sprang to its defence. In itself, very commendable. But the moment you lose your temper in Court and become anything other than totally calm and self-possessed will be the moment that Marshall will prise you open and cut you to ribbons. I assure you, Mr Butler, I know what I'm talking about – I've seen him do it. He can be deceptively pleasant, but he is totally ruthless in pursuit of his client's case. If he can provoke you to a show of volatility he will pounce on it and suggest to the Court that you are hot-headed, reckless, liable to do anything in pursuit of your own interests. The sort of man, in short, who would think nothing of cheating

401

another man out of a fair price for an estate.'

There was a long silence.

'Thank you, Mr Gunn,' said Butler at last. 'I can see now why Mr Newbery recommended you so highly.'

Gunn tapped Paget's Statement of Claim. 'Mr Butler, what sort of man is Paget? What other dealings have you had with him?'

Butler was grim. 'In eighty-one I caught him stealing my tea to improve his own.'

'I can confirm that,' interjected Charlotte.

Gunn's eyes flashed to her. 'You, Miss Noble? How?'

'I was there that night. My stepfather admitted stealing Tondip's tea and adding it to his own. I heard him – and saw him.'

Gunn brightened. 'Well, that certainly puts a different complexion on the case. If you are prepared to give evidence, Miss Noble, it will much improve our chances of winning.'

'I'm prepared,' said Charlotte, but Butler wasn't having it.

'You can't go into the witness box, Charlotte,' he said.

Charlotte was taken aback. 'Why not?'

'You've heard what's been said; they're going to try and ruin my character. They're going to paint me blacker than black. Somehow. I don't want you going in the witness box and being tainted by association with me.'

'I'm doing it.'

'You're not.'

'You won't stop me, John. You did all those things for Tondipgiri, but you can't save it on

402

your own. Not now. This time you need some help,' and she set her chin stubbornly. 'I'm quite determined, John. You won't stop me,' and her gaze was steady.

They stared at one another, neither prepared to back down, and Gunn broke the impasse.

'Were there any other witnesses?'

Butler looked away from Charlotte's set and determined face and needed a moment to gather his thoughts.

'He had a native helping him.'

'Where is he now?'

'He's dead,' said Butler. 'He fell off a rope bridge.'

Gunn nodded. 'Please continue.'

'Paget fixed the finish of the race in order to bankrupt me into selling to him.'

'Witnesses?'

'The Captain of the steamer.'

'Who, of course, benefited from what Paget did,' commented Gunn drily. 'He's hardly likely to be sympathetic to our case. Even if we can find him.'

'Paget tried to buy Tondip's earlier this year,' said Butler, and told Gunn about Brand's visit to the office. 'When I discovered Paget was behind it all I told him then and there that I'd never sell my estate to him.'

'Again, witnesses?'

'Just Brand.'

Gunn made a note and Butler suddenly straightened.

'My God, Changarai! How could I have forgotten?' and he snatched up the receipt.

'I beg your pardon?' asked Gunn.

'My foreman,' explained Butler excitedly. 'Look – that's his signature. And he used to work for Paget. He knows what sort of a brute he is – when I first met Paget he beat hell out of Changarai with a riding crop. He can give evidence for us.'

'And his character?'

'A good man,' said Butler stoutly. 'He runs my estate. I rely on him totally.'

Gunn nodded. 'Then I suggest you send him a telegram and tell him to get on the next boat to England. This case is already in the List but I think an adjournment for witnesses would pose no problem.'

Gunn put down his pen. He was sombre.

'If Paget wins this case – and I need hardly say, Mr Butler, that we will fight very, very hard against that possibility – he will first ask the Judge for a Writ of Possession on the one thousand acres he sold to you. In effect that means the Court takes the land from you and gives it to him. In addition he will also be asking the Judge to award a sum which reflects the revenue you have obtained from that land over the years and which, by implication, would have been his if he hadn't sold the land to you. He claims that as the land you bought from him now represents ten-elevenths of the new Tondipgiri estate he should, therefore, be entitled to ten-elevenths of the revenue derived.'

'Never!' exploded Butler, and his chair crashed onto the floor as he leaped up. 'Never, as long as I'm alive.'

There was silence. Charlotte and Kent were stunned by the force of Butler's reaction. Newbery said nothing and Gunn just looked at Butler mildly.

Butler realised his temper had got the better of him once more and he picked his chair up and sat down.

'I'm sorry,' he said after a moment. 'That won't happen again.'

The advocate went on as if nothing had happened.

'I doubt he'll get quite as much as he's asking,' said Gunn. 'But the Judge would certainly look to award him something in consideration of those revenues. Hence this supplement to his claim: Paget says he recognises that you would only be able to raise such large sums if you were to sell some of your Tondip's Tea business here in England – buildings, warehouses, other assets; so instead, he says, he is prepared to take the remaining one hundred acres of Tondipgiri in respect of his lost profits.'

'That means he'd get everything,' said Butler, horrified. 'It would be the end of Tondip's Tea if the estate goes; the estate is the heart of it all,' and he gripped the edge of Gunn's desk. 'That swine's not going to win; he's not going to get his hands on it. He's not going to win this case.'

'Mr Butler,' said Gunn carefully, 'I would be failing in my duty as an advocate if I didn't advise you to prepare for the possibility that you may lose Tondipgiri.'

Butler was stunned. 'In spite of everything?'

'In my judgement,' continued Gunn, 'this case

is going to prove to be very finely balanced. The steamer Captain and this fellow Brand are witnesses to what Paget's been doing, but if he's as unscrupulous as you suggest he's probably paid them to disappear. We will be pitting the evidence of Miss Noble and your foreman, Mr Changarai, against the alternative interpretation of the wording of the note, plus whatever it is about your character, your past, that's making them so confident they can win. The Judge is yet another factor.'

'But Judges are impartial aren't they?' asked Kent.

'In principle, of course,' said Gunn. 'But they all have their own view of the world, Mr Kent, their own varied experience of people. They have their own standards. And their own prejudices. We might get a judge whose view of the case is coloured by the character of the people involved. If Marshall successfully portrays Paget as a decent, wronged man and you, Mr Butler, as a hot-tempered fellow with a shady past...' Gunn let his words hang in the air. 'Well, you understand what I mean, don't you?'

Butler nodded. He understood only too well.

Outside Gunn's chambers Newbery took his leave and hurried away, leaving Butler, Kent and Charlotte looking at one another. Conversation was awkward.

'How's the Exhibition progressing?' asked Butler at last, trying to lighten the atmosphere, and Kent seemed relieved to have something else to talk about.

406

'It's going well, really well. There's a lot of interest in Tondip's.'

Butler nodded and there was silence again.

'I'd better get back there,' said Kent. 'Just to check on everything.'

'Thank you, Richard.'

They shook hands and Kent nodded and smiled, not knowing what to say, then nodded again and left them.

Charlotte looked at Butler with concern.

'John?'

'Mm?' Butler looked at her, torn from his thoughts. 'Sorry, I was thinking.'

'Let's walk,' she suggested, and took his arm. They took the path to the Embankment and Butler cast a gloomy glance at the Royal Courts of Justice – where the case was to be heard – as they passed. They reached the river and watched the boats for a few minutes then Charlotte ventured a comment.

'He seems a good man.'

Butler turned. 'Who? Richard?'

Charlotte smiled. 'Of course Richard's good; but no, I meant Robert Gunn. I think the case is in good hands, don't you?'

Butler nodded. 'He's very frank. Painfully so. But I suppose that's best; no point having a barrister who makes you believe everything's going to be all right and then it all falls down about you,' and he shook his head.

A gust of wind blew leaves around them and they walked on. Charlotte was silent, sensing that Butler wanted to say something else.

He cleared his throat.

'When I got started I took my very first tea to merchants in Colombo. I thought they would fall over themselves to buy it but they weren't interested. So I brought it to England and eventually I struck lucky – I found someone who believed in it as much I do. Then there was that business with the race. Right there on the quayside I thought I had lost everything; I thought I was bankrupt and there'd be no more Tondipgiri. But I was lucky again – we met Richard and Sir Henry Pickering and the tea shops were a success. So that's twice I've been lucky. Perhaps that's more luck than any man has a right to expect. And now this case – I don't know if I can be lucky a third time.'

'It wasn't luck,' said Charlotte indignantly. 'It was all due to your hard work. It was you who found a buyer, it was you who had the vision for the tea shops. It was you who persuaded Sir Henry. None of it could have happened if it hadn't been for you and everything you did.'

Butler brightened up a little. 'Thank you, that makes me feel better,' and he looked at her in mock suspicion.

'And when did you decide to be a witness?'

'As soon as you told me the summons was from my stepfather,' Charlotte said sweetly.

'You've known all that time?'

Charlotte nodded. 'And Mr Gunn thinks it's a good idea.'

Butter nodded. 'I suppose so,' he admitted ruefully. 'Thank you,' he added with genuine feeling, and Charlotte squeezed his arm.

Two

Monday 9th January, 1887
The Royal Courts of Justice

It's a surprise to all of us, Mr Butler,' Newbery was saying. 'Mr Gunn fully expected the case to be adjourned to February, or even March. I must say, I've never known such a short adjournment to be ordered.'

Butler shuffled restlessly. He looked up at the gallery and Kent gave an encouraging nod.

'Have you heard anything from Mr Changarai?' asked Newbery.

Butler turned. 'Nothing,' he said tersely. 'The lines to India and the Far East have been out of order for the last two weeks. They can't send and they can't receive. Anyway, what about that banker fellow, Dunlop? Any news?'

'Untraceable at the moment,' said Newbery. 'Gunn's going to ask for another adjournment to give us more time to find him.'

'What if the Judge doesn't grant it?'

Newbery looked worried. 'In that case Miss Noble is our only other witness. Is she calm?'

'Commendably so,' said Butler. 'She's waiting outside the court. She'll do well.'

He shifted his weight from one foot to the other then shifted it back again. He thrust his hands in his pockets and took stock of his surroundings.

From above halfway up, the walls were dull cream-coloured plaster either side of tall windows, but below them the wall panels and everything else were of dark oak, from the expertly worked Royal Crest above the Judge's bench, flanked with carved wooden pillars, to the Judge's bench itself and the Registrar's desk below that, then across the worn red flooring to the solicitor's benches and the barrister's benches behind them. On each bench seat were long, green leather cushions, cracked and shiny, their stuffing flattened.

Butler hunched his shoulders. The room was cold and he glanced up at the windows, rimed outside with frost.

Looking around the courtroom took him back to his law student days. He had barely begun his pupillage as a barrister before the infamous Rainford Lodge incident had taken place. An uncomfortable interview with the stony-faced head of his chambers had followed shortly after and that was the end of his law career. There had been little opportunity to learn from other barristers what he had used to dismiss as the 'tricks of the trade'.

He looked across at the witness box, placed to the left of the Judge's bench. He'd be in there soon enough and for a moment he wished he had paid more attention to his studies. At least that way he would have been better prepared for whatever Henning Marshall had in store for him.

'Our opponents are here,' said Newbery quietly and Butler looked round. Paget and two other men had entered the court. Paget glanced at

Butler and turned away disdainfully.

'Who are the others?' asked Butler.

'Paget's solicitor and Marshall's junior. And that's Marshall,' added Newbery as a stone-faced barrister entered, his silk robe billowing around him. The man's face had all the warmth of a chisel and when he looked at Butler his eyes reminded Butler of pebbles on a winter beach. He weighed Butler up, dismissed him in a single glance and started a discussion with Paget.

'Here's our chap,' said Newbery, relieved, as Gunn entered.

Gunn exchanged a nod with Marshall and crossed the courtroom. 'Good morning, Mr Butler. Are we ready?'

Butler nodded.

'Who's the Judge?' asked Newbery.

'The Lion,' stated Gunn flatly and Newbery muttered something to himself.

'Who?' asked Butler.

'Mr Justice Lyon,' explained Gunn. 'He has his good points but I could have wished for someone else.'

'The telegraph to the Far East still isn't working,' said Newbery. 'We don't know whether Mr Changarai is on his way or not.'

Gunn frowned.

'I was going to ask for an adjournment in any event,' he said heavily, 'but now it's even more important that we get one.'

The Registrar entered and everyone hurried to take their places. A door opened in the panelling by the Judge's bench and the Judge entered in scarlet robe and long-sided wig. He took his seat

411

under the Royal Crest and bowed to the Court. The advocates bowed in return, and the Judge sat down and immediately leaned forward to speak to the Registrar.

There was something about the Judge that seemed vaguely familiar to Butler – he was sure he had seen him somewhere before. Then Mr Justice Lyon straightened, the long sides of his wig bent and unfolded and Butler felt sick. He now knew exactly where it was that he had seen those impressive side whiskers.

He sat, frozen, as the Judge gave a cursory glance at the assembled Court and momentarily their eyes locked, then the Judge bent his head to study the bundle of documents before him. The Judge's face had been expressionless but Butler was certain that Mr Justice Lyon remembered him: the 'insolent young pup' at the Exhibition who, in the Judge's presence, had presumed to address Her Majesty without invitation.

Three

Butler stared at the surface of the desk in front of him and felt his stomach dropping away inside.

He straightened. No, dammit, this battle wasn't over yet. Win or lose, by the end of this case Paget was well and truly going to know he had been in a fight.

Butler's attention returned to the courtroom; Gunn was on his feet addressing the Judge.

'My Lord, this case has all its origins in Ceylon; the events in question happened there, the note of sale was written and signed there, the remedy that the Plaintiff seeks if he should win is there. In my respectful submission, I ask that the Court direct that these proceedings be transferred for disposition to the Court in Ceylon.'

'Thank you, Mr Gunn,' said the Judge briskly. 'Your concern for the disposal of this case is most commendable but, ultimately, unnecessary. I would remind you of My Lord Mansfield's Proposition Five in Campbell and Hall – when a territory becomes a colony it becomes subject to the laws applicable to colonies, when it becomes a British Possession it becomes subject to the laws applicable to British Possessions, when its inhabitants therefore become British subjects they become subject to the laws applicable to British subjects. In short, Mr Gunn, it is quite in order for this Court to hear a case regarding property located in Ceylon. Now, let us proceed. Mr Marshall?'

'My Lord,' persisted Gunn. 'There is another important matter I must bring to Your Lordship's attention. Several weeks ago those who instruct me sent a telegram to Ceylon requiring the attendance at Court of a witness whose evidence is absolutely vital to this case. He has not yet arrived in this country and I wish to take this opportunity to apply for an adjournment to give the witness time to arrive.'

'And I wish to take this opportunity to inform you, Mr Gunn, that I will not countenance any more adjournments to this case. It has been in the List for some considerable time; there has been ample opportunity for witnesses to be notified. I will hear you no further on this point Now, once more, let us proceed. Mr Marshall?'

Gunn sat down and Henning Marshall rose to open the case for Paget. As he did so Paget shot a triumphant glance at Butler and Butler pretended not to notice. His worst fears were realised – the Judge was against them. There could be no doubt. There could be no clearer indication.

'My Lord, may it please the Court,' began Marshall. 'The facts of the case are these. Mr Paget, a former officer in the Seventh Dragoon Guards, was, until the year eighteen eighty-two, the owner of a one-thousand-acre tea plantation in Ceylon. His plantation was prosperous and Mr Paget was highly regarded as an outstanding businessman. His teas were sold in this country with great success.'

Butler prevented himself making an exclamation. What Marshall was saying was absolute nonsense. He might have been describing someone else entirely, rather than that pig, Paget. Outstanding businessman? Butler recalled the day he had taken over Paget's estate and the horror with which Taylor and Thwaites had examined the fading tea bushes. As for the 'great success' of Paget's teas... Butler was determined to correct that lie when it was his own turn in the witness box.

Marshall was still addressing the Court.

'A matter came to the Plaintiff's attention which caused him much concern: his step-

414

daughter, Miss Charlotte Noble, a young and impressionable girl living here in England, was becoming a subject of interest to young men. Conscious of the impracticality of protecting her welfare in England whilst himself being resident in Ceylon, the Plaintiff concluded that he had only one option – namely, to sell his estate and return home. Accordingly, he announced that he was looking for a buyer for his estate.'

At this point Marshall looked down at the papers on the desk in front of him as if to check something, but Butler felt sure this was just for show. Marshall was far too fluent and relaxed in his presentation of the case to be in need of any reminders from his notes.

'Mr Paget had previously enjoyed entirely cordial relations with his fellow planters. He therefore found it completely inexplicable when they shunned him and, despite them being ambitious men, eager to progress, not one advanced an offer for his estate. Mr Paget could find no explanation for this. He grew concerned. Unless he could sell his estate he would be without the funds he would need to enable him to return home and provide protection, guidance and support to his stepdaughter. It was at this point that the Respondent, Mr John Butler, entered the picture. This man, the Plaintiff understood, had experienced some success as a tea planter. He had obtained the friendship of other planters and appeared to exercise a disproportionate influence on their deliberations. Mr Paget didn't trust him though. He suspected the Respondent of having made advances to Miss Noble on the occasion of her visit to the Plaintiff the previous year.

'The Respondent approached Mr Paget and made an offer for the estate. It was substantiall below what Mr Paget knew the estate to be wortl and, unsurprisingly, the offer was rejected. How ever, Mr Paget was unable to find anyone els interested. The other planters, all friends of th Respondent, continued to decline to make an kind of offer. The Plaintiff had no doubt that th Respondent had subtly imposed his will on thos potential buyers, but by now Mr Paget had n other alternative than to sell to the Respondent

Marshall paused for a sip of water from th glass on the desk and Butler shifted restlessly Judge Lyon fixed his eyes on him for a moment then returned to Marshall.

'Mr Paget returned to England. He expended considerable effort and considerable resources t protect his stepdaughter's interests and, ver reluctantly, concluded that it would be impracti cable to begin an action against the Respondent given that the Respondent was in Ceylon and M Paget was in England. The Plaintiff concluded that he had no alternative but to put the whol thing down to experience – bitter experience That, he supposed, was the end of his dealing with Mr Butler. Two years later though he wa startled when Mr Butler arrived in England or board a ship engaged in a "tea-race",' and Marshall gave a small smile. 'You may remembe the episode, My Lord,' and there was a murmu of amusement, quickly stifled, in the court.

The Judge said nothing and Marshall con tinued.

'The Plaintiff's memories of his dealings with Mr Butler were understandably painful and Mr Paget, by now a senior official in the firm of Wilkinson's Teas, made no approach to Mr Butler, save to make an offer at auction for the cargo of tea that the Respondent had brought from Ceylon.'

At this point Marshall glanced over at Butler.

'The Respondent's conduct at the auction gave the Plaintiff further cause to suspect that the Respondent harbours some secret enmity towards him. Mr Paget made the highest bid, but Mr Butler abruptly jumped up and declared that his tea wasn't for sale, thereby depriving the Plaintiff of the chance to make a perfectly open, genuine, honest purchase of tea.'

Marshall held the lapel of his robe with one hand and gestured to Paget with the other.

'The Plaintiff, My Lord, is an intelligent businessman. He recognised that the tea Mr Butler was now producing was of high quality; not surprising given that he was growing it on the Plaintiff's former estate and, not unnaturally, the Plaintiff wished to recover that which he felt had been unfairly bought from him. Mr Paget, however, is above all a practical and sensible man. The Respondent seemed to harbour strong antagonism towards him and would be sure to reject out of hand any offer the Plaintiff might make. Accordingly the Plaintiff, now promoted to the position of General Manager of the Great Eastern Tea Company, resolved to make an offer for the Tondip's Tea Company, as Mr Butler's company was now known, through the agency of a discreet intermediary. For the Company, the estate in Ceylon, all the Company's assets and liabilities the Plaintiff offered the considerable sum of five hundred thousand pounds.'

There was a murmur in Court and all eyes turned to Butler. Butler looked rigidly ahead and Henning Marshall continued.

'Mr Butler, with little ceremony or civility, rejected the offer. The intermediary returned to make his report and Mr Butler trailed him through the streets to Mr Paget's office, where he was abusive and swore that the Plaintiff would never get the land back. After long and careful deliberation Mr Paget resolved to take legal advice and, reluctantly, he brings the action that is now before this Court.

'My Lord, the Plaintiff seeks a Writ of Possession ordering the return of those one thousand acres. Additionally, he seeks an order directing the paying-over of monies that Mr Butler has derived from those acres whilst he has been in possession of them. But Mr Paget is not an unreasonable man. He recognises that those monies represent a considerable sum and that for the Respondent to make that payment in cash would necessitate the sale of many of the Tondip's Tea Company assets. The Plaintiff has no wish to deprive Mr Butler of that which has been built up by honest effort and so is prepared to accept as full payment, instead of cash, the adjacent one hundred acres of the Respondent's estate in Ceylon.'

Marshall paused.

'My Lord, that is the Plaintiff's case.'

Butler shook his head. This was worse – much worse – than he had ever expected it to be. Marshall had only got as far as completing his opening speech and already Paget was the wronged man and Butler a sly and dishonest rogue; he had even managed to infer that Butler had dishonourable designs on Charlotte Noble. He understood now what Gunn had meant when he said Marshall was sharp, but the man was far worse than that – he was lethal.

Four

'Mr Paget, why did you sell your estate?'

Paget sighed at Marshall's question and spoke slowly, the considered words of a man seeking to be open and honest and helpful to the Court.

'I had to sell because I realised that I couldn't give my stepdaughter the protection and support she needed if I was living in Ceylon. I could have employed a lady's companion for her, but there are times in a young woman's life when only the presence of a father – or, in my case, a stepfather – will do. This was one of those times.'

'And why did you sell your estate to the Respondent, John Butler?'

'It was never my intention to sell to him,' said Paget. 'I had formed an unfavourable impression of him ever since he paid court to my step-daughter when she came out to Ceylon for a visit in eighty-one. When I made the decision to sell I

419

first went to the Planters' Club; that's a club where most of the planters and estate owners go. I explained the circumstances, my reasons for selling, and I offered my estate for sale but no one was interested; I couldn't understand it.'

Paget paused.

'John Butler was there at the time.'

Marshall gave a small nod and there was a moment's silence in the courtroom. A very skilful operator, this Marshall; by punctuating Paget's words with small reactions – pauses, nods of the head – he was turning a straightforward statement of fact into hints of something suspicious, a suggestion of some dark motive or purpose on Butler's part.

'What happened next?' prompted Marshall.

'I was worried. Who wouldn't be? I needed to sell my estate and return to England as soon as possible. I went back to the Planters' Club at one point to see if I could drum up some interest but the place was empty. Except for him. It was as if he was waiting for me.'

'"He" being?'

'John Butler.'

'What happened then?'

'He made me an offer for my estate. I rejected it; it was much lower than the estate was worth. I told him so. He said "You won't get any other offers."'

More damned lies! Butler gripped the seat to stop himself jumping up and wished he had the control of Gunn, who was sitting quietly making notes. Every instinct in Butler screamed out to denounce Paget for the base liar he was, but such

420

an outburst would play right into Marshall's hands.

To hell with it!

'That is an absolute lie,' he stated as he stood. 'There isn't a single word of truth in anything he says.'

Butler felt Newbery's hand pulling at his sleeve but he ignored it.

'Mr Butler,' and Judge Lyon's voice was like cold gravel. 'Sit down, sir. I will not tolerate such outbursts in this Court,' and he glared at Butler until Butler sat down.

'Continue, Mr Marshall.'

'Thank you, My Lord. Mr Paget, you said the Respondent's words were "You won't get any other offers."'

'Yes,' said Paget, 'and it turned out he was right. There were no other offers, just as he said, not even an enquiry. I was very worried.'

'Then what happened?'

'I had no choice. I needed to sell, needed to get back to England. So I agreed to sell to him. He came to my house accompanied by an illiterate native and had the Bill of Sale with him.'

'The Bill of Sale, My Lord, is document number one in the first bundle,' interjected Marshall, and the Judge nodded. The document was passed up and the Judge inspected it.

'The general wording of the note is not an issue between the parties, My Lord; I think my learned friend, Mr Gunn, will confirm that?' and Gunn rose, nodded and sat.

'The point of disagreement concerns the interpretation of the words that Mr Paget appended with his signature: "Received under duress from J. Butler."'

Judge Lyon nodded. 'Continue, Mr Marshall.'

Marshall turned to Paget.

'Mr Paget?'

'I didn't want to sell,' said Paget. 'The price was much less than I needed. I knew that when I returned to England I would need funds to re-establish myself, to provide for a household, to ensure that my stepdaughter had all the clothing and other things that a young woman needs, to provide for trips for her education and development; I wasn't happy about the price at all. But I had no choice. So I signed.'

'Would you explain to the Court why you chose to sign the note with that particular form of words?'

Paget took a breath, the very picture of a wronged man having to recall the painful memory of a profound injustice.

'I had no doubt – no doubt at all – that I was being manoeuvred into selling to John Butler. It was entirely out of character for all those other planters – ambitious men, interested in building up their estates – to make no offers, nor even make any enquiries, nothing. And then the only offer was his. It was ridiculously low, he knew I *had* to sell and he was so smug I knew at once that he was behind it all; he had orchestrated matters so that I was compelled to sell to him. But what could I do? I signed the note, but I wanted him to always remember that he had obtained the estate dishonestly. So I signed that I had received his money but only due to the

422

duress he had put me under.'

'And then?' prompted Marshall in the silence.

'I came back to England. I thought that was the last I would see of John Butler. I knew I couldn't begin a Court case against him; he was in Ceylon and I was in England. Besides, I had my stepdaughter's welfare to think of. So, reluctantly, I concluded that I would just have to accept matters the way they were. I began to establish myself in England and it was a great honour when I was asked to preside at the reception committee for the two ships in the tea-race. When they arrived I was completely taken aback – there he was on the clipper. As President of the committee I was aware of course that someone called Butler was owner of one of the cargoes but I never dreamt it was *him*. Seeing him there was like ... some kind of nightmare. After that I thought about things for a few days. I'm not vindictive, I knew how good his tea had become since he had added my estate to his, and as a senior manager with Wilkinson's I had a responsibility to make purchases of good teas. So at the auction I made an offer. I was the only one left in the bidding – and he knew it – when he jumped up and declared "No Sale". It was most strange.

'Over the next few months I gave the matter a lot of consideration and decided to make an attempt to recover the estate. Clearly, he has some secret hatred of me and would never deal with me personally, so I employed an intermediary. Butler rejected the offer and told me I'd never get my estate back. I felt I had no other option but to bring this case.'

'Thank you, Mr Paget,' said Marshall, glanced at Gunn and sat down.

Gunn stood up and Butler prayed that he could undo some of the damage of Paget's 'evidence'.

'Mr Paget, you said that Mr Butler was present when you first went to the Planters' Club to sell your estate.'

Paget nodded. 'That's right.'

'He had a perfect right to be there, didn't he?'

Paget shrugged. 'It was strange though.'

'Mr Butler was an estate owner – a planter – so, I ask you again, he had a perfect right to be there didn't he?'

Paget hesitated for a moment.

'I suppose so,' he conceded.

'In fact, you had seen Mr Butler in the Planters' Club on several occasions previously, hadn't you?'

'He had been there once or twice.'

'And on the second occasion you visited the Club: again, Mr Butler had a perfect right to be there, didn't he?'

'If you say so.'

Gunn's tone sharpened. 'Mr Paget, this case will proceed a lot more smoothly for everybody if you don't waste the Court's time with prevarication. I ask you again: Mr Butler had every right to be there, didn't he?'

'Yes,' admitted Paget, but he didn't look happy about making the admission.

'Had you told anyone you were going to the Planters' Club on that second occasion?'

'No.'

'So Mr Butler didn't know you were going there. He could hardly have been "waiting for you", as you put it, could he?'

Paget glared at Butler.

'Mr Paget? Answer the question please.'

'Put like that I suppose I would have to agree.'

'Thank you. Did you ever witness any conversations between Mr Butler and other planters in which Mr Butler discussed the sale of your estate?'

'Well, he'd hardly let me see that, would he?'

'You mean you did not witness any such conversations?'

'No, he was too clever for that.'

'So you have no evidence that he conspired with them to prevent them buying your estate?'

'My Lord.' Marshall jumped to his feet. 'At no point has it been alleged that Mr Butler "conspired" with the other planters; the Plaintiff has suggested nothing more than that the absence of offers from those other planters seemed strange to him.'

'A rather fine distinction, Mr Marshall, but I will allow it.'

'Thank you, My Lord,' and Marshall sat.

'I suggest you rephrase your question, Mr Gunn.'

'My Lord,' and Gunn bowed his head. 'Mr Paget, those other planters listened to what you had to say, decided it wasn't good enough and they chose not to make an offer, isn't that the case?'

'My Lord,' interjected Marshall with an air of tiredness. 'I must protest. It is hardly possible for

425

Mr Paget to comment upon what was or was not in the minds of other planters.'

'I agree,' said Judge Lyon. 'Mr Gunn, if you wish to continue with this line of questioning I suggest you do it with the greatest circumspection.'

'Thank you, My Lord,' said Gunn, and moved on to a different subject.

'At the auction, Mr Paget, Mr Butler had a perfect right to withdraw his tea from sale if he wished, didn't he?'

'It was very strange though,' began Paget, but Gunn was having none of it.

'Mr Paget, I asked you a question. I am not asking you to comment upon it. It is the case, is it not, that Mr Butler had a perfect right to withdraw his tea from sale if he so wished?'

Paget breathed heavily.

'Yes,' he said, and Gunn moved to his next point of attack.

'You sent an intermediary to present your offer to Mr Butler,' he commented. 'Why did you do that?'

'Well, I knew Butler wouldn't deal with me directly. He harbours some hatred of me and–'

'Mr Paget, it is your contention that Mr Butler obtained this land by dishonest means; in your view he has something that is rightfully yours. Is it the act of a man who believes his property has been as good as stolen from him to employ an intermediary to *buy* it back for him?'

Butler cheered inside.

'I didn't see what else I could do,' began Paget, but Gunn drove on relentlessly.

'If Mr Butler had chosen to accept the offer he would eventually have had dealings with *you*, wouldn't he? You were the principal behind the offer, weren't you?'

'I might have had to deal with him—'

'*Might?* Mr Paget, you were the one making the offer, you were the one seeking to negotiate this purchase. That offer was a sham, wasn't it?'

'No, it was not!' responded Paget heatedly. 'It was a genuine offer.'

'It was a ploy, wasn't it, Mr Paget? A ploy that you knew John Butler would reject and which you could then adduce as supposed "evidence" of his enmity towards you?'

'Mr Gunn,' interrupted the Judge.

'You've been planning this case for a long time haven't you, Mr Paget?'

'*Mr Gunn!*'

'You're trying to recover that land because you've seen John Butler make something of it where *you* couldn't, isn't that true?'

'MR GUNN!' thundered the Judge, and Gunn ceased the attack.

Judge Lyon breathed heavily. 'Mr Gunn, this case has been brought for the Court's consideration and it will be the facts that will be considered, not speculation about the motives of the Plaintiff in bringing the action. Is that clear?'

'My Lord,' said Gunn respectfully, with that small bow of the head. 'I have no further questions of the Plaintiff,' and he sat down.

'My Lord, I have no questions in re-examination,' said Marshall. 'That concludes the case for the Plaintiff.'

'Commendable restraint on your part, Mr Marshall,' commented Judge Lyon. 'The Court will recess for lunch until two o'clock and I will see Counsel for both parties in my chambers immediately.'

He rose and there was a rustle of gowns and papers as the barristers got to their feet. The Judge gave the smallest of nods to the Court, glanced stonily at Butler, then swept out.

Gunn crossed to Butler. 'I'll need to speak to you before we begin again this afternoon. I'll see you outside the courtroom at half-past one,' and Gunn left.

Butler let out his breath and turned to Newbery. 'That Marshall fellow's damned sharp. What do you think the Judge wants to see them about?'

'I suspect it's to tell them he wants more decorum in the conduct of the case,' said Newbery. 'Judge Lyon's very ponderous. Nothing wrong with his mind,' he added hastily, 'but he's a stickler for correct behaviour.'

'Will it have damaged the case?' asked Butler.

'I don't think so,' said Newbery. 'But I don't think it'll have made matters any easier for us.'

Butler didn't know what to say to that. He looked round at the now empty courtroom.

'I'll see you after lunch,' he said and Newbery nodded.

Five

Butler, Charlotte and Kent sat in one of the new tea-rooms of the Aerated Bread Company, but none of them were very hungry.

'What's going to happen this afternoon?' asked Charlotte.

'I don't know,' said Butler. 'Perhaps that's what Gunn wants to talk to me about. Marshall finished his case this morning so it's time for us to put ours. How do you feel about going in that witness box?'

'I'm all right,' said Charlotte. 'I'm a bit nervous but I'm going to do it.'

'Marshall's a nasty piece of work,' said Kent. 'I can see why Paget wanted him on the case,' and Butler agreed.

When they got back Gunn was waiting outside the courtroom.

'I don't suppose there's any news about Mr Changarai?' he asked.

'Nothing,' said Butler.

'I'll go to the telegraph office,' said Kent. 'They might have some idea when the lines will be working again.'

'I suggest you make haste,' said Gunn. 'I'll draw the case out as long as possible but there's a limit to how far we can go with this Judge.'

Kent nodded and hurried away.

'What happened after this morning's session?' asked Butler. 'Why did the Judge call the two of you to see him?'

'It was nothing more than I expected,' said Gunn dismissively. 'He gave us a lecture about conduct in his Court. He's a bit stuck in his ways, thinks everything should be respectful give-and-take. It's been a while since he was involved in the cut-and-thrust of advocacy work.'

'Is he against us?'

'He's neither for nor against anybody,' said Gunn. 'But there's no need to antagonise him unnecessarily. This morning was all right though – it was early in the case and I could see Paget wasn't happy so I laid it on a bit. We got some useful admissions out of him. Our problem now is that Marshall's probably going to try something similar with you this afternoon. I'll take you through your evidence and then Marshall will cross-examine you. He'll try and provoke you to make some heated response, but don't fall for it; he'll be onto you in a second. Stay calm, answer his questions and keep your wits about you.'

'Mr Butler,' said Gunn. 'Several times this morning the Plaintiff suggested that you harbour some secret enmity towards him. Is this true?'

Butler chose his words carefully.

'I would say I have a low opinion of him.'

'And why is that?'

'There are several reasons,' said Butler. 'The first time I met him he was beating a native. I stopped him. The second time I had dealings with him was in eighty-one; I was in England, my

430

tea was selling well but then sales began to fall off. I went out to Ceylon and found that poor-quality leaves were being mixed in with my tea. I discovered that Mr Paget was taking tea from my store and adding it to his own, then adding poor leaves to my tea to make up the weight.'

Out of the corner of his eye Butler saw Paget leaning over to his solicitor, who in turn leaned over to Marshall. Butler concentrated on giving his evidence; whatever they were cooking up he'd find out about it soon enough.

'The third occasion was when I arrived home at the end of the tea-race. We were the first to get a line ashore and tie up. I saw him whisper something to the Captain of the other ship and a few minutes later Mr Paget declared that tea-races were traditionally won by getting cargo ashore. At that point the rival ship landed some cargo, so they won the race. I believe that the whispered comment he made to the Captain was an advance instruction to unload his cargo; he was giving the other ship an unfair advantage over mine. The fourth occasion was when he sent his intermediary to buy my company. I gave the offer genuine consideration but decided against it. I admit I wondered if Mr Paget was behind the offer so I followed the intermediary to see who had sent him. He went to the offices of the Great Eastern Tea Company, and that made me think it wasn't Paget who had sent him after all. I thought Paget still worked for Wilkinson's Teas, you see. I was still curious though and I followed the man inside. I found him with Paget. I told Paget I would never sell to him and he said I would change my mind one day. I left.'

'The Bill of Sale that Mr Paget signed,' said Gunn. 'What is your interpretation of his words "Received under duress from J. Butler"?'

'It means he was forced to sell because his estate was declining. It had been declining ever since I stopped him adding my tea to his own.'

'Mr Butler, did you cheat the Plaintiff out of a fair and proper price for his estate?'

'Absolutely not. I made a good offer and he accepted it.'

'Thank you, Mr Butler.'

Gunn sat down and after a moment Marshall got to his feet. He made a show of searching his notes as if hunting some errant fact, then suddenly looked up.

'You hate Mr Paget, don't you?'

'No,' said Butler. 'As I said, I just have a low opinion of him.'

Marshall grunted. 'You claim you saw Mr Paget beating a native; were there any witnesses to that?'

'None that I'm aware of,' said Butler. 'Only the native himself – a man called Changarai. He's now my foreman and he's one of my witnesses.'

'Is this man in the building?' asked Judge Lyon.

Gunn stood. 'Not yet, My Lord. Mr Changarai is the witness for whose attendance I sought an adjournment. His evidence is crucial to my client's case.'

'Then you'll just have to do the best you can without him, Mr Gunn. There will be no more adjournments. Proceed, Mr Marshall.'

This was ridiculous, thought Butler. The Judge

might indeed be as impartial as Gunn claimed but he was being damned awkward. He–

'Mr Butler?'

He realised Marshall was talking to him. 'I'm sorry?'

Marshall made a show of long-suffering patience.

'I'll ask you again, Mr Butler: do you make a habit of interfering in the staffing arrangements on other estates?'

'No, but–'

'So this was an exception, was it?'

'Well, yes, only–'

'This is all nonsense, isn't it, Mr Butler?'

'No it isn't nonsense,' retorted Butler, rattled by the speed and tone of Marshall's questions.

'You claim the Plaintiff was taking your tea; did you actually catch him on your property with his hand in a tea chest?'

There was a ripple of smothered amusement in the Court and the Judge glared round sharply.

'No,' said Butler. 'I saw a native doing it and I followed him to Paget's estate. I confronted Paget and he admitted what he had done. He said there were no witnesses; but his stepdaughter, Miss Charlotte Noble, was there and she heard everything. She's going to give evidence.'

Marshall held up a weary hand and Butler paused.

'Please, Mr Butler, one thing at a time. Miss Noble will have an opportunity in due course to tell the Court her version of events. Meanwhile, let us confine ourselves to the native; where is he now?'

'He's dead,' said Butler. 'He fell off a rope bridge.'

Marshall raised an eyebrow. 'Indeed? So we have only your word for it that he was attempting to steal from you?'

'He was stealing all right.'

'Isn't it the case, Mr Butler, that at the time of this "theft" the native was one of your employees?'

'Yes.'

'Are you a violent man, Mr Butler?'

'No.'

'Do you treat your workers well?'

'Yes.'

'Yet you ask us to believe that one of your well-treated workers suddenly decided to steal your tea and sell it to someone you despise – sorry, have a low opinion of.'

'He was a lazy man and I had reprimanded him for it before.'

'So he was frightened of you?'

'I wouldn't say that–'

'Did you beat him, Mr Butler, as you allege Mr Paget beat a native?'

'No.'

'You mean "No, Mr Paget *didn't* beat a native"?'

'No. I mean *I* didn't beat him.'

'Was he scared of your temper, Mr Butler?'

'I don't have a temper.'

'You're impulsive, aren't you? Hot-headed? Violent?'

'No, I'm not. I've already told you. Why don't you listen?'

The pause that Marshall left after that one

seemed deafening, and Butler knew Marshall was doing it for effect. He groaned inwardly.

'On the occasion of the tea-race, Mr Butler, on the dockside; did you actually hear what Mr Paget said to the Captain of the other vessel?'

'No, he whispered it to him.'

'How far away were you when this happened?'

'I don't know. About forty or fifty feet.'

'Was there a crowd?'

'Yes.'

'Noisy?'

'Yes.'

'So Mr Paget could have been saying anything, couldn't he? You wouldn't have been able to hear it.'

'No, but–'

'Mr Paget could have been saying "Congratulations, Captain," couldn't he?'

'The Captain spoke to one of his men who then hurried away–'

'The Captain could also have been saying anything, couldn't he?'

'They hadn't landed any cargo; the man went to tell them to get some ashore,' said Butler desperately, conscious that his voice was rising despite his efforts to control it.

'I see. So Mr Paget tells the Captain, the Captain tells a sailor, the sailor tells some other sailors,' rattled off Marshall. 'Come now, Mr Butler, this is all nonsense, isn't it? Vindictive nonsense.'

'No,' said Butler tightly. 'It isn't. It's the truth.'

He breathed heavily and Marshall regarded him enquiringly for a moment, then moved on.

'At the auction Mr Paget offered a higher price

than anyone else, yet you rejected it; was it because the offer came from Mr Paget?'

'No,' said Butler.

'Did you reject it because he is your enemy?'

'No, I tell you.'

'Do you mean he *is* your enemy but that wasn't why you rejected his offer?'

'No. I rejected his offer because I didn't want to sell to him.'

'Why?'

'Because – because–'

'Yes, Mr Butler? Do tell us. We're all waiting for your answer.'

Butler could feel the sweat trickling down his forehead and he wiped it away with his hand. 'It's my choice who I sell to and I chose not to sell to him. It's as simple as that.'

Marshall folded his arms and fired another question.

'Are you a sensible businessman, Mr Butler?'

'What?'

'I said, Are you a sensible businessman?'

'I like to think so,' said Butler.

'Are you not sure?'

Damn the man!

'I regard myself as a sensible businessman, but I don't boast about it.'

'What kind of sensible businessman is it that rejects an offer of five hundred thousand pounds for a concern worth considerably less than that?'

'It's not worth "considerably less" as you put it,' replied Butler, stung.

'So you mean it was a fair offer, yet you turned it down?'

'I chose not to sell,' said Butler. 'I've built the company up–'

'What kind of respectable businessman goes running around the streets chasing messengers?'

'I wanted to know where he went and–'

'What kind of honest businessman sneaks into buildings rather than announce himself to the doorman?'

'He was busy with two other men–'

'You burst into Mr Paget's office, didn't you?'

'No.'

'You were abusive to him, weren't you?'

'No!'

'You swore he would never get his land back, didn't you?'

'He never will get his land back!' burst out Butler, goaded beyond endurance, and at once regretted his choice of words. 'I mean, he'll never get *that* land back,' but Marshall pounced.

'At last. Now we're getting to the truth. "His" land you said, Mr Butler.'

'No, I meant to say "that" land. Look, it's not his, it's mine. He sold it to me.'

'You mean you cheated him out of it.'

'No!'

'You stopped the other planters from making a fair offer to Mr Paget, didn't you?'

'No, I didn't!'

'You put unfair pressure on him, didn't you?'

'I did not!'

'You put Mr Paget under duress and compelled him to sell to you, that's the truth isn't it, Mr Butler?'

'No! No! No!' Butler's shouts echoed round the

437

courtroom and his fist thumped the rim of the witness box on each word.

The echoes died away and the court was silent except for Butler's breath coming short and ragged. Marshall spoke and his voice was soft and wheedling and contempt dripped from every syllable.

'But you don't hate him, Mr Butler, do you? Oh no, you just want to make us believe that you have only a low opinion of him,' and Marshall stared at Butler's bowed head for a moment.

'I have no further questions for the Respondent, My Lord,' he said coldly and sat down.

The Judge nodded. 'Mr Gunn?'

Gunn stood. 'My Lord, may we recess for ten minutes whilst I take instructions?'

The Judge nodded again and got up. 'We will recess for ten minutes.'

Charlotte was waiting outside the courtroom, not allowed in until it was time to give her evidence, and she stood as they came out.

'I made a hash of that,' said Butler, trying to still his trembling hands. Charlotte looked at him with concern.

'I thought you did rather well, actually,' said Gunn.

'Really?' said Butler with a hollow laugh.

'Oh yes, I've seen him do that sort of thing before,' said Gunn, and Newbery nodded in agreement. 'It looks very effective, but if you take it apart all it amounts to is a lot of rhetoric.'

Butler nodded, not entirely convinced. 'You said you wanted to take instructions. What do you want to know?'

'Nothing,' said Gunn. 'That was just a ploy to give you a rest; you looked as if you needed it. Ah, Mr Kent is back,' and Butler turned. Kent was hurrying up the corridor.

'Anything?' asked Butler eagerly.

'Nothing,' said Kent. 'They don't know when the lines will be working again. How's the case going?'

Butler blew out his cheeks. 'You just missed seeing me getting grilled to a cinder by Marshall. Charlotte, when you give evidence be very, very careful. He won't give you time to think and he'll provoke you into saying the wrong things. He's dangerous.'

'I'll be careful.'

'It's as we thought,' said Gunn. 'Marshall's attempting to paint you as the sort of vindictive hot-head who would have no scruples about trying to cheat someone out of a fair price.'

'Are they succeeding?' asked Charlotte.

'They're having a good crack at it,' conceded Gunn. 'But in my opinion they haven't done enough to be convincing.'

'I don't think this Judge will have any problem being convinced,' said Butler. 'You haven't seen him yet, Charlotte; it's that fellow who was with the Queen at the opening of the Exhibition, the fellow who tore me off a strip.'

Gunn was interested.

'Tell me more,' he said, and Butler told him about the incident at the Exhibition. Gunn raised his eyebrows but made no comment.

'Be brutally frank with me, Mr Gunn,' said

Butler. 'What are our chances of winning this case without Changarai?'

Gunn considered. 'If the case finished right now and The Lion was giving his judgment I think he'd rule in our favour. They've presented no real evidence to support their case, but that's exactly what worries me. I've seen nothing yet to account for Marshall's confidence in taking this case on. He tried to rattle you in there–'

'He succeeded,' put in Butler.

'–but that was just standard cross-examination. He's not done anything spectacular. Whatever he's planning he hasn't done it yet.'

'You seem very sure he's up to something,' said Charlotte.

'He has to be,' said Gunn. 'We've heard their only witness, there are no more documents to introduce and he's had his shot at cross-examining you, Mr Butler. So what's he got left? Unless he's got something to surprise us with, the only thing I can imagine is that he plans to discredit Mr Changarai's evidence, or make it work against you in some way. Perhaps they're depending on Mr Changarai's evidence as much as you are.'

'*They're* depending on him?'

'Perhaps,' said Gunn. 'Are you absolutely sure of his loyalty?'

'Totally,' said Butler. 'I've got no doubts at all about him.' He shook his head. 'I can't believe, I *won't* believe that he isn't coming. I told him to get on the first available ship to London and I won't accept that he hasn't. We need more time. Mr Gunn, how much longer can you draw the case out?'

'I'll endeavour to get matters carried over until tomorrow,' said Gunn, 'but The Lion won't stand for much more prevarication.'

'We'll just have to do the best we can,' said Butler and looked at Charlotte.

'You're next,' he said. 'Good luck.'

'I won't let you down,' said Charlotte, and ignoring Gunn and Kent and Newbery, careless of other lawyers and their clients nearby, she reached up and kissed Butler's cheek. Then she turned to Gunn.

'I'm ready,' she said.

Six

'Miss Noble,' said Gunn, 'you visited your stepfather's plantation in eighteen eighty-one; did you ever see the Respondent, John Butler, on that property?'

Charlotte's voice was clear. 'Yes, I did.'

'Will you tell the Court the circumstances?'

'It was one night on the estate. I hadn't realised Ceylon was so hot and I couldn't sleep. I got up to open a window and I saw someone running to the storehouse. Then I saw someone following. I got up and looked for my stepfather but he wasn't in the house. I didn't know what to do, but I thought I should see what was happening. So I went across to the storehouse.'

'Very brave of you, Miss Noble,' commented Gunn, and Charlotte smiled nervously.

'Thank you. I went inside and had to hide quickly – a native was running out. I could still hear voices so I went further into the store. I found my stepfather and Mr Butler talking,' and Charlotte recounted what she had heard in the storehouse.

'What happened then?'

'My stepfather and I had an argument,' said Charlotte, and her chin came up. 'He shouted at me but I told him I was disappointed that he could ever have done such a dishonourable thing. He was angry but I was right.'

Silently Butler cheered.

'Thank you, Miss Noble,' and Gunn sat down. After a moment Marshall stood up.

'Miss Noble, when did you first meet John Butler?'

'On the ship going to Ceylon.'

'What impression did you form of him?'

'He seemed pleasant.'

'Was he polite to you?'

'Yes.'

'Did you ever have any conversations?'

'Yes.'

'Did you talk to him during dinner?'

'Yes.'

'Did you ever go out on the deck of the ship?'

'Yes, I did.'

'And did you ever talk to John Butler there?'

'Yes.'

'Did he have nice manners?'

'Yes, he was very civil.'

'By the time the voyage ended did you dislike him?'

Charlotte was surprised by the change in tone of the question.

'No, I didn't dislike him.'

'You liked him, then?'

'I thought he was very pleasant.'

'I see.' Marshall seemed to be considering his next question.

'When you saw the figures running to the storehouse did you recognise John Butler?'

Charlotte shook her head. 'It was too dark.'

'When you went to the storehouse what were you wearing?'

'My nightdress.'

'Anything else?'

'No, it was very warm.'

Marshall raised an eyebrow and Butler silently cursed him. Marshall was treading the finest of lines but he was doing it with consummate skill. With the greatest subtlety he was managing to imply that Charlotte's conduct in the night was rather less than ladylike. Yet he hadn't actually suggested anything.

Marshall moved on.

'Did you ever see John Butler again?'

'Yes. Two days later I decided I should go and apologise to him for my stepfather's behaviour.'

'*You* decided?' asked Marshall incredulously. 'Did you consult your stepfather in this matter?'

'No, I decided myself.'

'And what did you do?'

'I went to Mr Butler's estate—'

'Who accompanied you?'

'No one, I was on my own.'

'I see; you went unchaperoned to the estate of

443

an unmarried man. What happened next?'

Charlotte's lips tightened; she knew exactly what Marshall was trying to do.

'I went to the estate, to Mr Butler's bungalow,' and she stopped.

'Yes?' asked Marshall, and Charlotte hesitated, realising the corner she was painting herself into.

'He was busy, so I left.'

Marshall hadn't missed the hesitation and he pounced.

'What was Mr Butler busy doing?'

'Er, he was with someone.'

'Who was he with?'

'Someone.'

'Who, Miss Noble?'

'One of the workers on the estate.'

'How did you know it was one of the workers on the estate?"

'I saw him with her,' and she paled, immediately regretting saying 'her'.

'Was anyone else there?'

'No,' said Charlotte, and her voice was low.

'Speak up please, Miss Noble, the Court wishes to hear your answer; was anyone else there?'

'No.'

'Mr Butler was alone in his house with a female worker from his estate. What was he doing?'

Gunn jumped up. 'My Lord, I protest. The purpose of this case is to establish whether the Plaintiff sold his estate under duress or not; how Mr Butler runs his own estate is not an issue here.'

Marshall disagreed. 'My Lord, I submit that it is very much an issue. The question before the court is whether the Respondent is the sort of unscrupulous, dishonourable person who would do anything he thinks necessary in order to get what he wants. I submit that how Mr Butler conducts himself when alone with female workers on his estate is entirely relevant to that central issue.'

Judge Lyon glanced at Charlotte then fixed a stern look on Marshall.

'You may proceed, Mr Marshall, but a lady is present. I expect you to exercise the greatest care in what you suggest.'

'Of course, My Lord. Thank you for your assistance in this matter,' and Marshall made a small bow.

He looked at Charlotte. 'I have no wish to offend your sensibilities, Miss Noble, but this is of great importance. Please tell the Court exactly what you saw.'

Charlotte looked at Butler and his face was set and tense.

She swallowed. 'He, er, he was in the back room of the bungalow,' and she stopped again.

When Marshall spoke his voice was soft and coaxing.

'Miss Noble, were you able to see what sort of room the back room was?'

'It – it–' and she looked at Butler again, apology and desperation in her eyes.

'Miss Noble, what sort of room was it? Please tell the Court.'

'It was – it was–'

'It was the bedroom, for God's sake,' shouted Butler, jumping up. 'I was in the bedroom with a

445

native girl. Is that good enough for you?!'

The Lion looked thunderous but his voice was low.

'I have warned you once, Mr Butler. I will not warn you again,' and his voice began to rise. 'If I have one more interruption from you I will hold you in contempt. *Now sit down.*'

Butler glared at the Judge, then sat down. The silence was oppressive.

'Thank you, Miss Noble,' said Marshall pleasantly. 'I have no further questions, My Lord.'

Charlotte left the witness box and looked helplessly at Butler as she passed. He shrugged and made an apologetic smile. His outburst had given Marshall more ammunition and simultaneously deprived Gunn of any opportunity to spin the case out. Almost certainly any chance they had of winning was now destroyed, but the despondent look on Charlotte's face hurt him far more.

'I have another witness to call, My Lord,' Gunn was saying and Butler knew how much of a bluff that was. 'But I am conscious of the hour and would suggest we take that testimony in full tomorrow.'

'Thank you, Mr Gunn,' said Judge Lyon. 'I agree. The court stands adjourned until tomorrow morning.'

Outside the courtroom Charlotte was distraught and angry at the same time.

'I'm sorry, John, I'm so sorry. How could I have been so stupid? I didn't realise what his questions might lead to.' She shook her head. 'I've ruined the case. I've ruined it for you. If only I'd realised what he was trying to do I could have been more careful about what I was saying. I'm so sorry, John. If the Judge rules against you after this it'll be all my fault.'

Butler took her hands and tried to console her. 'You were marvellous in there, Charlotte. You said all the right things; you told them exactly what happened in the storehouse and nothing can change that. And if I lose this case it'll be no one's fault but mine; I was the one who jumped up and shouted out. I could see exactly what he was trying to do so I thought I might as well admit it.'

He squeezed her hands.

'This isn't going to last much longer anyway. Gunn and Marshall will make their closing speeches tomorrow and then it's up to the Judge. How long he'll take before giving judgement I don't know, but after what I did today I shouldn't think it'll be very long.'

'It's not over yet,' said Charlotte hopefully. 'Changarai might arrive.'

Butler hesitated. 'I'm worried about Changarai,' he said. 'He might not come,' and at her confused look he explained.

'I thought it was Changarai that was stealing the tea and I hit him and told him to get off the estate – him and Mirissa. I apologised of course when I found out the truth, but did he really forgive me? Then Mirissa died and I was too busy driving everyone to put a cargo together for the tea-race to give any thought to his feelings, his grief. I trampled all over his pride and self-respect and I've been kicking myself for it ever

447

since. If there was ever an occasion for getting hi own back, for getting some revenge, this is it.'

There was a long silence between them and Charlotte finally voiced the unthinkable.

'What will you do if you lose?' she asked 'There wouldn't be any reason to go back to Ceylon, would there?'

Butler grunted. 'There might be. There'd be no Tondipgiri, no Tondip's Tea Company,' and he shook his head ruefully. 'But I'm not a business man, Charlotte, not in the way Richard is; I'm a planter. I wasn't, once, but it's what I've become Yes, Richard and I built up the Company together, but planting tea's what I know about. I I lose the case the only thing I can do is go back to Ceylon and try to build another estate. It'd be hard work of course, but I did it before and could do it again. There'd be nothing to stay in England for.'

Charlotte nodded in understanding and mur mured her agreement, but Butler's last sentence made her turn her head away so that he couldn' see the hurt in her eyes.

Seven

'Any sign of your man yet?' asked Gunn the following morning.

Butler shook his head. 'My partner called earl to say a steamer's been sighted in the Channel He's gone to meet it, but whether Changarai's or

448

board we've no way of knowing.'

'I'll make an application for an adjournment but I don't expect The Lion to allow it,' said Gunn. 'However,' he added briskly, 'we must be optimistic and hope your man arrives. We may as well go in; we'll be starting soon.'

'I'll watch from the gallery,' said Charlotte.

'Thanks,' said Butler. 'Right, Mr Gunn, let's return to the fight.'

Butler took his seat and looked up at Charlotte in the Gallery. She smiled encouragingly and Butler smiled back. Also in the Gallery were three men who hadn't been there yesterday. They were exceedingly well dressed and wore an air of affluence. When Paget entered they returned his nod and Butler wondered whether they were friends of Paget's or whether they were business colleagues from the Great Eastern Tea Company. Probably there to congratulate Paget if he won, he supposed; without Changarai's evidence Paget's triumph looked certain.

Butler's speculations were cut short as Gunn stood.

'My Lord, I am of course conscious of your ruling regarding adjournments in this case but I *must* make a further representation to you. As I outlined yesterday there is another witness to this case but it is not known whether he will arrive in time. A ship is due in today from Ceylon, but due to failures in the telegraph we have no way of knowing if the witness is aboard. I must therefore ask that you reconsider my request for an adjournment. I am conscious that this case has been in the List for some time, but I must advise Your Lordship that the witness in question is crucial to the Respondent's case. It is of the utmost importance that the Court has the opportunity to hear his evidence.'

'Thank you, Mr Gunn,' said Judge Lyon drily. 'But, as I said yesterday, I will countenance no further adjournments. If the witness is not present the case must proceed without him.'

'My Lord, the witness has vital evidence–'

'Then he should have been here earlier,' snapped the Judge. 'There will be no adjournment, Mr Gunn.'

'My Lord–'

'No adjournment. Now proceed with your case.'

'As Your Lordship wishes,' said Gunn heavily, and looked down at his notes. Butler knew the barrister was searching for some means of prolonging matters in the hope that Changarai might yet arrive, and he looked across at Marshall and Paget in frustration.

Whilst Gunn had been arguing for an adjournment a Court official had entered and spoken briefly to Paget's solicitor. The solicitor was now talking intently to Marshall. Marshall stood up.

'My Lord, I have a matter of the utmost importance to bring to Your Lordship's attention.'

Gunn glanced at Marshall then looked in query at Butler. Butler shook his head and shrugged and Gunn sat down.

'Yes, Mr Marshall.'

'My Lord, in the course of preparing instructions for this case the Plaintiff hoped to locate a certain witness. The witness was not found, much to the Plaintiff's disappointment, and accordingly no mention was made of that hoped-for witness in the pleadings. However, I have just been informed that the witness has been found and is at this very moment outside the court-room, ready to give his evidence.'

'I must protest, My Lord.' Gunn's voice rang out sharply.

'Who is this witness?' asked the Judge.

'My Lord, it is a former business associate of the Respondent, a man named Vincent Vincent–'

'Who?' interrupted the Judge as if unable to believe his ears.

'Mr Vincent Vincent, My Lord. I understand that the evidence of his dealings with the Respondent will prove extremely illuminating.'

Judge Lyon stared at Marshall for a moment.

'Vincent Vincent,' he repeated sceptically.

'My Lord, yes.'

Gunn saw his chance. 'My Lord, I must have an adjournment. This witness comes as a total surprise to the Respondent. I have had no time to prepare. There has been no witness statement for me to consider. I cannot properly conduct my client's case unless I have time to prepare for this witness's testimony.'

'My Lord,' and Marshall was all reasonable-ness. 'I too am conscious of Your Lordship's earlier comments regarding adjournments of this case and I submit that my learned friend will find he has ample opportunity to make his response to the witness's testimony. The man is here, he stands ready to give his evidence, to be cross-examined for as long as the Court wishes. His evidence can only help the Court, not hinder it.'

Judge Lyon stared long and hard at Marshall.

'I do not approve of surprise witnesses,' he said. 'I am almost tempted to refuse your application, Mr Marshall. However, if the man is outside the courtroom I will, very reluctantly, allow it.'

'My Lord, if those are your directions I must ask for a recess so that I can take instructions,' insisted Gunn stubbornly.

The Judge nodded.

'That seems only fair in the circumstances,' and he stood. 'The Court will recess for half an hour.'

'Who,' said Gunn, barely holding his temper, 'is Vincent Vincent?'

They were in a private room and Gunn was pacing, unable to sit still.

'As Marshall said, he was an associate,' said Butler.

'Mr Butler,' said Gunn, near to boiling point. 'I once asked you whether there was anything, anything at all in your past that Henning Marshall could use against you, so why, *why* didn't you tell me about this man?'

'Because there's nothing wrong,' said Butler. 'It was fifteen years ago and there's nothing in my dealings with him that can damage me. In fact, *he's* the one with the shady past.'

Gunn was stern. 'I don't for one moment believe that tale Marshall spun about having only just found this man. This is what they've been leading up to; whatever this man is going to say is what makes Marshall think he can win this case. So tell me, what were your dealings with Vincent Vincent? Leave nothing out. If I'm to represent you I need to know *everything.*'

'Back in seventy-two I owned a half-share in a racehorse called The Rascal,' Butler explained. 'Vinnie Vincent – as he was known then – owned the other half. Vinnie and I always decided together which races to enter her in; sometimes I'd suggest a race, sometimes it was Vinnie. She was a good horse and we had some wins with her. But then she started winning races where she was an outsider. As an owner you don't mind that; after all, your horse has won. You mind it even less if you've got a bet on. You shouldn't get wins like that very often, but we did and I got to wondering about it. I noticed it was always the races Vinnie had suggested where The Rascal won against the odds. I followed Vinnie and found out he had a scheme going. He was bribing other jockeys to pull their horses, getting friends of his to put bets on The Rascal at long odds then sharing the winnings with the jockeys.

'I wanted no part of it. I sold him my share for next to nothing and got out. The wins against the odds continued so I sent a letter to the Jockey Club. I don't know what they did but I never saw Vinnie on a racecourse again. I never saw The Rascal again either. So you see what I mean? None of it damages me. I wasn't party to any of what Vinnie was up to.'

'Did you tell him you had found him out?' asked Gunn.

'No,' said Butler. 'I just sold him the share and got out of it.'

'Did the Jockey Club contact you?'

'No. They couldn't. I sent the letter anonymously.'

Gunn reacted to that. He stared at Butler.

'Why anonymously?'

'I didn't want any of it coming back to me; I just wanted to be shot of it. I didn't want to be caught up in any of Vinnie's dodgy dealings.'

'So we have no way of proving that you were the one who sent the letter,' said Gunn.

'Is that a problem?'

Gunn shrugged. 'It would have been better for us if you had signed the letter – it would have looked more open and honest – but perhaps it's not critical. Is there anything else that he might say?'

'Nothing I can think of,' said Butler.

'Right,' said Gunn decisively. 'Let's go back in there and see what this fellow has to say.'

As they were about to re-enter the courtroom Kent hurried up. He was grim.

'He's not coming,' he said. 'Changarai wasn't on board.'

Butler shut his eyes. So Changarai hadn't forgiven him after all. He supposed he deserved it but it hurt, really hurt.

'Well. That's it then,' he said heavily. 'It's all over.'

'Not yet, Mr Butler,' said Gunn. 'We've got "Vinnie Vincent" to deal with first.'

'I call Mr Vincent Vincent,' said Marshall, and

454

waited whilst Vincent was called. He sidled into the courtroom, a short thin man in a brown-checked suit, and was shown to the witness box. He was sworn in and looked furtively around the courtroom as if searching for the nearest bolt-hole. Butler glanced up at the Gallery. To his surprise Charlotte wasn't there.

'Mr Vincent,' said Marshall, 'are you acquainted with the Respondent in this case, Mr John Butler?'

'I am, sir. That's 'im,' and Vincent pointed at Butler.

'Thank you, Mr Vincent,' said Marshall. 'Will you tell us, please, the extent of your dealings with Mr Butler?'

Vincent ducked his head and shot out his chin.

'Well, it was like this, see. I had a half-share in a horse, he had the other half. Nice mare she was, called The Rascal. A right rascal she was too; caused some upsets she did.'

'What sort of upsets?'

'Winning when she shouldn't have. Yes, she was good, but what was she doing winning all those times at fifty-to-one; seventy-to-one; a hundred-to-one?'

'Tell us from the beginning, Mr Vincent.'

'Well, like I said, we had half-shares and we did all right – sometimes she'd win, sometimes she wouldn't. And then she started winning when you wouldn't expect her to. There'd be other horses in the field and you'd think to yourself, "She's not going to win today, not against them," but then she'd go and win. Nice for us, but I couldn't help wondering. It was happening too often, see? So I

455

started watching a bit closer. On those races where she was getting long odds, who was betting? It took a few races before I figured it out and it was the same faces every time; up they'd pop and put money on whenever The Rascal had long odds. There were four of 'em and it was never the same one making the bets; it was a different one at each course. I could have reported them – right there and then – but I didn't.'

'Why was that?'

'Well, The Rascal won other races where there was nothing suspicious and I asked myself, "How do they know when The Rascal's going to win at long odds?" There was only one answer: they had something going with the jockeys. The jockeys had to be pulling their horses. It was about then that Johnny Butler over there sold me his share. And that was funny, too – dirt-cheap he sold it. She was worth a lot more than that, but he insisted; said he didn't want it no more. Well, fair enough, I thought. But it didn't answer how they were rigging the races, so I thought, "Right, Vincent, you'd better be a bit clever," and I worked out how I could catch them paying the jockeys off. But then I got pulled up by some blokes from the Jockey Club. They had coppers with them and they marched me off the course. Said they'd been told what was going on, said they'd had a note about it from someone. I tried telling them I had nothing to do with it but they didn't believe me.'

'What did the Jockey Club do, Mr Vincent?'

'It was nasty what they did, sir; nasty. They struck some jockeys off and put the word out to stop me owning a horse. Put the word out to stop me ever going on a course again too. Those were hard times, gentlemen, hard times. I've found work on the edges but they won't let me do what I love best: being there, at the Turf,' and Vincent Vincent finished his evidence managing to look pious and wronged simultaneously.

'Did you ever find out who sent that note, Mr Vincent?' asked Marshall.

'No sir, I didn't. But I'll tell you this: to put the finger on those punters and on those jockeys it had to be someone who knew what was going on – someone with inside knowledge,' and Vincent ticked off on his fingers. 'They had names, they had dates, they had places. How did they know? I ask you. That note was from someone who was part of it, if you ask me. That note–'

Gunn stood quickly. 'My Lord, the witness's speculations are not evidence.'

'Thank you, Mr Gunn,' and the Judge turned to Vincent. 'We are only interested in what you actually know, Mr Vincent. Do not speculate and do not guess at events or the identities of others. Continue, Mr Marshall.'

'Thank you, My Lord. Mr Vincent, did you ever see Mr Butler again?'

'Not once. It was strange, that; we used to be friends and now it was as if he was avoiding me.'

'Thank you, Mr Vincent,' and Marshall sat. Vincent nodded and took a step to leave the witness box.

'Not so fast, Mr Vincent, if you please,' and Gunn was on his feet. 'I have a few questions for you.'

Vincent made that head-ducking and chin-shooting movement again and gripped the edge of the box.

'What do you want to know?'

'Mr Vincent,' and Gunn seemed to choose his words very carefully. 'Did *you* ever bet on The Rascal?'

'Sometimes.'

'Did you ever bet on her when the odds were long?'

'I might have done.'

'What does that mean, Mr Vincent?' said Gunn sharply. 'Did you or didn't you?'

'All right; yes, I did.'

'Have you been involved with "the Turf" for a long time, Mr Vincent?'

Vincent was thrown by the sudden change of subject and glanced at Marshall and Paget. Marshall had his head down and Paget was expressionless. Vincent shrugged.

'Yes, I've been involved for a long time. Since I was a lad.'

'Would you describe yourself as being quite knowledgeable about it?'

'I know a fair bit.'

'What does it mean when a horse is given long odds?'

'It means it probably isn't going to win.'

'You've just told us you betted on The Rascal when it had long odds – when it "probably wasn't going to win". Why would such a knowledgeable man as yourself bet on a horse under those conditions?'

'Well, it was my horse. Our horse.'

458

'But you knew it was unlikely to win, Mr Vincent. So why bet on it?'

'I can have a flutter if I like, can't I?'

'What's the point, when the horse is unlikely to win?'

'There's no law against it.'

'You bet on The Rascal at long odds because you knew the other jockeys had been paid to pull their horses so that The Rascal would win; isn't that the truth?'

'No, it isn't.'

'*You* paid off those jockeys didn't you, Mr Vincent?'

'I never. I never did.'

'Why did The Rascal win all those races?'

'She was the better horse.'

'What, at a hundred to one? Did all those tipsters and racing experts get it wrong? Not once but several times?' and Gunn glared at Vincent. 'You're lying aren't you?'

'No, I'm bloody well not.'

'Knowledgeable men don't bet on a hundred-to-one outsider,' said Gunn, boring in relentlessly. 'Not unless they know something that no one else knows – such as the existence of a plan for the other jockeys to pull their horses. Your entire testimony is lies isn't it, Mr Vincent?'

'No, it's the truth. It was 'im that was behind it,' and he pointed to Butler.

'Nonsense,' snapped Gunn. 'You were the one who continued to put bets on at long odds, even when – you claim – you suspected something was wrong. It was *your* racket, wasn't it, Mr Vincent? You were fixing the races, weren't you?'

'I wasn't. I didn't. I never.' Vincent spread his arms helplessly and looked to Paget again. Paget didn't meet Vincent's eye.

'I have no further questions for this – witness,' said Gunn with an air of disgust and sat down.

'My Lord?'

It was Marshall.

'I have one question in re-examination, My Lord.'

The Lion nodded.

'Mr Vincent,' said Marshall. 'We've established that the men who orchestrated this betting deception put bets on at long odds; did Mr Butler ever put a bet on The Rascal when she was going to run at long odds?'

'Yes, sir, he did. He certainly did, just like them other fellers,' and Vincent pointed at Butler. 'He bet on her.'

Butler grunted like a fighter taking a low blow and Marshall sat triumphantly. He had won now and knew it. Gunn's suggestion that only someone involved in the scheme would bet at long odds was an attempt to reveal Vincent's involvement and discredit him, but Marshall's last question had turned that suggestion around and implicated Butler.

That was it; the case was lost.

Vincent Vincent left the box and scuttled from the courtroom. Judge Lyon looked at Gunn.

'Has your witness arrived yet, Mr Gunn?'

The Judge knew full well that no one else had come into Court, that no messages had been passed to Gunn.

'Not yet, My Lord.'

'Have you any other witnesses to call?'

Judge Lyon knew the answer to that one as well.

'No, My Lord, there are no more witnesses for the Respondent.'

'So that concludes the case for the Respondent, does it not?'

'Yes, My Lord.'

'Very well,' said the Judge briskly. 'I will hear counsels' closing speeches. Mr Marshall?'

'My Lord,' and Marshall made a small bow. 'When I opened the case for the Plaintiff I made reference to the Plaintiff's belief that the Respondent harboured some secret enmity towards him; during the two days of this case we have witnessed that enmity emerge and there can no longer be any doubt – the Respondent is bitterly resentful of Mr Paget. When sales of Mr Butler's tea started to decline he rushed out to Ceylon in search of a scapegoat, rather than staying to examine his business arrangements here as any sensible man would. In Ceylon he victimised an employee who then sought sanctuary with the Plaintiff; the Plaintiff subsequently became the next recipient of the Respondent's base and baseless accusations. When the Respondent lost the tea-race – and lost it fair and square under traditional tea-race rules – the Respondent was such a bad loser that he concocted an absurd tale of Mr Paget passing some kind of message to the rival Captain. He went on to vindictively deprive the Plaintiff of the chance to make an honest purchase at auction. He would not even countenance the sale, at a most generous price,

461

of the Tondip's Tea Company. In this very Court his volatile and hot-headed nature—'

The door to the Court banged open and Charlotte rushed in.

'Stop! Stop! He's here! Changarai's here!'

Documents and legal volumes were knocked to the floor as barristers and solicitors turned. The Judge roared from his bench.

'Young lady!' he thundered and the courtroom fell silent. 'How dare you burst in here, into a Court of Law, of Justice—'

Charlotte was having none of it.

'If you carry on there'll be no justice!' she shouted. 'He's here, he's coming, the only man who can prove that John Butler's telling the truth.'

'Young lady, I will not have this Court interrupted...' the Judge trailed off and stared at the man who had come in at the side of Richard Kent.

'Thank God,' breathed Butler. 'Thank God.'

It was doubtful that a stranger figure had ever been seen in that Court. He was wearing rough sandals, his legs were bare up to the knee and he was wearing an extremely baggy pair of wrinkled canvas trousers. Hanging loosely about his top half was a woollen jersey of such a worn and faded nature that it wasn't possible to tell what colour it might originally have been. Over all this was an open black oilskin jacket and he was holding a broad-brimmed white hat with frayed edges.

The manner of dress was ridiculous, but there was nothing ridiculous about the man wearing it.

The wrinkled skin was as leathery as ever, the beard whiter than Butler remembered, but the dignity of the little man was unmistakable.

He looked at the Judge and in a clear, firm voice called out:

'Good morning, Mr Judge-Sir. I am here to tell you about John Butler-Sir.'

The Lion's eyes bored into him but Changarai stared right back, frank and unafraid.

'Mr Changarai, I presume,' said the Judge finally, and Changarai nodded. There was silence.

'Come forward.'

Marshall was indignant. 'My Lord, I protest and in the strongest possible terms. Counsel for the Respondent has already stated that he has closed his case. As Your Lordship stated there has been ample opportunity for the Respondent to ensure the presence of his witnesses. There can be no justification now for the Respondent to make further representations to the Court. The Respondent cannot–'

'Mr Marshall.'

Paget's counsel fell silent.

'I permitted Mr Vincent to give evidence and I would remind you that that gentleman was not even mentioned in the documents. However, I allowed his evidence, exceptionally. This gentleman – Mr Changarai – has at least been mentioned in advance, even if he has been unable to attend until now. I can hardly permit your surprise witness, Mr Marshall, yet deny the Respondent the evidence of a witness on whose behalf, I should mention, I have had repeated representations,' and The Lion looked at Gunn with the ghost of a half-smile.

Gunn rose, nodded in acknowledgement and sat.

'Let the witness be sworn,' said the Judge. 'Come and stand here, Mr Changarai,' and he indicated the witness box.

Charlotte and Kent sat at the back of the courtroom. Changarai came forward and stopped when he saw Butler. They looked at each other and Changarai gave a small smile and bobbed his head. Impulsively Butler reached out and shook Changarai's hand.

'Mr Changarai,' said the Judge. 'If you please,' and Changarai released Butler's hand and entered the witness box. The Registrar held out the Bible and Changarai stared at it blankly.

The Judge watched. 'Are you a Christian, Mr Changarai?'

'I am a follower of the Buddha, Mr Judge-Sir.'

Judge Lyon looked at the Registrar. 'Do we have provision for the swearing-in of Buddhists?' and now it was the turn of the Registrar to look blank.

'I'm afraid I've never – er–'

'Very well,' said the Judge and took the matter into his own hands. 'Mr Changarai, do you affirm, by all that is sacred to you, that you will tell the truth, the whole truth and nothing but the truth?'

Changarai nodded. 'Yes, Mr Judge-Sir.'

'Do you understand what I mean?'

'Yes, Mr Judge-Sir, I will tell only truth.'

'Very well,' and the Judge leaned back. 'Your witness, Mr Gunn.'

'Thank you, My Lord,' and Gunn stood.

'Mr Changarai, tell the Court, if you please, about the first time you met John Butler.'

'I was worker for Mr Paget,' said Changarai, and it suddenly struck Butler that Changarai didn't add the respectful 'Sir' to Paget's name. A new wave of affection swept over him as he recalled that there had never been an occasion when Changarai had addressed him as anything other than Butler-Sir.

'He beat me with stick,' Changarai was saying. 'Butler-Sir stopped him.'

'Why did he beat you, Mr Changarai?'

'Mr Paget in bad temper. Store book was wrong and he have bad head. He drink many bottles night before.'

'Thank you,' said Gunn, but Changarai continued.

'He beat me plenty times. He have bad head very often. He drink many, many bottles.'

Butler glanced at Paget. He was glaring at Changarai, and Marshall was very still next to him.

'He beat other workers plenty times, too. He drink much every day.'

'My Lord, this is preposterous.' Marshall was on his feet. 'The evidence of this witness cannot be accepted by the Court. He's clearly prejudiced, there are no witnesses to these foul and baseless allegations. This is yet another attempted distortion of the truth by the Respondent.'

'Mr Marshall,' and the Judge's voice was sharp. 'You attempted, as you were entitled, to portray the Respondent in a bad light. But by choosing to make Mr Butler's character an issue in the case, Mr Marshall, you must accept that your client's character can be made an issue in return. Continue, Mr Gunn.'

'Mr Changarai,' said Gunn, 'what happened the next time you met Mr Paget?'

'Butler-Sir was in England, selling tea—'

'If I may interrupt you, Mr Changarai. My Lord, to clarify, this would have been between the years eighteen seventy-seven and eighty-one. I don't believe my learned friend will dispute these dates,' and Gunn glanced at Marshall. Marshall, for the first time, seemed unsure, caught off-balance by the nature of Changarai's evidence. He hesitated, then shook his head.

'No dispute, My Lord,' he said, rising slightly and the Judge nodded.

'Thank you, Mr Marshall. Thank you, Mr Gunn. Please carry on, Mr Changarai.'

'One day Mr Paget came to Tondipgiri. He say he wants to speak to me about Butler-Sir. He say he will give me money if I will secretly give him tea from Tondipgiri.'

Butler started. Changarai had never told him this.

'I say No. He say he will give me much money to steal Tondipgiri tea. I say No. He not happy.'

The Judge, until now staring intently at Changarai, now looked at Paget. Paget was pale. Under the Judge's cold stare he shifted restlessly and licked dry lips.

'Butler-Sir came back. He found bad native stealing tea. Butler-Sir is a good man; he work hard. He make my granddaughter very happy.

He try to save her from elephants in storm but she is crushed by them.'

'Thank you, Mr Changarai,' and Gunn sat down. Changarai, unaware of the niceties of court etiquette, didn't stop though and carried straight on.

'Mr Paget is very bad man, Mr Judge-Sir. While Butler-Sir was in England Mr Paget came to Tondipgiri again—'

'My Lord,' protested Marshall. 'This is nothing but personal abuse. This is a Court of Justice – it cannot possibly accept the so-called evidence of this ragged native. His claims are complete nonsense and his late attendance is itself suspect. I suggest he has been coached by others in what to say. My Lord, this cannot—'

'He wanted my granddaughter.'

Changarai's voice was loud and clear and rang round the courtroom. The Lion glared at him fiercely and Butler would have wagered that that look had quelled countless rebellious advocates and witnesses, but Changarai was unaffected by it. His eyes were fixed rigidly on Paget and after a moment the Judge leaned back.

'You are overruled, Mr Marshall. Continue, Mr Changarai.'

Changarai continued to stare at Paget and his face was solemn.

'Butler-Sir was in England and Mr Paget came to Tondipgiri again. He see my granddaughter, Mirissa. Very pretty little girl. Mr Paget say he will give me much money for her.'

Butler was frozen. Changarai hadn't told him any of this either.

467

'I say No, I not sell her. He say he will give me more money. I say No, I not sell her. He say he will shoot me if I do not give him my granddaughter. I say No.'

Changarai fell silent.

Marshall was quick to rise. 'My Lord, this is a preposterous fabric of falsehoods. I must insist that I be allowed to recall Mr Paget in re-examination. He must have the opportunity to defend his good name and rebut this foully concocted series of lies.'

'Very well,' said the Judge.

'Thank you, My Lord. I call William Paget.'

There was total stillness in the courtroom and Marshall, irritated, turned to Paget, expecting him to rise and re-enter the witness box as bidden. The seconds passed with no movement from Paget and the silence was broken only by the rustling of cloth as those in the courtroom turned to look at him. Without exception, they had been stunned by what they had just heard and all were eager to learn how the man would refute the appalling allegations. But Paget, his face shrunken to the colour and texture of old parchment, made no reaction, made no movement, and his silence condemned him. Gradually the curiosity of those looking at him faded, displaced by utter disgust as the realisation of the truth sank in.

The court was horribly quiet. Marshall was rigid, his jaw and lower lip trembling, then he turned to the Judge and his voice was glacial.

'My Lord, I can no longer represent the Plaintiff in this case. With your permission I must withdraw.'

The Lion regarded Paget with barely concealed revulsion.

'Granted, Mr Marshall. Mr Paget, you no longer have counsel. Neither, I have decided, do you have a case. This matter is dismissed, with costs to the Respondent. Mr Gunn, unless you have the calculations to hand I trust you will submit a detailed application for those costs in due course.'

'My Lord.'

The Lion stood, everyone in Court followed hastily and the Lion bowed and left. There was a moment's silence, then the courtroom exploded with noise. Charlotte and Kent came from their seats at the back, Butler shook hands with Gunn and Newbery, then went straight to the witness box and pumped Changarai's hand. Changarai looked baffled but was soon smiling as he realised that Butler had won and he pumped Butler's hand in return.

'I thought you weren't coming,' Butler kept repeating, and his eyes were moist.

'I found him wandering along the Strand,' said Kent excitedly. 'He was right outside; he didn't know this was the place,' and Kent shook his head, bemused. 'He was on the ship after all. He must have come down one gangway as I was going up the other.'

Butler turned, Charlotte was right there in front of him, her eyes shining, and he hugged her. He held her hands and looked over at Paget.

Paget was sitting very still.

Marshall's junior and Paget's solicitor were gathering documents as if they couldn't leave the court quickly enough, then Marshall gave the barest of nods to Gunn and left without even glancing at Paget. Paget was still for a moment longer, then he stood up. He looked up at the Gallery and Butler followed his gaze. The three well-dressed men were leaving and their faces were grim. One looked down on Paget and shook his head and made an angry dismissive gesture with his hands, then he followed the other two. Paget paled and stared in disbelief.

'Well done, John,' Kent was saying. 'You did it.'

'No.' Butler shook his head and turned round. 'Changarai did it,' and those bright eyes in the leathery face smiled back at him. Tondipgiri was saved and Butler knew who he owed it to. He gripped Changarai's hand again.

'Thank you, old friend,' he said simply. 'My God, thank you for everything.'

Eight

Three weeks later

The bitter wind rolling up the river from the sea was a better spur to the labouring dockhands than any sharp-tongued foreman. They bent their backs and hurried about their work; it was the only way to keep warm. Casks and bales and barrels and coils of rope built up in heaps on the

470

quayside, then the heaps diminished as other dockhands either took the cargoes aboard vessels tied up at the quay or else trundled the loads off to nearby warehouses. Movement and shouting and activity were the order of the day, no one wanting to stand still and freeze, everyone goading everyone else to work harder.

But a huddled knot of people on the foredeck of one particular steamer were conspicuous by their stillness. They were conscious that the moment for departure was drawing near and conversation was difficult.

A gust of wind rattled the steamer's cables and the group stirred at the blast from the ship's whistle.

'Just six weeks aboard and you'll be back home, Changarai,' said Butler, and after a moment added, 'I wish I was coming with you.'

'It will be much warmer,' said Changarai, and Butler laughed, glad to relieve the tension.

'Yes, much warmer.'

'Thank you, Changarai,' said Charlotte, and kissed him on the cheek. He blinked in surprise and Kent shook his hand.

'Thank you for coming. We owe you so much.'

Changarai bobbed his head, embarrassed at all the praise, and the awkward silence returned.

'Changarai,' asked Charlotte suddenly. 'Do *you* know how Tondipgiri got its name?'

'Yes,' said Changarai.

Butler stared at him in amazement. 'You know?'

'Yes,' repeated Changarai and he explained. 'Very long time ago was King Tondip. Men came from the forest to take his land. They wanted to make his people slaves. But King Tondip stood on the hill and would not let the men from the forest take the people.'

'He did that on his own?' asked Charlotte incredulously.

'So it is told,' said Changarai.

'He must have had some help, surely,' said Kent.

Changarai shrugged, an expressive gesture with hands and arms and shoulders.

'King Tondip stood on the hill,' he repeated. 'He saved his land and his people. That is why it is called King Tondip's Hill.'

'Must be something in the earth there,' commented Kent, and looked pointedly at Butler. 'Something that makes a man dig his heels in and not let go of it.'

A voice rang out from somewhere near the steamer's stern.

'All ashore that's going ashore!'

'Right, that's us,' said Butler, and straightened. 'Thanks again, Changarai. Good luck.'

'Thank you, Butler-Sir. May you find much happiness.'

Butler nodded and gripped Changarai's hand, wanting to say something beyond mere words of appreciation, something that expressed how he felt about this man to whom he owed so much. But all he could think of was how things had been in Ceylon when he and Changarai had worked the estate together and now Changarai was going back there. Butler realised he envied him.

The words he wanted to say didn't come and finally Butler gripped Changarai's hand once more then followed Charlotte and Kent down the gangway. He joined them on the damp and blustery quayside and thrust his hands deep in his coat pockets.

Changarai nodded and smiled at them from the ship's rail and Charlotte waved. Changarai waved back.

'He's a good man,' she said. 'I wish he could have stayed longer, I really like him. When I saw him in that witness box I remembered Tondipgiri again, and so clearly too; all those vivid green tea bushes covering the hill, the women in their bright colours picking the tea and singing. And Changarai looks after it all.'

'He's one in a million,' agreed Kent. 'A good sound man to run the estate. That's what a plantation needs all right: a foreman you can rely on to get the leaves picked properly, to turn them into tea—'

'Oh, the hell with it!' and Charlotte and Kent turned at Butler's sudden outburst.

'Wait here,' he ordered, and ran back up the gangway. He ran past the startled Changarai to the stern of the steamer and spoke animatedly to the man standing there, a well-built fellow with a beard and peaked cap. The man listened to Butler, then shrugged and nodded. Butler ran back along the deck and the gangway bounced as he ran down it. He stopped in front of Charlotte and took her hands in his. The intensity of his expression startled her.

'Marry me, Charlotte.'

473

'What?!'

'Marry me.'

She stared at him, speechless. 'John–'

'Never mind that; will you marry me?'

Her lips moved but no words came out.

'Well?'

She blinked. 'Yes. Yes, I will.'

'Good, come on,' and he took a step toward the ship.

'What? What do you mean?'

'We'll get married in Ceylon.'

'In *Ceylon?!*'

'Yes, come on.'

'John, I can't.'

'Why not?'

'Well, I – I–'

'What?'

'Well, I've got nothing with me. No luggage.'

'So? Neither have I.'

'But what about the business?'

'Richard can take care of it. You can do tha can't you, Richard?'

Kent was as much taken by surprise as Charlotte and could only nod.

'There you are, he can take care of it,' and Butler looked at Charlotte. 'I can't stay ir England, Charlotte; I'm a planter, Ceylon's where I belong,' and he gripped her hands tighter. 'Bu being out there, being back on Tondipgiri again won't mean a thing unless you're there to share i with me. What do you say?'

The rattle of the first of the two gangways as i was pulled away from the ship made Butler turr his head. The dock-hands came along the quay towards the remaining gangway and Butler looked at Charlotte urgently.

'Charlotte?' he asked, imploring.

'I can't, John, not Ceylon.'

'Charlotte–' and Butler turned to the dockhands. 'Leave that!' he ordered and the dockhands stood back uncertainly.

'Charlotte, listen, you'll be fine. When I first went out there I knew nothing about the place. I didn't want to go, believe me. But it's my home now; I want to go back there. I *need* to go back there – and I need you to come with me.'

He searched her face for some sign of encouragement, but all he saw was confusion and doubt.

She took a step back. 'No.'

'Charlotte–'

'No, John, I can't.'

'Leave that gangway, I said!' snapped Butler, and the dockhands stopped and pushed their caps back in exasperation. The steamer's whistle blasted again and Butler stepped closer to Charlotte.

'The ship's about to go. They can't wait any longer. I've got to get on it, Charlotte, I'm going back with Changarai,' and he was silent, waiting for her response, hoping desperately that she would say yes. Charlotte couldn't meet his gaze and dropped her eyes, taking her hands from his. She turned away and couldn't look at him.

Butler winced as if hit and his shoulders drooped. He stood like that for a moment then took a breath and straightened. He swallowed, took a step closer to her and whispered softly.

'Goodbye, Charlotte. I'll never forget you. Never.'

He turned to Kent. 'I don't have to say "Look after the company," Richard; I know it's in good hands.'

'We've done all right,' agreed Kent, feeling the need to mark the occasion somehow, feeling that something profound still needed to be said. 'We've come a long way since that meeting in Mrs Carey's shop.'

'It's been the challenge you were looking for?' asked Butler, and Kent nodded.

'We'll go on to do even better,' he said confidently.

'The announcement about the Royal Warrant's due next month,' said Butler. 'If we've won it you'll have a lot of work to do.'

'I've been thinking about that already,' said Kent. 'And we'll win all right. But if you're in Ceylon you'll miss it all.'

Butler smiled and shook his head.

'I don't mind,' he said. 'I can't think of anyone I'd rather have handling it. I'll still be at sea when they make the announcement, so telegraph ahead and let me know how we've gone on.'

'I will,' promised Kent. 'Good luck.'

'And to you,' said Butler, and they shook hands. Butler glanced again at Charlotte. Her back was still towards him, her head bent, and Butler hesitated, then turned and ascended the gangway. He joined the open-mouthed Changarai at the rail and called to the dockhands.

'Right, you can move it.'

The dockhands looked at each other, raised

476

their eyes heavenwards and shook their heads, then set about untying the securing ropes.

'Charlotte?'

She turned and looked at Kent and he frowned at the damp trails on her cheeks.

'Charlotte, my dear—'

She shook her head. 'I'll never see him again.'

'Of course you will. He'll come back.'

'No, he won't. He once told me that he's got Tondipgiri in his soul. He's gone for good, he won't be coming back,' and her voice was choked. 'He'll never come back.'

Kent took in her stricken face and the distress in her eyes and shouted to the dockhands. 'Hey, you – leave that gangway alone.'

'Now look 'ere—' began one of the men.

Kent ignored him. 'He's there on the boat, Charlotte. He's waiting. You know what to do,' and he added gently with mock annoyance, 'for goodness' sake, go to Ceylon and marry the fellow.'

She stared at him, her mouth open. 'But Richard, I—'

'You'd better hurry, they're about to move that gangway.'

Charlotte turned and looked up at Butler, standing pale-faced but determined at the rail, and the steamer's whistle blew impatiently. Abruptly Charlotte whirled, kissed Kent on the cheek and ran to the ship. Even as she was running up the gangway Butler was running along the deck and he met her at the top of the gangway, swinging her off her feet and wrapping her in his arms.

Kent watched, grinning, then noticed the dock-hands standing about.

'Well?' he said genially. 'Have you never seen two people in love before?' and he gestured to the gangway. 'Come along now, chaps. Look lively.'

Despite the cold, Kent stood on the quay until the steamer disappeared over the horizon, only the long black plume of smoke from her funnel signalling her position. Not until the smoke had finally dispersed did he turn away and then he strolled along the quay whistling to himself.

He came level with a clipper ship and stopped, startled. It was the *Elizabeth Miller*, looking distinctly battered now, but it was her nameboard that caught Kent's eye: *'Elizabeth...'*

A memory came, unbidden, of someone he had once known, and Kent looked out to sea again. If John and Charlotte could make a new start then so could he.

Butler, Charlotte and Changarai were going home to Tondipgiri, and Kent decided it was time he went home too. He had a visit to make tomorrow.

The publishers hope that this book has given you enjoyable reading. Large Print Books are especially designed to be as easy to see and hold as possible. If you wish a complete list of our books please ask at your local library or write directly to:

Magna Large Print Books
Magna House, Long Preston,
Skipton, North Yorkshire.
BD23 4ND

This Large Print Book for the partially sighted, who cannot read normal print, is published under the auspices of

THE ULVERSCROFT FOUNDATION

THE ULVERSCROFT FOUNDATION

... we hope that you have enjoyed this Large Print Book. Please think for a moment about those people who have worse eyesight problems than you ... and are unable to even read or enjoy Large Print, without great difficulty.

You can help them by sending a donation, large or small to:

The Ulverscroft Foundation, 1, The Green, Bradgate Road, Anstey, Leicestershire, LE7 7FU, England.
or request a copy of our brochure for more details.

The Foundation will use all your help to assist those people who are handicapped by various sight problems and need special attention.

Thank you very much for your help.